A TRUE LIKENESS

A TRUE LIKENESS

Tessa Barclay

This first world edition published in Great Britain 2002 by
SEVERN HOUSE PUBLISHERS LTD of
9–15 High Street, Sutton, Surrey SM1 1DF.
This first world edition published in the USA 2002 by
SEVERN HOUSE PUBLISHERS INC of
595 Madison Avenue, New York, N.Y. 10022.

British Library Cataloguing in Publication Data

Barclay, Tessa
    A true likeness
    1. Missing children – Fiction
    I. Title
    823.9'14 [F]

ISBN 0-7278-5640-5

Typeset by Palimpsest Book Production Ltd.,
Polmont, Stirlingshire, Scotland.
Printed and bound in Great Britain by
MPG Books Ltd., Bodmin, Cornwall.

One

As she waited for her client, Lindsey thought over what she knew about her. Very little, when she came to consider. Mostly what Old Oliver had said yesterday at the evening conference.

Old Oliver was more correctly known as Mr Ollerenshaw, the head of the law firm of Higgett, Ollerenshaw and Cline. Mr Higgett and Mr Cline had long since gone to that judgmental courtroom in the sky but Old Oliver remained, looking like a benign character out of Charles Dickens. But this was misleading. He was a very sharp and cool-headed old man and, like everyone else on the firm, Lindsey Abercrombie had to pay attention to what he said.

What he'd said about Mrs Guyler, the client for whom she was waiting, was that she must pay the strictest respect to what she wanted. 'Mrs Guyler has been a client of ours for some fifteen years,' he pronounced, 'and her retainer to us for our services is very substantial. But, of course, those have been for commercial contract development, not for family matters. To have her ask for advice on a family topic is very unusual.'

He fixed Lindsey with his piercing grey eyes at this point and she felt constrained to say something. But what? She had never met Mrs Guyler, had never taken part in any of her contract negotiations, and so was at something of a loss. 'I'll certainly do all I can to help her—'

'If help is what she needs,' Old Oliver broke in. 'Bear in mind that Ursula Guyler is a self-made millionaire. Her cosmetics sell throughout Europe. So "help" hardly seems to be in the picture. I imagine it will be something about a will – she has a lot of money to bequeath and probably has very firm ideas, so you'll go along with her wishes – yes?'

'Certainly, Mr Ollerenshaw.'

Old Oliver gave her another of his piercing glances. He saw a pretty young thing – young in his estimation, although he knew her age to be about thirty, because that was one of the reasons he'd engaged her. Young blood, young *female* blood. He'd picked up signals from his fellow lawyers that it was needful these days to have young women on the firm, good for an up-to-date image and moreover surprisingly popular with women clients. She looked fresh and youthful with her pale skin and her fine dark hair, but he knew that under that silky thatch a watchful intelligence was always working. You could tell that by the mildness of the hazel eyes, the steadiness of the calm voice.

'She specifically asked for someone accustomed to handling family matters.' He paused. 'I ask myself now if she used the word problems? No. No, I can't imagine Mrs Guyler would have a problem of that kind because my understanding is that she *has* no family . . . a husband, yes, he came with her to our Christmas party last year . . . or was it the year before? What I am trying to convey is that if Mrs Guyler is thinking of making a will, such family as might benefit from it may be distant relatives. So I want you to be very particular in getting her exact intentions, since distant relatives can be difficult to find when the regrettable necessity arises.'

'I quite understand,' said Lindsey, knowing that the others seated around the conference table were suppressing smiles. One of Old Oliver's many faults was that he insisted on telling people things they already knew.

'Very well then, Lindsey,' he said, about to turn to some other topic. 'And remember – kid gloves, kid gloves! She's a very important lady.'

So here she sat, in her office at Higgett, Ollerenshaw and Cline, with the September sunshine spilling though the old sashed windows and the sound of the traffic drifting down the lane from Colmore Row. Mid-morning wasn't a busy time on the roads of Birmingham yet the city was never quiet. Mrs Guyler, she knew, would sweep up to the door in a chauffeured limousine, driven from a fine house near the Botanical Gardens but nevertheless perhaps delayed a little by trucks and lorries and therefore glad of a cup of coffee. Lindsey had ensured coffee would be ready the moment she rang for it. She considered lowering the blinds in case the sunshine might bother her client but decided the low table and cushioned chairs would be just out of range of the sunbeams by the time Mrs Guyler arrived.

She looked through the dossier she'd put together since Old Oliver gave her the assignment on Monday. Photocopies of articles and mentions in the *Birmingham Post*. Mrs Guyler played her part in the social round, was known for her contributions to charity, attended big events at Symphony Hall and opened fetes and fairs. She employed fewer people than Lindsey would have expected but Andrew had explained that.

'She contracts out almost all the manufacture,' he'd told her. Andrew knew all about it because he took part in drawing up Mrs Guyler's business contracts which were such an important part of the law firm's work. 'That place she has on the industrial park is for packaging, mostly. So her actual wages bill isn't all that big, but the turnover of the business is really something. She's got her head screwed on all right, sweetie, so watch your step with her.'

Excellent advice, but then Andrew always gave excellent advice. He'd befriended her when she joined the firm two years ago. She owed him a lot because, knowing no one in Birmingham, she might have spent a lonely time outside office hours. But Andrew Gilmore had made life pleasant – more than pleasant, often wonderful, especially when he took her in his arms and made her share in that brief, transient joy of physical love.

With a start Lindsey drew herself back to the moment as the receptionist rang through. 'Mrs Guyler for your eleven o'clock, Miss Abercrombie.' Lindsey was at her door when Mrs Guyler came out of the lift at the second floor.

'Good morning, Mrs Guyler. So nice to meet you. May I take your coat?'

The civilities allowed her to take stock of her visitor. She was a very handsome woman, somewhere in her mid or late forties, elegant in a tailored trouser suit of raw silk and a black velour reefer coat. A mop of what looked like carelessly

3

combed blonde hair, but Lindsey knew it had been under the hands of an expert hairdresser that very morning. Hands beautifully manicured, feet gleamingly shod in fine leather – a woman to whom appearance was of the first importance. Lindsey rather regretted not having made a bigger effort with her own clothes today. She was in one of her muted outfits of jacket, blouse and skirt – neat, not gaudy, as Shakespeare advises.

Coffee was offered and accepted. They sat down in the comfortable chairs by the low table. For a few minutes they made conversation: Lindsey said she was delighted to have the chance to be of use to one of the firm's most valued clients; Ursula Guyler replied that she'd been doing business with Higgett, Ollerenshaw and Cline for well over a decade; they agreed that today's weather was a blessed relief from the rains of the past week, and then it was time to get to work.

'I'm told by Mr Ollerenshaw that you specialise in family affairs,' Ursula said, eyeing the girl across from her with some doubt. To Ursula she seemed rather young.

'That's been the case,' Lindsey agreed. 'It just turns out that I get very reasonable results, so I've been given most of the clients who come with family problems.'

'Mm . . .' A pause. 'I need help over something that's come up, but the beginning of the story goes back a long way. Seventeen years, in fact.'

Lindsey's heart sank. This was going to be one of those tales of a family row, started over some triviality but now needing to be healed because . . . well, some small piece of property was to be inherited, or someone was going to write a family history which would make Mrs Guyler look bad, or something equally tedious.

Mrs Guyler was still hesitating. Lindsey gave her an encouraging smile.

Mrs Guyler said, 'Seventeen years ago my three-year-old daughter went missing.'

It was all Lindsey could do to stifle a gasp. This was totally unexpected.

'Missing?'

'From a beach in Wales. It was August, we were there on

4

holiday, and Julie was building sandcastles on the beach under the eye of her nanny. Nanny – that was Kristel, we got her through an agency, very reliable and good – came to me distraught – mid-afternoon, it was, time for Julie's nap – she'd gone to fetch her from the sandcastles but she wasn't there.'

Here Ursula Guyler stopped. She seldom spoke of that afternoon. It rose up before her now in all its terror, all its anguish. The Austrian girl's tear-blotched face, the wild run down the stairs from the holiday apartment and out into the clogging, shifting sand, and then the shallow hole with its little sandpies, the plastic red spade and the blue and yellow bucket . . .

'Yes?' Lindsey prompted in a gentle voice.

It dragged Ursula away from that searing vision. She blinked once and went on, 'The police searched everywhere, questioned everyone. Kristel said she only took her eyes off Julie for a minute, to find a towel in the beach bag so as to wipe the dampness off before bringing her indoors. I believe her. I never held her to blame.'

'Go on.'

'When almost a year had gone by, everybody began to advise me to give up searching. In the nicest way, you know, but . . .'

'And did you?'

'No, it was almost exactly a year since I lost her so I put an advertisement in all the papers, saying that any news of her would get a big reward. Billy was against it. Billy's my husband, you know.'

Lindsey nodded. She'd gleaned that from the file she'd put together: pictures of William Guyler wearing a sports jacket, standing in the background while Ursula awarded a cup to a croquet player, and wearing an evening jacket while Ursula sparkled in sequins at a premiere.

'He was against it?'

'He'd been persuaded by the experts, the counsellors who were supposed to help me get over it. "It's time to get on with your life," they'd say. And about the adverts, they told me I'd get a crop of cranks. And of course I did.'

'So did you decide to listen to them after that?'

5

'Well, yes, but I couldn't bring myself to . . . to give up hoping. Among those letters there were a few things about some little girl turning up somewhere unexpected and I had a security firm look into those – the security firm that supplies watchmen for my premises in Walsall, you know . . .' Her voice faded for a moment, but then she continued, 'None of them was my Julie. Yet I couldn't help thinking, "There *are* children who don't seem to be in their right place, and one of them *could* be Julie," so I kept the ads going for a while. But in the end I had to cancel because nothing really came of them.'

'What did you do then?'

'I just let it all go for a bit. But when the anniversary came around the next year, in August, I couldn't ignore it. So I put the ad in again, and I've done that every year ever since.'

'For seventeen years?' Lindsey said, aghast.

'Yes. "A will of iron," that's what they say about me,' Ursula remarked with a grim smile. 'And it's true. That's what got me to the top in my business, and that's what's brought me here today.'

'How do you mean?'

'This was the seventeenth year. Julie would be twenty if she were alive, and I've always believed she was still alive. So this year that TV programme – you know – *Last Seen*?' Lindsey shook her head. 'Oh. Well, it's on early evening – I daresay you don't get home in time to watch it even if you wanted to. Anyhow, they decided to do a short insert in their programme about Julie because she'd be twenty – they thought it was a point to make – two decades – oh, I don't know, maybe they just needed something to fill a spot, it gets pretty boring, you know, lists of people who've gone missing and only old snapshots to show . . . Well, they did what they call a "spot" about Julie in August – about how I'd never given up, and how that next year when the ad came out it would be Julie's twenty-first . . .'

'Yes?'

'And a girl called the phone number and they talked to her.'

'Go on.'

'Edie Maybury.' Mrs Guyler stopped, fixed her gaze for a

6

moment on the vase of gladioli on Lindsey's document cabinet, then resumed. 'She said her mother had died about eighteen months ago and she'd found some strange inconsistencies in the papers she'd had to deal with afterwards. She said she'd come to the conclusion Mary Lois Maybury wasn't her mother at all. The team that produce the TV show have some experience about that kind of thing and they told me they thought there was something there.' She stopped again, then repeated, 'Something there . . .' She gave a little nod at the memory. 'So I told them to give her a number to ring but not my home number, you understand – because it might have been a hoax or a swindle.'

'And did she ring?'

'Yes.'

'When was that?'

'The beginning of September.'

'And what do you think?'

'I don't know what to think.'

'What did she say?

'I don't exactly remember. I . . . I've got to confess I was in a flap. I meant to tape the conversation so I could go over it again later but I . . . I don't know exactly how, but I seem to have switched the recorder off at some point and I didn't get much.'

'Tell me what you can remember.'

'She talked again about her mother's death – how she'd had to find her and her mother's birth certificates and things to get possession of the house – and the birth certificates didn't match up.'

'In what way?'

'Oh, I don't remember! Something about . . . her mother was in her fifties when she died but the birth certificate was for a younger woman . . . And there was more, but it's complicated.' Ursula made a sound of annoyance and shrugged. 'I'm not usually feather-headed but I went to pieces, I admit it. I couldn't take it in.'

'It's very understandable,' Lindsey said soothingly, knowing she must keep her client from blaming herself over such a simple matter. She already had a burden of guilt over the loss

7

of her child, from the implied negligence that always goes with such a grief-filled event. 'You were flustered because you felt you might be talking to your lost daughter.'

'She can't be my daughter!' Ursula burst out. 'She's nothing like what my Julie would be if she were still alive!'

Lindsey drew back. She felt a little spark of discovery. Was this the key to the problem? 'In what way?' she murmured, scarcely above a whisper so as not to alert Ursula to the disclosure she was perhaps about to make.

'She's so *common*! She talks like someone behind a stall in the market! And no manners – interrupting everything I tried to say – she seems to think she's the only one in the world who has the right to speak and nobody's to disagree or argue! She *can't* be Julie! I won't believe it!'

The handsome features had flushed with outrage, the unflinching dark blue eyes sparkled with tears. Lindsey rose, went to her desk, and spoke quietly into her intercom, ordering fresh coffee because she thought it might help, but mainly to give Ursula Guyler a chance to recover.

When she resumed her place her client was stuffing a handkerchief into her Gucci bag and giving little shrugs as she regained her self-control. 'Sorry,' she said. 'I thought I could discuss it calmly. But she's such a little . . . brat.' Brat, that was the word. Graceless and mannerless – the impact of those first words of conversation still sent a shudder through Ursula Guyler as she recalled them.

'That must have been a big surprise—'

'A shock! A terrible shock! They never mentioned that she was a scrapper! Those TV people had done nothing to prepare me for anything like that. I picked up the phone expecting to hear—'

'What did you expect to hear, Mrs Guyler? You couldn't have thought it would be a little three-year-old girl.'

'No, but Julie . . . Julie was such a sweet child, so full of smiles, so eager to chatter to you in her little way, so *gentle* – she didn't have an ounce of defiance in her. Whereas *this* girl wants to take on the world – full of her own opinions, and so . . . so uncouth!'

'But then you don't know what her life has been, Mrs

8

Guyler. If she is Julie, there's a gap of seventeen years when things have been very different from what she'd have had with you.'

Ursula sighed and looked at Lindsey with unwilling appreciation. 'That's what I've tried to tell myself. I don't want to be unjust. In business I try never to let my emotions get the upper hand, and that's what's happening here.'

The door opened and the receptionist came in with fresh coffee. There was a little pause while she gathered up the used cafetière and took it out.

As Lindsey poured from the new one, she asked the question that had to come next. 'What is it you want from me, Mrs Guyler?'

'I want you to meet this girl. I want you to check up on her story, about her mother and the birth certificate and all that. I want you to examine all the dots and commas, and if she's trying to pull a fast one I want you to scare her back to wherever she came from.'

'And if the matter of the birth certificate checks out as genuine?'

Her client accepted the coffee cup and looked down into its brown depths. 'That still wouldn't mean much, would it? Some mix-up over the mother's birth dates – a slip of the pen – that could be anything, after all.'

'That's possible.'

There was a moment of silence then Ursula said, 'What I've told you is in absolute confidence.' She sipped her coffee and set the cup down. She waited until Lindsey had done likewise then fixed her with a cold blue stare. 'I don't want anyone to know a word about this. If, God forbid, that girl is my daughter, I want to deal with it quietly. If it's a deception, I don't want anyone to know that I got entangled even to the smallest extent. I have my business reputation to consider, I don't want to be seen as a fool.'

'I understand.'

'I mean it – absolute confidence. I'd prefer that you didn't discuss it with colleagues here.'

'Oh, but—'

'Mr Ollerenshaw handles a lot of my legal negotiations. We

9

have a good working relationship. I don't want him beginning to think I'm a nitwit who can be swayed by emotion. Because I'm not! And that's why I'm twice as wary of this chit of a girl as most women would be. I suppose she thought I'd fly to her with my arms wide open and we'd cry over each other and then she'd ask me for a couple of thousand—'

'But Mrs Guyler, does she know you have money?'

Ursula frowned. 'Well, she knows I've got more than *she* has! *Last Seen* preserved my anonymity, of course, and the first contact was through their own free-phone number. But in the broadcast they referred to me a couple of times as 'a businesswoman' and of course they said Julie was snatched while her nanny was distracted for a moment. Poor people don't hire nannies, Miss Abercrombie.'

'Well, that's true.' Lindsey recognised the shrewdness behind the woman-of-fashion appearance. 'When you spoke on the phone, did she mention money?'

'Of course not!' Ursula replied with contempt. 'She's far too sly for that! But that's coming, I can feel it in my bones. So I want you to vet her, to hear her story out in full and report back to me. There's no way I am going to get involved with her until I find out what she's up to. And that's where you come in. Will you see her and check her out for me?'

'Of course. How do I get in touch with her?'

Ursula took from her handbag the sheet of paper on which she had personally typed out the girl's name, address and telephone number. 'You shouldn't telephone her until after seven in the evening because she has some grotty job in a mini-supermarket and doesn't get home until then.'

The paper showed an address in Hobston, a small Cheshire market town. 'I don't expect you to go there,' Ursula observed with some amusement as Lindsey took in that fact. 'I imagine it's the back of beyond. Fetch her to Birmingham, put her up somewhere decent overnight, and of course I'll pay all expenses.'

A very businesslike plan. 'Very well,' Lindsey agreed. 'I'll try to contact her this evening and set it up.'

'Please yourself about the timing, but of course the sooner the better. Keep me in touch with what's going on. But I need

10

hardly tell you I don't want her to find out where I live or my home telephone number. I don't want to be harassed.'

'Oh, I hardly think—'

'You didn't hear her on the phone,' Ursula cut in. 'She's no fool, believe me. So if you have her here in the office, don't leave any papers lying about where she could get at them, no files with my name on them or anything like that.'

'So how am I to refer to you when we talk?' Lindsey enquired, trying not to sound too formal about it. To lighten the question she added, 'I could call you Mrs X, if you like.'

'Don't be silly,' said Ursula. She wasn't in the mood for jokes. 'When *Last Seen* handled it they used a version of my first name – my parents used to call me Shula. That's how this girl asked for me when she telephoned – "Can I speak to Shula," she said.' Her face changed at the thought, a momentary softness played around her lips. 'I can't tell you what I thought and felt at that moment . . . I thought I was going to find Julie.'

'And perhaps you did,' Lindsey said, wanting to keep that possibility in play despite Ursula's reluctance.

'*No*! That was never my Julie,' cried Ursula, and made for the door.

While helping her on with her coat and seeing her down to the hall, Lindsey made small talk. 'I'll get straight on to it and be in touch as soon as I can. Shall I call you at home or at your office?'

'Either, if it's anything really important. If you just find out she's a trickster – which I'm sure she is – I'm not bothered to be put in the picture at once. I'd like you to take whatever steps you think best in that case – scare her off with threats of the police, or something like that. The less I hear of her the better, really. Well, goodbye, Miss Abercrombie. I appreciate your help.'

As Lindsey was making her way back to the lift, Mr Ollerenshaw's secretary put her head out of a door. 'Mr Ollerenshaw would like a word, Miss Abercrombie.'

Lindsey went into his anteroom. The secretary said into her intercom phone, 'Miss Abercrombie, Mr Ollerenshaw.' She

11

listened, nodded at Lindsey, and ushered her into the inner sanctum.

Old Oliver had the best office in the building – walls panelled in Victorian mahogany, a bay window out of whose left-hand panes he could get a glimpse of St Philip's Cathedral, a thick ash-grey carpet which was like walking on marshmallow, and splendid chairs in buttoned maroon leather.

He waved her to one. 'So,' he began, 'you've seen Mrs Guyler?'

'Yes, sir.'

'And what did she want?'

Lindsey knew this was going to be awkward. 'She asked me not to discuss it with anyone, even within the firm.'

'What?'

'It's a very personal matter, Mr Ollerenshaw. Perhaps by and by, when matters are straightened out a bit, she'll empower me to speak about it.'

'My dear Lindsey, I have been a friend of Mrs Guyler's for many years. Surely there's nothing she could want in the way of legal advice in which I couldn't be useful?'

It always irked her that he could call her by her first name but that she had to call him Mr Ollerenshaw or sir. It was so terribly old-fashioned. In most law firms, even junior members were regarded as near equals and everyone would be on first name terms.

'I'm sorry, sir,' she said, 'but it was Mrs Guyler's specific wish that nothing she said this morning should be discussed.' She knew how to stem his curiosity. 'You could of course telephone Mrs Guyler and speak to her on that point if you like.'

'Oh no, no, certainly not. If she wishes an entire confidentiality she is of course entitled to it.' The idea of facing an irritated Mrs Guyler clearly didn't appeal to him. But he wasn't going to give up just yet. 'However, you are about to take some action on her part, are you?'

'Yes, I am.'

'Will it be a lengthy process? Because if so, you will keep good time records, I hope. Our accountant likes to have precise times for the audit of our billings.'

'Certainly, I'll be very particular about it.'

'It would be helpful to know if you are going to be out of the office much?'

'I don't know exactly what I shall be doing yet.'

'Oh? On what does that depend?'

She could see that the only way to end the enquiry was to give him a satisfactory hint. 'I have to interview someone on Mrs Guyler's behalf. Until I've set that up, I don't know what will happen.'

'I see,' said Old Oliver, nodding. Not a will, then. Blackmail, he said to himself. It's a case of blackmail. Well, well, I wonder what Ursula Guyler's been up to? Or perhaps it's Billy – I would never blame Billy if he were to break out and take a mistress. He allowed a faint amusement to crease his rosy cheeks. 'Very good, then, Lindsey, of course Mrs Guyler's wishes must be respected. However, there may come a time when you'd want to consult.'

To consult – that meant to go to some other member of the firm and ask for an opinion over a sticky point. In the end, Old Oliver was consulted over almost everything. He was, after all, the head of the firm and a solicitor of vast experience. Confident that before too long he'd hear all about it, he smiled and dismissed his junior colleague. 'I hope to hear more when the matter is ended. Thank you.'

Lindsey too was smiling as she made her way up to the second floor and her own less sumptuous office. Thought he'd fathomed it, did he? Old fox. But even he with all his experience could never imagine what she had heard from her client this morning.

She was pleased with herself for having fended him off. But she had it all to do again when she went out for lunch with Andrew Gilmore, fellow member of the law firm and the man of the moment in her life.

'I got a glimpse of her as she swept in,' he told her. '*Very* smart. So what did she want, our Mrs Guyler?'

'Can't tell, Andrew. She made a point of complete confidentiality.'

'What, even within the firm?'

She nodded, eyeing her limp salad with distaste. Why was it that you couldn't get a decent salad without going miles to eat at a veggie restaurant? Andrew had been tucking into his steak baguette with enthusiasm but now paused to study her. His bright black eyes were full of curiosity. 'You can tell *me*,' he urged.

'No I can't. And I didn't tell Old Oliver, either.'

'You're joking.'

'No, the whole thing is a no-no until she says otherwise.'

'But why? Why's it so hush-hush? Her stuff is usually about financial contracts leading forward for three or four years – or else she's suing some manufacturer for sub-standard ingredients. I mean, we've all taken snips and snaps at her contracts – why's this one so different?'

'I'm not at liberty to say.'

He cut another section of baguette but then pushed it around his plate. 'Wait a minute, wait a minute! I wasn't really paying attention at the conference last night but it comes to me as a faint echo – didn't Old Ollie say it was farmed out to you because of your special talent in family matters?'

'I leave it to you to look up your notes on that point, Andrew – if you took any.'

'I always take notes,' he protested, although they both knew he didn't. Andrew Gilmore was valued by Mr Ollerenshaw for two things in particular – he was good in the magistrate's court, tall and bright and always helpful to their worships, and he was very much on the old-boy network with barristers when a case had to go to a higher court. Lindsey had to acknowledge that he sometimes got by on spin-doctoring, but he was a successful solicitor in a city where the competition was fierce and had brought in some very lucrative clients.

'Family matters,' he mused, glancing at his watch. He hurried to finish his baguette, he had an appointment at two thirty. 'Why should the owner of the famous Gylah Cosmetics firm need your help over a family matter? The only family she has is poor little old Billy, isn't it?'

'As far as my file on her goes, it seems she has few relations. She was an only child, her father died years ago, her mother has money of her own and is in a posh retirement village in Spain.'

'And Billy?'

'If you're interested you should do your own research,' Lindsey teased him, knowing he wouldn't do anything of the sort. Andrew concentrated his efforts on what he thought would do him the most good, and since the Guyler file wasn't his domain, he had only a normal curiosity over it.

'I've got more interesting things to do than research,' he told her, with a little grin. 'This evening, for instance – dinner at eight? I'll pick you up.'

She shook her head. 'No, I can't this evening. I'm going to stay at the office a bit – there's something I have to see to.'

'Oh, come on, the office closes down at six and so should we.'

'But not when we have to see to things that can't be dealt with before six.'

'Burning the midnight oil isn't going to impress Old Oliver, Lin. He's one of the old school, thinks solicitors should organise their days so that they can relax over a good bottle of port in the evening.'

Lindsey shuddered, she hated port. 'I really can't make any date for this evening, Andrew. I've got something important to do.'

'But it's not going to take *all* evening, surely?'

'It might go on till about nine o'clock.' If Edie Maybury got home about seven from her supermarket job, presumably some time between seven and nine would be a good time to speak to her on the phone.

'Well, then, I'll tell you what. Drop in on me after you've finished up with whatever it is you're going to do.'

'I don't know, Andrew. I'm going to be pretty tired.'

'All the more reason. A nice little drink and a cuddle or two before you have to take that dreary suburban train home. Come on, say yes, it's on your way to the station anyway.'

She knew that he was hoping to persuade her to stay till morning. It was happening more often recently. She'd allow herself to tempted by the pleasure he offered, the bliss of joining with him in that great forgetful moment of wonder . . . Yet the mornings always brought regret, there was the scurry to get to her own home for fresh clothes, or else it meant planning ahead and bringing an overnight case, and somehow

15

in Andrew's cramped little bachelor flat there was never room for a hairbrush or cosmetics or spare shoes. How practical and domestic that sounded as she thought of it – was that what love came down to, in the end – the domestic details, the problems of train timetables?

She drew a deep breath. 'I really can't, Andrew,' she said. 'This is important, this piece of work. And after I've done it I need some peace and quiet to think about the results. And you know—' she chuckled – 'I never get any peace and quiet with *you*.'

'Fair enough,' he agreed, rather flattered. One thing that was so nice about Lindsey – she was always ready to show appreciation. He reached for her hand, gave it a little squeeze of affection, and his dark eyes sparkled with pleasure in her company. 'Okay, then, but I get first dibs on tomorrow evening, right?'

'I'm not promising anything,' she said. 'Let's see what tomorrow brings.'

They had to hurry back to the office. The afternoon was taken up with work on the problems of other clients. She heard the office emptying, goodnights being exchanged as her colleagues left. The receptionist called to say she was switching the telephones to overnight mode, meaning that the solicitor allotted to take emergency cases would be called at home, and Lindsey said she would use her mobile. She finished up her day's stint, ensured that all timings were correctly transferred from her palm-top to the accountancy file on the firm's computer, then went to make herself a cup of coffee. From her drawer she took the sandwich she'd bought on the way back from lunch.

She ate while she listened to the news on her portable radio. At seven she tidied away the sandwich wrappings, took the coffee mug out to the corridor kitchen for the early morning cleaners to deal with, and washed her hands. At about ten minutes after seven, she got out the piece of paper with the telephone number that Ursula Guyler had supplied. She tapped in the numbers on her mobile and heard the ringing tone.

The receiver was picked up. 'Hello?' said a voice.

Lindsey wondered if she was about to speak to Ursula Guyler's daughter or to an impostor.

Two

L indsey chose the venue with care. The Grange Wharf had
once been a coaching inn on the edge of one of the old
canals. Refurbished, it was now a medium-grade hotel, much
favoured by those coming to Birmingham for the weekend to
attend events at Symphony Hall. Since today was a Thursday,
there were few guests except businessmen who, at lunchtime,
could be relied upon to be elsewhere. The restaurant, called the
Granger, was therefore very quiet.

Last night's phone conversation had been brief, with little of
the antagonism Lindsey had been led to expect. Edie Maybury
had agreed without argument to the invitation to come to
Birmingham 'for a chat'. Asked if she could get a day off
from work at the mini-market, she'd said, 'No problem.' She
herself chose the following day for the meeting.

'Do you know Birmingham?'

'Never been there.'

'Take a taxi from New Street—'

'Where's that?'

'The railway station.'

A sound of amusement. 'No trains at Hobston. I'll be coming
by coach.'

'Oh, then, take a taxi from the coach station, ask for the
Grange Wharf—'

'What's that?'

'It's a hotel. I thought we'd have lunch, if you agree.' She
paused for a response and, taking silence for consent, went on,
'I'll meet you there, in the restaurant at one thirty – just ask
for me.'

'Okay.'

'Of course all your expenses will be paid.'

'You bet!' said her guest, and that was the only real sign of aggression in the conversation.

Lindsey had arrived in good time. She knew the problems of Birmingham's roads and so at this hour of the day had caught a bus. Though she could drive, she'd found it totally frustrating to run a car in this city of permanently tangled traffic. Sometimes even calling a taxi was a waste of time, and the bus stop was just across Colmore Row from the office.

She wanted to have the chance to make at least a moment's assessment as the girl was shown in. She sat at their table, drinking a Cinzano and watching the other lunch guests – middle-aged couples mostly by the look of them, here for the shopping.

The door of the restaurant was swung open by the hall porter to allow the entrance of a girl in a short black leather skirt, bare legs, and clog-like black plastic shoes. Her upper half was clad in a black jacket of thick cotton under which she wore a black T-shirt piped with white. Her face was very pale, helped to that tint by some thick cosmetic. Her lipstick was of a red so dark it looked almost purple. Her eyes were heavily made up with kohl. Her hair had been cut very short and dyed to a matt black, lustreless and dull.

She was clearly into some fashion form – Dragons and Dungeons, perhaps, or the Dracula's victim style. It was no wonder that the other people in the restaurant stared as she was ushered to Lindsey's table.

'Hello there,' said Lindsey, offering her hand. 'I'm Lindsey Abercrombie.'

'Hi.' Edie Maybury took the hand, shook it once, and sat down as the waiter drew out her chair.

'How was your journey?'

'Boring.'

'Did it take a long time?'

'Had to change at Crewe, there was a bit of a wait, know what I mean?'

'You're ready for a drink, then. What would you like?'

'Lager.'

'Any particular brand?'

18

'Something foreign, since you're paying.'

The wine waiter, hovering, said, 'German? Belgian? Mexican? Japanese?'

She gave him a hard stare from unexpectedly blue eyes. 'You taking the mickey?'

'No indeed, madam.' He was accustomed to deal with hesitation over choosing drinks. 'May I recommend the Japanese? Very refreshing.'

'Okay.'

The table waiter reappeared as he withdrew and handed them menus. The main dishes were mostly run of the mill – chicken in a basket, steak and chips, roast lamb and mint sauce, ham salad. The starters never rose above prawn salad, fruit juice, or soup of the day. Lindsey's guest ordered shrimps and chicken, then felt in her shoulder bag for something. Lindsey sighed inwardly: if Edie was going to bring out cigarettes she would have to tell her it was a no-smoking restaurant. What she produced, however, was a rather worn manila envelope.

'These are photocopies of the birth and death certificates,' she explained. 'You can't really understand what I'm on about, know what I mean? unless you see them.'

Lindsey took it but laid it aside. 'Let's eat first,' she said. 'We can have coffee in the lounge afterwards and that will be a better place to look at papers.'

'Please yourself.'

It was time to try for a much more friendly tone. 'I think I was told you work at a supermarket. Is that right?'

'Yeah. Boring.'

'The job's in Hobston is it? What's Hobston like?'

'Boring.'

'You've always lived there?'

'Nah.'

'I understand you inherited a house—'

'Nah. It was just a yearly lease, ran out in March.'

'Oh, I'm sorry. So where are you living now?' Lindsey asked

'With Graham.'

It was like getting blood from the proverbial stone. Luckily the lager arrived and provided enough diversion to let Lindsey

19

summon her patience. After all, it was a scary situation for this girl. She'd come up from a rural market town to a big city, to face a solicitor whom she'd never met, with the intention of somehow proving she was the daughter of someone whom she had also never met.

So Lindsey took a reviving sip of her Cinzano and picked up the conversation. 'Living with Graham. A relative, is he?'

'My boyfriend.'

'Ah. Anything serious?' She smiled to let her guest know that they were moving towards a woman-to-woman chat.

The only response was a shrug.

'So where did you live before you came to Hobston? Always in the country?'

'Yeah. Mum made these – you know – soppy country things – corn dollies, willow wreaths, that sort of thing. Had a stall in the market once a week in summer, for the folk driving through to Wales. Did well then.'

'Is there a living in it?'

A thin little smile. 'If you could call it that.'

'There's been no mention of your father,' Lindsey said very gently. 'What was he like?'

'Never knew, did I? Mum was a single parent. At least that's what my birth certificate shows – if it *is* my birth certificate.'

'So it was just you and your mother—'

'If she was my mother.' She shrugged. 'No, there were "uncles" now and again, know what I mean? Uncle Bert, Uncle Donnie. Never lasted long, it always ended in a row.'

'Temperamental?'

'Up and down like a yo-yo.' She tried the lager, raised her eyebrows in appreciation. 'What did that guy say – refreshing? – it's certainly better than what Graham always drinks.' It seemed that she was unbending a little.

'What does Graham do?' Lindsey asked.

'Garage.'

'He's not into country crafts or anything like that?'

'Motorbikes.' After a moment she added, 'I can do things with wicker, you know – and reeds – but it hurts your hands. Of course Mum wore special gloves. I threw them out.'

'You didn't want to do that kind of work?'

'No, I threw them out because she'd made me so angry.'

'Because you found out she wasn't your mother.'

'Liar,' the girl said flatly. 'She was always a bit of a liar. Lived in a sort of fantasy world, know what I mean? Every boyfriend was going to be *the* one – faithful, kind, never going to leave her. Then he'd take off, and it was then she'd remember I was around and she'd say, "*You* love me, Edie, don't you?"'

'And what did you reply?' Lindsey murmured.

'I'd say yes, because at times like that I did love her. She needed me then, made me feel I was important to her.' She paused. 'After all, who else was there?'

The first course came and was placed before them. There was some admiration in the way Edie surveyed the pretty glass dish and the contrast of pink sauce against green lettuce. 'So,' she said, picking up her spoon, 'you're a solicitor, eh?'

'Yes.'

'And you're working for this Shula.'

Ah. At last the name had been mentioned. 'Yes, you could put it that way.'

'And what's your part in this game, then? Look me over and get rid of me as fast as you can?'

That was so near the truth that Lindsey had to suppress a shiver. 'Oh, no, you mustn't think—'

'Listen, Abercrombie, I'm no dummy. Her Highness didn't fancy me, she made that quite clear. Well, you tell her it's no skin off my nose. If she doesn't care—'

'But she does care,' Lindsey put in quickly, before the antagonism could mount between them. 'Don't forget, she's been looking for her little girl for seventeen years.'

'Not very hard, though, eh? It'd have been nice for me if she'd caught up with us some time when things were bad at home.'

'Surely she told you when you rang her – she hired detectives—'

'Yeah, yeah, she spent money – I bet your Mrs Shula thinks that solves everything. She's rich, isn't she?'

'She's not poor, at any rate,' Lindsey allowed.

'And she thinks I'm working some kind of a scam, doesn't she? That's why she's dragged in her solicitor.'

'No, no – it's just that this is a very poignant situation and she felt she—'

'She felt she ought to keep me at arms length or even further. Well, tell her I'm not bothered about that. All I want is to know who I really am. One thing's certain, Mary Maybury wasn't my real mum.'

'You learned that from the death certificate? That must have been a big shock for you when you saw it?'

'Yeah.' There was a musing expression on the heavily made-up features. She took a long sip of her drink. 'But even before that . . . She used to come to collect me from school, and I'd look at her and at the other mums, and she was so much older than them – they were all fresh-faced and in bloom, know what I mean? And she was – she had the crow's feet round her eyes, and there was grey in her hair, and she just . . .' She made circles with the lager glass on the table top. 'One day,' she said reflectively, 'I was about ten, I think, I said to her, I don't know what made me say it, I said, "Are you my granny really?" Because there was a kid in my class, he was being brought up by his granny 'cos his real mum had done a bunk. And she slapped me, but then after a minute she burst out laughing and said, "No, I'm not your granny or anybody else's. You could say I made a mistake and fell, after more than thirty years of being careful. And you're the result."'

'Meaning that she was in her thirties when you were born.'

'Yeah, if you could believe what she said. But you could never be sure. She was so wrapped up in herself . . . If she'd told me then that I was adopted, I'd have believed her. But when I eventually saw my birth certificate, there was nothing on it about adoption.'

It was said with a grim calmness. The shock of discovery was long past for her, Lindsey could see.

There was a little silence while the main course was brought. Lindsey said, 'You thought she was too old to be your mother.'

'The hospital doctor told me she was probably in her early to mid fifties and had never had a child.'

22

'She died in hospital?'

'Yeah, of a brain thing – haemorrhage. The hospital was quite interested about it. That's why they talked quite a lot to me about it and did a post mortem.'

'Did you have to handle that all on your own?' Lindsey asked with concern.

'Who else? We didn't have friends – Mum didn't make friends, except for the uncles, and there wasn't one around when she went.'

'I'm so sorry, It must have been awful.'

'It was more like . . . peculiar. I mean, if she'd never had a child, where did I come from, know what I mean? I'm not talking about the stork, either. I wasn't hers by birth, and she hadn't adopted me. I found that out when I had to find the papers about inheriting – a big flap about nothing, she'd almost nothing worth inheriting but I had nowhere to live, you see, if they didn't let me take on the lease . . . Well, I found what was supposed to be my birth certificate. I worked out that she'd had to have that for when I started school.' She nodded as if at the envelope which she'd given to Lindsey. 'Well, you'll see for yourself. That and the other things.'

'You've had time to come to terms with it to some extent—'

'Don't you believe it,' the other girl riposted. 'I'm never going to sit down under this! I was lied to all my life – and I end up Miss Nobody. You think I'm happy with that? I'm never going to rest until I've found out who I am.' Then she turned her attention to her food. She attacked her chicken with vigour. 'This is nice, eating it proper. I never like getting my fingers greasy in the fried chicken places.

'Glad you like it.'

'Ummm. Classy place this, isn't it?'

Lindsey had chosen it because it was so un-classy, though entirely respectable. But it was a relief to get some words of approval so she explained about the hotel's history; and conversation about that and the renovation of Birmingham's canals took them to the end of the meal. When Edie refused a pudding they went to the lounge for coffee and mints.

The lounge was pleasant, decorated with enlarged photographs of the old barging days and colourful bargees' buckets

23

and water carriers. There were plenty of comfortable armchairs. Once settled, Lindsey took out the papers in the envelope.

They consisted of a birth certificate and three death certificates. The birth certificate was the topmost document, announcing the arrival of Edie Maybury to Mary Lois Maybury, aged twenty. No father's name was entered.

The next document was a death certificate for Mary Lois Maybury. But the cause of death was given as multiple injuries on a date seventeen years earlier. Lindsey looked up in astonishment.

'Yeah,' Edie agreed to the unspoken comment. 'My mum's dead – but look at the next one.'

Lindsey unfolded it. It was a death certificate for Edie Maybury, aged three years, from the same causes.

'So I'm dead too,' Edie said. 'Isn't it a hoot?'

'My God!' Lindsey was so stricken that the papers fell from her hands. They fluttered to the floor. It took her a moment to retrieve them, during which she was able to get her breath back after this devastating discovery.

The last document was for Mary Lois Maybury, aged approximately fifty-five. Cause of death, a subarrachnoid haemorrhage.

'But this is a false document!' she heard herself say, her solicitor's training taking over. 'Her name can't have been Mary Lois Maybury. Mary Lois Maybury died years earlier.'

'They didn't know that at the time. When I went with her in the ambulance to the hospital, I had to give her personal details at the reception place and of course I said she was Mrs Maybury – my mum – who else? Then when she died and the doc started chatting me up to find out more about her, it got clear that she *wasn't* my mum. But she was Mary Lois Maybury as far as any of us knew. I registered the death at the council place as Mary Lois Maybury – what else would I do? I thought that's who she was. I haven't told them different, since I found out the truth.' She paused. 'You're a solicitor – have I done anything to get me in trouble?'

'You did all this?' Lindsey asked, touching the documents. 'You yourself searched the records?'

'Well, wouldn't you? When I saw my so-called birth certificate I knew it couldn't be right. No way was she twenty when she had me. So I asked at the Citizen's Advice and they said I should go up to London and look in St Catherine's House. So I took a day off work and went and did that – it took hours, looking at things, asking what to do next, so I only got a bit done the first time. I went back, though, and did more. And in the end I got what you've got there. The only thing I haven't got is a marriage certificate for Mary Lois Maybury – it seems she was what they call a single parent.'

Lindsey spread the papers out on the upholstered arm of her chair and gazed at them. 'It looks as if Mary Lois Maybury and her little three-year-old were killed in an accident seventeen years ago.'

'Yeah.'

'The Mary Lois Maybury you lived with wasn't your mother.'

'Oh great. You actually get it. I tried to explain all this to your Mrs Shula but she wouldn't hear me.'

'Well . . . It *is* difficult, Edie.'

'It's a problem just right for *Who Wants to be a Millionaire*. What does it mean?'

A waitress brought their coffee. While she poured it, Lindsey tried to make sense of what she'd learned. Edie watched her closely, waiting and wanting to hear someone explain the mystery that had plagued her for over a year now.

'I think it's clear,' Lindsey said, 'that your mother – your foster-mother – stole the identity of a dead woman.'

'Go on.'

'You said it yourself. She had to have a birth certificate to enter you in school—'

'And for a passport,' Edie put in. 'We went abroad occasionally – to craft fairs – Munich at Christmas, she made money there with wicker animals and such. So she had to apply for a passport and she'd need a birth certificate for that, but I think I was on her passport as her daughter.'

'Yes, that's been changed now, but that's not relevant. The point is, every time your foster-mother needed an official document, she used the identity of the real Mary Lois Maybury.'

They stared at each other.

'She was clever,' Edie said in grudging admiration.

Lindsey didn't say that it wasn't so terribly clever. The whole process had been explained in a well-known thriller years ago. You find someone whose personal details are a match to your own and apply for birth certificates, marriage certificates, anything you might need for a life using that identity. The only thing you don't apply for is the death certificate because you don't want anyone to know that person has died – no, no, she's alive and well and living inside your skin.

When Edie's so-called mother had to have papers, she'd used the dead woman's name. She'd chosen a woman who died along with her three-year-old daughter. In fact, that had been the *reason* for the choice – the fact that she and her three-year-old child had died together. The age problem of the mother couldn't be solved – that would have been too much to expect. Mrs Maybury was perhaps fifteen years older than the woman whose name she took over. But hardly anyone would challenge a woman about her age, and especially not over a passport photograph.

The woman known in Hobston and elsewhere as Mrs Maybury thus accounted for the presence of the little girl who had grown up to be this young woman now sitting with Lindsey in the lounge of the Grange Wharf Hotel. The child was not hers.

Perhaps she had been stolen from a beach in Wales seventeen years ago.

It was Edie who resumed the conversation. 'See, I'm not Edie Maybury. She's dead long ago. So who am I?'

'Was there anyone among your mother's friends – I mean, your foster-mother . . . Lord, it's difficult to know what to call her.'

'I still think of her as Mum, though God know she was never very motherly. You'd best tag her as Mrs Maybury.'

'Well, could it have been any of her friends who . . . you know . . . like the kid at school whose granny took him over.'

'You mean she took on somebody else's kid to bring up?' The scorn was burning hot. 'Out of the goodness of her heart? You didn't know her!'

26

'Well, then . . . Money could have been involved. Somebody paid her to take you over, perhaps.'

'Then she could have just have said she was minding me, know what I mean? She could have got a birth certificate for me by using my real name, whatever that was. She could have taken up a birth certificate in the name of my real mum, if it was important to change her name, though God knows why.'

She waited for Lindsey to respond. Lindsey found she couldn't. During past contacts with social workers she'd learned that many young women handed over their children to be 'minded', paying a relative or perhaps a friend. If the mother then disappeared – and that could happen, alas – the minder generally went to the local authority and was given the role of fosterer, for which there was a recognised fee from the local council. That was an easier solution than finding some twenty-year-old who died with her toddler in an accident.

'See,' Edie went on, 'she found somebody she could use to sort out the fact that she had a little girl – she wanted to be my mother as far as the rest of the world could tell.'

Lindsey nodded in acknowledgement, 'You've given it a lot of thought.'

'You bet! It's been on my mind every day since I found out I couldn't really be Edie Maybury. So that's why I thought I'd get in touch with this Shula person. I mean – her kid just vanished, didn't she? Stolen off a beach, they said on telly. So I thought, what if it was my mum who stole the kid, and then by and by had to provide us with names and papers and got them by claiming to be Mary Lois Maybury and daughter?'

'It could be.'

'You just don't want to admit it,' Edie said in a harsh tone. 'That's what this is all about, isn't it? Her Ladyship doesn't fancy me and you're here to find reasons why I can't be her missing daughter.'

'You mustn't say things like that. What I'm here for is to find out the truth.'

'Well, the truth is that I'm this missing Julie, right?'

'There's a lot to support that argument,' Lindsey said, speaking with the utmost calmness to cool down the atmosphere. 'A child went missing whose age would be the same as yours. You were brought up by a woman claiming to be your mother but who obviously was not. But there are whys and wherefores in all that, things we can't account for. Shula couldn't understand what you were telling her so she asked me to find out more so she could make a judgement.'

'Yeah, well, she's the one who gets to do all the judging, isn't she? What about me?' The purple-lipsticked mouth was set in a grim line. 'I have to have some say in all this.'

'Of course, and you've told me a lot that will be important. But it can't be done in a rush, Edie. It's got to take time. And we've got to be sure we're going the right way about it – you can see that, can't you?'

'Well, yes . . . I suppose so.'

'Have you got any family pictures?' Lindsey enquired, taking the chance to move off this shaky ground.

Edie shook her head. 'What, Mum and me at the funfair, that sort of thing? Nah, we were never into that.' She hesitated. 'Well, there were a few but tell the truth, I slung 'em out, along with her craft tools and her clothes and all the rest, when . . . you know . . .'

'I understand. None of yourself, either? I mean recent photos?'

'Only a flash thing from a disco – you can hardly see me and anyhow Graham's got it.'

'Well, then, would you mind? I brought along an Instamatic.'

Edie gave a knowing and angry grin. 'What's this – identity parade?'

'Well, you know . . . Shula needs to know whether you look anything like her missing daughter.'

'Oh, right, only seventeen years difference.' But she rose and went at Lindsey's suggestion out to the patio garden that led down to the canal bank. Here she stood with her arms straight down at her sides, glaring at the camera, as Lindsey took two snaps.

Edie studied them when they emerged. 'Could have done better in a passport booth,' was her verdict.

It was almost four in the afternoon. She said she had to leave. 'I'll miss my connection at Crewe if I don't get to the coach station for the four thirty.'

'You could stay overnight if you like,' Lindsey suggested. 'I could easily get you a room here.'

She could see the idea appealed, but in the end it was rejected. 'There's work tomorrow. I couldn't get there before midday and if I was late on a Friday . . . Not much of a job but I'd like to keep it, know what I mean?' She paused. 'You said I'd get my expenses?'

'Of course.' Lindsey had provided herself with plenty of cash, and handed over a good deal more than the coach fare. 'That's for a taxi to the coach station and in case you want a coffee or a snack at Crewe.'

'Well, ta. So what comes next. You have to report to headquarters, is that it?'

'More or less.'

'And then what?'

'I'll be in touch.'

Edie slung her bag on her shoulder and headed out to the foyer. 'So long then. Tell your Mrs Shula that next time round I want a photo of *her*.' With that she went out and walked quickly towards the main road in search of transport to the coach station.

Lindsey went back to the lounge where she sank into a chair. That had not been an enjoyable experience. She felt drained; the need to take notice of everything, keep Ursula's identity concealed, and deal sympathetically with this abrasive girl had taken every ounce of her concentration. She ordered tea for herself and while waiting for it got out her mobile.

Her call was answered by a secretary who put her through at once 'Well?' Ursula demanded. 'What did she say?'

'Can I come and talk to you about it?'

'Tell me first, what's she like?'

'Well, she's not easy—'

'Not easy? She was downright impossible when she spoke to me!'

Lindsey stifled a sigh. 'Perhaps she wouldn't win any points for charm,' she acknowledged, 'but I don't think her manners are the issue here. Can I come and see you?'

'When?'

'I leave that to you.' It was a test. If Ursula were unwilling

29

to hear what she had to say and put her off, the whole thing was hopeless.

'Well . . . This evening? We have dinner early, Billy and I. Could you come after that, about eight?'

'Certainly.' Well, that was a relief. Even if she didn't like the idea of Edie Maybury as her daughter, on some level Ursula was still willing to listen.

Back in the office, Lindsey called a couple of clients who had left messages and dealt with letters that had come from the word processing department. Andrew put his head in as she was preparing to leave. 'Are we set for this evening?'

'I beg your pardon?'

'Don't you remember? I told you I had first dibs on tonight.'

'Oh, Lord, I forgot! Well, I can't, love. I've got a business appointment.'

'Since when?' he said in an aggrieved tone.

'Since about an hour ago.'

'What's going on? You've been out almost all day and now you say your evening isn't free!'

'Look, Andrew, when you're dealing with family affairs you can't keep business hours—'

'Oh, so it's the cosmetics queen again, is it? Oh, then I understand. With money like hers she's quite entitled to have you running round in circles.'

'Listen, I don't have to be where I'm going until eight. How about if we go out and have a meal?'

'Oh well . . . You mean now?'

'Just give me a minute to change.'

'But six o'clock is so early to eat.'

'Andrew, that's the best I can do.'

He hovered on the verge of turning it down, but then smiled and nodded. She at once forgave him the critical tone in which he'd been speaking to her. When Andrew smiled, everything was all right.

She went to the cloakroom to freshen up and change. She kept an all-purpose, uncreasable dress in her documents cabinet which could be brought out for unexpected evening engagements – black, of course, very simply cut and made of

30

some sort of clingy crêpe which did quite a lot for her slender figure. For the office today she'd been wearing a beige suit, so the jacket went over the dress quite well.

As she changed she thought to herself once again that it would be a lot easier if she and Andrew moved in together. Then they would see each other every evening and every morning, and this continuous hassle of finding time to be together would be over. There was plenty of room in her flat, a capacious conversion in a big house out beyond Bromsgrove. The only problem was that Andrew disliked the idea of the suburbs. To him, living in the city centre was an important part of his life style.

She'd choose her time to put it to him. Not this evening – there wouldn't be time to set out the pros and cons properly and in any case she had a lot on her mind otherwise.

Notably, what to say to Mrs Guyler.

Three

The door was opened by an elderly maid or housekeeper with a foreign accent. She greeted Lindsey with the news that Mr and Mrs Guyler were in the sitting room and she'd been told to ask if Miss Abercrombie wished for any refreshment.

'Are they having anything?'

'Coffee and brandy.'

'I'll have some of that, then.'

'This way please.'

The room into which she was shown had not yet been lit, so that the evening sun shone in through west-facing windows. There was a sofa and several handsome armchairs in ivory-coloured loose covers, a parquet floor that glowed in the soft light and here and there Oriental rugs. Lindsey was no expert but she thought the rugs were antique.

Ursula Guyler rose to greet her, a silhouette against the evening light. Her pale blue silk dress made her seem wraith-like.

'Did you have any problem finding us, my dear?'

'None at all, thank you.'

'This is my husband.'

'How do you do, Miss Abercrombie.' He too rose, from a chair facing out towards the garden. He was closer to fifty than his wife, and by no means as striking. A little taller than Ursula, clad in an unlikely cream linen jacket by Armani and dark trousers, he had something of the air of a man on holiday in a resort he hadn't chosen.

'Did Erika ask if you wanted anything?' Ursula enquired.

'Yes, thank you, I'll have some of your coffee if that's all right.'

'Billy, tell her we want fresh.'

32

Billy went obediently to the door and called to the house-keeper. Meanwhile his wife waved Lindsey to a chair. 'What's she like?' she demanded without preamble.

'She's the right age and she's got blue eyes. I can't say about her hair, she has it dyed jet black.'

'Jet black?' She shook her head in wonder. A blonde all her life, she couldn't imagine anyone wanting to have jet-black hair. 'Could you talk with her? Converse?'

'Oh yes, sticky at first but afterwards no problem.'

'But she's difficult – admit it, you had your work cut out.'

It would have been silly to deny that. She nodded, and Billy returned as she was saying, 'The woman who brought her up wasn't the best kind of mother, I gathered. You have to make allowances—'

'Maybury?' Billy asked. 'I went to the library and looked up the phone book for Hobston and saw a Gilbert Maybury. Is that the husband.'

'There's no husband,' Lindsey said. 'May I tell you about it?'

She recounted the conversation, referring occasionally to notes she'd made as soon as she got back to the office. When she said she'd taken pictures, Ursula at once held out her hand.

'Let me see.'

Billy came to look over his wife's shoulder as she examined the photographs.

'A real little madam,' she said, shaking her head. 'Look at the way she's staring out at us. Sheer defiance, that's what it is.'

'Perhaps she's just putting up a front, dear.'

'Why should she, if she's really who she claims to be? And she's not, of course.'

'We shouldn't jump to conclusions.'

'Oh, Billy, *look* at her. Is she anything like our sweet little charmer?'

'No, but . . .'

'Mrs Guyler – Ursula – you have to remember that—'

'Of course you're going to say that years have gone by – but temperament doesn't change, personality doesn't change.'

'How can you say that?' Lindsey cried, amazed. 'Everybody changes, all the time. You're not the same person you were ten years ago, twenty years ago—'

'I know what I know,' Ursula replied, 'it's instinctive and I *know* she's not my daughter.'

'If you're going to take up that attitude, why did you have me meet her? You raise her hopes by having me make that contact—'

'Hopes of getting me totally trapped in some confidence trick.'

'Mrs Guyler, the entire time we talked, she never made any demands except for her day's expenses.'

'Of course not, all the big stuff is still to come—'

Lindsey was about to tell her client that she was being paranoid but at the back of her mind she could hear Old Oliver saying, 'Kid gloves, kid gloves,' so instead she said, 'I think you're mistaken.'

The maid came in with an individual cafetière on a small silver tray. Everyone fell silent while she put the tray on a little table close to where Lindsey was sitting and went out. Lindsey poured black coffee into the cup. Billy Guyler offered sugar and cream to which she shook her head. Ursula stared at the photograph. Billy set down the cream and sugar, then moved nervously around the room switching on table lamps

When the pause had gone on long enough to restore a complete calm, Lindsey began on a new tack.

'Just let's assume for a moment that these documents are genuine,' she said, touching the photocopies. 'I for one believe they are. This young woman has been living for years with a woman who claimed to be her mother but clearly was not. She sees an item on television that makes her think perhaps her real mother is out there somewhere and rings the number given. The television producers think there's enough in her story to pass on the news to you and you supply a number that she can ring.' She broke off for a moment, until Ursula met her gaze. 'If you had heard a sweet young thing speaking in BBC accents, would you have come to me to inspect her for you?'

'That's beside the point.'

'It very much *is* the point. She's not what you expected so you shy away. Don't you think that's very unfair?'

'Unfair? It's only good sense – good business sense.'

'But Mrs Guyler – Ursula – finding a lost child isn't a business matter, now is it? You engaged me to give you advice.'

'I did nothing of the sort!' Ursula cried. 'I hired you to go and look at her and report back to me. And all I get is a lecture as if I'm somehow in the wrong!'

Biting her lip to keep from crying, she leapt up from her chair and rushed out of the room.

Her husband got up as if to follow her, then changed his mind. Lindsey began to gather up her papers. 'I'd better go.'

'No, don't,' he said. He made flapping motions with his hands. 'She'll be back in a minute. You have to forgive her, this whole thing has upset her dreadfully.' He sighed. 'I've never seen her like this before. She's always so level-headed.'

'Well, this is a huge problem for her.'

'And she knows she's got to deal with it and she knows she can't do it by running away from it. So she'll be back.' He picked up the snapshots that his wife had thrown down. 'There's no denying,' he muttered, 'this isn't what she expected.'

Lindsey nodded. 'And of course Edie's manners aren't exactly pleasing, and the way she talks . . .' She thought of the little speech pattern, 'Know what I mean?' which she used so often and so pointlessly.

'I don't know anything about the way she talks,' Billy remarked. 'I've never heard her.'

'But when she rang?'

'Oh, I was there, it was at the office, using one of Shula's mobiles. But I only heard Shula's end of it. It didn't last long and she got more and more upset until in the end she scribbled down a telephone number and switched off. And then a minute later she screwed up the piece of paper and threw it in the wastepaper basket.'

'But she gave me the number and the address.'

'Yes, well, she rescued it afterwards and we took it home with us and talked about it all weekend. And then she decided to go to Mr Ollerenshaw, and he recommended you.' He stooped to direct an earnest, worried gaze at her. 'You will sort it out for her, won't you? Stick with it, I mean? She needs help, though of course she'd never admit it.'

Lindsey stifled a sigh. 'I'll do my best.'

'What we need is a drink. What would you like? We've quite an assortment – brandy? A double malt? A liqueur?'

She accepted a small measure of Armagnac, feeling she needed some reinforcement for what was turning out to be a terrible evening. As she was sipping it, Ursula came back. If she'd been crying, she'd covered the traces very well.

She sat down, accepted a whisky from Billy, then spoke in a very firm tone. 'I don't want to be unfair. I'm just trying to protect myself – my husband and me – from what might turn out to be some form of extortion. Those documents may be genuine as you claim, but the fact that this girl was brought up by someone who wasn't her mother doesn't necessarily mean she's my Julie. There could be other explanations.'

'That's possible.'

'Could you make some enquiries?'

'What do you have in mind?'

'Well, find out if there was a young Mrs Maybury, whether she died and if so how and when – that sort of thing. I mean, those papers are only photocopies and these days it's not difficult to forge things.'

'I can verify the documents easily enough.'

'No, no, I want you to do more than that. I want you to go to . . .' She picked up the papers and sorted through them. 'The place where she lived – Cartfield – I want you to go there, find out if she was a real person, what she was like, what her little girl was like.'

'But Ursula, she died seventeen years ago.'

'It's a small town, people remember people in a small town. I want you to go there and find out what you can.'

Lindsey considered this in silence. Next day was Saturday – she could give the weekend to it, although weekends weren't the best time for conducting business. Yet some of this – perhaps most – would mean seeking out family and friends who were quite likely to be at home on a Saturday or Sunday.

'Very well,' she agreed. 'But meanwhile, what am I to say to Edie Maybury? I promised to be in touch.'

'Did you say when?'

'No, but I hoped it would be soon. You have to realise, Ursula, this is a big thing for her too.'

'Oh,' said Ursula, making shrugging movements, 'a day or two can't make all that much difference. Leave that until you've got a bit more information about the existence or otherwise of Mrs Maybury and her daughter.'

'All right.'

'And let me know as soon as you have something positive.'

That seemed to be as far as Ursula was prepared to go at present towards a solution. Lindsey felt it was just a barrier that she was putting up to defer any actual contact with Edie. She made a note of mobile phone numbers and took her leave, rather thankful to get away. At the corner where this leafy lane met the main road, she found a telephone box and called a cab.

Once home she looked up Cartfield in a road atlas. It wasn't too far from Carlisle so her best plan was to take the train and then hire a car. She spent the remains of the evening sending voicemail to the office with instructions to defer any appointments for Monday in case she had to stay over. She found a Carlisle hotel by consulting her drivers' handbook, rang, and booked a room. She called a taxi firm to collect her at six next morning.

That done, she fell into bed exhausted, and slept at once. When her alarm woke her – it seemed only ten minutes later – she went through her wake-up routine still half asleep. She was on the platform waiting for the train when it dawned on her that she hadn't let Andrew know she'd be absent all weekend.

She didn't want to disturb him so early on a Saturday. It wasn't until they were drawing out of Manchester that she felt justified in ringing. Even so he sounded very disgruntled. 'You're where? What on earth for?'

'It's a business matter, Andrew.'

'But you never said a word about it yesterday.'

'No, it came up after we had dinner.'

'Oh, it's *la belle dame sans merci*, is it?' He snorted half in amusement, half in annoyance. 'Very well, then, we have to put up with it, Old Ollie made a big point, didn't he. Okay, then. When will you be back?'

'Monday, but I perhaps won't come into the office.'

'See you Monday evening, then?'

'I'm not sure, Andrew. I'll ring you when I know how it's turning out.'

'So where are you headed, on this train?'

'North,' she said, in mock heroic tones.

'To the tundra?'

'I'm not afraid,' she responded. 'Remember, I was born in the northlands.'

She was in fact born and brought up in Northumberland, in a little town not far from Newcastle-on-Tyne. The countryside to which she was heading wasn't unfamiliar to her. As she switched off and settled back in her seat she thought with amusement that it was easier to get from Birmingham to Carlisle than it had ever been to get to Carlisle which was only the short trip west from her home town.

But she knew the area well. She and her two brothers had been taken on family picnics along the banks of the dark brown rivers, had walked and cycled all along the region of the Roman wall, had played mock battles between the Roman legions and the Picts – she of course being always the defeated Pict while her brothers strode about brandishing plastic swords and wearing plastic helmets.

Her parents still lived in the old family home, her father was the leading solicitor of the town. One brother was in London teaching mathematics, the other was in Italy selling scientific instruments. Sometimes she thought that it would be nice to join Gilbert in Italy, perhaps handle the negotiations to buy old farms in Tuscany for English émigrés. But that would mean leaving Andrew . . . and she couldn't do that.

She reached Carlisle about eleven. At the hotel she registered, left her overnight bag, and went out in search of a car hire firm. Well before noon she was on her way to Cartfield, some ten miles to the south. The roads were much less busy than she'd feared although driving conditions weren't of the best – a dull morning, with a persistent drizzle, and autumn leaves on the surface making it difficult to see the traffic markings. But she rolled into it at midday, finding it a little more difficult to park than she'd expected. But then, she recalled, on Saturdays people came in from the surrounding villages to do their shopping at the local market. It had been so in her home town of Ellenham.

She drove round the town just to get the feel of it, and was pleased to see a double-fronted office on one of the main side roads with the name, Cartfield Clarion, Printers and Publishers. On the window was painted: YOUR FAVOURITE LOCAL PAPER!

She found a place to leave the car in a park-and-ride area intended for those taking the bus into Carlisle. She walked back to the newspaper office, which was open for the taking of advertisements. Today was the day when people put in notices of engagements, forthcoming marriages, and funerals.

'Might I be allowed to look something up in the back numbers?' Lindsey enquired when her turn came to approach the counter.

'I beg your pardon?

'The back numbers – do you have them here?'

'You don't want to place an ad?' said the girl, clearly flummoxed.

'No, thank you, I've come up from Birmingham to make some enquires and it would help me a lot if I could look up your files.'

'Did you ring up and ask?'

'I'm afraid not. I only realised there was a local paper when I got here this morning.'

'We-ell, I don't know . . .' Clearly no one had ever walked in and requested such a thing before. She hesitated. Those behind Lindsey in the little queue muttered in impatience.

'Is there someone you could ask?' Lindsey prompted.

'We-ell . . . There's Mr Holland.'

'Could you do that, then?'

'I can't leave the desk.'

'Could you ring him?' Lindsey enquired, nodding towards the telephone that stood nearby.

'We-ell . . . I suppose so.' She picked up the instrument rather gingerly, pressed buttons, and spoke with some hesitation. 'There's a lady here, Mr Holland, wants to look at the back number file . . . . Just a minute, I'll ask.' She turned to Lindsey. 'Could I have your name, please?'

Lindsey had a business card ready. The girl read out from it: 'Lindsey Abercrombie, Higgett, Ollerenshaw and Cline, Solicitors, Hanover Lane, Birmingham – yes, Mr Holland, Birmingham it says here.' She looked up. 'Mr Holland would like to know what it's about.'

'I'm afraid it's a legal matter concerning one of my clients but it's nothing that need trouble the newspaper – I just need some information, that's all.'

The message was conveyed. 'Yes, Mr Holland.' The advertising clerk put down the phone, raised a flap in the counter, and invited Lindsey through. The queue made approving noises. 'Through the door and turn right,' she said. 'Mr Holland will meet you.'

She pushed a buzzer that released the latch on the door. Lindsey followed the directions, to find herself in a small paved hall and at the foot of a flight of stairs. There was the clatter of heavy shoes as a figure came flying down. The light was rather dim but she saw a tall man with ruffled hair and in his shirt sleeves.

'Hello there. Miss Abercrombie, is it? I'm Keith Holland, managing editor.'

'How d'you do? I hope I'm not being a bother but I would very much like to look up something in your files.'

'Yes, yes, Betsy said all that. Something important, I take it if it's a law thing. Is it within the last five years?'

'No, considerably farther back than that.'

'Oh. In that case, come this way.'

He led the way along the hall to a door under the staircase. From this steps led down. He switched on a light, then led the way. 'Nothing up to date and efficient such as microfiche or computer files until five years ago,' he said. 'Back numbers before that are in bound volumes.'

The basement was dusty and smelt of old paper and leather. Large shelves of unpainted wood housed great rectangular books, each the size of a full newspaper page.

'What year?' the editor enquired.

'I'm not exactly sure but it will be about seventeen years ago.'

He raised thick dark eyebrows. 'Huh? Search for a beneficiary, is it?'

'No, nothing like that.' She followed him between the stacks of shelves. He found the series of volumes that might be of use, took hold of the strap fitted on the spine of one volume and heaved it out. A little cloud of dust came with it.

'This way,' he said over the top edge of the volume, and led her to a battered table under the dusty basement window. He set the leather book down with a thump.

'What are we looking for? It'll be births, deaths or marriages, I expect.'

'The death notices, please.'

'Well, you'll find them on page four of every issue. Each volume is six months issues bound together and this one is January to June. I'll bring you July to December and then if you need to go back or forward, I'm afraid you'll have to manage on your own.'

'Thank you. That's very kind.'

'What name are you after?' he asked, opening the volume and beginning to flick over pages.

'Oh, I'd rather not discuss that, if you don't mind.'

He gave a sudden grin. 'Solicitors. You're all alike.' He glanced over her shoulder but she was still turning pages. 'Okay, I'll fetch you the other six months.' Off he went, returning with another great book which he leant against the table leg. 'Got to go,' he said. 'I'm wrestling on the computer with an article for next week's issue and waiting for some extra info to be faxed through.' He went to the door of the dingy room. 'When you're finished, come upstairs and give a shout. I'll let you out of the main door – there's a security system.'

'Thank you very much.'

He hesitated a moment, gave her a little salute, and went out. Once he was gone, Lindsey closed the book on the table and hefted up the one on the floor. She knew the date of the issue she needed – she had it on the photocopy of the death certificate in her handbag. After flicking over a few yellowing pages she found the notices. There, sixth in the list, was the announcement.

> MAYBURY: Mary Lois Maybury in her 23rd year and Edie Maybury, aged three, beloved daughter and grand-daughter of Peter and Ada Maybury, on 6 July at Whelby Hospital, Carlisle. Funeral service at St John's Church Cartfield on 14 July, floral tributes to Gregg and Sons, 11 Rigley Road, Cartfield.

So it was true. There was nothing faked about the death certificate. Lindsey had never thought there was, but to please her client she had verified it. She copied down the details.

'Find out what you can.' Was this enough? Well, no, because she could have done this by telephone or e-mail, although it would have meant a certain crack in confidentiality. But she knew that Ursula Guyler had meant her to do more – to find out some personal details about the dead woman and her child.

Lindsey closed the book and set it back against the leg of the table. No need to give the inquisitive Mr Holland even the slightest hint of what she'd been looking up. She went up the stairs to the lobby and there called up to the first floor. 'Mr Holland! I've finished.'

'Just a sec,' came the call from upstairs. It was perhaps sixty seconds before he came down two steps at a time. 'Just had to capture that last literary gem,' he said. 'Find what you wanted?'

'Yes, thank you.' She moved towards the door that led out to the street. He went with her but paused with his hand above a pad of numbers. Clearly his reporter's instinct was urging him to find out more.

'If one of my townsfolk is about to inherit a fortune, it would be nice to know so I could go and interview him.'

'Nothing like that, I'm afraid.'

'Well, no, perhaps not, since you were looking up deaths. So is it something that's got stuck in probate?'

42

'Now you know I'm not going to tell you,' she said, laughing. 'Please open the door, I've got things to do.'

'Here in Cartfield?'

'I should have known you'd ask!'

'Had lunch?'

'Well . . . no.'

'And you're a stranger in Cartfield so you haven't a clue where to eat.' He glanced at his watch. 'Just hang on a minute while I save what's on the computer, and I'll take you to the best pub in the district.'

'Oh, no, thank you, but really—'

'Afraid I'll trap you into a damaging admission?' He shook his head and held up a hand in solemn oath. 'I promise – not a word.'

She chuckled. 'I know better than to believe the word of a journalist,' she said.

'You only know dreadful city journalists. Here in the sticks, we're all true and noble.' He turned back to the stairs. 'Wait there, ten seconds.'

He ran upstairs two at a time, which seemed to be the pace at which he took everything. When came back he was shrugging into a rather shabby sports jacket. He tapped some numbers into the security pad, opened the door, and they went out. Lindsey found she had accepted the lunch invitation without exactly knowing how.

Outside it was still drizzling. She nodded at her hire car. 'Do we go in that?'

'It's a five minute walk but we'll drive if you want to. You city folk,' he remarked, putting on an expression of mock disapproval, 'always rushing about in cars. Have you no regard for the environment?'

'We'll walk,' Lindsey said.

He started off at once and she found she had to move briskly to keep up with his long-legged amble. He was a tall man, loose-jointed, with ordinary brown hair above a high brow and light brown eyes. She thought he might be approaching forty, but it was hard to tell because his face was lined, mostly with laughter lines around his mouth and eyes which showed up against an outdoor tan.

43

'So,' he remarked, 'you're Miss Abercrombie from Litigant, Will and Codicil of Birmingham.'

'Close enough,' she agreed. 'And you're Mr Holland, of the *Cartfield Clarion*.'

'Keith Holland, managing editor and owner. Not much to manage but a lot to edit – I'm the eyes and ears of Cartfield.'

'What, all on your own?'

'No, no, I've an elderly lady who reports all the choir recitals and debating-society events, and a young hopeful who goes to watch our rugby team get slaughtered and takes all the pix. Incidentally, if there was anything you'd like photocopied from the bound volumes, the books are too big to go on the machine but Sammo could photograph the items and enlarge them if you like.'

'No thanks, I got all I needed.' To soften any abruptness in her response, she asked, 'Is the *Clarion* a give-away paper?'

'Absolutely not!' He turned an indignant eye upon her. 'You take a look in your Birmingham give-away and see how much space they give to reporting a wedding or the musical successes of the local brass band! No, the *Clarion* is one of the very few remaining local papers that actually takes an interest in the neighbourhood.' He took her elbow. 'Here we are.'

They'd been passing detached houses with pleasant gardens, clearly moving towards the edge of the little market town. Now they were at an old public house, with a flagstoned forecourt on which stood an old cart, its shafts resting on the stones and its body filled with tubs of white-blossomed geraniums.

'The Merry Carter,' Keith Holland said, leading her indoors. 'All local produce, I particularly recommend the ham sandwiches.'

They went into the saloon bar, which was quite full. Several of the customers nodded at her companion as they came in. An elderly man rose from a table saying, 'You can have this, Keith, I'm just going.'

They sat down. He handed her a menu. 'Take a look at that while I fetch our drinks. What will you have?'

'Mm . . . I'll have a lager, please.'

'Any particular brand?'

'Something foreign,' Lindsey said, smiling to herself.

44

'You'll be lucky! This is brewing country, you're supposed to support our local breweries.'

'You choose, then.'

He returned a few minutes later with their drinks. Setting them down he said, 'If you'd like something hot, they do a good lamb stew and a first-class vegetarian lasagne.'

'I'll have the lasagne, then.'

'You're a vegetarian?'

'Tut tut. There's no evidence to support that. I just like Italian food.'

He grinned, took a sip from his glass of bitter, then went to order. 'Ten minutes,' he said on his return. 'So while we wait let's get to know each other. You're a fully fledged solicitor, are you?'

'I am. And you're a fully fledged editor.'

'I don't know that you ever get fully fledged in this game. Something's always turning up to surprise you. You, for instance.'

'Oh, there's nothing surprising about me. I'm just beavering away on behalf of a client.'

'Somebody with a lot of money, obviously – you're from a city firm where I expect you've a lot on your plate but you're wasting your time ferreting around in a Cumbrian market town.'

'Oh, I'm not wasting my time,' she said, and regretted it at once.

He didn't smile in pleasure at having got that much out of her, because it was indeed very little. She interested Keith Holland very much, this calm bright visitor from the great city. Very few people came to the newspaper office except to place advertisements in the personal columns. He'd been owner now for nearly five years and this was the first time anyone had wanted to look anything up in the morgue. But it was going to be hard work getting her to tell him the reason.

'Will you be staying long?' he began again.

'Not very, I think.'

'If I can help you in any way, please don't hesitate. I know the district very well, I've got lots of friends that I could call on – here in this room,' he said, nodding about, 'there isn't a man I couldn't put a name to.'

'That only proves that you're a regular here. It doesn't prove you know the entire population of Cartfield.'

'Ouch.' He shook his head at her. She was a very smart lady. 'I'll walk you round the market after lunch. You'll see, I know everybody and everybody knows me. I could be a big help to you if there's something you need to do here in the town.'

She smiled. 'You talk too much, Mr Holland.'

'Huh?' He was taken aback.

'Part of my business, like yours, is getting people to confide in me, and experience shows that if I do all the talking, others fall silent.'

He had to give her full marks for that. 'I could say that folks hereabouts are not talkative anyhow, but that would be a cop out.'

A call from the bar announced that their food had arrived. He rose to fetch it, then set the plates and napkin-wrapped cutlery down on the table.

'Thank you,' she said. 'And tell your local brewery they make good lager.'

'Now there you are! That's just the kind of thing that I could use in my local chit-chat column.'

'Shall I say something more enthusiastic? The best I've ever tasted – but it means nothing.'

'Why not?'

'I almost never drink lager.'

'Well, now I know two things about you. You're not a vegetarian and you don't usually drink lager.'

'Much good may it do you.'

'Oh, little brushstrokes make up the picture,' he replied. 'A good journalist can make a lot out of little.' There. Shake her up a bit. Instinct told him there was a story here, big or small, he wasn't sure.

'You've always been a journalist?' Lindsey said, well aware he was baiting her.

'I ought to be ashamed to admit it, but yes. But not here in Cartfield. I worked in Manchester when I started and then got a great job in London.'

46

'So why are you here?'

'Oh, disillusionment, I think. The great job turned out to be sleazy so I left and went freelance, and was lucky enough to land a couple of very big exclusives – so with the money and a loan from the bank, I bought the *Clarion*.' He paused abruptly. 'I'm doing all the talking!'

She ate another forkful of lasagne. 'You were right,' she said, 'this is very good.'

He drew in a breath and let it out in a big sigh. 'Do you do much work in the magistrates' court? I bet you're a whizz at it.'

'No, I don't do much court work.'

'Well, let me start again,' he said, gathering his forces for a different approach. 'You're staying in Carlisle?'

She nodded, busy with her food, because she'd discovered she was ravenously hungry.

'At the Sceptre?'

She couldn't quite hide her surprise that he'd guessed so correctly. He grinned. 'It's in the drivers' handbooks,' he said. 'A lot of people put up there because they give it such a good rating. Did you get the discount for the special long-weekend package?'

She studied him in silence for a moment. 'I seem to recall,' she said, 'that when you offered to show me where to eat, you promised not to ask any more questions.'

'I did? Never! Asking questions is second nature to me.'

'I'm enjoying my lasagne very much, thank you. How is your steak?'

'Excellent. Is Abercrombie a Scottish name?'

'I believe so. Is Holland a Dutch name?'

He burst out laughing. 'Well, at least tell me your first name.'

'It's on the card I gave your advertisement clerk.'

'Mine's Keith. That's Gaelic and I believe it means battlefield soldier, which is very suitable because of course the newspaper world is a battlefield, but my parents didn't know I was going to be a journalist when they chose it. Does your first name have anything to do with the law?'

'No, but it begins with L.'

47

'Victory! You've actually volunteered something! Well, I'm happy now. I'd begun to think my interviewing technique had rusted away completely. If you've finished your lasagne, let me recommend the apple pie.'

'No, thank you.'

'Coffee?'

'No, thanks, I'll just stick with the lager.' She didn't really want any more, and in fact was rather eager to get away from this lively, questing mind. A fencing match can be fun but it must end with the buttons still on the foils.

They had a friendly wrangle over whether he would pay the bill or whether they should go Dutch. She let him win. She knew he thought it would let him lead on to something else, and sure enough on their walk back to the newspaper office he said, 'Have you plans for this evening?'

'I don't know yet.'

'I'll ring you, shall I? We could have dinner at the Sceptre – the food there is rather good.'

'It's very kind of you, but I may be busy. And if not, I think I may be pretty tired, so I'd like an evening alone.'

'Oh, but that would be a cold thing for a visitor to our region. No, no, you must let me—'

'No, no, you're very kind, but really I may be otherwise engaged.'

'Doing what?'

'Doing what solicitors do.'

'I'll ring,' he said.

When they reached her car, parked near the newspaper office, he said, 'Can I give you directions to anywhere?'

She laughed. 'I haven't seen a copy of the *Clarion* yet,' she said, 'but I begin to think it must be absolutely full of things you've ferreted out. Goodbye, Keith Holland, and thank you for the lunch.'

'Goodbye, Miss L. Abercrombie, I'm going straight to the advertisement counter to find out your first name.'

She got in and drove off. She could well have left the car there, it wasn't in a parking zone and she knew it wasn't far to walk to the town centre, but she had a strong desire to get out from under the inquisitive eye of Keith Holland.

She found what she was looking for not far from the market, still busy though the afternoon was waning – an old-fashioned bookshop with some travel books among the window display. She went in and bought a thin book called *Street Maps of Carlisle and Neighbouring Towns*, after ensuring that it contained Cartfield.

But after sitting in the car for ten minutes looking first in the index and then through the pages, she couldn't find Millers Road, the name on the death certificate of the Mayburys, mother and child.

She went back into the shop. The salesman was elderly and perhaps the owner. She asked if she could trouble him for a moment. 'I bought this book to look for Millers Road, Cartfield but it doesn't seem to be there?'

'Millers Road? Er . . . That rings a bell . . . Millers Road . . . Oh, of course, that was that dreadful long winding road going out to the west. Millers Road – yes, I'm very sorry, miss, but that was all bulldozed away when they built the bypass ten or twelve years ago.'

'Oh.'

Her disappointment was so obvious that he tried to be more helpful. 'Did you want a particular address?'

'Number 127 – the people who lived there were the Mayburys.'

'The Mayburys, the Mayburys . . . No, sorry, don't know the name.' He gave a rueful smile. 'Only know those who come in and buy books, you see. The Mayburys probably weren't book readers.'

It was a setback but she was used to those. 'What happened to the people who lived along Millers Road – can you recall?'

'Umm . . . er . . . Seems to me they were mostly resettled on one of the council estates. They built two around that time, I recall – Wheelwright Park and Cathaby . . . Yes, I think that's where most of them went.'

To find out who had gone where would mean visiting the council housing department which of course was closed on a Saturday afternoon. She was about to thank the bookseller when she was struck by a thought. She felt in her bag for the envelope with the photocopies, brought out the death certificate

49

for mother and daughter, and asked, 'Can you tell me if Gregg and Son the undertakers are still in existence?'

'Gregg's? My word yes! Been there for getting on seventy years now, I should think – certainly since *I* was a boy. In Rigley Road – do you want to go there? Here, let me show you.' He opened her book at the Cartfield pages, and put an unerring finger on the line of the road. 'You're driving? You'll have to go round the one-way system, then. Really, it would be quicker to walk. Just cross Market Square, go down Victoria Street, see it? You can't miss it, it's got the chemist on the corner. Then you see Rigley Road is the second turning on the right.'

She thanked him and he walked her to the door. 'Just leave your car there, it's quite safe.' And with heartfelt thanks to the good-citizenship of country towns, she did so and walked off in search of Gregg and Son.

It had been her experience as a family solicitor that people tended to stay with the same undertaker. She had actually had a client say to her while making his will, 'Put in that Jepperson's to bury me. They do you a good burial at Jepperson's.'

Since Gregg had been in existence so long it was probably not Gregg or Son who greeted her when she went into the mahogany-panelled interior. He wore a sombre suit over a portly stomach, but his manner was un-stuffy. 'How may I help you, madam?'

She gave him one of her business cards. He looked only slightly impressed. 'A legal matter?'

'It's just an enquiry, there isn't a problem,' she hastened to reassure him.

He smiled. 'Happy to hear that. What can I do for you?'

'Do you by any chance remember the Maybury family?'

'Maybury, Maybury . . .' He rubbed the tip of his nose. 'Angus Maybury? Died about two years ago? No? Gladys Mary Maybury – she was two years short of her hundred, poor soul. No?'

'This would have been about seventeen years ago – a mother and little girl who died together—'

'In a traffic accident? Let me see . . . Mary Louise . . .'

'Lois.'

'Mary Lois and . . . and . . . Enid?'

'Edie.'

'Ah yes. A little toddler. Very, very sad. I'd only just started in the business as young Mr Gregg's assistant. I remember it upset me a lot. And the poor parents – now I'll tell you their names in a minute, I seldom forget a name or a face. Peter and Alice. No, Ada.'

'That's who I'm looking for, Mr and Mrs Maybury.'

'Ah, I fear you won't find *him*. We arranged his funeral about two years after his daughter went. Broke his heart, you know, to lose those two – I remember he said to me, "It's all wrong, Stilworth, a daughter dying before her parents, but a granddaughter's unbearable." And then you know, they pulled down all those nice old houses in Millers Road and moved everybody off to housing estates, and it was just the end of poor Mr Maybury. Two, maybe three years after his daughter and granddaughter.'

'And Mrs Maybury?' Lindsey said, holding her breath.

'Oh yes, she's still alive and well. Pillar of the church. She often does the flowers at churches where we're involved with the funeral service. I see her from time to time – yes, yes, alive and well, alive and well.'

'Could you by any chance give me her address?'

Mr Stilworth gave a little frown. 'I don't know whether . . .'

'Is she in the phone book?'

'Well, yes, she is, of course . . . Oh then, there seems no reason to withhold her address. She's living in . . . just a moment, let me check.'

He went from the handsome front office to another room where she could glimpse a workaday desk and filing cabinets. She heard a steel drawer being opened and the sound of files being pushed on their hangers. Then Mr Stilworth returned with a slip of paper. 'There you are, twenty-two Ankery Row – that's about three-quarters of a mile down the by-pass road and then off to the right, where there's rather a nice little group of bungalows.'

'She's not on one of the council estates, then?'

'No, there was insurance and so on at her husband's death, I think, and she didn't like living in a council flat so she bought

51

the bungalow.' He paused. 'Give her my regards when you see her,' he ended.

'I will. Thank you.' Lindsey went out, wondering if she really would pass on the good wishes of an undertaker.

She went back to her car and set off. Getting on to the by-pass necessitated going around the one-way system and she chose the wrong lane at the roundabout. So it was nearly six o'clock before she saw the signpost – Ankery Vale. She drove slowly down a road bordered with laurel and rhododendron, found what looked like an imitation village green, and saw that off that was Ankery Row, about a dozen newish bungalows with neat front gardens and with autumn-tinted trees on the pavement.

Outside number twenty-two were tubs with dwarf Michaelmas daisies. She rang the bell. No reply. She rang again, then knocked. In the next house a small dog yapped, and its door opened. Out came a grey-haired lady saying, 'Quiet, Nicky, quiet, it's only a visitor.' To Lindsey she said across the neatly trimmed hedge, 'Can I help you?'

'I was hoping to speak to Mrs Maybury.'

'I'm affeared she's out.'

'Any idea when she'll be back?'

'No till late-ish. She's at the church social, and though they dinna last till late, she stays on to help clear the tables and do the dishes.'

Lindsey sighed. But it had been too much to hope that she would contact Ada Maybury so easily. 'I'll come back tomorrow, then,' she said.'

'Ach, she'll be at the morning service,' said the neighbour with a slight shake of the head. 'Aye at something to do with the church . . . I'd leave it till afternoon if I was you.'

'Thank you very much. I'll come back then.'

'Shall I say to her you're coming? She might very well go out to help with Sunday school or something!'

'Oh . . . I suppose that's true. Well, could you say someone would just like a word with her, nothing very important. My name is Abercrombie.' She didn't offer a card, thinking the word solicitor might scare both the neighbour and Mrs Maybury.

She drove back into the town, thinking about how to approach Mrs Maybury. The fact that she'd decided not to leave her business card was a signal that it was going to be a difficult interview. Exactly what could she say? 'I'm a solicitor and I've come to ask about your granddaughter'? That raised the idea of an inheritance, she'd always found. But then, 'I know somebody who's using your granddaughter's name and birth certificate,' was neither kind nor useful.

Some slight subterfuge was called for. When she reached the town centre she parked without difficulty, since the market was emptying and the stalls closing down. She bought a clipboard and a sheaf of writing paper at a newsagent, then went into the shopping mall. There she found, as she'd hoped, a machine offering the instant printing of visiting cards. She put in her money then printed out a set which said: Lesley Abercrombie, representing the Traffic Reorganisation Inquiry, and after that her address at the law firm in Birmingham.

That done, she drove to the Sceptre. She was very tired by now and longing for a long hot shower, a meal, and early bed.

The first two were easily accomplished. She enjoyed a fine *sole meunier* and a glass of rather good Chardonnay, refused coffee, then went upstairs to make hot chocolate from the supply in her room. But before she did so she must ring Andrew.

He was out. Of course – Saturday night. Why would a young man about town be indoors at nine o'clock on a Saturday? She left a message on his machine, and was just tearing open the packet of drinking chocolate when the phone rang. She picked it up, expecting Andrew.

It was Keith Holland.

'Good evening, Lindsey Abercrombie,' he said. 'I said I'd ring, didn't I? How are you? Have you found the Sceptre up to expectations?'

'Ah . . . yes, thank you.'

'Had dinner yet?'

'Yes.'

'It really is a good menu, isn't it?'

'I found it very pleasant.'

'So what are you going to do now? Watch television? There's a good film on Sky.'

'No, I intend to have an early night.'

'For an early start back home in the morning.'

'No.'

'You're staying on?'

'I am.'

'Coming back to Cartfield?'

She sighed. There was no reason to deny it, but she had an instinctive resistance to telling him anything. Journalists weren't to be trusted.

'If you're going to see Mrs Maybury, I'll meet you there,' he went on.

She stifled a gasp. For a moment she was dumbfounded.

'Hello?' said Keith Holland.

'How did you know I was going to see Mrs Maybury?'

There was laughter in his voice when he replied. 'My spies are everywhere,' he said.

Four

Lindsey had been so tired she'd almost been asleep on her feet. But after Keith Holland's phone call she found she was wide awake. The hot chocolate, now tepid, had no effect. She lay awake wondering what she should have done.

But she'd known as they were speaking that nothing she could say would deflect him. Nor in fact had she the right to stop him. 'It's a free country,' as the saying goes. He had a perfect right to be at Ankery Vale tomorrow afternoon.

She had no doubt it was the undertaker who had given him the information. The owner and chief reporter of a local paper must be on friendly terms with the people who serve his community: no doubt it was well known that if you sent in little items of news or gossip, the *Clarion* would treat you well with regard to advertising space or favourable comment. Or perhaps even give small cash payments to the man or woman in the street.

So he would be there tomorrow. She could do her best to avoid him – turn up early, be on the watch for Mrs Maybury returning from church and go in with her. But that would hardly be favourable for a friendly chat because Mrs Maybury would be needing her lunch . . .

Round and round it went in her mind. At last she fell asleep and, as a result, woke late and was just in time to get to the breakfast room before the buffet service closed at ten.

Overnight her unconscious had to some extent settled the problem. There was nothing she could do about Mr Holland's activities. So she would ignore them, go to see Mrs Maybury as planned, and retain an absolute silence to Holland about the reasons for the visit.

She read the Sunday paper over breakfast, strolled out about eleven, and went for a walk around the city of Carlisle. The weather was still unfriendly – not cold but not warm, with a slight breeze blowing a sea mist in from the coast.

Close to the railway station she found a cyber cafe. There she composed a questionnaire such as might be used by an organisation enquiring into the results of road-building and traffic reorganisation. 'Were local shops destroyed? Were local transport services altered? Were they (a) improved? (b) worsened? (c) discontinued?' And so on. She printed out half a dozen, then returned to the hotel to scribble pretend answers on some of the sheets. She put them all, scribbles and blanks, under the clip of her clipboard and put the clipboard in her capacious shoulder bag. There! She was an investigator taking a poll, with all the correct paraphernalia.

By now lunchtime was approaching. But she was too full of breakfast to want anything so instead, for old times' sake, she got in the car and drove east along the River Eden towards Brampton and Hexham. The sky had cleared and a watery sun had come out. Everything shone with a silvery glint from the moisture of the morning. She looked fondly at the familiar landscape, the rolling hills, the birch trees, the sheep like dots of ivory on the green pasture.

A few more miles and she'd be not too far from her parents' house – but she had to turn back before long and head for Ankery Vale and its bungalows.

When she drew up at the beginning of Ankery Row, Keith Holland was sitting on a low wall bordering a municipal flowerbed and reading a book. He rose as she got out of the car. 'Good afternoon, Lindsey. Did you sleep well?'

'Thank you, yes.'

'Mrs Maybury came home about an hour ago, I should think she's had her lunch by now.'

'You've been here an hour?' she exclaimed, amazed.

'In the course of duty, no sacrifice is too great. Shall we make a joint approach?' He made as if to walk with her towards the house.

'No, we certainly shall not,' she said, standing quite still.

'Oh, come on. I'll find out what you talked to her about

56

one way or another. We might as well do the interview together.'

'No.'

'It's something to do with Peter Maybury, isn't it?'

'It's none of your business.'

'I looked up the Mayburys as soon as I heard you were interested in them. He died about fifteen years ago. Was he up to something? Nobbling the horses at the race track? Secret love affair?'

'Why don't you go back to your office and do something useful,' she suggested.

'Nobody seems to remember him particularly. If he was leading some kind of a double life, he was good at it because nothing seems to ring a bell with anybody.'

'Have you been asking people about him? Good heavens, the way you're going on, you'd think it was a federal case!'

'Well, is it? That's what I want to know. You come all the way up from Birmingham, you're taking a lot of trouble—'

'The only trouble I have is you,' she riposted. 'Now, let's get this clear. I am going to have a chat with Mrs Maybury, and I'm going to do it without any interference from you. If you insist on harassing me, I'll call the police on my mobile.'

She marched away, and he had the good sense not to try to accompany her. He could see he had really angered her, and that might be a good thing or a bad thing, because people tended to let things slip when they were angry. On the other hand, he didn't want to be on totally bad terms with her. There was something very engaging about this swallow from the south, with her clear hazel glance and her quick intelligence.

He watched her go up the path of Mrs Maybury's house. A slight figure in a navy Caractere jacket, matching skirt, and medium heels. Very non-specific, not likely to alarm a widow living on her own.

Lindsey smiled and held up her clipboard when the door opened. 'Mrs Maybury? I called yesterday but you were out.'

'Oh aye, Violet told me. Miss Abernethy, is it?'

'Abercrombie. I wonder if you could spare me a few minutes to answer some questions?'

57

'Och now, what's it about?'

She had the lovely accent of the Borders – softened consonants, a slow lilt to her speech. She was taller then Lindsey by a few inches, strong-looking, a hint of grey in the tawny hair – a colour so often seen in the old raiding grounds of the Vikings.

'It's a survey about traffic,' Lindsey said, 'about the effects of road building on the local community, and in particular my questions are about the by-pass—'

'Oh, the by-pass!' cried Ada Maybury. 'That wicked thing! Come in, come in, I can tell ye a life's history on that – I have a loath for it!'

Lindsey followed her into a narrow passage and then into a room at the front of the house. It was sparklingly clean and smelt of Mr Sheen. Starched curtains of old cotton lace hung at the windows. As she approached them Lindsey could just make out the irrepressible Keith Holland sitting on the stone wall. She smiled to herself.

'The by-pass! One way or anither it was the ruin of my life,' said Mrs Maybury, gesturing her to an armchair of dark brown velour. 'It killed all of my family! If it wasna for the by-pass I wouldna be here in this poky wee house all on my lone.'

There was absolutely no need for the fake questionnaire, thank goodness. Lindsey said, 'How did that happen, Mrs Maybury?'

'Ach . . .' Her hostess sat down in the armchair opposite, sighing with the pains of memory. 'First it took my daughter and her lovely wee girl. We lived in Millers Road then, and I willna deny it was a bad, bad road, long and winding and wi' hollows and dips that made it hard for the drivers. But there were "Slow" notices all along it, and lines to prevent the cars going into the wrong lane . . . Well, that's common, isn't it? But it didna stop a great hulking lorry from hitting the pair of them and then driving on and leaving them all broken and bleeding in the road . . .'

Her fingers pleated and kneaded the lace protectors on the arms of her chair.

'I'm so sorry,' Lindsey said in a very low voice, careful not to disturb the process but inwardly distressed at its results.

58

'Well, the ambulance took them to Carlisle. But they'd died on the way, so they told me.'

'That was – when?'

'Seventeen years ago – my wee Edie would have been twenty now – ah, what a pretty little lassie. She'd have made a beauty if she'd lived to see it. Wait, then, I'll show you.' She heaved herself out of the chair, went to a sideboard, and took out a photograph album.

Unhesitatingly she opened it at the right place. She held it out to Lindsey who took it, to see a small dark-haired child in a party frock, holding a stuffed penguin in her arms. 'That was her third birthday – and look, there's her mother, my Mary . . . They were a pair, pretty and blithe as blackbirds, took after my husband – that's him, bringing in the birthday cake – Peter . . .'

She let the album go into Lindsey's hands. She sought for a tissue in the pocket of her church-going dress and wiped her eyes.

'They're lovely, your daughter and granddaughter,' said Lindsey. 'Both beautiful brunettes. What colour are the little girl's eyes? I can't quite make out.'

'Brown, of course, I telt ye, they took after Peter. Not a speck of me in the pair of them, nor of that villain that left her with a bairn in her arms – well, she was better off without him, whoever he was . . .'

Peter Maybury was in some of the snaps on an earlier page – a burly man, with a quiet gaze and a head of dark hair already beginning to recede from his forehead.

Seeing Lindsey's eyes on the picture, Mrs Maybury began again. 'He died two years after the accident. Poor man, never recovered from the loss of the bairns, our own and my daughter's. Then came the by-pass, and the landlord got a compulsory purchase order on the row of houses, and ours among them so we had to go. Where did they send us? To a flat on a council estate.' She sat down in her chair again. 'Not that it was a bad place as council estates go, I'm not saying that. But Peter and I, we'd aye had our front door and a bit of a garden . . . He just . . . dwindled away. His heart took him off in the end.'

'So you decided to move?'

'Aye, this was a new development at the time, nice wee houses and a bit of a garden. And to me an important thing was, it's near the cemetery where my dear ones are buried. I take them flowers every week. And then there's a bus into the town twice a day from Ankery Green, even on a Sunday, so I can get in to church, and friends in the Mothers Union will pick me up at other times. Oh, I've little to complain of compared wi' some, but I'll never forgive the building of that by-pass road.' She stopped, summoning a smile. 'So you can tell them that sent ye that though it may have made life more convenient for the motorists, there's mony that curse the day it was ever started.'

'I understand how you feel,' Lindsey said. She turned over a few more pages of the album to encourage Mrs Maybury's recollections, but there was little more to be learned: Mary Lois Maybury and her daughter Edie had both been dark-haired and brown-eyed, they had both died under the wheels of a truck and were buried nearby. The Edie Maybury whom Lindsey had met was living under a false identity.

After another ten minutes Lindsey gathered her handbag and rose. 'I want to thank you for spending so much time with me.'

'Now you're not going to go without me offering you a cup of tea.'

'Thank you, but I have more work to do.'

'Of course, of course, I understand. Well, I hope this has been useful.'

'Very, very useful,' Lindsey said, shaking hands. 'Thank you very much.'

She was shown out, and as she made her way down the short path she saw Keith Holland rising to meet her from his place on the wall. She sighed.

'Give me a lift back to Cartfield?' he suggested.

'What!'

'I took the morning bus. No further transport towards town until four o'clock.'

'Well, for running, standing and jumping effrontery!'

'Come on, be a pal. It's coming on to rain again.'

On reflection, it seemed better to take him away from the

neighbourhood rather than have him go pestering Mrs Maybury with a fishing trip. 'All right,' she said.

'You're really very nice, for a solicitor,' he said.

When they were back on the by-pass, she enquired, 'You know what you were asking – about whether Peter Maybury had been up to something – would you *really* put that in your paper?'

'Well, has he?'

'You're not answering my question. The man has been dead fifteen years, his widow has a hard burden of memories, would you *really* publish something to make her life less happy, just to fill up space?'

He looked momentarily perturbed. 'Well . . . If you put it like that . . . No, of course I wouldn't, unless something else was going to emerge to make it newsworthy. If there was going to be an enquiry by the Jockey Club about something he did at the race course.'

'Peter Maybury did nothing except fall sick and die,' she said with vehemence. 'And his widow has done nothing except grieve, put her life together again, and help out at her church. Leave her alone.'

'All right, all right! But you still haven't explained why you're here.'

'And I'm not going to, so give it up.'

He began to laugh. 'Never in the history of human news gathering has so much time been spent on so little and so forth. You've fought me to a standstill, I must confess. So let me pay tribute to you by offering you afternoon tea.'

'No thank you, Mr Holland.'

'Oh, come on, there's a stately silver service at the Sceptre, with teensy sandwiches and cream cakes – you'd enjoy it.'

Now all at once she discovered she was hungry. Breakfast had been some four and a half hours ago. She longed for a cup of tea. And now that he had admitted defeat, it would be possible to relax and treat him as a fellow human being, not a threat.

'All right,' she said. 'I'll drive you to Carlisle so you can pay for my tea. But you promise to behave?'

'Cross my heart.' He made the motion with his finger. He

looked all at once very unthreatening, someone with whom it would be pleasant to spend an hour or two instead of sitting alone in a corner of the lounge watching the rain come down.

Afternoon tea at the hotel proved all he had promised. There were quite a few other guests – it seemed an outing for afternoon tea was an established custom with those who could afford the price, which was considerably more than a doughnut and a plastic beaker in the local Macdonald's.

'Do you do this sort of thing a lot, Lindsey?' he asked when they had sampled the sandwiches. 'Jaunt around the country for your clients?'

'Sometimes,' she confessed. 'And I wasn't too put out at coming to Carlisle – I was born just the other end of the Roman wall.'

'Ah, a native! Now you see, I'm an incomer. After five years I think they've begun to accept me.'

'I noticed in the pub yesterday most people seemed to know you.'

'Oh, yes, they even call me by my first name, which is Keith, by the way. I wish you'd use it.'

'All right then, Keith.'

'I'm sorry if I upset you last night by telephoning. I thought afterwards it was rather a mean thing to do.'

'You spoiled my hot chocolate.'

'It was just that I sensed – mistakenly, it seems – that there was an interesting story there. My instincts as a reporter are seldom wrong, but I apologise.'

'Well, in return I'll tell you that I've accomplished my work for my client and I'll be leaving in the morning.'

'So soon?' He appeared genuinely disappointed. 'I hoped we might have a chance to get to know each other a little better. I could show you around a bit – I could even offer you a meal at my place, I'm quite a good cook, and the house is rather nice, an old one-up one-down cottage on the banks of the Eden.'

'You do your own cooking?'

'Oh, sure, no wife, no family. I was married once but it didn't take. You?'

She shook her head.

'Stay on a day or two. The forecast is for better weather.'

'No, I really can't. I'm expected back in Birmingham.'

He ate the last of the sandwiches, looking thoughtful. 'I can find something to bring me to Birmingham,' he mused. 'Or I could even decide not to put it on the expense account and come for a weekend break. I've got your Birmingham number on that card – shall I ring you one day soon and fix it up?'

She was about to say, 'Why not?' when she remembered Andrew and what he might say to it. 'I don't know,' she said, 'I'm kept pretty busy.'

'"Getting and spending, we lay waste our time,"' he quoted, then held up a finger. 'That's an idea. Let's meet in Stratford and take in some Shakespeare.'

She decided she had to break the conversation. She got up. 'I think I'll just wash my hands, I've got mayonnaise on them.' She hurried away, and was about to enter the ladies' room when she realised she'd forgotten her handbag. She went back for it.

And there was Keith going through it, pulling out the clipboard with its heading about a traffic survey.

'What on earth!' she cried, incredulous.

He turned his head, not the least bit repentant. 'It was falling out of your handbag,' he said, with a smile that said he didn't expect to be believed.

'Not only a sneak-thief, but a liar – and not a very good one!'

'I wasn't going to steal anything! I just wanted to know what the clipboard was for.'

'Goodbye,' said Lindsey, picking up her belongings, about to take her leave.

'Oh, hang on a minute. You can't blame me for trying—'

'I shan't be available to ferry you home to Cartfield. I hope the next bus back is tomorrow morning. Goodbye, Mr Holland.'

Five

That evening she rang Ursula Guyler to say she'd done what she came to Carlisle for and would be back in Birmingham next day.

'Come straight to my office,' Ursula commanded. 'I want to hear all about it.'

Lindsey really wanted to get to her own office and write a report for her own files but she recalled the 'kid gloves' instruction and, sighing, agreed. She was packing in preparation for an early departure in the morning when her bedroom phone rang.

'Yes?'

'A bouquet has arrived at the desk for you, madam. Shall I send it up?'

'By all means,' said Lindsey, intrigued.

A knock on the door a few minutes later revealed Keith Holland holding out a bunch of twenty red roses wrapped in cellophane.

'Oh! I thought it would be a pageboy!'

'If you'd like me to be a pageboy, I'll be a pageboy. Just so long as you forgive me.'

'Where on earth did you get roses at nine o'clock on a Sunday night in Carlisle?'

'Contacts, contacts,' he said. 'Do you like them?'

'No one could ever have anything against red roses.'

'Do you like *me*?'

'No.'

'Please come down to the bar for a drink so we can negotiate.'

'No.'

'Have I antagonised you for ever?'

64

'Yes.'

He gave an exaggerated sigh. 'I'm not alone in being weak. Oscar Wilde once said he could resist anything except temptation.'

'Goodnight,' Lindsey said, and closed the door.

A moment later there was a knock at the door. She didn't open it. 'Go away,' she said.

She stood there, waiting. But after a time she heard his footsteps receding. Thank goodness, she told herself.

When she reached the premises of Gylah Cosmetics next day it was nearly noon. Mrs Guyler rose with unexpected haste, coming round her desk to greet her with outstretched hands. 'Well, tell me!' she cried, taking Lindsey by the arms in a fierce grip.

Lindsey's instinct was to say, 'Calm down.' Instead she managed a smile and gave a little shrug. From his place by the window Billy Guyler said, 'Shula!' Realising what she'd done, Ursula let Lindsey go.

They all sat down, Lindsey on a chair facing Ursula's desk as if she were applying for a job, Ursula in the executive chair, Billy to one side. 'Would you like anything? Tea, coffee?' he asked.

'No thanks, I'm fine. Let me tell you what I found out as briefly as I can. Mary Lois Maybury and her daughter were killed in a traffic accident seventeen years ago. I've seen pictures of them both. Baby Edie was dark-haired and brown-eyed, like her mother and grandfather. The girl I met, who was using the name Edie Maybury, is the right age, has blue eyes like yours, and underneath the black dye may have fair hair. I think it's more than just possible she is your daughter Julie.'

Ursula sat as if frozen. Billy looked at his wife with anxiety and sighed. Lindsey waited.

No one spoke for what seemed an aeon. Then Billy said, 'So what do we do now?'

'I can't accept it,' Ursula said.

'Dearest, you can't just ignore it.'

'But she's so *awful*!'

'Members of a family don't necessarily always like each other,' Lindsey remarked. She knew this only too well from her work. 'You can dislike her, yet she can still be your daughter.'

'That's not what I . . . What I was . . . hoping for.'

'I understand that.'

'What should come next?' Billy persisted.

'Well, perhaps you ought to meet—'

'*No!*'

'Ursula, what do you want to do? Handle it with tongs? Pretend it never happened?' Lindsey challenged.

'I wish it hadn't! Oh, I wish it hadn't'

'We have to move on,' Lindsey insisted. 'Either you meet her and try to come to terms with the fact that she's probably your daughter, or you tell her that you don't want to have anything to do with her. In that case I think it would haunt you all your life, and Edie might not accept it.'

'Not accept it?'

'Edie has a part in this too, Ursula. It's a game of two players.'

'Oh, God,' groaned Ursula.

'We could meet,' Billy murmured. 'Take a look at her.'

Lindsey understood that here she had an ally. 'Meet,' she urged. 'Better still, spend some time with her.'

'Spend time?'

'Invite her to stay—'

'I don't want her in my home!'

Checkmate again. Lindsey took a moment to re-group. 'Okay, then, on neutral ground?'

'Neutral?'

'This is neutral,' Lindsey said, glancing about. 'But it's too commercial, too . . . unbending.'

'What about the Juvena?' said Billy.

His wife frowned, played with a pen on her desk.

'The Juvena?' said Lindsey.

'It's a health club we go to attached to a hotel in the Lake District – the Old North Star – a few miles outside Kendal, we spend time there quite regularly.'

'That might be good,' Lindsey said, though she felt that a

hotel meeting still lacked warmth. She glanced questioningly at Ursula.

'I don't know.'

'Suggest somewhere else, then.'

'I mean I don't know that I want to—'

'Shula, we have to do something. It's tearing you apart as it is, dear. Don't you think we ought to take some sort of step?'

It occurred to Lindsey, not for the first time, that they were talking about a girl who was very likely *his* daughter too. She'd called it a game of two players, but perhaps there were three. Yet they were discussing it as if only Ursula mattered. Self-effacing, unassuming . . . Yet Billy was trying to play his part.

'Just the weekend?' Ursula said.

'That's what we usually do, go for a long weekend,' Billy explained to Lindsey. 'What would you think of that?'

'It sounds like a possible idea. Not too long, not too short.'

'Well . . . perhaps.'

'Who should suggest it to her?' Billy went on.

'Not me!' cried Ursula.

'And not me,' Billy said. 'I wouldn't know how to handle it.'

They both looked at Lindsey. She knew she would have to take the next step. 'Would you like me to speak to her about it?'

'I think you should,' said Billy. 'It needs to be handled very calmly.'

'Very well. You're suggesting next weekend, I take it?'

'Well . . . yes . . . I suppose so. What do you think, dear?'

'If we must, we must,' Ursula said with grim acceptance. 'You'll see to that, then?' she said to Lindsey.

'Very well.'

'This evening?'

'Yes'

'And let me know at once.'

'Yes.'

'Tell her we'll pay for a car to collect her on Thursday evening.'

'Thursday?'

'A long weekend – four nights, Thursday to Monday morning. We'll have her picked up – get her address in – wherever it is.'

'Hobston.'

'And she'll be ferried to the hotel, it's the Old North Star. We'll meet her there.'

'Wouldn't it be better if you called and collected her, took her with you?'

Ursula shook her head, sighed, and shrugged. 'Do you think I want to be cooped up in the back of the car with her all the way to Kendal? It's going to be hard enough finding anything to talk about in civilised surroundings – I don't believe we've got a thing in common. At the hotel we can meet and have a bite to eat and then it'll soon be time to go to bed and that will give us a chance to recover.'

'Shula, Shula, it'll be all right,' soothed her husband.

His wife had opened a folder on her desk. From it she took the polaroid snaps. She shook her head as she studied them. 'Tell her to wear something decent,' she muttered.

Not on your life, thought Lindsey. It was going to be hard enough without that. It was a far from ideal arrangement but it seemed the best Lindsey could achieve. She agreed to telephone Edie that evening and report back.

Billy escorted her down to the entrance. 'She's not convinced the girl is Julie,' he murmured to her in the lift. 'She doesn't really want to meet her and besides that she doesn't want her to know where we live.'

'Oh, for goodness' sake! What about at the hotel? You'll be registered there under your own names, surely?'

'But she won't get our address.'

'It would be perfectly easy to get your address once she knew your name,' Lindsey pointed out.

'I suppose it would.'

'Mr Guyler – Billy – this grudging attitude is very bad. No matter who she is, this girl *is* owed something, don't you think? She was encouraged to contact the TV producer, she was given a telephone number to call, her hopes were raised—'

'Her hopes?'

She laid a hand on his arm. 'Don't you see,' she said, 'that

68

Edie may be as eager to find her mother as Shula has been to find her daughter?'

'Oh,' said Billy Guyler. 'I never thought of that.'

Back at the law offices there was catching up to do, but she went home early all the same. She put her head in at Andrew's door to say she needed time to recover from her trip north and that she'd see him in the morning. She was very weary. Interceding in family troubles always took its toll, she found.

A long hot shower, a pot of tea and a quickly assembled meal revived her. In cotton track suit and thick woolly socks, she settled down for some television. At eight o'clock she rang Edie Maybury's number. The call was answered by a male voice – young, terse, unwelcoming.

'Yeah?'

'May I speak to Edie, please?'

'She's busy, who's this?'

'This is Lindsey Abercrombie.'

'Oh, the s'licitor. Hang on.' Off-side, but only too clearly audible, he roared, 'Edie! It's that Birmingham tart!' Then, to the phone, 'She's coming.'

Edie picked up the receiver. 'Yes?'

'Edie, I've been talking to—' She caught herself up, about to say Mrs Guyler. As yet, Ursula Guyler wished to remain anonymous – a mistake, in Lindsay's opinion, but that was what her client preferred. 'I've been talking to Shula and she says she thinks the two of you should meet.' A slight untruth, but she wasn't going to say to this troubled girl that Mrs Guyler had been talked into a meeting.

'Oh? Oh, well . . . Oh, good. I'm glad to hear that. Er . . . I can get the day off again, be in Birmingham tomorrow.'

'Well, in fact, she was suggesting that you should join her for the weekend – this coming weekend.'

'Oh? Yeah . . . I can see that would be better . . . That would be what? Saturday and Sunday? I'm s'posed to be working both days.'

'You are?'

'Course I am. Saturday's the busiest day. Sunday – Sunday's voluntary, so that's not so hard, I can just say I don't

69

want to come in but it means I lose six hours' pay, special rate.'

Lindsey wondered whether she should say that Mrs Guyler would recompense her, but it seemed too commercial . . . and Edie was already hurrying on: 'But it's okay, it's special, isn't it, so it's got to be. Let me get a piece of paper and a pen to write down the address . . .' Her voice faded, she was gone for some seconds then said, 'Okay, tell me where to come.'

'It's . . . In fact it's a hotel, Edie.'

'A hotel? My mum works in a hotel?'

'No, she'll be staying there for the weekend.'

'In a hotel in Birmingham – what, that place where we had lunch?'

'No, it's in the Lake District.'

There was a long, shocked silence.

'She doesn't want to see me at her house?' Edie asked faintly.

Lindsey could sense the disappointment and the feeling of offence. 'She felt . . . She thought it might be best to meet . . . elsewhere.'

'Why's that?' Edie recovered from the affront. After all, it had been clear from their first conversation that this old witch wasn't going to join an Edie Maybury fan club.

'It's just how she felt about it, Edie.'

'Oh, it is?'

'She very nervous . . . very upset—'

'Upset? I'll tell you what it is! She doesn't like me. I could tell that from the way she clammed up on the telephone that first time. Well, tell her – tell her I don't think much of her either, come to that! And if she thinks I'm going to run after her to a hotel as far away from her posh home as she can manage, tell her to think again. Goodbye!'

'Edie! Edie! Don't hang up! Edie!' But the phone had gone dead. Lindsey depressed the button and pressed redial. It rang and rang.

At the other end Edie stood looking at it, thinking, Ring, you bother-box, all you ever bring is bad news!

'Ain't ya goin' to pick the thing up?' Graham shouted from the kitchen, where he was heating up a tin of soup for supper.

She put it to her ear and said, 'Well?'

'Edie, let's try to be calm about this,' Lindsey began. 'Never mind for the moment about what *she* thinks and what *you* think, consider the situation. You may be mother and daughter, you've got to come together to see what you can discover about each other, what you can work out. You're angry, she's scared – perhaps a neutral place is a good idea.'

'A neutral place? How about a boxing ring?'

'I understand that you're indignant—'

'Indignant? Is that what I am? Pissed off is what I am! I do all the work, make the efforts, rush about on the buses, get on the wrong side of old Brinksy at work, and for what? So this stuck-up cat can tell me she doesn't want me on her own doorstep, I've got to go swanning off somewhere that suits her better—'

'Edie, calm down! I apologise, I'm sorry if I've handled this badly.'

'It's not your fault,' Edie cut in. 'It's that big-headed bag who's paying you to front for her. Who does she think she is? The queen of snoggin' Sheba?'

'She's got a lot of anxiety and apprehension—'

'Oh, I scare her, do I? Well, good! I'd hate to think I was the only one having a bad time!'

There was some faint trace of humour in the last few words. Taking that as a good sign, Lindsey decided on a step forward. 'So will you come on this weekend thing?'

'Why *should* I? What's in it for me?'

'You'll see what she looks like. You'll see her husband – your father, perhaps.

That brought her up short. 'Yeah,' Edie said slowly, 'there's that.'

'Say you'll come.'

'Well . . .'

'You'd kick yourself afterwards if you refused.'

'Yeah . . .'

'It's a nice place. There'll be a pool, a beauty salon, all that kind of thing, I imagine. Saturday night, there's probably a disco or something.'

'Where's this place?'

'A few miles outside Kendal, in the Lake District. A car will collect you in Hobston on Thursday evening—'

'Thursday?'

'Well, that would be best.'

'You know all this is going to be docked off my pay packet? A weekend, I thought you meant Saturday and Sunday.'

'Well, Shula is going to be there from the Thursday evening until the Monday morning. You could join her just for the Saturday and Sunday if you'd rather.'

'No – no, if we're gonna meet, we might as well take a good stab at it, know what I mean?'

'So you'll arrange to get time off for the whole three days? If there's any problem about money—'

'You mean she'll give me a couple of quid in my pocket to take home, eh? I might just ask her for it – she seems to be loaded.' But she was grinning to herself as she said it.

'What time should the car come for you?'

'It'd have to be late Thursday – Thursday's late shopping night. Late for Hobston, that is, but it only means eight o'clock.'

'No problem. Say about eight thirty? Nine?'

'All right.'

'And it'll bring you back on Monday morning in time for work.'

'Oh, will it.'

'Is that all right?'

'It's all a bit sudden, know what I mean? I dunno that I want to be rushed into things like this.' But she'd really decided to go by now.

They spent another few minutes arguing about details but in the end Edie accepted the plan. 'You going to be in touch with her?' she asked.

'Yes, of course.'

'Tell her I agree, then. But you tell her this, too. I'd rather have had a cup of tea with her in a caff than go through all this stupid hoo-ha. For all her faults, old Ma Maybury never acted too big for her boots.'

Lindsey murmured something non-committal and discon-nected. She was wondering if she could put in a claim for danger money. Handling these two difficult women was like dealing with a couple of tigresses.

But things were progressing. They would meet, get to know each other a little, begin to come to terms with their problem. She thought it unlikely they could ever reach the stage of loving mother and daughter, but at least they would no longer be living in limbo.

Now Lindsey's part was a waiting game. After the weekend she would hear from each of them and perhaps get some idea if they wanted to take any further steps.

Thankfully she thought she could go back to the more normal work at the office – wills, estate enquiries, mortgage negotiation, all very dull in comparison with the Guyler case.

On Thursday afternoon there was a telephone call through the office switchboard. She picked up the receiver expecting it to be a financial adviser for a client, and heard Keith Holland's velvety voice.

'Forgiven me yet?'

'Good heavens!'

'I heard you left my roses behind at the hotel. I found that very disheartening.'

'And you think that worries me?'

'Listen, Lindsey, I think I need to explain something to you. I picked up some very bad habits during my time on the nationals. I bought myself into the Cartfield *Clarion* to make a fresh start, be a more responsible journalist – but I find there's a bit of backsliding now and again.'

'Very touching. I'm busy right now, Mr Holland.'

'No, wait, I just want you to say you understand and you forgive me for poking around in whatever it was you were doing in Cartfield.'

'Very well, that's agreed.'

'You forgive me?' he said, delighted.

'Yes.'

'And we can be friends?'

'No.'

'Oh.' There was a sound, half a sigh, half a laugh. 'You're not easily bamboozled.'

73

'I hope not. Goodbye, Mr Holland.'

'Please stop calling me Mr Holland—'

'I'd be delighted not to speak to you at all. Goodbye.'

'Lindsey, I'm coming to Birmingham on Wednesday of next week for a thing at the National Exhibition Centre. Could we meet for a drink in the evening?'

'No thank you, Mr Holland.' She replaced the receiver neatly, thinking to herself, That's got rid of you.

But she was smiling to herself all the same. What a gamester! No wonder he had pulled off some big exclusives in the world of journalism. He just refused to give up.

Andrew walked into her office just at that moment. 'What are you smiling about?' he enquired.

'Oh, nothing, just an oddball on the phone.'

'Are we doing anything this evening?' he asked.

'It's going to be a lovely evening. How about a drive out to Stratford, to look at the swans?' A lovely thought – the big pool on the river at the front of the theatre, the evening light gilding the tawny leaves on the trees.

'Swans?' said Andrew.

'On the Avon.'

'Oh . . . you know . . . going too far of an evening, I never enjoy battling the traffic . . . There's a new Balti house opened near Colmore Circus, I thought we might try it?'

She laughed. 'Is it your ambition to sample every ethnic cuisine in the city?'

'Why not? I might write a book about it one day – Travels with my Chopsticks.' He shared her laughter, and his dark eyes sparkled with enjoyment.

She thought to herself, Never mind the swans, it will be nice to spend the evening with him in some little restaurant and then go home with him to make love.

Better that than worry about what might be happening at the Old North Star Hotel this evening. Or thinking about the quick-witted caller on the telephone.

Six

Lindsey was buying groceries on Saturday afternoon when her mobile rang. She delved into her big shoulder bag to find it, expecting to hear Andrew confirming that he would be coming to dinner and other pleasures that evening. Rain was coming down hard so she sheltered in a doorway.

She didn't at first recognise the voice.

'Is that you, Miss Abercrombie? Lindsey?'

It was Billy Guyler, extremely distressed.

'Yes, it's me. What's wrong, Mr Guyler?'

'Everything here is an absolute disaster, Lindsey. Shula and the girl are at daggers drawn and Shula just said . . . just said she was going to tell the hotel she wouldn't pay the girl's bill as from now.'

'What?'

'She wants her gone. She says she's not going to pay board and lodging any more for a girl who's so unpleasant.'

'She hasn't done that, surely?'

'Not yet. She's upstairs in our suite, crying. I'm using the phone in the foyer. Lindsey, please come—'

'What, to Kendal!'

'Please come. We need someone to . . . to sort of . . . mediate.'

'But Mr Guyler, it's Saturday afternoon.'

'I know, I know, but this whole thing is going straight down the drain without someone to help us. You could be here in time for dinner if you started now.'

'What, straight away?'

'Please come, Lindsey.'

Nothing but the direst extremity would have brought him to this point. He said his wife was in tears and he sounded close to that himself. She didn't in the least want to be involved in a row – it was the weekend, Andrew was coming to dinner, they would spend the night in each other's arms and then there was all of Sunday.

'Shula needs to know that she's right to give out this ultimatum. If you could talk it through with her.'

'I don't know what good I'd be.'

'We need *someone*,' he cried in desperation.

'All right,' she said, hearing panic in his voice. 'I'll be there as soon as I can.'

She hailed a taxi, told him to wait at her door, threw a few things in a bag and was out and on her way to the station within twenty minutes. She changed at Birmingham, and got herself to Penrith, where a good-hearted taxi driver was willing (for a somewhat inflated fee) to drive her the thirty miles or so to Kendal. Through darkening rain-swept hill country she was carried to the entrance of the Old North Star Hotel by about eight in the evening.

Billy Guyler was in the foyer, sitting in a capacious leather armchair and pretending to read a magazine. He leapt up as she came in.

'Oh, Lindsey! My dear girl! Such dreadful weather! I'm so grateful!'

He ushered her to the reception desk then rushed to give money to the hall porter for the fare to the taxi driver. Lindsey learned that a room had been reserved for her. Well, that made sense, she was clearly going to have to stay at least overnight.

'You'll want to freshen up and hang up your coat,' Billy said when he returned, puffing. 'There's a dinner dance on tonight –' he nodded towards the muted thump of music coming from somewhere beyond handsome plate glass doors – 'so dinner's in the breakfast room, if you'd like to join us there. I'll tell Shula you're here. Shall we say a quarter of an hour – twenty minutes?'

The bellboy was already taking her bag towards the lift and she agreed, and then followed him. Billy headed for the bar, where presumably Ursula Guyler had been waiting out the time until she arrived. But where was Edie? wondered Lindsey as

76

she rose in the lift to the second floor. Where was the cause of all the upset?

When she came down again Mr and Mrs Guyler were waiting for her on a tapestried bench outside the breakfast room. Within, in a well-designed effort to make the place look attractive as a substitute for the dining room, there were pink-shaded lamps on each table and little flower arrangements. There were few diners there – most seemed to be patronising the disco dinner.

Ursula Guyler was very chic in a very plain brown silk shift with a single strand gold chain round her throat. Billy was in a dark suit, but not in evening jacket. Lindsey didn't feel out of place in her travel clothes of black skirt and French Connection top. Wine was ordered, menus produced, but only Billy paid any attention to the idea of a meal. The two women were looking at each other, each wondering how to begin.

'Tell me what's been happening,' Lindsey said.

'I don't know why I ever agreed to this,' Ursula burst out. 'The minute I actually saw her—'

'Where is Edie?' Lindsey put in.

'She's gone out! Gone out! She simply walked out on us!'

Perplexed, Lindsey looked at Billy for an explanation. He however was busying himself with ordering food. His wife surged on, 'All because of that dreadful boy—'

'What boy?'

'Her boyfriend. Graham. He's awful – worse even than *she* is.'

'Ursula, calm down.'

'There was never any mention of her bringing a boyfriend – if I had known she meant to do that—'

'Could we go back to the beginning?' Lindsey suggested. 'She arrived on Thursday evening, and brought the young man to stay here with her?'

'No, no, he came zooming up on Friday about midday on a motorbike. The hall porter wasn't going to let him in.'

'What?'

'Well, if you'd seen him – rings and studs through his brows and ears, and greasy jeans.'

Lindsey drew in a breath and turned again to Billy. He

had no refuge any more, the waiter having departed. He said unwillingly, 'He's not the type that they expect to come in through their front door, Lindsey. I quite understand that they tried to tell him he was in the wrong place. But then he asked for Edie, and they came in and told her he was here, and she rushed out to him.'

Wine was brought and poured, there was a pause until the waiter had gone. Lindsey took a reviving sip before resuming the conversation. 'This was – what did you say – lunchtime yesterday?'

'Yes, just before lunch. You know, the weather had turned bad so Shula decided to have a treatment in the salon, and then we were having a drink and talking about the afternoon.'

'And when I said it would be a good idea to go shopping in Kendal – because there are some very nice little boutiques in Kendal – she all at once flew up in the air and said she didn't come to the Lake District to drag around a shopping precinct, and then this Graham arrived, and she just dashed out. And the next thing we knew she was gone, on his pillion.'

Lindsey couldn't help thinking that if she had come to a hotel to get to know someone and that someone shut herself up in a cubicle in the beauty salon, she too might have felt an urge to rush off with a friend. But she said, 'Was she gone long?'

'Until it began to get dark,' said Billy. 'Then she reappeared, so they tell us, with mud all over her boots and soaking wet. Shula and I had been ringing her room and ringing the desk to ask if she'd come back, so they rang me to say she'd come in. I went along to speak to her – to her room, you know – but she said she was changing out of her wet clothes and she'd meet us downstairs. So we came down and then we said we'd ordered a table for dinner at eight, and Shula asked her what she was going to wear—'

'And she said, "This, of course". And if you could have seen it! Black jersey dress that looked as if it had been cut from just the *sleeve* of somebody's sweatshirt, and a choker – a choker an inch wide! – of black wooden beads. I wouldn't have been seen dead with her in an outfit like that.'

'So Shula suggested something a bit less bizarre—'

'And she said, "Doesn't matter, I'm going out anyway."'

And with that she was gone. We never saw her again last night. Now I ask you, Lindsey – is that any way to behave? She was supposed to be here so as to get to know us.'

'And she's made absolutely no effort—'

'But what happened this morning?' Lindsey put in between their words of complaint. 'Why did it suddenly get so urgent?'

'Well – there's this disco dinner – and we thought she would like that, but she didn't come down to breakfast at all so Shula rang her room at ten and after trying two or three times she answered.'

'And I said there was this disco tonight and we thought she would enjoy it, and how about if she and I were to go to Kendal to buy her a nice dress.'

'And really, she was terribly sulky – I could hear on the extension.'

'But she said she'd have to ask Graham if he would like a disco, and I said we weren't inviting Graham—'

'And she slammed the phone down—'

'And we haven't seen her all day.'

'So where do you think she is now?' Lindsey asked.

'Out on a pub crawl with Graham, if last night is anything to go by,' Billy groaned.

The food arrived. Billy looked around in surprise, then said apologetically, 'I just ordered what I thought you'd like.'

Smoked trout was set before them, the waiter placed brown bread and a little dish of sauce, they picked up knives and forks. But then Lindsey set hers down.

'What is it you want me to do?' she asked. The situation seemed to her to be almost past mending. Neither side had made any real move towards a relationship, and the one attempt at friendship from Ursula – the offer to play fairy godmother, buy Edie a dress, and 'take her to the ball' – had been wrong-footed to say the least.

'We thought you could talk to her,' Ursula said. 'You seem to understand her at least to some extent. Neither Billy nor I can get her to say more than "yes" and "no".'

'But you must have talked,' Lindsey insisted. 'On Thursday evening, when she arrived?'

'Oh . . . well . . .' Billy looked faintly guilty. 'We said,

"How d'you do" and "Did you have a good journey?" and things like that.'

'But Billy, you surely knew you had to do better than that.'

'It was such a *shock!*' Ursula cried. 'Face like a zombie, black hair like a hank of wool, clumping about in clog-things.'

'But you'd seen the photographs? You knew she wasn't going to look like a debutante.'

'But we thought you'd have warned her to dress a bit decently,' Billy said. 'You let us down there, Lindsey – you should have told her this wasn't the kind of hotel where they'd expect a trashy appearance.'

Lindsey felt a pang of indignation, but made no response. They needed someone to blame, and she was prepared to be that someone. She thought it better not to say that she'd had a hard enough time persuading Edie to come at all, never mind lecturing her on what to wear.

'Have you actually had *any* conversation with her?' she enquired. 'Talked about the birth certificate, the stolen identity?'

Neither of them made any reply. They gave their attention to the hors d'oeuvres. It was perfectly clear that they'd made no efforts in that direction – perhaps from embarrassment, or fear or – on Ursula's part – an unwillingness to believe the girl could be her daughter.

Well, tomorrow was another day. If Edie was out on a pub crawl, it was no use trying to speak to her tonight. Tomorrow morning Lindsey would see what could be done. For the moment, her role was to let the Guylers unload their dismay, their resentment and their sense of failure on to her, so that they might feel somewhat ready for a fresh start.

When they all went upstairs to bed about eleven, Edie still hadn't reappeared. Lindsey didn't expect to sleep – she thought she'd have too much on her mind – but in fact she dropped off almost at once and was down to breakfast by eight thirty next day.

Ursula was there in a strawberry-pink velvet sweatsuit and a matching headband. Glowing with health, she'd clearly been in the gym for an early morning session. Lindsey felt like a

80

sparrow alongside some exotic bird, for she'd brought no fancy exercise gear – in fact, didn't own any. She was wearing the skirt she'd travelled in and a white cotton sweater.

Outside the rain beat down, pulling the last of the tawny leaves from the trees. Lindsey saw an expanse of sodden lawn, a small ornamental pond, and an exercise trail. Not really very enticing.

'Good morning, Ursula.'

'Good morning, though it's not good at all, really. What with the weather and what's likely to come.'

'Have you rung Edie's room?'

'No, I rang the desk and they said she came in after midnight so I left it. I thought it would be better if you . . . well . . . Don't you think?'

'Yes, all right. Later. What's her room number?'

'She's in number fourteen – it's a lovely room, with a four-poster and everything.'

'Fine. After breakfast then – I'll see what I can do.' She rose to go to the breakfast buffet. 'Where's Billy?'

'Oh, Billy's not an early riser. He'll be along when he's got himself together.'

During breakfast Lindsey learned that the couple followed separate regimes at the health centre. Ursula went in for exercise, ran the fitness trail, used the awesome gym equipment. Billy liked the sauna and the massage. 'He's a lazy man,' Ursula said, with fondness. 'Letting himself go to seed a bit, I feel. I used to try to get him to take part in the cosmetics business but . . . oh, I don't know . . . he was only ever interested in the packaging – he was a packaging designer, you know . . . And now it's such big business I have the packaging done in Italy.'

'So what does he do these days?' Lindsey asked.

'Oh, a little bit of PR, stands in for me if I can't open a fair or award a prize. He's listed as a PR assistant on the books but you know really . . . Well, we're all different, aren't we? Myself, I couldn't bear to fritter away my time.'

As Lindsey finished her coffee she asked what should follow on after she had her conversation with Edie.

'What do you suggest?'

'Well, you really need to sit down together and talk. Don't you think so?'

Ursula suppressed a shudder. 'I suppose we must.'

'Otherwise it's pointless, Ursula.'

'I just feel it won't work. But my business sense tells me we've got to move on somehow. All right, ask her if she'll come and have a chat in our suite – we've got a little sort of sitting room, and it's private.'

'Yes,' agreed Lindsey, thinking that raised voices might ensue from any 'talk' between these parties, so privacy was desirable.

It was now nine thirty and Edie had made no appearance in the breakfast room. Service ended at ten. From what Lindsey had heard of her behaviour so far, it was unlikely she'd be down in time for any food. She suggested that if and when she got Edie to the Guylers' suite, some sort of refreshment might be welcome.

She went up to the first floor to tap on the door of number fourteen. No reply. She knocked louder, waited, tried the door handle and found that the door opened. She knew better than to go in. She could hear the sound of the shower. She withdrew, quietly closed the door, and waited a good three minutes before knocking again.

'Yeah?' called a grumpy voice.

'Edie, it's me, Lindsey Abercrombie.'

'What?'

'Can I come in?'

'Half a mo'.' A slight pause and the door was opened by Edie Maybury, barefoot, clad in the big fluffy bathrobe supplied by the hotel and with her black hair in the little polythene shampoo cap.

Seen like this, she wasn't nearly as alarming as her usual self. The matt white-ish make-up was absent, so that a clear creamy skin could be seen. Without the black eyeliner, her blue eyes looked less fierce, more girlish. Her neck was hidden by the big towelling collar but the legs and feet below the robe seemed too thin, almost skinny.

'So you turned up at last!' she exclaimed. 'Why weren't you here when I arrived?'

'Me?' Lindsey was taken aback. 'But it was never proposed that I should be here. This weekend was for you and Shula and Billy.'

'Oh, was it? So how would that work, if she was in the salon with gook all over her face and he's in that hot-tub thing?'

'Oh, not all the time, Edie—'

'No, the rest of the time she wants to go shopping. Shopping! When there's all that great hill country to see, and them lakes – have you seen the lakes? But for that pair, the outdoors is nothing, what they want is shopping malls.'

'Edie, stop moaning at me and let's have a conversation.'

Edie made a grimace and waved a hand at a chair. 'Take a pew. I'm never at my best first thing in the morning. Hang on while I make a cup of coffee.'

She busied herself with the tray of supplies while Lindsey took a seat. It was a pretty room, as Ursula had implied, with a double bed hung with sprigged muslin, a swagged dressing table, and cretonne curtains still closed against the morning light.

With a cup of steaming black coffee, Edie came to the bed, plumped up the pillows, and climbed back in. 'Well,' she said, after a sip, 'what's the message?'

'The message is that Shula and Billy would like you to come along to their suite and have a chat.'

'About what? About how she offered me one of her dinky-pink training outfits because she thought my gear was common? About how they wouldn't let Graham come to their rotten disco last night? About how *she* wanted to take me to a shop for a "more suitable" dress? Eh? Is that it?'

'Edie, they didn't expect Graham to be here.'

'Why not? He's my boyfriend, in't he? And it's not costing 'em anything, he's got a bed and breakfast through the motor-bike club he belongs to.'

'Now you know very well it's nothing to do with what it costs them.'

'You can say that again! Rolling in it, you can tell by

the way they order whatever comes into their heads! And that,' Edie said after a big swallow of the reviving coffee, 'is what's wrong, know what I mean? They're afraid I'm after their dough.'

'You've got to accept that this is a very frightening situation for them, for Shula particularly. It might well be that you're their daughter, and that means taking on responsibilities.'

'I don't need them to be responsible for me!' flashed Edie. 'I never asked them to be responsible for me! All I asked was a bit of decent chit-chat, to work out whether she really could be my mum, but if you want it straight I can't stand her so it's best we just say ta-ta and let it go.'

'No, Edie.'

'I'm off as soon as I get dressed. Graham's collecting me – what time is it? – well, in about an hour or so, he's like me, Graham, never at his best of a morning.'

'So there's time to talk to Shula before he comes, isn't there?'

'I dunno that I *want* to talk to her.'

'Oh, come on, you ought at least to give this thing a chance, Edie. You've been at odds with each other ever since the first moment, now haven't you? And you just said you wanted a bit of a chat – here's your chance.'

'But what's the point? She'll only talk high hat at me.'

'No she won't. I promise.'

'Will you be there?'

'Ah . . .' It would be better if they could try to communicate without any outside help. But Lindsey could see that they needed an intermediary. 'All right.'

'Okeydoke,' Edie said grudgingly. 'Just let me get my things on.'

'Edie . . .'

'What?'

'Could I just say . . . I think it would help . . .'

'What?'

'Don't put your make-up on.'

'Are you kidding?' Edie snorted. 'That's me, take it or leave it.'

Lindsey sighed and nodded. Her armour – she'd feel naked

without it. 'See you along in their suite when you're ready then?'

'Right.'

The Guylers were waiting for her with anxiety. Billy, somehow overdressed in slacks and a blazer, was eating from a breakfast tray at a little table. Ursula was pacing to and fro in front of windows thrown wide open to the cool damp air, taking deep calming breaths.

Lindsey explained that Edie was getting dressed and would be along. She didn't tell them that Edie was planning to leave almost within the hour. She still hoped that could be averted. One more day – surely they would agree to give one more day to the attempt at getting to know each other?

When the knock came, everyone stiffened. Billy slammed down his cup and stood up. Lindsey opened the door to admit the girl who might be their daughter. Edie, much as they had seen her hitherto – skimpy black leather skirt, thick black tights, black T-shirt edged with white, black boots in need of a good clean after tramping up Lakeland hill tracks.

Ursula's sigh of disapproval was quite audible.

'Would you like some breakfast?' Billy blurted. 'There's coffee here, and croissants and things – please – help yourself.'

Edie sauntered across to fill a cup for herself. 'Well,' she said, 'here I am. What's the next move?'

'I wondered if you'd like to tell Shula a little bit about your life with the Mrs Maybury who brought you up,' Lindsey said.

'Oh, I told all that to you. Didn't you tell them?'

'Yes, but it would be nice if they could hear it in your own words.'

'Oh. Well . . .' Oddly enough, Edie seemed embarrassed. She fiddled with cream and sugar for her coffee.

'What I'd really like,' Ursula cut in, 'is if you could remember anything about your life before that. If you remember the house we lived in then – there was a little red swing in the garden—'

'For Pete's sake, I could only have been three – d'you expect me to remember the pattern on the wallpaper?'

'But the seaside – do you remember the seaside? And nanny helping you to make sandcastles?'

'Nanny? My grandma?' asked Edie.

'Your nanny – Kristel.'

'So I had a nanny,' snorted Edie. 'What was the matter – too posh to look after me yourself? No wonder I got lost!'

'You didn't get lost, some awful woman *stole* you!'

'She wasn't an awful woman, she was all right and at least she kept me with her and didn't hand me off to a *servant*.'

'Kristel wasn't a servant, she was a lovely girl, I took every care to find someone really suitable—'

'So as not to have to be bothered yourself, is that it?'

'I don't need any criticism from you, you ill-mannered little chit.'

'Oh, so you can't be criticised – but it's okay to give snooty looks at my clothes and tell me which fork to use when we're eating, is that it? Let me tell you, Mrs Guyler, you're no winning number when it comes to good manners.'

There had been a noticeable start of alarm from Ursula when her last name was used. Edie, carried forward by her anger, stopped short and gave a triumphant grin.

'Oh, yeah, *Mrs Guyler* – if you wanted it to be a secret you should have told the staff to keep their traps shut. "Yes, Mrs Guyler, certainly, Mrs Guyler, I'll see to that at once, Mrs Guyler" – bunch of creeps, and don't you just lap it up! It's true I don't know what my real name is, but whoever I turn out to be I'm never going to make people crawl to me the way you do!'

Ursula had flushed with anger and resentment. Billy was making soothing gestures with his hands, though he didn't quite know at whom. Lindsey sought desperately for something to say but nothing came.

Edie rounded on her. '*You* should have told her! I thought you understood!'

'Told her what, Edie? I'm trying to understand! I'm trying to help the two of you understand each other.'

'You can give up the attempt, Miss Abercrombie,' Ursula said in a voice that had icicles in it. 'This matter and your part in it is at an end, is that clear? And you, miss –' she wheeled round on Edie – 'you can go back to whatever gutter it was you came from because your scheme to trick me has failed. Though how you ever thought I would *believe* that you were any kin of mine, I'll never comprehend.'

'Yeah, yeah,' sneered Edie. 'Hoity-toity to the end. I wish I'd run up a huge bill for you to pay but I missed out on that 'cos I couldn't stand to be in the same building with you. Ta-ta then, don't forget to hug your moneybags!'

And she was gone with her long-legged stride out of the door and in a few moments more out of the hotel.

Lindsey started to go after her, but Billy caught her at the door and closed it. 'It's no use,' he said. 'Let it be.'

'But Billy—' He shook his head, then went to put his arms round his wife. 'Don't, dearest,' he murmured. 'She isn't worth it.'

Lindsey left them to comfort each other. She went to her room, packed her bag, then wrote a short note to leave at the desk.

> Dear Ursula
> You said that my part in your dealings with Edie Maybury was over. I accept that as an instruction to close the file. I'm sincerely sorry that it wasn't possible to come to a happier conclusion. I hope however it will not affect your relationship with the senior members of our firm.
> Yours sincerely
> Lindsey Abercrombie

She was glad to see the back of the affair. But she knew that if Old Oliver lost any business because of this failure, she would suffer for it, hence the plea to her client not to visit her vengeance on him.

She was back in her own home by early evening. Andrew proved to have gone out so she spent the hours till bedtime going over what had happened and trying to see how it could have been managed better. On her lap-top she wrote a report for Old Oliver, skirting round any definite details but merely sketching her part in a 'personal problem of the Guyler family' and stating honestly that she'd been unable to resolve it.

*   *   *

87

Old Oliver called her into his office to cross-question her. She simply maintained that she hadn't had permission to discuss the matter with him, but if and when she did she would give him full appraisal of the facts. He humphed and harrumphed but accepted it, the more so as the bills she had put into the accounts computer were very satisfactory indeed.

On Wednesday the receptionist rang through about two in the afternoon. 'There's a Miss Maybury to see you, Miss Abercrombie.'

'What?'

'A Miss Maybury?' Meg's voice dripped with disapproval. 'She *says* she's a client.'

'I'll come down.'

Edie was standing in the foyer looking irritated. 'Oh, there you are. I want to talk to you.'

Lindsey conquered her surprise. 'We'd better go up to my office.'

'Nah, I don't like the vibes here. Let's go across to the shopping centre, find a caff.'

'Just a minute, let me get my jacket.' By the time she'd got it from her office and returned, Edie was outside on the steps kicking her clumpy heel against a Victorian foot-scraper. 'What a dump,' she said.

'It's old, Edie, it has atmosphere.' They set off across the cathedral green. 'Why are you here?'

'Graham said I ought to look you up, know what I mean?'

'He did?'

'I was a bit leery, but he said you'd see me all right. So as I had a half-day due, here I am.'

'But why? You walked out on everything on Sunday.'

'Yeah, well . . .' She fell silent, so that they walked on towards the busy facades of the shops and cafes with Lindsey divided between hope and anxiety.

They went into a Starbucks. They ordered coffee and settled in a corner where they could see the crowds hurrying about in the main street.

'See, Graham and I talked it over,' Edie began, 'and the thing is – have I got legal rights?'

And at that, Lindsey's heart sank.

Seven

The two women were almost heads together across the tiny round table in the corner of the coffee shop. Lindsey took a moment to think what to say.

'I have to explain something to you, Edie,' she began. 'I can't be your solicitor.'

'What d'you mean?' exclaimed Edie in disbelief. This was the woman who'd always been there, ushering her towards the Guylers, explaining the Guylers, smoothing things over between her and the Guylers. 'You *are* my solicitor.'

'No, I'm Mrs Guyler's solicitor. She asked me to make contact with you, after you made that first phone call. *She* hired me. I can't give you legal advice.'

'Because she's got the money to pay you and I haven't!' The reproach leapt to her lips before she could stop it.

'It's nothing to do with money, Edie. I can't act for two people who have opposing interests.'

Edie made a grimace. Was this true? She thought she'd heard it before, perhaps as part of the story of some film she'd seen. 'Well, I'm not asking you to act. I'm just asking for information,' she ventured.

'Then go to someone else.'

'Who, for instance? The Citizens Advice Bureau? The TV people who started all this in the fist place?'

Lindsey could just imagine how Mrs Guyler would like it if the TV company got hold of it again. Naturally they would want to pursue it on air. As for the Citizens Advice Bureau, Lindsey had the highest opinion of them but she didn't think they could handle anything as delicate as this.

'Well . . .'

'I just want to know where you think I stand.' Edie tried to

89

put pathos into the plea. Seeing that Lindsey was hesitating, she went on, 'Graham says—'

'What the devil does Graham know about it?' Lindsey burst out in exasperation. 'I hope you don't take advice from him all along the line.'

'He's got his head screwed on, has Graham! You can't pull the wool over *his* eyes.'

'Who's talking about pulling wool? There's no deception of any kind in this, now is there? It's a straightforward problem of identity.'

'Then if it's so flippin' straightforward why can't you tell me what you think?' she demanded. 'Where do I stand? Can I make a claim on the Guylers?'

Seeing no help for it, Lindsey decided to make a few points clear. 'You have no *legal* claim on Mr and Mrs Guyler—'

'Even if they're my parents and they've got heaps of dough and I've got none? Don't be daft!'

'It's not as simple as that. You're not a minor, you're over eighteen and earning a living. You're not in need of their support.'

'Wha-at?' Edie groaned. This was quite different from Graham's reading of the matter. 'Graham said they'd have to fork out.'

'Graham is talking through his hat. Children who have displeased their parents get disinherited every day.'

'Yeah, but they bring court cases, don't they? You see it in the papers – tycoons' fortunes being haggled over.'

'After the death of the parent, yes, and in those cases there's no doubt of the legitimacy of the heirs or of their identity. You can't sue the Guylers for refusing to acknowledge you as part of their family, and even if they agreed you were the long-lost Julie, they don't have to take any responsibility for you.'

'That can't be right!' It sounded too different from everything she'd been hearing from Graham. She stared at this clever-clever woman in challenge, demanding some justification of her opinion.

'Listen to me, Edie. You walked out on them on Sunday. You rejected them just as they rejected you. Why are you here now groaning about how they owe you something?'

90

'Well, they do! They do owe me! You heard the old girl on Sunday – when I said she'd let me get lost, she said, "You weren't lost, some woman stole you" – she knows fine and well that I *am* the missing kid, that I'm her daughter and she's my mum.'

Shula's words seemed to have burned themselves into Edie's brain. At the time, she'd been too wrapped up in the row they were having to pick up on them and make them an issue, but they kept coming back. 'You weren't lost, some awful woman stole you.' That had been her mother speaking to her, accepting her in that one moment of dolorous recollection.

Lindsey too had noted that exchange: she'd sensed that somewhere deep inside herself Ursula Guyler accepted the fact that Edie was her lost child. But two changes were necessary before anything could come of that. First Ursula had to agree consciously that Julie and Edie were one and the same. Second, she had to accept Edie in all her disagreeable aspects. To Lindsey, neither seemed at all likely in the near future. And certainly not if Edie began making ill-founded threats about legal action.

She said, 'I'll concede this much. There may be a moral responsibility. Mrs Guyler let the TV people make their programme and when its producers sent on your name to her, she agreed to let you get in touch. There's *some* accountability. But I don't think you could ever make it stand up in court.'

'Huh . . .' Edie thought it over. Perhaps it was time to move over to the attack, as Graham had phrased it. 'Well, then . . . what if I didn't take it to court. What if I took it to the newspapers?'

'What?'

'What if I told them she was turning her back on her own flesh and blood, know what I mean? Adding even more suffering to what I've already gone through? Seventeen years pretending she wants me back but it's all been a sham?'

'You wouldn't do that!'

'Why not? I had seventeen years of misery with old Ma Maybury because my real mum was careless and let me be snatched.'

That took the wind out of her sails, thought Edie. Graham

91

was right – attack is always better than argument. And even this clever lady solicitor seemed at a loss now she'd really stuck it to her. 'Well?' she insisted.

Lindsey could tell this was very dangerous ground. The influence of the boyfriend seemed strong and very harmful. It was certainly true that this was the kind of human-interest story greatly beloved by the tabloids. Big blocky headlines and of course pictures sneaked by telescopic lens . . . Very hurtful to Ursula and Billy, and the damage to the hoped for relationship would be irreparable.

'What you're suggesting is extremely cruel, Edie,' she ventured. 'You just said a minute ago that you thought Mrs Guyler really feels you are her daughter Julie. Given time, that might bring some good result. But if you go shouting insults in the newspapers you kill that chance.'

Edie was surprised at the genuine concern in the solicitor-lady's tone. She felt something like a pang of regret. But Graham had said she was to stay on the attack until she got what she wanted. Still . . .

'I'm prepared to be reasonable about it,' she said. 'Providing I can get some . . . some damages.'

'Damages?'

That was the word Graham had told her to use. He said it was a good legal word. 'Yeah, damages. For all the time I've wasted, all the running about I've done, for the way I was treated at that snooty hotel, for the problems I've had at work about taking time off.'

'Is this what Graham's counted up for you?'

'Well, who else have I got to turn to? He says I've been badly treated, and if you want to know,' Edie said, to her own surprise feeling tears well up, 'I think so too!'

'I see. So what do you want next?'

'I want you to tell Mrs Toffee-Nosed Guyler that I expect something for my trouble. And not just peanuts either, know what I mean?'

'What sort of sum did Graham have in mind?' Lindsey said with irony.

'Don't get sarky! We talked it through and we agreed that I ought to get a couple of grand for every year she let me stay

92

with old Ma Maybury having a bad time. So seventeen years at two thou a go is thirty-four thou, and we thought a round figure of thirty-five would be neater.'

'Thirty-five thousand.'

'Yeah. Or else.'

'Or else you go to the newspapers.'

'Yeah.'

'Edie, she's almost certainly your mother. You'd really do that to her?'

Suddenly it was all too much. Edie felt the cafe surroundings begin to swim around her. A great sob rose in her throat. She jumped up, heading for the door and an escape from what she'd just done. 'Tell her, that's all,' she managed to croak before she rushed out.

For a few minutes Lindsey sat alone at the table. The friendly girl at the counter enquired, 'Is your friend all right?'

Far from it, thought Lindsey, but only smiled and nodded as she got up to go back to the office.

There, sitting on a chair in the foyer, was Keith Holland. He rose as she came in. Meg the elderly receptionist said quickly, 'This gentleman said you were expecting him, Miss Abercrombie, but he's not on the appointments list.'

'I'm sure he isn't,' Lindsey agreed. To Keith she said curtly, 'What are you doing here?'

'It's Wednesday, remember? I told you I'd be here for a conference at the Exhibition Centre – and thank heaven that's over and so I took the train straight to thee, my love.'

'I'm sorry you've wasted your time, Mr Holland. I'm rather busy.'

'But not this evening. Remember we were to go out for a drink in the evening?'

'You have a very fanciful imagination. I have work that I expect will take up most of my evening.'

'You're working of an evening? That seems hard.'

'Even if I weren't, I have other things to do.'

'But just a drink, for old times' sake'

It was hard not to smile at his quick footwork. Perhaps at any other time she might have given in. But the interview

93

with Edie Maybury was still at the forefront of her mind, with all its awful implications. She said with calculated sharpness, 'Mr Holland, I have something very important that needs my attention. Please go away.'

This time there was no bantering response. He studied her. 'Something's upset you?'

'Will you *please* mind your own business!' She turned and hurried to the lift, leaving him standing somewhat shaken in the hall.

When she got through to Ursula Guyler at her office, she was greeted with impatience and dismissal. 'I thought I told you that I had no further need of your services, Miss Abercrombie.'

'Mrs Guyler, this is serious. Edie came to see me this afternoon and she's making threats.'

'Threats?'

'Yes, and I think—'

'What kind of threats?'

'I don't think we should discuss it on the phone. May I come and see you?'

'I'm in the middle of a meeting here – I came out of it to take this call.'

'This evening? It's important, Ursula.'

Ursula made a huffing sound. 'Billy and I are going to a thing at the university this evening.'

'What time?'

'Well, it starts at eight.'

'Could I see you before that?'

'We-ell . . . We have a room at the Lamont where we're going to change . . . In the bar there, say six thirty?'

'Fine. I'll see you then.'

Lindsey had a client coming in almost immediately to discuss problems with a landlord. Then there was the usual Wednesday afternoon conference about the week's work, at which Old Oliver decided to hold forth for ten minutes about efficiency and time-keeping. She barely had time to wash and freshen her lipstick before she headed for the hotel. Luckily it was within walking distance so she didn't have to try for a taxi in Birmingham's evening rush hour.

*   *   *

Ursula Guyler was alone at the bar when Lindsey walked in. She felt this was a pity for though Billy contributed little in the way of thought, he had a calming influence on his wife. And a calming influence was certainly going to be needed in the next few minutes.

She ordered a drink then drew her client away to a table by the window. She reported her conversation with Edie. Ursula's anger flared up at once. 'That's blackmail!' she cried.

'I agree with you.'

'She wouldn't actually do it. It's a bluff!'

'Perhaps.'

'From what you say it's that awful boyfriend who's putting her up to it.'

Lindsey nodded. 'That's rather my feeling too.'

'I knew he was trouble the minute he showed up at the Old North Star! Designer stubble, studs in his eyebrows and about six rings in one ear.'

'Never mind what he looked like. It's clear he's got a lot of influence—'

'How can she even bother with what he says?'

'Maybe it's because she's got no one else to turn to.'

'What?'

Lindsey met Ursula's gaze. It was startled, troubled. She said very gently, 'That girl's been through a lot, Ursula. She's been twice bereaved.'

'Twice?'

'The first time when Mrs Maybury died. She thought she'd lost her mother. The second time when she found out Mrs Maybury wasn't her mother. That's a shock I wouldn't want to face. From what she told me she and Mrs Maybury didn't make any friends and were unpopular with their neighbours – so who else can she turn to except Graham?'

'I see what you mean,' Ursula admitted. 'But she doesn't even *try* to make people like her.'

'True enough. But I think she's had to fight her own corner all her life.'

'And now she's got herself hooked up to a boy who's a blackmailer.'

'That's the way it looks.'

95

'You do see now how impossible it is that she could really be my Julie. She's so hard, so spiteful.'

'But she has a point.'

'What?'

'You've been advertising for seventeen years to find this child and now you may have found her you repudiate her because she's not the kind of girl you like.'

Ursula slammed her fist on the table. 'Don't you dare speak to me like that!'

'You were prepared to have her turned out of the Old North Star because you were annoyed with her.'

'But she's so *unpleasant.*'

'Ursula, if you keep disapproving of her, of course she's going to react. Give as good as you get – that's been the motto she's had to live by.'

'I don't know why you keep making excuses for her!'

'Because I think she's having a hard time.'

'And me? Do you think I've been enjoying myself?'

'No, of course not. It's been terrible for you, I realise that. So I think you ought to ask yourself if you've always acted wisely, if you haven't let your emotions run away with you.'

'Billy says I've been on an emotional helter-skelter since she first telephoned,' Ursula acknowledged with a rueful grimace.

Lindsey nodded.

'I'm not really an emotional type, you know.'

You could have fooled me, Lindsey said inwardly. But she didn't say it aloud.

'So what do you think . . . what should I do?' Ursula faltered. 'I'm not paying out any money. Once start that, you never see the end of it.'

'Quite right.

'So what then?'

'Meet her again.'

'What?'

'Meet her. Try to close your eyes to the peculiar clothes and the anti-good-looks make-up. Try to remember that the way she speaks isn't her fault – it's how she was brought up. Give her the benefit of the doubt.'

'Ha!' said Ursula with the toss of a well-groomed blond

head. '"The difficult we do at once, the impossible takes a little longer". You're not asking much.'

'It's worth a try. Don't you think so?'

'Well . . . all right. But –' and she held up a finger for emphasis – 'just a short meeting. No being cooped up with her in a hotel, no embarrassing meals where she turns the smoked salmon starter into a sandwich with the brown bread.'

'Invite her to your home.'

'No!'

'Ursula, she understands the implied insult in not being allowed in at your front door. She's not a fool, you know. Ask her to your house.'

'No! No, that seems to be saying that I . . . that I . . .' She came to a wavering halt. 'I can't do that, Lindsey. It's too much to ask. I just can't have her in my house, where my own dear little girl ought to be.'

There was no use pressing the matter any further. 'All right, how about my office, then?'

'Your office? Well, when?'

'As soon as possible.'

'Not tomorrow. I'm not ready for that. Let's say . . . Friday. Friday, my diary's not too crowded, I could come in the afternoon, about three.'

So they made arrangements, and parted, Ursula to go upstairs to change into her evening dress and Lindsey to go home on the train, thinking what to say to Edie Maybury on the phone.

When Lindsey rang the telephone was answered at once by Edie, so promptly that she might have been sitting by it.

'Edie, I spoke to Mrs Guyler.'

'Yeah?'

'She'd like to have a talk with you.'

'Yeah? Changed her tune, has she? Glad enough to see the back of me at that high-hat hotel, but now she's worried.'

'She suggests Friday afternoon.' There was no way at present to make the conversation sound friendly: Edie's tone was full of pre-rehearsed antagonism.

'Friday afternoon? That's a busy work day.'

'I realise that—'

97

'It means more time off. I just took today off already, to come and see you. I'll lose another day's pay and Old Brinksy'll moan and groan.'

'Of course your loss of pay and any expenses will be refunded.'

'Great, that sorts that out then, doesn't it. Anything can be solved by offering money, know what I mean? Is she going to be as ready to fork out for a little bit of silence, eh?'

'That's what we're going to talk about.'

'We? You gonna be there?'

'Yes, the meeting's in my office.'

A slight pause. When Edie spoke again Lindsey thought she heard relief in her voice. 'Well, that sounds more like it. In your office, all business, we're gonna talk about how much it's worth to her to settle this without a fuss. Mebbe it should have been like that from the first, know what I mean? None of this sentimental rubbish about mother and daughter feelings, eh?'

The bitterness with which it was said clearly signalled the hurt that lay behind the words. Lindsey searched for some alleviation. 'Shula is hiding behind a business facade, Edie, because she's in a terrible emotional state. I think it's a defence mechanism.'

'Oh yeah? Well, this is an attack mechanism. You tell her I'm not gonna be treated like riff-raff by her or anybody else, get it? I'll be there on Friday afternoon, but tell her not to worry, she doesn't have to take me out to *luncheon* –' she said in an assumed cultured voice – 'and watch me put ketchup in my soup.'

Nothing about the discussion boded well for Friday. If she could, Lindsey would have called the whole thing off, would have put it off until feelings on both sides were calmer. Yet how long might that be?

Andrew came into her office next morning to say that they ought to go to hear the new jazz pianist in the bar of the Gladwyn so how about a meal there that evening and an overnight at his place? To hear him offering some normal love and companionship was so touching that her voice almost broke when she agreed.

'What's the matter?' he asked. 'Catching a cold?'

'No, just a morning frog in my throat,' she said. And broke a long-standing rule by giving him a big hug while they were on business premises – mixing business with pleasure had always been forbidden.

'Wow!' he said. 'I take it that's just a foretaste.'

'Quite right. More this evening.'

He gave her a wink of his gleaming black eye and went out.

She began Thursday in a much more cheerful mood. But Friday was coming. In only twenty-four hours she would have two very unhappy, angry women to deal with – and she didn't know if she was up to the task.

It turned out worse than she expected. For Edie brought Graham.

Eight

The morning had started quite well. Wakening early, Lindsey had bestowed a kiss on Andrew's cheek before rising and dressing quietly. She caught a nearly empty train and was home in good time to shower, dress, and have a relaxed breakfast of toast and fruit before heading for the office.

There she arranged to have the conference room from three to five in the afternoon. This raised a query from Old Oliver, but the magic name Mrs Guyler removed his doubts. 'All going well, I hope?' he remarked.

'Not exactly, Mr Ollerenshaw. This meeting is going to be rather delicate and I may need to consult later.'

'By all means, by all means.' He was divided between pleasure at being needed and alarm that something was going wrong for the rich Ursula Guyler. But he knew that he mustn't ask for further details at present.

Lindsey's morning's work presented no problems. She put rough outlines of the day's letters on her computer, ready for the word processing room to make fair copies for her to sign. She dealt with a bank manager who was being unnecessarily difficult to one of her clients. She had lunch with a woman friend who came to the city once a month from an artists' commune in the Welsh Marches.

Ursula Guyler arrived rather early. Although she tried to hide it, she was very nervous – or nervy, perhaps. Unsettled, unable to follow any topic of conversation.

'Your husband couldn't come?'

'No, a golf date with a business friend. It's the kind of thing you can't change because it lets the others down. But anyway, Billy wasn't keen to come. He doesn't like rows.'

100

'But we're not going to have a row,' Lindsey corrected gently. 'This is going to be a nice calm discussion. Too much to expect it will be friendly, but let's try for peaceful, shall we?'

'Peaceful? When this awful girl is trying to extort money by threats?'

'Listen, Ursula, I think what she's doing is forcing you to pay attention. I'm not sure that money is really the point.'

'That's nonsense. I *did* pay attention to her.' She made putting-together motions with the palms of her hands. 'Over that weekend – we could have had long conversations if she'd only been willing to fall in with my suggestions but no – she had to go dashing off with that repulsive boyfriend!'

Lindsey thought it better not to argue any further. She was about to ask if her guest would like tea brought up when her phone rang. The receptionist announced: 'Miss Maybury, as you were expecting, Miss Abercrombie. But she's brought someone with her.'

'Oh? Who?' Lindsey asked, her heart sinking.

'A Mr Graham Walker.'

'What's happening?' Ursula asked, seeing the change in Lindsey's expression.

'I'll be down in a moment, Meg. Keep them there.' To Ursula she said, 'She's brought the "repulsive boyfriend" with her.'

'I'm not having him here!' Ursula cried.

'Ursula, we don't want to antagonise them further—'

'If he comes in that door, I walk out!'

Lindsey had risen to go downstairs. She paused. 'I'm going down to talk to them. But let me make this clear – I think Edie has brought him because she feels the need for some support.'

'She's brought him just to make things difficult.'

'Don't be silly, Ursula! Put yourself in her place.'

'Don't you call me silly! How dare you? You've absolutely no respect for my feelings.'

'I'm going down to the hall. Pull yourself together. When I come back I'll probably have the repulsive boyfriend with me and if you can't be polite, at least hold your tongue.' Firmness seemed the only tone to take.

101

'Don't you dare bring him up.'

'This is my office, Ursula. If you don't want to share the room with whoever I bring in, then go. But I thought you wanted to sort out the problem, not make it worse.'

'Why, you – don't you understand – I – I . . .'

'You probably have about five minutes to get a grip.' It was something of an ultimatum. With that she went out, and walked down the stairs instead of taking the lift so as to stretch the interval in which her client might calm down.

Edie was standing uneasily with Graham Walker nearer to the door than to the receptionist's desk. Lindsey thought they looked as if they were expecting to be thrown out. She said to Edie, 'I didn't expect you to bring anyone.'

'No, I reckon you didn't. Walk into the lions' den, two to one against me – that was the plan, wasn't it?'

'Oh, don't talk nonsense,' Lindsey said almost crossly. Really, what was wrong with these people? They had a delicate problem to resolve but they wanted to go at it with pickaxes. 'Mrs Guyler is waiting upstairs in my office. Before I take you up –' she held up a hand to emphasise her point – 'I want to establish some ground rules. Everybody is going to be polite. If we come to an agreement of any kind, I want to tape-record it. You –' she gave Graham a cool look – 'were never invited, but I'll allow you to be present. However, you are not to cloud the issue by giving ill-informed legal opinions. Is that clear?'

'Oh, hoity-toity,' he said. He was a good-looking young man who, like Edie, seemed to want to make himself unattractive. Three days' growth of dark beard, rings in his left earlobe, studs through his left eyebrow, hair the same matt black as Edie's and his clothes funereal in colour though not in style – leather jacket, leather trousers tucked into calf-high boots, a black T-shirt bearing the motto 'Garage Forever!' Lindsey was unsure whether that referred to his job or to the kind of music he preferred.

She waited a moment to see if there would be argument about her ground rules, but when they said nothing she led the way to the lift. They rose to the first floor in silence. She could tell that Graham was impressed against his will by the sombre elegance of the premises, their air of solid respectability.

102

With some trepidation she opened the conference room door. Ursula Guyler was sitting at the table in a chair with her back to them. She turned her head casually as they came in, raised her eyebrows, and turned back. Utterly neutral, no sign of emotion or antagonism. Well done, Ursula, thought Lindsey, you've got yourself under control.

Then she added to herself, so far.

'Well, here we are then,' Graham said in a hearty tone. Lindsey found that encouraging. He was floundering, completely out of his depth and knew it. Perhaps he'd have the good sense to stay quiet.

She offered seats to her guests. Edie chose a spot not quite at the far end of the conference table, which seated twelve. Graham sat next to her. Lindsey chose a chair from which she could see all the parties without having to crick her neck. A quick glance told her that they were all extremely stressed: Edie drumming her fingertips silently against the table top, Graham flicking glances at the panelled walls and the portraits of former solicitors, Ursula nibbling at her underlip.

'Now,' she began in a quiet voice, 'let's make a start.' Her gaze was directed at Edie. 'We're here, as I understand it, because you feel you have some claim on Shula for the disturbance she has caused in your life over the past few weeks.'

'Right,' Edie said. 'Days off work, loss of pay, upheaval in my normal way of living, and . . . and . . .'

'Emotional distress,' Graham supplied.

Ursula said nothing. Lindsey said, 'When we spoke on Wednesday, you mentioned a sum you were going to ask for in compensation.'

'Thirty-five thousand.'

'That's out of the question.' This was Ursula, utterly cool.

'It's quite a reasonable amount when you think you left me for seventeen years with old Ma Maybury—'

'My client might be willing to consider some compensation for the time and disturbance since you first telephoned her, but that's only a matter of about a month.'

'None of that!' Graham interrupted, waking up to the fact that negotiations had started. 'We're not going to be fobbed off with a few bob for a month's upset!'

'Mr Walker, you aren't a party to this discussion. There's no "we" about it. This matter is between Mrs Guyler and Miss Maybury—'

'She's not Miss Maybury, she's Miss Guyler, her *daughter*. That's what we're talking about.'

'No we are not! We're talking about a crude attempt at blackmail,' cried Ursula.

'You can call it what you like, Missus, but you know damn well you owe her something.'

'Ursula, let's not use terms like "blackmail". I think we can agree that Edie has been put to some inconvenience over the last few weeks and there might be a feeling that she should be paid something in recognition—'

'Recognition! Right, that's the word!' Graham jumped in. 'We want her to recognise her own daughter and since she don't seem to want to be friends with her, we want something in damages for the way she's neglected her and refused to take reasonable care—'

'Will you hold your tongue, you impudent fool!' cried Ursula. 'You don't have a clue what you're talking about, all you want is to screw money out of this situation.'

'Well, you've got plenty of it, and Edie here deserves her cut.'

'If you think I'm going to pay a penny, you're living in cloud cuckoo land, my lad. You'd only get it out of her – it's easy to see you think you're on to a good thing here.'

'Ursula, Ursula . . . please, let's lower our voices. Shouting belongs at a football match.'

'*She* started it,' Graham grunted.

'Yes, I did,' Ursula responded, surprisingly. 'I was a fool to think I would ever really find my little girl again. All those years of hoping, and this is what I get! A pair of crooks!'

'What you get is your daughter,' Graham declared. 'You just don't want to believe it.'

'She's not my daughter,' Ursula insisted. 'A mother would know her own daughter. She's no child of mine.'

'Oh, maternal instincts, is it?' Edie queried, speaking at last. 'You'd know me if I was really yours – your heart would go "thump" and we'd rush into each other's arms, eh? Well tell me this. If I'm not your daughter, whose am I?'

'That's your affair! You delved about among the birth and death certificates, go back and delve some more! You'll find your real parents, but you won't accept them because they won't have money and position in society.'

'Oh, you mean they'll be peasants, like me, is that it?'

'You said it, I didn't.' There was contempt in Ursula's tone.

'Will you behave?' Lindsey burst out. 'You should listen to yourselves – you sound like a bunch of schoolchildren.' A sudden silence fell. No wonder, she thought: this is most unsolicitorly behaviour. 'Now, can we get back to what I was suggesting? A reasonable sum of money for the inconvenience—'

'Not a penny,' Ursula declared. 'Except for expenses. She doesn't *deserve* anything more.'

'You're really tight-fisted the minute we start talking about money,' said Graham.

'And you're just a leech trying to bleed me for money for a girl who's nothing to me.'

'She's your daughter, Julie!'

'No she's not—'

'Wait,' Lindsey said in despair. 'There's a way to establish the truth or otherwise of that.'

'What way?' Graham said, surprised.

'DNA testing.'

Everyone looked at everyone else. Edie, who had been frowning in anger, sat back in her chair, made a little moue of thought, then shrugged in acceptance.

'No!' cried Ursula.

Lindsey was taken aback by the vehemence of the response. She'd expected reluctance but not so extreme. She'd thought that, as a businesswoman, Ursula would agree to have the matter tested and, if it proved that Edie was her daughter, make some businesslike arrangement – a legal acknowledgement of the relationship and then perhaps a reasonable monthly allowance, although with strict rules about non-interference in each other's lives. She was about to say something about the advantages of having the facts verified. But Edie intervened before she could frame the words.

'See? She doesn't want to know! She's dead set against me and I knew that from the first! If she thinks I care whether I'm really—'

'Edie, don't get in a state!' Graham interrupted, making calming motions. 'I'm sure if we just chat this over, we can—'

'Chat it over?' cried Ursula. 'There's a phrase for you! And she brings an idiot like this to a serious discussion! We're wasting our time.'

'Who're you calling an idiot?' Graham exclaimed. 'I dunno who the devil you think you are—'

'She's just an uppity old girl with too much money,' Edie said. 'Come on, Gray, let's split.'

'Right! I didn't come here to be insulted.'

'No, you came to see what you could screw out of me but you got more than you bargained for! I meet types like you ten times a week, trying to sell me rubbish in my office – well, they get shown the door and so do you!'

'Come on, Gray,' Edie urged, ready to leave.

'No – hang on.' He had remembered there was money involved. 'She's got to stump up for what she's made you suffer.'

'A cheque for expenses and loss of earnings will reach you by post,' Ursula said, addressing Edie exclusively.

'Keep your rotten money!' Edie cried. 'You and everything to do with you! I wish I'd never heard of you, you stupid old crow!'

She marched out. Graham hurried after her, looking like a man who has somehow lost the plot.

Ursula cast a glance of triumph at Lindsey. 'There you are! Do you really think a girl like that could be my daughter?'

Only too easily, Lindsey thought. They were so alike in character that it sometimes seemed to glare at you, it was so obvious. Stubborn, pugnacious, proud – mother and daughter shared attributes that were never going to make life easy between them. That is, if they ever at any time came together.

Lindsey was sure in her own mind that they truly were mother and daughter. All the evidence, although circumstantial, pointed to it. Only the fact that Ursula had taken instant dislike

106

to Edie prevented them from developing an affectionate, or at least a friendly, relationship. It was true that Edie wasn't particularly lovable. What she might have been under different circumstances, no one could say. But an upbringing with an unstable woman, who seemed to have abducted her almost at random . . . It wasn't any wonder that she was difficult and aggressive.

Alas, Ursula wasn't prepared to make the slightest allowance. Disappointed and distressed by their encounters, she too had taken up a combative stance. In a situation calling for patience, there was irritation, where there should have been gentleness there was antagonism.

And now there was the repulsive boyfriend as an additional nuisance. He worried Lindsey. She felt sure he had his eye on the main chance. He was almost the worst adviser Edie could have chosen. But then who else was there? Moved about from country town to country town, Edie had had scant opportunity to make friends among people of her own age, and as for friendly elders – it seemed Mrs Maybury had been on bad terms with her neighbours wherever they went.

This passed through Lindsey's mind while she tried to take stock of her client. Ursula was very close to tears. Something stronger than afternoon tea was called for. Lindsey took a bottle of Remy Martin and a glass from the lowest shelf of her document cupboard and poured a stiff drink.

Ursula accepted it without demur. She gulped, coughed, made sounds that were half a cough, half a sob, and allowed herself to be patted gently on the back.

'Well,' she said when she recovered, 'that's that. I've called their bluff. Make out a cheque for whatever is due to her in the way of expenses and send it with a compliment slip or something.'

'Ursula, don't you think—'

She held up a hand to stop any argument. 'I know what I'm doing. I've seen off more than one man like that, believe me – trying to pull a fast one on me in a business negotiation.'

'This isn't just business, Ursula – feelings are involved,'

'Not so far as I'm concerned! I'm done with making myself

107

miserable over that insolent little cat. Just pay her off and you'll
see – that'll be the end of it.'

Far from it.

Three days later Lindsey was standing in her kitchen eating
toast for breakfast and listening to the local radio which
supplied her with information about the train service as well
as a time check. The linkman was chatting about the morning
papers in his usual casual way.

'Here's a thing in the *Morning Banner* that might interest
you folks,' he remarked. 'It's about someone who lives right
here in little old Birmingham. "Millionairess Slams Door on
Daughter." Dramatic story: "Mrs Ursula Guyler, owner of
bestselling Gylah Cosmetics, has barred her own flesh and
blood". That turns out to be Edie Maybury, who says she's
the long-lost daughter . . .'

Lindsey waited for no more. She dashed out of the kitchen,
out of her flat, and ran downstairs to the little shop that supplied
newspapers and emergency supplies such as milk and instant
coffee to the residents of the building. There she bought a copy
of the *Banner*.

The big letters of the headline stood out above a photograph
of Ursula, taken at the opening of a school fete. In the main
story, Edie was quoted as saying, 'I find it hard to forgive. All
this pretence of wanting to find me but it was a sham. Ursula
Guyler is a hard-hearted hypocrite.' 'Mrs Guyler refused to be
interviewed,' was the last line of the report.

Dear heaven, thought Lindsey. Edie, how could you! But
her next thought was that this was Graham's doing. Foiled in
his attempts to get money from Mrs Guyler, he'd gone instead
to the tabloid newspaper with a story that would fetch a good
price. A human interest story – but in whose interest was it?
Graham might have got a handsome sum from the *Banner* but
to Lindsey it was a terrible defeat. It meant that Ursula would
never now be persuaded to think of Edie in friendly terms.
Never ever.

And moreover . . . it meant Lindsey would have to tell Old
Oliver all about it. And be told, with perfect truth, that she'd
handled the whole thing badly.

Nine

When Lindsey tried to phone Old Oliver, his wife told her that he'd already left for the office. She was about to ring the office when her mobile rang. She fished it out of her handbag.

Billy Guyler said without preamble, 'Shula's very upset.'

'Yes.'

'We've got reporters here.'

'Yes.'

'What're you going to do about it?

'I'm trying to reach Mr Ollerenshaw—'

'He's not in the office, I tried there first.'

'I'm just going out to the train – I'll ring him en route.'

'We want this stopped!' Billy said in what was almost a shout. 'Do you understand that?'

'Of course, Mr Guyler.'

'You've let us down! Get it sorted out!'

Her house phone was ringing now. She heard Billy switch off and dashed to her desk. To her astonishment, the voice on the line belonged to Keith Holland.

'Saw the *Banner*.'

'I'm busy.'

'That's why you were looking for Mrs Maybury.'

'Mind your own business!'

'Wait! Mrs Maybury's going to be upset when she sees her name in the papers.'

That was only too likely. She said with regret, 'There's nothing I can do about that.'

'There'll be reporters at her house by midday.'

'Mr Holland, you're wasting my time.'

'I'm trying to help. I'll get to Mrs Maybury within the next

109

half hour, sign her up for an exclusive with the Cartfield
Clarion – how about that?'

'What?'

'If she's signed up with me, she can't say anything to any
other paper – that's the rule.'

'That wouldn't hold up in a court of law.'

'We're not talking about the law, we're talking about rules
that reporters live by.' His tone was matter of fact, and
somehow she found it comforting.

'But they'll badger her – after all, the Cartfield *Clarion*
is—'

'Insignificant – yes, okay – I'll tell her to say she's signed up
with "another paper" – they'll think it's the *Sun* or the *Mirror*,
and give up.'

She paused to collect herself. 'How did you get my home
number?' she demanded.

'Got it from directory enquiries, of course – where else?
Remember, I'm an investigative reporter.'

She could tell he was grinning.

'Why are you doing this?'

'Because I like you.'

'What?' she said faintly.

'And because Mrs Maybury is practically a neighbour. She
deserves a bit of help.'

'Well, that's . . . that's . . .'

'Noble of me?' He laughed. 'Don't forget, I'm getting an
exclusive.' He rang off, and she was left holding the receiver
and listening to the empty line.

Snatching up her shoulder bag and mobile, she scurried out
of the flat. A neighbour just about to drive to work gave her a
lift to the station. She rang the office as she waited for her train,
to be told by the receptionist that Mr Ollerenshaw wanted to
see her *at once*! I'll bet, she thought, and assured Meg that she
was on her way. She'd no sooner folded up the mobile when it
rang. It was Andrew, speaking from the office.

'Lindsey, what were you thinking of?' he asked with something like incredulity. 'To let things get to such a bad stage?'

'What? How do you . . . ? How are you involved in this,
Andrew?'

'Well, of course, as soon as I saw the *Banner* I tried to ring Old Oliver, but he was on his way to the office, so I hopped over here in a taxi. That's the advantage of living in town, Lin. I was here on the doorstep when he arrived.'

'Oh.' She hesitated. 'What's he saying?'

'He's breathing fire and flames.'

Her train rumbled to the platform. 'I can't talk now, Andrew, I've got to get on the train.'

'See you when you get here. And put on your asbestos apron, sweetie, you're going to need it.'

He couldn't have uttered a truer word. The receptionist gave her a sympathetic glance as she scuttled in, but she hardly noticed. She took off her coat, threw it over a chair in the corridor, and went to Mr Ollerenshaw's office. His secretary greeted her with the words, 'Go straight in.' The inner door was ajar. As she tapped on it she could see the senior partner sitting in his stately leather chair, staring at his computer screen. Andrew was at his elbow, pointing to something on it.

They both looked up as she came in.

'Would you care to explain?' Old Oliver demanded.

'I did say to you on Friday that I might need to consult—'

He grunted, his white brows coming together in anger. 'That was the understatement of the year. Please let me have an account of your dealings with this disastrous affair.'

She had had time to get herself together on the way there. She started at the beginning with Ursula Guyler's seventeen years of advertisements offering a reward for information about her lost daughter, then went through what had happened since Edie first rang.

'So on Friday we had a meeting, but unfortunately Edie brought this young man with her. I'm sure he was the one who contacted the *Morning Banner*.'

'Really?' said Old Oliver in icy tones. 'Did it never occur to you that this girl was a fraud, trying to extract money from a vulnerable woman?'

'Mr Ollerenshaw, that's too big a leap to make. I told you about the enquiries I made in Cartfield. Someone stole the name of Mary Lois Maybury and her daughter Edie – the only reason I can think of is that she – the false Mrs Maybury

– needed a birth certificate for the child she snatched from the beach.'

'There's no evidence for that. The new Mrs Maybury needed false identities, that seems clear, but there's no evidence that the child in question had anything to do with Ursula Guyler.'

'But I think there *is*!' she insisted. 'They're so alike—'

'Alike? This little swindler and our client?' Mr Ollerenshaw was so astonished that for the moment he was without further words.

'That's a bit emotional, Lindsey,' Andrew suggested.

She wanted to say that in dealing with family problems, emotions had to be taken into consideration. But she knew that her boss wouldn't like that, and Andrew was giving her a warning glance. No use in getting Ollie's back up, he was saying.

'The thing now, sir, is to limit the damage,' he suggested.

'Quite true, Andrew. I . . . er . . . I think I should have a telephone conference with Mrs Guyler . . . clearly she can't leave her house at the moment . . . I gather there are reporters besieging it.'

'If I might suggest something, Mr Ollerenshaw,' said Lindsey. She turned to Andrew. 'Could we try for an injunction?'

'Ah. Er . . . ?' he said in a questioning tone.

'To restrain the press. This can't be said to be a matter of national importance – I think a sympathetic judge might see it as an intrusion into personal affairs.'

Andrew seemed to be considering it. He left it to the boss to make the decision.

'Well . . . that is a possibility, certainly.' Old Oliver frowned and rubbed his nose. 'Andrew my boy, I think you might get going on that. You have some good contacts in the courts, I know.'

Lindsey was startled. It was *her* case, so she should plead for the injunction.

But the chief was waving Andrew out of the door and saying to Lindsey, 'And as for you, young lady, you'd better get on the telephone and apologise as best you can to Mrs Guyler. Andrew and I have been reviewing her account with us, and really if she goes elsewhere because of this, we stand to lose a great deal in monetary terms, to say nothing about the blow to our reputation.'

But the telephones at the Guyler house were never picked up. Not even an answering machine. She tried the office telephones. There was a recorded message: 'If you wish to place an order, press one. If you wish to check despatch, press two. If you wish to speak to a member of the executive staff, press three.' But pressing three only got you a recorded message offering the sales manager, the transport manager, the advertising manager and so on. None of them offered the owner and managing director, Ursula Guyler. The last option was the message: 'If you require any other service, please press five.' But five only got you a message saying: 'We regret that no other services are available at this time. Please call again.'

In other words, the Guylers had made themselves incommunicado.

Lindsey thought it best to deliver this news in person rather than by intercom. 'I'm afraid no one answers at either the Guyler home or the office, Mr Ollerenshaw.'

'Oh?'

'To avoid having to speak to reporters, I imagine.'

'Of course. Very shrewd.' He harrumphed a few times. 'What do you suggest?'

'I think I'll have to go there, sir.'

'To the house?'

'I'd say that's where they are. The reporters probably camped out there as soon as the first editions of the *Banner* came out – and that's about two in the morning, I think.'

'So early? Good Lord!' He took in this fact, sighing and glancing at the clock. 'If they got to Mrs Guyler at 2 a.m., no wonder she's switched off her phones. She's had about eight hours of it.'

'Yes, it must be horrible.'

'How do you intend to get past the reporters? And if you do, will the Guylers let you in? I imagine you're persona extremely non grata with them at the moment.'

'Well . . . Billy Guyler did ring me at home this morning.'

'He did? I don't think you mentioned that.' A moment's consideration. 'That may mean we're not entirely out of favour,

113

then. Very well, see if you can make personal contact. And if you do, assure them that we're doing all we can to handle this affair.'

'Of course, Mr Ollerenshaw.'

Having received his blessing, she dashed back to her office to cancel some appointments and rearrange others, then looked in on Andrew. 'How are you getting on with the injunction?'

'Can't move on it. I need the Guylers' instruction.'

'I'll get that.'

'How d'you mean, you'll get it? They're not answering phones or anything.'

'I'm going to the house.'

'They'll shoot at you from the window,' he said, laughing.

'Oh, don't, Andrew! It's not funny!'

'No, it's not, and how we're ever going to repair the damage I don't know.' Sobered, he shook his head at her. 'This is a big blot on your copybook, sweetheart. If we lose the Guylers because of this, Old Ollie will hang you up by your thumbs.'

'Thanks a lot for the encouragement,' she said, and went out.

There was a sandwich shop which did deliveries just beyond the cathedral from whom members of the firm ordered in sandwiches when they didn't want to go out for a meal. She went there, asked to speak to the owner/manager, and explained her problem. He heard her out, beginning to smile after the first few sentences.

'Right you are,' he agreed. 'Only one thing – can you ride a motorscooter?'

'I'm a quick learner,' she said.

He raised his eyebrows, but he was an immigrant from a war-torn country where everyone had had to be a quick learner. He led her to the side alley where two scooters stood at the ready for the late-morning deliveries of sandwiches, cakes, soft drinks and coffee. The scooters had plastic open-meshed carriers fixed on the back. While Andreas gave her a quick course on the controls of the scooter, an assistant came out with light cardboard containers of sandwiches which he put into the carrier.

He handed her a jacket. It was of navy-blue nylon and

across its front were stitched the word; 'EATS'. On the back the stitching read, 'ANDREAS'. Lindsey took off her black cloth coat, donned the jacket, and got on the scooter. With little waves of encouragement, they stood back to let her take off. After a wobble or two up the alley, she stopped, restarted, turned in a neat curve and rode away to the main road and the route to the Guylers.

There were at least seven reporters, male and female, camped at the gates. Photographers on light aluminium ladders were sighting over the railings towards the door and windows. A van for the local TV station was parked a little further along, one for a national network was just behind it.

Everyone turned to stare at Lindsey. But their interest only evoked murmurs of, 'Cook's gone on strike, has she?' They resisted her efforts to elbow her way through with her containers of sandwiches, but someone suggested the Guylers might open the gate for her and they might get a pic. So they allowed her to get to the front.

Once there, she waved vigorously and called the name of the housekeeper she'd seen on other visits. 'Erika! Erika!'

There was a long pause. Then the gates opened electronically, just enough to let Lindsey slip past. The woman reporter who tried to follow got her foot squeezed and retreated, exclaiming in anger and a little pain. Lindsey hurried to the front door, where Erika let her in through the narrowest possible opening.

She took the cardboard containers from Lindsey without comment. 'In there,' she said, nodding towards a door down the hall.

The room might have been described as a study, furnished with dark leather and panelling. But its chief use seemed to be to house Billy's golfing trophies, of which there were quite a few but not of any great merit – local clubs, regional competitions, pro-am matches for charity.

The Guylers were sitting hand in hand on a leather-upholstered couch. Lindsey thought that Ursula looked quite ill, her usually perfect hair pulled back in a clasp, her make-up carelessly applied. Billy was pale and drawn but that seemed more because Ursula was upset than that he himself was affected.

They stared at Lindsey in her navy nylon jacket. Hastily she discarded it. 'I couldn't get through by phone,' she explained.

'No. We've switched them off.'

'We'll need a way to communicate if you intend to keep them switched off. What about your mobiles?'

'They're not listed but they seem to have got hold of the numbers.'

'Well, I'll leave you mine when I go. When it rings, you can answer without any anxiety – you may get my family and friends calling but just say you're borrowing my phone, and in any case it'll probably be someone from Higgett Ollerenshaw.'

'Without any anxiety! This is torture!' Ursula gasped. 'The phone began to ring at half past two this morning and it never stopped until we cut it off. And those ghouls outside – I'm a prisoner in my own home.'

'What's the plan?' Billy asked, gazing at Lindsey, his grey-blue eyes full of trust. She was here now, had managed to bring help through the siege line. She must have a good plan.

'Mr Ollerenshaw is asking for an injunction to prevent the press from hounding you—'

'An injunction? You think that lot will pay any attention?' Ursula demanded.

'Oh yes, otherwise it's contempt of court and prison until they promise to behave. And a heavy fine, perhaps. They'll obey the injunction.'

'So when does it come into force?'

'That's why I'm here. The plea can't be entered until you give us instructions. Look, I brought up a form letter on the computer – it gives us power of attorney to act for you for the next three days. That way, we can take whatever steps seem best.'

'Three days? You think they're going to stay there for three days?' Ursula wailed, aghast.

'It's just a temporary measure, three days is logical and if it's not needed we can cancel it immediately. You have a fax machine?'

116

'At the office. I leave all that behind me when I come home.'

'Well, never mind. We can take your instructions by telephone as a temporary method. I'll write that in on the letter of agreement – is that okay?'

'This is awful!' Ursula cried. 'It's like being trapped in a cage. I'm not used to doing business like this.'

'I know, I know, but this is a difficult situation – unless you feel like leaving the house?'

'What, and have them shoving microphones in my face, asking me how I *feel* about having that loathsome girl claim she's my little Julie?'

Billy squeezed his wife's hand, murmuring soothing words. Lindsey waited until Ursula had calmed down, then tried to make plans for the next few hours. She hoped that by the end of the day the press would have been ordered away by court order.

When she went out again, the reporters crowded round her. 'Did you see Ursula Guyler? Did you speak to her? What's she saying? Did you call the servant by her name? Did you speak to her? Has she anything to tell?'

But when she merely walked on without a reply, they soon turned back to their survey of the house. She mounted the scooter and rode back to Andreas Eats, where her safe arrival was greeted with cheers.

Mr Ollerenshaw was pleased when she delivered the temporary power of attorney and even more so when she reported leaving a viable phone with the Guylers, its number unknown and unsuspected by the press. Andrew set off for the chambers of a friendly judge, to get the injunction. In Old Oliver's office, the telephone conference was set up, he at his desk, Lindsey on an extension, and the secretary at hand with a notebook to take any instructions.

The conversation was dominated by Ursula, full of complaints and demands. Old Oliver was at his rather grandiose best, soothing, persuading, reassuring. Lindsey was never once called upon for a contribution. As the call was coming to an end Old Oliver said, 'Don't worry, my dear lady, within an hour or two those persecutors will all be cleared away and you can go about your life just as usual.'

'Nothing will ever be as usual again,' Ursula mourned. 'That girl has done a tremendous amount of damage.'

'Well, well, we'll deal with her by and by,' he said comfortingly. 'The law can be brought into play in a case of harassment or defamation.'

'Yes . . . well . . . nothing can restore my good name. People are going to look at me with a funny expression from now on, Mr Ollerenshaw.'

'Nonsense, nonsense, after all that you and your husband have done for charities? No, no, we'll show her up for the little harpy that she is, and it will all be forgotten.'

'You really think so?'

'Certainly, not a doubt of it.'

Lindsey sighed inwardly. She was by no means sure that he was right. And . . . though she would never dream of putting this into words . . . what about Edie in all this? She was being cast in the role of villain yet to Lindsey's mind, Ursula had played a part in her own troubles. Well, she wasn't supposed to think like that, she told herself. Higgett, Ollerenshaw and Cline were paid to regard Ursula Guyler as the wronged party in all this, so that's what she had to do. But she found that it troubled her.

After lunch Andrew Gilmore returned from the courts, subdued. He put his head in at Lindsey's door. 'Come with me to see Ollie.'

'What's up?'

'The circuit judge refused the injunction.'

'Oh, Lord!'

Mr Ollerenshaw's secretary could tell that something was seriously wrong. Two members of the firm didn't come unannounced to her desk asking to see their boss unless it was important. She went to the inner door, tapped, entered and murmured the news to her employer. From the outer office they could hear Old Oliver's exclamation. She came out, nodded them in, and closed the door behind them.

Their boss had been reading a thick document, a will

recently revised yet again by a troublesome client. He set it aside.

'What's this?' he growled, his thick white eyebrows raised in surprise.

'I'm sorry to say, sir, that Justice Arkull refused the injunction.'

'Refused?'

'Yes, sir.' Andrew gazed at the corner of the room for inspiration but, finding none, continued. 'He says the matter is within the public domain and has been for a long time, due to the actions of Mrs Guyler herself.'

'Oh, but—'

'He heard me out then said that as she had been putting advertisements in the newspapers for seventeen years, she had engaged the resources of the press. She can't now claim that it's none of their business.'

'That's absurd! Is he saying that if someone announces an engagement in the papers, he forfeits his right to privacy?'

'Not at all, sir. He bases it on the length of exposure, seventeen years, and the "continuation of the effect" in her co-operating with the TV company's programme.'

'But that was in the attempt to *find* her child.'

'I tried that one, Mr Ollerenshaw. He said that people who invite the press into their lives can't choose how long they'll stay there. The thing's become a matter of public interest and certainly isn't a "trivial" thing – I tried to argue for that, but although he said he felt no approval of the way the *Banner* treated it, they didn't "trivialise".'

Old Oliver frowned grimly. 'This is terrible. I promised Mrs Guyler that the reporters would be gone by the end of the day.'

'I'm sorry, sir.'

Seeing him look so downcast, Lindsey tried a rescue attempt. 'If Mrs Guyler will just stay quietly in her house for another day or two, the press will find something else to run after,' she suggested.

'Oh really?' her boss said with a glare of irritation. 'Is that the advice we're to offer our client? That she hides in her home because we can't do anything to help her?'

119

'Well . . . in fact that's how things stand . . .'

'Thank you for your input.' He turned to Andrew, waiting for suggestions. But Andrew had nothing to suggest.

'Very well. Mrs Guyler will have to be told that we have failed her.' He nodded at Lindsey. 'And since she is after all your client and it's due to your inability to control the situation that we're in this plight, I think you must be the one to convey that message.'

'Yes, sir.'

'Please let me know what she says.' He nodded his dismissal at them. They went out without another word until they reached the corridor.

Then Andrew stopped, his hand on Lindsey's arm. 'For heaven's sake be careful what you say to Mrs Guyler. If she withdraws her business from the firm, it'll be a disaster.'

'I know that, Andrew.'

'You've handled this like an amateur from the very beginning, Lindsey! Surely you must have seen that the girl was setting up a scam?'

'No, I didn't. And I don't think so now.'

'Oh, for the love of mike! She makes demands for money, and when she doesn't get it she runs to the tabloids?'

'We don't know how the *Banner* got into it—'

'You're not going to say that they found out by having it drop from a passing carrier pigeon? Of course she sold them the story. And a nasty vicious thing it is to do!'

Lindsey lost her temper. 'You don't know the first thing about it!' she exclaimed. 'And you didn't do all that well yourself with your friend Judge Arkull, did you?'

'It was *your* idea to apply for an injunction.'

'But I expected you to have done some research before you dropped in on him with a simple shot like that. Didn't it occur to you that he might cite previous co-operation on her part.'

'What else was there to use except invasion of privacy.'

'You could have tried business detriment – the bad publicity will probably do harm.'

'Oh, fine, you had all these good ideas but you never let me know about them.'

'What chance did I have? And besides, that was *your*

120

department. I had to get to see her and get the temporary power of attorney.'

'The fact is, you've let yourself get emotionally involved in all this, Lindsey, and you should have known better. And now look where it's landed us!'

He stalked away. She had the impression that when he said 'Look where it's landed us,' he didn't mean the law firm, but the trouble the two of them were in with Mr Ollerenshaw. She for her failure to stop Edie Maybury from causing trouble, and he for failing to get the injunction despite his reputation for having good contacts at the courts. Andrew wasn't the kind to enjoy being wrong-footed.

With a heavy heart, she went into her own office and picked up the telephone, trying to think of a way to tell Ursula Guyler that for the present she would have to endure continuing press interest.

It wasn't going to be a pleasant conversation.

Ten

L indsey's prophecy proved correct. Next day a big story broke, concerning the love life of a pop star. The crew of reporters and cameramen decamped from the front of the Guylers' house except for one local journalist, to whom Ursula Guyler was more important than a London-based singer. He, in his turn, was summoned away by a scandal to do with a local borough councillor.

Keith Holland rang from Cartfield to say that the real Mrs Maybury had suffered very little from press attention.

'Though she told me to tell you that you were a bit sneaky when you came to see her,' he teased her. 'You said it was something to do with traffic on the by-pass road, and all the time it was about her daughter.'

'We-ell . . .'

'But she forgives you, Lindsey,' he went on. 'She says you're a nice lass.'

'Oh.'

'What's happening your end?'

'Oh, it's mostly died away. My client was very upset, of course.'

'Your client being Mrs Guyler, the "Mum Slams Door" character.'

'I can't discuss that.'

'Okay, okay – but it stands out a mile. I've asked around among my cronies in the business magazines, and they say she's a bit of a tartar.'

'No comment.'

'This kid Edie – I don't agree with what she did, but she does seem to have been treated with very little sympathy.'

'Look here, I can't chat with you like this.'

122

'Chat? I'm the one who's chatting, you're saying nothing. But that's all right, I'm the type that likes to hold the floor.'

'I've noticed,' she said, unable to resist.

'Oh, so you've got as far as noticing things about me? That's a step in the right direction.'

'Keith, you're impossible!'

'Not impossible, just a bit far fetched. And speaking of being far fetched, I feel too far away from you. Are you free this weekend?'

'Why do you ask?'

'Because I'll come to Birmingham if you'll be around.'

'We-ell . . .'

'Is that a yes?'

'Oh, now, Keith, are you coming just to find out what's been going on in the Guyler business, so as to get a scoop?'

'My dear *girl*, nobody uses the word "scoop" any more. But no, I'm not coming to pick your brains. I'm coming for the pleasure of your company.'

It was rather nice to have someone sound so approving. In the last few days Mr Ollerenshaw had not been pleased with her, nor were the Guylers kindly disposed. The relationship between herself and Andrew had suffered too: a coolness had developed. She couldn't get over how he had rounded on her as they came out of Old Oliver's office. Andrew for his part seemed inclined to keep some distance between them, as if she had the plague.

And of course she had – the plague of having made a mistake.

'As a matter of fact . . .'

'Yes?'

'I hadn't anything planned for this weekend.' There, she'd said it. Should she have said it?

'How would you like to go to a concert performance of *La Traviata* at Symphony Hall?' Keith enquired, wondering what her tastes might be.

'Oh . . . too weepy, Keith. I'm in the mood for something more up-beat.'

'A touring company doing *Annie* in Malvern?'

'No, nothing to do with orphans, if you don't mind!'

'You're hard to please, young woman. How about a charity market near Lichfield on Saturday and a decent lunch at the Fox afterwards?'

'That sounds better.'

'It's a deal. I'll pick you up, shall I? About eleven, at your place. Give me directions how to find you.'

'No, no, it makes more sense if I come north while you're coming south.'

'But I shan't be coming south, I'll be at the Normanton in Birmingham on Friday evening.'

'Oh, I see. Well, in that case, it makes more sense if I come to the Normanton to meet you – you don't want to come all the way out to Bromsgrove and then drive back north.'

After some amicable wrangling they agreed that Keith would pick her up in his car at Birmingham New Street. As she hung up, she felt for the first time in days a sense of warmth and approbation.

The office week ended, Saturday came. She took some care over her appearance although it was just a day to be spent wandering round some muddy field looking at home-made cushions and sampling farmhouse cheeses. She put on boot-leg jeans, brown leather jodhpur boots, a brown silk shirt under a blue sweater, and a watch cap to keep her ears warm in the early November breeze. For make-up she used only a little eye-shadow and lip gloss – elaborate make-up would be too noticeable for a day in the open.

As she came out of the station, Keith drew up beside her in a sturdy-looking Shogun, not new but gleaming from a recent wash and wax. Keith himself was a good match for his car, in a faded blue flannel shirt under a dark red guernsey. It looked as if his shaggy brown hair might recently have had the attentions of a barber.

He made to get out and usher her to her seat but she waved him back and hopped in as he opened the door for her.

'Well, hello.'

'Hello to you. Your train was right on time.'

'Being Saturday! On working days it's generally late.'

Why were they talking about train times? The idea seemed

to occur to them both at the same moment because, as he turned out into Queensway each of them began a new sentence.

'It's so nice to see you—'

'I'm so glad to be out and about after—'

They broke off and laughed. 'You first,' he said.

'I was going to say it's nice to be out and about on pleasure. This has been a really miserable week.'

'Well, we'll put Mrs Guyler and her troubles behind us and simply enjoy ourselves. Although I'm not sure what sort of pleasure this event is going to provide.'

'Never mind. So long as it has nothing to do with family relationships, it'll be grand.'

'Been difficult, has it?'

She sighed. 'Let's not talk about it.'

He put himself out to entertain her on the drive to Lichfield. He told her about his meeting with Mrs Maybury, who had forgotten any ill-feeling over Lindsey's interview when soothed with what she called 'a posh afternoon tea with squishy cakes'.

'I put a bit in the *Clarion* saying she'd been very surprised to find herself mentioned in the strange business of Mrs Guyler's lost daughter. One or two people rang up and we got a few letters expressing indignation or condemnation – of the late so-called Mrs Maybury, I mean. I responded this week with a few words about how people learnt the trick from reading thrillers, and that's the end of it.'

'But not as far as poor Edie Maybury is concerned,' mourned Lindsey.

'You're sorry for her?' He was pleased to hear that note in her voice. He had a poor view of the law and solicitors in general, since he'd often found them a problem in his days of investigative journalism. But Lindsey wasn't that kind of solicitor, he was glad to find.

'I am – well – concerned about her,' she admitted. 'She's not the most lovable person you could happen to meet, but she's having a tough time at the moment, in my opinion. Unfortunately, she hasn't the know-how to sort things out – she blunders about, you see, making things worse . . . Oh, well, there's nothing to be done about it, and I oughtn't to be talking about it.'

Keith gave her a sidelong glance. A nice lass, Mrs Maybury had said, and he was in thorough agreement with that. Knew it the minute I met her, he told himself in self-congratulation.

Since she clearly meant what she said about not wanting to discuss the Guylers, he began to talk about something else. 'You know Lichfield was the birthplace of the Grand Panjandrum?'

'Dr Johnson? Yes, I know.'

'Oh? Hang it all, I was going to astound you with my literary knowledge but you already know!'

'I looked it up in the gazetteer,' she said, laughing.

'Well . . . So did I. So, that's one more thing we have in common – we like to know where we're going.'

'Could we also say we like to try to impress others with our literary knowledge?'

'Could we? *I'm* trying to impress *you* – it would be very nice to think *you're* trying to impress *me*.'

She shook her head. 'It's nothing personal, one-upmanship is part of the legalistic background. You have to try not to be at a loss.' And then she sighed. She'd been at something of a loss ever since Edie Maybury and her boyfriend walked out of her office on Friday.

It would have been so nice to discuss the whole thing with Keith. Normally it was to Andrew she turned for opinion or advice, but at the moment Andrew wasn't around much. Keith struck her as someone who would see matters from her point of view – that although Ursula Guyler was her client and must come first, it was important to deal not only fairly but kindly with Edie.

She shook herself mentally. It was nothing to do with Keith. It was nothing to do with Andrew either. Ursula Guyler had come to her for help and advice, and it was up to Lindsey to support her in every way.

But as yet she didn't see what the next step should be. Nor was Ursula ready for it yet. Perhaps on Monday . . . She would ring, and arrange to meet, and they would talk things through. Lindsey couldn't accept that a total break had occurred between these two troubled women. There must be some way to build a bridge . . . But at the moment she couldn't see how, and perhaps it was best to put it out of her mind, to enjoy the outing and let herself be refreshed for what might come next.

The charity market was more interesting than either of them had really expected. Keith began taking notes, as a basis for putting up the idea to Cartfield parish council. Lindsey bought things – home-made plum jam, onions strung together in a plait, a tea-cosy. Lunch at the Fox was a mushroom omelette and, for Lindsey, a glass of surprisingly good wine. Keith, though he grumbled, contented himself with mineral water.

They went to Dr Johnson's house in the afternoon, and it was while they were examining his portrait – heavy square face, great dark grey wig – that her mobile rang.

'Lindsey?' It was Andrew. 'Where on earth are you?'

'I'm in the Dr Johnson House in Lichfield. Why?'

'Need you ask? It's the Guylers.'

She remembered that Andrew was duty solicitor today. Each of the junior members of the firm had to be ready in turn to go to the aid of a client over the weekend, and this was Andrew's weekend.

'What's the problem?'

'It's the girl and her boyfriend again. Mrs G. wants you on the double.'

'Why didn't she ring me? She has my mobile number—' But then she recalled that she'd given her mobile to Ursula. The one she was carrying now was a temporary replacement until she could reclaim her own. 'Oh. Well, I'll ring her at once.'

'You'd better.' He disconnected with a snap that was almost audible in her ear.

Keith was looking at her as she turned back to him. 'Trouble?' he asked. He could tell it was, from her anxious expression.

'I'm afraid so. I have to get back to Birmingham at once.'

'Okay.'

'Okay?'

'I'll get the car.'

'But it seems such a shame to ask you to—'

'You mean you feel it's wrong to drag me away from Dr Johnson?' He grinned in amusement. 'Come on, let's get going.'

While he went to fetch the Shogun she dialled Mrs Guyler's number. The phone was picked up at once. When Lindsey announced herself Ursula said in annoyance, 'Where were you?'

'I'm in Lichfield—'

'Lichfield? What on earth are you doing there?'

Enjoying myself, she nearly responded. Instead she said, 'What's been happening?'

'That dreadful young man – he's been trying it on again.'

'He rang you?'

'No, it was a letter – such a ridiculous effort – he can't spell, his writing's like a ten year old. He says—'

'I'm on a mobile, Ursula, better not say anything.'

'Well, you'll see it when you get here. Make it quick, for heaven's sake!'

'I'll be there as soon as I can.'

Only sixteen miles to cover, but because the traffic was heavy it was an hour later that they drove into Birmingham. Keith had offered to take her wherever she wanted to go, but she thought it would be very unwise to let him drive her to the gates of the Guylers' house. She trusted him – well, she thought she trusted him – but to take a newspaperman to the house was asking for trouble, so he dropped her at New Street, where she had no difficulty getting a taxi.

The gates stood wide, and Billy Guyler was waiting to open the door to her. 'Thank goodness,' he cried, and almost clasped her in his arms. 'Shula's in such a state!'

And when she read the letter, Lindsey didn't blame her. Graham Walker issued what he probably thought of as veiled threats.

You beleive its over but youll see, there's lots more I can tell the papers especialy the big Sundays who like a jucy bit. Think it over, do you want to divvy up and get some peice or do you enjoy be hated and pointed at by everrybody. Same terms as befor for a quite life.
Yrs
Graham Walker

128

'What a fool,' Lindsey muttered.

'A fool? He's a crook, that's what he is!'

'Yes, that too. But he's signed the letter. We could have him charged with extortion.'

'Good God, girl!' exclaimed Ursula. 'The last thing we want is a court case!'

'Of course. I know that. But we can scare him off by threatening him with the charge—'

'You can do that?' Billy asked in a tone in which desperation was giving way to hope.

'Certainly.'

'Then why did that young man recommend we make a counter offer?'

'I beg your pardon?'

'That young man who took my call when I rang. I couldn't get you at your home address, and of course I didn't know if you had another mobile or what number it would be,' Ursula explained in a rapid, fluttery voice. 'When I rang the office this man answered.'

'Yes, the duty solicitor.'

'I blurted out what was in the letter, more or less,' she hurried on, 'and he said he'd get in touch with you and you'd sort it out but it wouldn't be difficult – just offer them a lot less to shut them up.'

He didn't, Lindsey thought to herself. He couldn't have. Nobody in their right mind would give advice like that.

She herself had thought at one time that a small outlay to help Edie with her life might solve the problem. But that was before Graham Walker showed his colours. Now it would be wrong to give in at any point. Edie had had a cheque for expenses and loss of earning, and that was all that was going to be paid.

'I'll see to it,' she said. 'May I take the letter?'

Ursula nodded agreement. Lindsey put it back in its envelope, put it in her shoulder bag, retrieved her mobile from Ursula, and used it to call a car-hire firm. When the car came to the door, she signed the forms and took possession. She dropped the driver back at his office then set off for Hobston. It was about five o'clock on a drizzly November evening and not at all how she'd envisaged the end of her Saturday.

She sighed to herself. Was she actually missing Keith?

The drive to the little market town was uneventful. She asked the way to Bergiss Road, where Graham lived, and found the address without trouble. The building was a block of council flats. There was no reply when she rang the bell at number twenty-two. A neighbour with her hair in heated rollers put her head out. 'Looking for Graham? He's prob'ly down the pub – it's quiz night, he fancies hisself.'

'Thank you,' Lindsey said. 'Which pub is it?'

'King's Head, o' course.'

'Thanks a lot.'

She'd passed the King's Head on her way to the flat, a pub with strings of coloured lights across its front and a big placard in orange. She drove back the way she'd come, and within minutes could read the orange placard: Quiz Contest, King's Head Royals v. Red Bull Bullets. She parked and walked back to the entrance.

There was the thump of music from a hi-fi, but it wasn't overpowering. She went in, to find the clientele settled at tables and on benches with all their attention centred on a young man in a red blazer who was holding a mike.

'Come on, Red Bulls,' he was urging. 'Give it to you again, shall I? In American football, what's the pitch called? Do you want a clue? Two points deducted if you take a clue. No? Give up? Right, home team, the Royals – your turn. What's the pitch called in American football?'

'The diamond!' shouted a voice.

'Wrong! Sorry, Royals, you lose an extra point for not answering through your captain—'

'Nay, we're not having that!' Hubbub broke out. Glasses and tankards were thumped on tables.

Lindsey threaded her way between the quiz fans, to reach the man who had called out the wrong answer. 'Hello, Graham,' she said.

He turned from his argument with a neighbour, gaped at her in astonishment. 'What . . . ?'

'Can we have a word?'

With a great effort he gathered himself together. 'Brought the money, have you?' he enquired.

130

'Let's go outside.'

He shook his cropped black head. 'It's wet out there – and I'm busy here.'

'Busy giving wrong answers,' she observed. 'Come on, out where we can talk in private.'

He grimaced and took a gulp of his lager, but followed her out to the porch of the pub.

'Gave the old girl a start, didn't I?' he remarked with a grin of confident expectation. 'So what's your offer?'

'Three years in jail from a circuit judge.'

'Wha-at?'

'Demanding money with menaces is a crime, Graham.'

'You what?' A mixture of alarm and disbelief dawned in his slate-grey eyes.

'Didn't you know that? Your education's been sadly neglected, it seems, not only with regard to American football.'

'Aw, come on, you can't come that with me! Who's gonna believe—'

'Hard evidence,' she cut in, flourishing the envelope which she'd taken from her shoulder bag. 'Signed, sealed and delivered.' Without taking out the letter, she quoted from memory, '"Do you want to divvy up and have some peace or do you enjoy being hated and pointed at? Same terms as before." That shows a continued intention to extort money. You might get five years, not three.'

'That don't say nothin' about threats,' he protested. 'That just asks if she enjoys—'

'Barristers are a lot cleverer than you, Graham. When you're in court, do you really think you can stand up to one if he reads that out?'

'Here, there's no need to talk about court!' Now he was really scared. He swallowed hard and tried for a man-of-the-world tone. 'We can settle this easy enough, all Edie and me want is our rights.'

'*You* have no rights. You're meddling in something that's none of your business and trying to make money out of it.'

'Of course we want to make money! Dammit, the old girl's got pots and pots and Edie deserves a share.'

'No, she doesn't. I already explained all this to Edie. She has

131

absolutely no legal claim of any kind, and you, you idiot, are committing a criminal offence.'

'Don't you call me an idiot! I know my way around.'

She laughed. 'If you could hear yourself! You don't even know enough to score a point in a pub quiz!' He coloured up at that, and for a moment she thought she'd gone too far, that he was going to hit her. She said quickly, 'Listen, Graham, I'll make it easy on you, here's some good advice. Forget about making money out of Ursula Guyler. She's built up a business from nothing, and runs it personally. She can hire solicitors and barristers and see you in prison if she wants to, and she's *never* going to give you a penny, no matter how hard you try to exact it from her. Do you understand what I'm saying?'

She'd talked him back into uncertainty. The hand he had raised to slap her fell to his side. He shifted uneasily on his thick black boots. 'You're saying I'm boxing outside my class?' he muttered.

'Exactly. Some other woman, you might have had a chance with, but not Ursula Guyler. I'm speaking for her now – and I tell you, back off, back off *now* while you're still free and enjoying life!'

There was just enough play-acting in this to impress him. 'Cor . . . !' He pouted, looking much younger than his twenty-some years. A whining tone came into his voice. 'All we want is a few quid.'

'You were asking for thousands.'

'But we could negotiate.'

'No we couldn't. Mrs Guyler will go to the police and you'll have them on your doorstep within a week.'

'She wouldn't do that to her own daughter.'

'She'd be doing it to *you*, you fool. You're the one that signed the letter. But –' she held up a warning hand – 'don't think you can start again with Edie signing the letters.'

'What letters?' said a voice. And Edie herself appeared through the swing doors of the pub, in black to match her boyfriend and looking puzzled as she recognised Lindsey.

Graham jumped about a foot in the air. 'Edie! I thought you and Bess—'

'Yeah, well, Bess has gone off with her feller. What's going on?'

'Nothing, nothing.'

'He didn't tell you he'd written to Shula?' Lindsey enquired, understanding at once that Graham had acted on his own.

'He what?' She took him by his elbow and pulled him to face her. 'You wrote a letter?'

'We-ell, everything was grinding to a halt.'

'You did it without telling me?'

'Well, you always get in such a tizz when I—'

'You rat!' she cried. 'You rotten snake! Who gave you the right to butt in like that?' She turned on Lindsey. 'What did he say? In the letter?'

Lindsey knew better than to get caught in the middle of this oncoming row. 'I leave it to him to tell you,' she said. And to Graham, by way of farewell, 'Remember the long arm of the law!'

She left them there, their faces tight with resentment and their voices already harsh with conflict. She thought, I've set the cat among the pigeons. But they weren't pigeons – more like two black crows quarrelling over some discarded scrap of meat.

She was pleased with herself at first. But a few miles down the road on her way home, she began to think. Edie Maybury had first contacted Ursula Guyler in hopes of finding a family. Now, it seemed, she might be losing even her stupid boyfriend.

It seemed nothing to triumph over, now that Lindsey came to think it over.

Eleven

An hour later Lindsey pulled up at a service station, suddenly aware that it was some nine hours since she'd eaten. She was hungry and thirsty, she was tired.

A sandwich and a mug of strong coffee revived her. She saw pay-phones, and decided to ring the Guylers before it got too late.

Billy answered at almost the first ring. 'Lindsey?' he asked.

'Yes, it's me. Sorry it's late.'

'Never mind, what happened?'

'I don't think you'll have any more trouble. I spoke to Walker.'

'Thank God! Shula's been *so* upset – I persuaded her to take a sleeping pill so she's gone to bed. So in the morning I can tell her . . . ?'

'I don't think you'll hear any more from that quarter.'

'Great, great, perhaps we can have some peace now. I can't *tell* you what it's been like for us! Well, we've learned our lesson.' His voice was full of fatigue, perhaps from further back than the advent of Edie Maybury. 'Shula's given up any hope of ever finding Julie. It's time, you know . . . Seventeen years she's gone on . . . I should have put my foot down years ago.'

The idea of Billy Guyler putting his foot down would have been amusing in other circumstances, but a pay-phone on a motorway wasn't the place.

Lindsey said, 'Well, I think it's over as far as Edie and her boyfriend are concerned. If anything else arises don't hesitate to get in touch.'

'Thank you, but I hope there won't be the need. Not that you haven't been great,' he added hastily.

'I understand. Goodnight, Mr Guyler.'

'Goodnight, Lindsey.'

When she got home there were messages on her answering machine: Andrew asking if she'd settled the Guyler problem, then again asking what was happening; then Keith saying he hoped everything had turned out all right whatever it was and he hoped to see her again soon; and lastly Andrew saying in a vexed tone, 'What's going on? I expected to hear from you by now. I've logged it in the day book as an on-going case at this present time, eleven forty-four p.m.'

She wiped the tape, switched off the phone, and fell into bed.

She slept late next morning, Sunday. When she prised her eyes open far enough to look out of the window, it was raining. She groaned inwardly, then decided to have a day of self-indulgence indoors. She had a big pot of green tea and lots of toast, a long luxurious bath with some of her tea-rose bath oil, a manicure and some experimental hair styles, a trying-on session with her clothes leading to the decision that she ought to buy a new winter skirt, and finally lunch with the Sunday papers spread around her.

From these she was roused by a call on the entry-phone 'So you *are* there! Why aren't you answering your phone?'

It was Andrew, both annoyed and alarmed.

'Oh, sorry, I switched it off last night – I was dead beat, didn't want anything to wake me. Come on up.'

She had the flat door open when he appeared. He kissed her rather unlovingly on the cheek and marched in. 'Did you play back my calls?'

'Yes, but it was so late—'

'Good Lord! I waited up till well past midnight expecting you to report back! How do you think it's going to look in the day book? You respond to a call from a client and then everything goes dead for almost twenty-four hours.'

'Oh, Andrew, don't be such a martinet! I'll do a full report for Ollerenshaw on Monday.'

'You'd better do it before that! Naturally I got in touch with him when you didn't report back.'

'You didn't!'

'I certainly did! Mrs Guyler is one of our most important clients—'

'How could you! That was like making a crisis into a catastrophe. I was *dealing* with it, Andrew. It's all settled.'

'Settled?'

'Yes, I went up to Hobston and found the boyfriend.'

'That's where you were all evening?'

'Yes, of course.'

'But you didn't answer your mobile!'

'I had it switched off. I didn't want the Guylers ringing and asking what was going on, it's too insecure on a mobile.' All of a sudden, she was exasperated. 'Andrew, why am I having to explain my actions to you? I tell you, I handled the situation, it's all okay and I'll report to Mr Ollerenshaw tomorrow.'

'You'd better ring him today. He's quite worried about it.'

'Why on earth did you alert him about it? There was no need!'

'Well, I didn't know that, did I?' he grumbled, beginning to look a bit unsettled. 'I'm "duty" until office hours tomorrow, I hate it when things happen on my shift.'

'Sounds to me as if you got in a flap,' she said, trying to recover her good humour and end the discussion.

'Well, no . . . I wouldn't say that . . .' He looked put out. 'But Ursula Guyler is such a big noise and we didn't handle things well – I mean, her name in all the papers, it's not what she expects, Lin.'

'No, I admit that.' She couldn't deny a pang of guilt on that score. 'The boyfriend Graham was responsible for that, I'm almost sure. But I've dealt with him.'

'How much did he settle for? I bet it was only a couple of hundred in the end.'

She frowned at him and shook her head. 'You should never have suggested to the Guylers that money came into it again. Mrs Guyler was always dead against paying out anything by way of blackmail.'

136

'Yes, but these two were such nitwits – a couple of hundred and they'd have—'

'No money was involved. I talked him out of it.'

'Talked him out of it? What on earth does that mean?'

'Never mind. It'll all be in the report and then you can hear any details at the weekly conference.'

'But, good heavens, a chap like that isn't going to be put off with *words*. You should have—'

'Andrew, I had a very tiring day yesterday and to tell the truth I've had it up to here with the Guylers, the Mayburys, and everybody else in between. Would you please drop it?'

'What?' he exclaimed, startled by a tone he'd never heard from her before.

'Would you like some coffee? I just made it.'

'But Lindsey, I have to make an entry in the day book.'

'Put in what you like. I'm going to sit down and have my coffee and some cheese and crackers. Would you like some?'

'Well . . . But surely you want to talk about it.'

'Andrew! Cease, desist, withdraw, fall silent, become mute. If you speak again, talk about the weather, the score at yesterday's football match, or the value of the euro. But if I hear another word about the Guylers, I'll have to throw you out!'

He stared at her in amazement. Despite the joking tone, he could see she was totally in earnest. It was the first time he'd ever been aware that there was steel under the silken exterior.

He pulled himself together, and managed a smile. 'In that case,' he said, 'I'll have a cup of coffee.'

There was an awkward silence between them as she cleared the newsprint from chairs and sofa. Andrew sat down, and Lindsey went into the kitchen for the coffee. When she handed him the mug he saw it was just as he liked it, lots of cream and doubtless well sugared.

'So . . . well . . . Did you say you were in Lichfield yesterday?'

'Yes, looking at Samuel Johnson's portrait when you rang.'

'I didn't know you were interested in Samuel Johnson.'

'I'm not, particularly. But that happens to be his birthplace.'

'I meant, why did you go there?'

'To visit a charity market.' She found she wasn't saying

137

anything about Keith Holland. She told herself she had good reasons. Keith Holland was a newspaperman and the mere mention of his occupation would send Andrew into fits. The press had not been well thought of by her colleagues at Higgett, Ollerenshaw and Cline during the publicity over Edie Maybury. Nor, in fact, did any of them think well of reporters in general. Too inquisitive, too careless with facts.

She said, 'What did you do with your Saturday, apart from worrying about the Guylers?'

'Oh well . . . you know . . . not much. I went to a jazz club in the evening, but of course they don't like people to have their mobiles switched on during performances. I switched it to the silent ring, but once Ursula Guyler began fussing, I had to leave.'

'Poor you.' But it seemed to him she didn't sound very sympathetic.

Andrew was in a difficult position. He knew she was vexed with him for what she probably thought of as lack of support when Old Ollie gave her a wigging last week. Switching off her phone last night was probably understandable, but now he wanted to know what had happened with the Maybury girl and her boyfriend, because when reporting Mrs Guyler's phone call in the day book, he'd scribbled, 'I recommended a small monetary inducement' and now it seemed Lindsey had solved the problem without spending a sou. However, it appeared that Lindsey was in a bad mood and wouldn't talk about it. So he didn't know how to amend the entry in the day book. Awkward.

Luckily his eye was caught by an article in one of the Sundays, a review of a book by an American solicitor turned novelist. He asked if she'd read the review, which led on to a discussion of American law as compared with British, which led on to a more companionable conversation about a tax case that was coming to trial the following week.

The coffee pot was empty, Lindsey's cheese and crackers were cleared away and she put the lunch things in the dishwasher. Then she rang Mr Ollerenshaw's home, and was grateful to get his answering machine. She left a short, businesslike message: 'All's well with the Guylers, no further problem expected, a full report on your desk in the morning.'

It was about four in the afternoon, the rain had eased off and a mild, rather muggy evening was coming on.

'How about going out for a walk?' Andrew suggested. 'Then we could have an early dinner somewhere nice, and perhaps take in a film. Anything you want to see?'

Rather to his dismay she chose an Italian film at an art cinema. But he fell in with her choice. He wanted her to be pleased with him again. Rather to his surprise she'd done very well yesterday, and it was always a good idea to be friends with people who were doing well.

For her part Lindsey was happy to fall in with his suggestions. She didn't want to be bothered with decisions today. Yesterday had been tiring physically and exhausting emotionally. The apprehension she'd felt on her drive north-west, the need to appear confident – even aggressive – with Graham Walker, the feeling of having hurt Edie Maybury yet again as she drove home . . . In a way, Andrew was a comfort. So she went walking with him along the canals, accepted his decision over where to eat, laughed and mourned over *Il Postino*, and when afterwards he took it for granted she would spend the night at his flat, she didn't demur.

Kisses and embraces, fervour and languor, the reassurance of well-known joys . . . Perhaps these would wipe away the feeling of having been heartless in dealing with someone very vulnerable.

Next day, Mr Ollerenshaw was pleased with her report on the Guyler affair. Her stock at Higgett, Ollerenshaw and Cline went up a little. If she had been inconsiderate as regards Edie, she told herself, it was justified. After all, what had she done? She had carried out her client's wishes effectively. That was what she was paid for.

She was fast asleep when her bedside phone rang very late on Tuesday night. She rolled over in bed, eyed the clock – twenty-five past one – and reached for the receiver, unwillingly coming awake. Who could it be?

Mrs Guyler again? Oh, please, no, she groaned to herself. 'Hello?'

'Is that Miss Abercrombie?'

'Yes.'

'This is William Cross, of Positif Security. I'm at HOC's offices in Lamb Lane—'

'I beg your pardon? Who did you say you were?'

'Positif Security, miss. I'm just doing my second round.'

'Second round of what?'

'Security patrol.' She could hear him draw an audible breath of annoyance at her lack of response. 'Miss Abercrombie?'

'Yes?'

'This is the security patrol at your firm's offices.'

'Higgett, Ollerenshaw and Cline?'

'Yes, your offices in Lamb Lane. Could you please come—'

She was now awake. 'It's half past one in the morning!' she exclaimed.

'I know that, miss. I'm sorry to wake you, but there's a young woman here who says you can vouch for her.'

'What?'

'A young woman. Sitting on the steps outside the office. I found her here when I came round on my second patrol.'

'Sitting on the steps?'

'Yes, the three steps outside the main door.'

Lindsey was sitting up now, brushing her hair off her forehead and clutching wildly at reality. 'There's a young woman sitting on our steps?'

'Well, sleeping, she was, actually. But she's awake now and she says you can vouch for her. She says her name's . . .'

'Edie Maybury,' she said at the same time as he pronounced it.

'Oh, you know her?'

Alas, yes. 'Did you ask her what she's doing there?' she enquired.

'She says she's waiting for you to arrive for work in the morning.'

'Good Lord.' That was nine thirty tomorrow. Over eight hours away.

'I can't leave her here, miss,' said William Cross in worried tones. 'I mean, it's not on. She's got a backpack and for all I know she's got tools for a break-in in there.'

'No, no,' she said. 'That's not why she's there.'

'Well, if you say so, miss. But what am I going to do? Since she mentioned your name, I looked you up in the staff list folder and I'm ringing you from inside my van. I'm keeping an eye on her – I can't really leave her here, now can I?'

Lindsey's mind was reeling. She said into the phone, 'Wait a minute.' There was a carafe of water on her bedside table. She poured some water on her hand, patted her face with it, and began to feel more normal.

'You say you have a vehicle, a car?'

'A van, miss.'

'Could you take her to sit in it?'

'But I've got to get on, miss, I have to do a time-check at two on the other side of Colmore Row.'

'Whereabouts?'

'Outside Taypes the jewellers.'

'Right. I'll meet your there in half an hour. Just let me ring for a taxi and I'll—'

'Oh, you're coming? Well, look, no problem with transport, we have a van that patrols your area – you're in Passally Mansions, right?'

'Yes – Flat 1a.'

'Okay, I'll contact Trimmett, he'll pick you up in – say, ten minutes?'

'Right.'

'A blue and white van, says Positif on it.'

'I'll be outside on the porch.'

She threw on the clothes she'd taken off last night, grabbed her handbag and hurried out and downstairs. As she quietly closed the outside door of the old building behind her, the van drew up.

'Miss Abercrombie?'

'Yes.' She got in beside the driver, an elderly man with bushy eyebrows under an official-looking peaked cap. He spoke into a two-way radio as he drove off.

'Passenger aboard, eta two-oh-five.' He flipped the off switch. 'Warm enough? I can turn up the heater.'

'I'm fine, thanks.'

They sped along silent roads with only a shadowy cat to glance up at them. As they neared the city a few cars passed them but the journey was much faster at this hour of the night than any commuter could ever hope for.

At Colmore Row her driver reduced his speed, spoke into the radio again. 'Positif Four, this is Positif Ten. We're at the corner of Temple.'

'Received, Positif Ten. I'm at corner of Newhall and Great Charles. Quickest for your passenger is to proceed on foot.'

'Received.' He turned to Lindsey. 'Your best plan is to go via the pedestrian precinct. Would you like me to accompany you?'

'No, no, I'm sure it'll be all right. Thanks for the lift.'

'No problem, miss. Mind how you go.'

As she hurried away she could hear him muttering once more into the mike, relating her progress.

The van was in an alley behind the shops. Edie Maybury was sitting beside the driver with a backpack on her lap. She and William Cross got out simultaneously, the security man watching her all the while.

'Edie!' cried Lindsey. 'What's this all about?'

Edie stalked up to her, holding out the back-pack like a weapon, a battering-ram. 'Look what you've done!' she said angrily. 'You were s'posed to sort things out and now I've lost everything!'

'Edie, calm down—'

'Calm down! Calm down! It's all right for you, you selfish cow! You ever been thrown out with not a soul to turn to?'

'Thrown out?'

'He threw me out,' Edie wailed. Tears gushed down her pale cheeks. 'He . . . he . . . called me a stupid bitch and shoved me out the door!'

Twelve

Edie stood on the pavement outside the office, hugging her rucksack and crying like a waterfall. William Cross of Positif Security took Lindsey by the elbow so as to turn her away for a private word.

'You her probation officer or something?'

'Good heavens, no!'

'A relative?' But he was shaking his head as he said it. To his mind there could be no relationship between this stray cat all in black and the nice-looking girl he'd summoned to the scene. 'Are you gonna do something about her?' he asked. 'I can't leave her on site – more'n my job's worth.'

'Well . . . no . . . of course she can't stay here.'

'You gonna take her some place? There's a shelter for the homeless—'

'No, no!'

'Well, what?' He was glancing impatiently at his watch. Clearly he had another checkpoint to reach and his time was running out.

'I'll see to it,' said Lindsey. 'Er . . . could you call a taxi for me? I came out without my mobile.'

'Sure, no problem.' He spoke into his radio, relayed her request, waited a moment or two then nodded. 'Five minutes.' He hesitated. 'Want me to hang around till he comes?'

'No, that's fine. Thanks a lot. You've been great.'

'Don't want me to put this in a report, do ya?'

'No, if that's okay. Nothing criminal, you know. She's just upset.'

'Okeydokey. Simpler for me. So long then.' He got into his van, gave a wave of farewell, and drove out of the alley.

Lindsey was left with the weeping girl. She surveyed her

with a mixture of remorse and resentment. Why on earth was she being dragged into her affairs again? She wanted to shake her, tell her – like Professor Higgins – to cease this unseemly boo-hooing.

'Edie. Edie! *Edie!* Please stop crying!'

'I can't! I just . . . I don't . . .' And she went on wailing, the backpack held up to her chin for dear life as if it were the only connection between her and stability.

The taxi nosed up. The driver stared out at them. He got out and opened the door for them, looking unwilling.

'Dry up, Edie, or the driver will refuse to take us.'

Edie mopped at her eyes with the back of one hand. The rucksack slipped. The driver caught it and moved towards his vehicle. 'Come on,' Lindsey said.

Edie made a heroic effort and stifled her sobs. 'Wh-where are we going?' she quavered.

Lindsey heard herself say, 'You can spend the night at my place.' Oh, God, she added internally, what am I doing?

Edie was dumbfounded. She climbed into the cab, fell back on the seat, and wiped her wet cheeks with both hands. Lindsey handed her a tissue from her pocket, crumpled but serviceable, and she wiped her face dry, heard Lindsey give an address to the driver, and began to feel that her misery might abate.

Once again the drive out to the suburbs was swift with only big trucks and trailers on the roads. Lindsey paid off the taxi, unlocked the main door of the block of flats and led the way upstairs. Edie followed with her backpack.

'Leave it there for the moment,' Lindsey said as they entered the vestibule of her flat. 'Are you hungry?'

Edie shook her head. She was in too much of a state to feel hunger. But when she was sitting in Lindsey's kitchen with slices of brown bread and a big mug of instant soup, she found herself making instant inroads.

'Now,' Lindsey said, sitting down opposite. 'Tell me.'

'We had a row.'

'Yes.'

'It went on for days – from the minute you left us outside the pub, until tonight – I mean last night. About half nine – he suddenly shouted at me to get out, and I said I would, never

144

thinking he really meant it. Know what I mean? So I slung my things into my bag and I thought he'd come to his senses when he saw I'd packed, but he just grabbed me and shoved me out on the landing and threw my pack after me.' Tears threatened again. She choked on a piece of bread, coughed, and there was a long pause while she recovered.

'What was the row about?' Lindsey enquired.

'Well . . . you.'

'Me?'

'You and what you said. When you spoke to him outside the King's Head. He said you'd threatened him with the police and it was all my fault, and *I* said he'd no right to send threatening letters without ever telling me what he was up to, and he said I was as thick as a brick for not using my chances proper, and I said I never wanted to screw money out of them, that wasn't the point. Know what I mean? And he said I didn't have the brains to see the point, which was that the Guylers were loaded and would cough up if we went about it the right way, and I said again that I didn't want money, and he made as if to hit me, and I told him if he touched me I'd walk straight out and he said, "Go on then, you dimwit, what a millstone *you* turned out to be", and that was when I started packing, but he didn't try to stop me and I think he's a rat and I don't know what I ever saw in him!'

More tears. Lindsey provided kitchen towels. Edie mopped herself and blew her nose. 'Oh, crikey, what a fool,' she muttered.

'It certainly wasn't a very sensible thing, parking yourself outside the office.'

'Where else was I to go?'

'But Edie, you must have known there'd be no one there at that time of night!'

'Well, I wasn't thinking straight, was I?'

'How did you get there?'

'Hitched.'

'Hitched! Edie, that's dangerous!'

'Well, I haven't got much money, have I? They gave me the push from the supermarket. Poor attendance, they said, but the real reason is that I was bad news. Know what I mean?

145

Customers stared at me because I was the girl who said she was Ursula Guyler's daughter. Caused a jam at the checkout.'

'But they must have paid you severance pay?'

'Oh, sure, but I left *that* on the mantelpiece in Graham's flat, didn't I?'

'Oh, Edie . . . !'

'Yeah,' she said, sighing in agreement. 'Not too bright, am I?' She yawned enormously. 'Oh gawd, I'm tired! Am I really going to kip here?'

'Yes, just for tonight. I'll show you the spare room.' Lindsey led the way, switching on the light and was surprised at the reaction.

'Wow, this is great!' cried Edie. She thought it was the prettiest room she'd ever seen, with its white iron bedstead and hand-quilted cover. 'And your kitchen – all that plain wood and tiles – you've got a really nice place!'

'The bathroom's just across the hall. I'll put out some towels for you.' Lindsey didn't say that she had put out towels some days ago, intending to ask Andrew to come and stay. But somehow that had all got pushed into the category of 'unlikely', which was probably just as well because what would she have done with this homeless waif otherwise?

'Yeah,' said Edie yawning again. Half asleep, she fetched her backpack from the hall and began to unbuckle it with fingers that didn't seem to belong to her.

'What you need is a good night's sleep. We'll talk in the morning.'

''Kay.' She was sitting on the bed, ferreting about in the bag for night things, things she'd need if she were to get to bed. A toothbrush, was that what she was trying to find? She didn't really know.

'Goodnight, then,' Lindsey said.

'Night.'

Lindsey closed the door on her, went to her own room and undressed again. She got into bed, exhausted, expecting to drop off at once. But it was a long time before she slept, torn by feelings of guilt, annoyance, sympathy, regret, anxiety . . . Anxiety, because she didn't know what would come next.

*   *   *

When her alarm woke her she rose, heavy-eyed and still weighed down by the burdens of the night. She looked in on Edie, who, it seemed, had fallen asleep at the very moment Lindsey had left her – seated on the bed, delving into her backpack. She was bowed over the pack, her arms still loosely around it.

Sighing, Lindsey eased her back on to the pillows, raised her legs, took off the half-boots with their clumpy soles, removed the backpack, covered her with a blanket, and left her.

She had no appetite for breakfast. She drank orange juice and then coffee, lots of it and as black as pitch to get her lacklustre brain to work. When it was time to leave, another glance at Edie showed her still fast asleep. She went back to the kitchen, took down the shopping reminder board and wrote a list of where things were to be found – tea and coffee on the shelf above the stove, milk and juice in the fridge, cereals in the cupboard above the workbench, and so on. She ended with, 'I'll ring.'

There was a full morning of appointments awaiting her, but she found time between them to ring home. No answer at eleven, at eleven thirty, at noon. At twelve thirty she had a lunch engagement with a client, at two p.m. she was due at the bank of one of her clients where there was trouble over the terms of a loan.

When she got back to Higgett, Ollerenshaw and Cline at three, telephone messages needed replies but not one was from Edie. By now Lindsey was anxious. Was the girl still asleep? It had been nearly three a.m. when she left her in the spare room, it was now twelve hours later. It was possible to sleep twelve hours, particularly if you'd been going through the mental turmoil that Edie had known. All the same . . .

She snatched a moment to ring again, but no response. She went back to business, and then awoke to the fact that today was conference day, when reports and/or problems were discussed by as many of the staff as could attend. Lindsey must be there because Old Oliver would be talking about her report on the Guyler affair.

He was rather kind to her. 'A satisfactory outcome of the latest intervention from the young man, I gather. Lindsey? Would you comment?'

'He isn't as clever as he thinks he is, and he's not brave,' she said. 'I'm sure I frightened him off permanently—'

'The more so as, from your account, it seems he and the Maybury girl were having a quarrel when you left?'

'Quite right. I gathered that in writing to Mrs Guyler he had acted without telling her and she was very angry.' She took a breath, intending to report what had followed. 'The next event—'

'Was a very complimentary telephone call from Mrs Guyler to me,' said Ollerenshaw with a satisfied smile. 'I had been quite apprehensive about her view of the matter, and we all realise, I hope, that withdrawal of her legal business would have been a serious blow to the firm. However, nothing of the sort was mentioned. She said she was sure that Graham Walker – whom she calls "that obnoxious young man" – was the bad influence and that our young colleague here had silenced him. A good result, as I believe our sporting friends might say. Now,' said Old Oliver, putting his fingertips together and adopting a judicious air, 'the next item on the agenda is the question of prompt entries in the computer files. There is no objection to paying quite substantial expenses, but they must be validated by immediate logging on the computer . . .'

Lindsey's moment was past. She had not mentioned the arrival of Edie Maybury on their doorstep last night. Should she interrupt? Insist on speaking again? And say what? All she could report were the bare facts: Edie had left her boyfriend and was now at home in Lindsey's flat.

But what followed from that? She was pretty sure Mr Ollerenshaw would be aghast. He would order her to throw Edie out immediately. But Edie had had too many rejections in her life already and who knew what would follow if she was left to sink or swim in the shifting currents of Birmingham?

If anything bad happened to her, it would be on Lindsey's conscience for ever.

And besides, why shouldn't she offer Edie a bed for the night? She was sure in her own mind that Edie had no mercenary intentions towards the Guylers. Graham was the one who had criminal thoughts, and Graham was no longer part

148

of Edie's life. So there was no conflict of interest in befriending Edie in her hour of need.

All the same, Lindsey realised that to let anyone know Edie was at that moment probably pottering round her flat, making herself something to eat, taking a long hot bath, getting herself together after the dramas of the last few days, would cause uproar. No matter how neutral it might seem in the formally legal sense, to her colleagues it would have the scent of irresponsibility.

Irresponsibility . . . one of the most dreaded crimes in the legal world. As in chess, every move had to be planned very well ahead so as not to fall into any traps. Lindsey knew that the moment she mentioned Edie in a sympathetic tone, there would be an outcry. 'You've been irresponsible! You acted impulsively! How dare you side with the enemy!'

She came out of this reverie to find that the weekly conference was winding up. One of the senior partners gave her a commendatory nod as he went out, two of the junior partners lingered to make complimentary remarks. Andrew was waiting to accompany her out of the room, and say as they went to fetch their coats, 'Came out of that well! How about a celebration dinner somewhere?'

'Ah . . . no . . . thanks all the same, Andrew, but . . . er . . . I've got a bit of a domestic crisis to deal with.'

'Oh, anything I can help with? TV set gone bust? Need a plumber? I've got a couple of phone numbers for repairs if you—'

'No, thanks. It's just . . . oh, nothing much . . . but I'd like to get off home, if you don't mind.'

'Tomorrow then?'

'We'll talk about it in the morning, shall we? I must dash.'

She caught her train then rang home on her mobile. Still no reply. Now she was worried. Was Edie ill? All that emotional upset last night – had it been the onset of something serious, a psychological crash? She thought of the contents of her bathroom cabinet but there were no serious medicines there, nothing of use to a girl weary of life.

She went into her flat calling, 'Edie? You there?'

No reply.

She's gone, she thought. And then, Oh, good! But then she was ashamed. To feel relief at having got rid of her – that was uncharitable in the extreme.

She knocked then put her head round the door of the spare room. The rucksack was still there, perched on a chair. A few garments had been taken out and were now over the chair back. Cosmetics were laid out on the dressing table.

Lindsey's heart sank. Gone, but not far. She was out, but clearly intended to return.

Her instinct was to back out of the room, close the door, and try to pretend she hadn't invited this unwanted guest. But that was foolish. Facts were facts. The problem of Edie was yet to be faced.

Lindsey was in the kitchen making preparations for an evening meal for two when the entry-phone rang. She knew who it was before she asked.

'It's me – let me in.'

'Push the door when you hear the buzzer.'

Lindsey went to open the flat door. Edie appeared coming quickly up the stairs, alive with energy and smiling broadly. Anything less like a creature heading for clinical depression would have been hard to find.

Edie had wakened about midday in the pretty room, at first unable to think where on earth she could be. Then she'd remembered. She'd broken up with Graham, been befriended by Lindsey, and now here she was. Ratty old Hobston was behind her, the big city was ahead of her, she had someone decent to turn to if things went wrong and if – as might happen – Lindsey was a bit unwilling, well . . . There were things she might say to persuade her to play along.

'Hello, glad you're back!' she sang out as she came in. 'Thought I might have to park on the doorstep here as well! What time d'you get off work, then?'

'It varies,' Lindsey said. 'I tried to ring you half a dozen times today – were you asleep or did you go out early?'

'Oh, dashed out soon's I could get my eyes open. No time to waste, y'know! So the good news is, I got a job!'

'What?'

'Yeah, went to the Job Shop, saw this notice about a sales assistant in a boutique, went straight there, got taken on. Start tomorrow nine o'clock.'

'A boutique?' Lindsey echoed, trying not to sound surprised. What kind of boutique would hire this startling amalgam of black denim, black hair dye, chalk-white make-up and steel ear loops?

'Yeah, a leather boutique – knew it was me the minute I saw it. Know what I mean? It'll be great, everybody there's young, not like the supermarket where most of them are about forty and love the Bee Gees.' She was taking off her jacket as she spoke, glancing at the pot on the stove and sniffing in approval. 'Smells great, what is it?'

'Carbonara sauce for the *conchiglie*.'

'You what?' Some foreign rubbish, presumably.

'Pasta with sauce. I thought we'd have that with a salad.'

'Aw, if I'd known you had nothing for a proper meal, I'd have brought in some hamburgers.'

'Don't you like Italian food?'

'Italian? Spaghetti bolognese – sold that in the supermarket, slithery stuff. Of course, there's pizza.' A bit sticky when you held a slice in your hand, but okay. 'Yeah, I like pizza.'

'This is a different thing, it's lots of little shells made of a sort of pastry and the sauce goes over them, made of cream, eggs and bacon.'

'If you had all that why couldn't we just have bacon and eggs?' she asked in bewilderment.

Lindsey turned to the stove. 'If you don't like it you don't have to eat it,' she said over her shoulder. 'Plenty of bread and cheese in the larder.'

There was a chill in the tone. She'd obviously said something to annoy Lindsey. 'Oh, gee, you don't have to get narky.'

'Yes I do.' Lindsey turned back, annoyance taking over. 'You're my guest, so I want to be hospitable. But that doesn't mean I have to put up with bad manners. You can eat what I'm having, or not, just as you please. And you can lay the table while you think how to apologise for your bad manners.'

'Whoops!' cried Edie, giggling. 'Was it something I said?' Bad manners? What had she said that was bad manners?

She was in such careless good spirits that Lindsey found it impossible to stay angry with her. They sat down at last at the kitchen table, the great dish of pasta and the salad between them and a pot of coffee waiting to be poured.

'This isn't bad.' Edie allowed when she'd eaten a couple of mouthfuls. 'What's its name again?'

'Pasta carbonara. So now tell me, what do you intend to do?'

'Eat a lot.'

'No, I mean, with your future. What are your plans?'

'I haven't worked it all out yet,' she explained through a mouthful of *conchiglie*. 'But the job's a start, see. Oh, it's great! I always wanted to work somewhere with a bit of life in it, but in Hobston – well . . . Anyhow, that's all behind me now. The shop's just the beginning. Of course the pay's not great but, as Mrs Knott said, I have to learn my way round the merchandise.'

'Where is it? In Birmingham?' Lindsey was encouraged. The girl was eager to take steps to change her life.

'Yeah, at the back of City Plaza.'

'How did you find it? How did you *get* there?'

'Hitched, didn't I? Easy, that's a busy road out there.'

'Edie, you mustn't do that! It's not safe.'

'Oh, go on, think I don't know that? Most of them that pick you up, they're only after one thing. But I know how to handle 'em. Know what I mean?'

Lindsey was shaking her head. 'You'll have to find somewhere to live that's closer to the job.'

Edie paused with a forkful of salad halfway to her lips. She felt a sudden quenching of optimism. 'Find a place? I thought I was gonna live here.'

'What?'

'Well, I am, ain't I?'

'Edie . . .'

Edie laid down her cutlery, leaned across the table and wagged a finger at Lindsey. This was crunch time. 'You owe me,' she said in a voice in which she tried to combine pathos and bitterness. 'It's your fault I haven't a roof over my head.'

'Oh, come *on*!'

'If you hadn't steamed up on Sunday night, doing your clever dick performance, Graham and I'd still be together.'

'And you'd still be tied up to a young criminal – and not a very good one at that,' Lindsey cried. 'Do you really think it would be a good thing to be living with a man who goes behind your back, tries to carry out extortion in your name?'

Time to give a little, Edie thought, to show some willingness. 'Oh, okay, okay, I grant you, Graham was one of my big mistakes.' She sighed and shook her head. 'But you know . . . when there isn't anybody else . . .' Edie glanced at her hostess from under her lashes, assessing the weight of this plea.

Lindsey could think of no reply. After a moment Edie went on, her voice full of regret and reasonableness, 'I s'pose I always knew he was a twister. But at least he meant a roof over my head. And then when I thought I'd be tying up with Mrs Guyler, I hoped I'd leave all that behind me. Know what I mean? But she didn't want me, and at least *he* did – or I thought he did.'

'Oh, Edie.' Lindsey sighed.

'Well, now I'm making a fresh start, and I've got a job, and if you'll just put me up for a bit – until I get a couple of weeks' wages – then I'll look for a room somewhere.' She produced a nicely calculated smile, half rueful, half hopeful. 'I know you and me are two different sorts. But I'll keep my mouth shut and try to be a good little girl as long as you'll let me get started on this new life thing.'

It wasn't a prospect that appealed to Lindsey. Yet what was she to do? It was already after seven, so that the thought of turning Edie out this evening didn't even occur to her. The best time to look for accommodation would be the weekend because in the intervening days Edie would be at the boutique. And after all, the weekend was only a couple of days away – surely she could put up with this troublesome girl through Thursday and Friday?

The words, 'You owe me,' echoed in Lindsey's head. She knew that in logic they weren't true – Edie had no real claim on her. But something within her argued against that view. She'd

153

handled Edie badly from the start, underestimated the delicacy of the situation, imagined that because the girl expressed herself so aggressively that she had no finer feelings.

She'd been wrong. Edie was capable of being hurt, though she might not show it. And to turn her back on her now, when she was about to start a new life and needed all the encouragement she could get . . .

That wasn't within Lindsey's capacity. She shrugged then said, 'A few days, to let you get settled in your job and so forth.'

'Oh, *great*!'

'Just a minute. There are some rules.'

Edie grinned at her. 'Yes, teacher.'

'No hitch-hiking. You'll take the train or the bus into Birmingham.'

She hesitated. 'I ain't got much left in the way of ready cash . . .'

'I'll lend you some money for fares and lunches.'

'Oh, I can take a sandwich.'

'All right. Rule two, you'll be starting out earlier than me in the morning so you get yourself up, you make breakfast and all that *quietly*, and make sure you close the flat door and the outside door properly as you leave.'

'Be quiet, close doors – okay – anything else?'

'Let's see – tomorrow will be late shopping day – what time will you be home?'

'Half eight?'

'Right, supper at nine. Rule three, no noisy programmes on TV, and if you've got a radio you play it quietly.'

'No problem, got a Walkman.'

'Rule four, no undies or tights hanging to dry in the bathroom – you use the washer-dryer.'

'Washer-dryer – check.'

'You make your own bed, you pick up after yourself, you don't make long distance calls on my telephone.'

'Bed making, pick up, don't use the phone. Right.'

'And Rule five, the most important – no boyfriends here, especially Graham.'

'No fear,' Edie said with extreme seriousness. 'He's lost and

154

gone forever, believe me.' She added after a moment, with some admiration, 'You worked all that out pretty fast.'

'Oh, I've had experience. At university I shared a flat two or three times, and, anyway, I was brought up with two brothers – there had to be rules or you got trodden underfoot.'

'You've got brothers?' All at once Edie felt odd. She'd conned her way into staying at this really nice place, taking advantage of its owner because that was the best she could envisage at present. It had almost been as if Lindsey wasn't a real person, only a means to an end. Now all of a sudden she said something that made her genuine, real, part of a family.

Lindsey got up to fetch biscuits to serve as dessert with the coffee. 'They're off on their careers now, same as me. But we keep in touch.'

'You got . . . like . . . your mum and dad?'

'Yes, back home in Ellenham – that's a few miles outside Newcastle-on-Tyne. My father's a solicitor, my mother designs and makes costumes for amateur dramatics and pageants and that sort of thing.'

'And so you grew up with, like, a whole family and then you went away to university and now you're a solicitor like your dad and you live here on your own . . .' Edie couldn't keep the deep-seated envy out of her voice. 'Got a boyfriend?'

'Have a biscuit,' Lindsey said, proffering the packet.

For a moment Edie wanted to go on with her questioning, but the sight of the Bahlsen biscuits distracted her. 'What are *those*? We never sold anything like that in the supermarket!'

'One of my weaknesses. Try the one with the half-chocolate coating.'

Edie did as suggested, nibbled a corner, then said with a sigh of pleasure, 'This isn't going to be half bad, being your lodger.'

If Lindsey felt an inward shudder at the term, she didn't let it show.

The rest of the evening passed quite amicably. Edie spent time in the spare room unpacking and listening to her Walkman. Lindsey tidied up in the kitchen then got some work out of her briefcase. Before she went to bed she put out some cash and a spare key on the kitchen table, tapping on Edie's door to tell her so. She was weary after last night's loss of sleep and a hard day today. She heard Edie pottering about for a while, but soon drifted off to sleep.

In the morning Edie had gone out to her job. She seemed to have skipped breakfast except for a cup of instant coffee, the washed mug was upturned in the drainer.

So far so good, thought Lindsey to herself. But that only lasted until the evening.

When she got home about six, expecting to have the flat to herself for a couple of hours, she found Edie lolling moodily in one of the armchairs, sipping lager from a can.

'You're home early!' Lindsey remarked. 'I thought this was late-shopping night?'

Edie banged the can down on the coffee table so hard that lager spouted out of the opening.

'Gave me the push, didn't they? In the middle of the afternoon.' She was furious. After all her hopes and expectations . . .

'You got the sack?'

'Yeah.'

'Oh, Edie . . .' Lindsey's heart went down into her shoes. 'What happened?'

'Stupid lot! Said they didn't like my attitude.'

Thirteen

The story was short but not sweet. A troublesome customer, who had tried on half a dozen skirts and jackets, decided she liked one outfit, but wanted the skirt lengthened. In Edie's view, leather skirts couldn't be too short. She told the customer it was a stupid idea to try to lengthen this one.

The customer walked out, vowing she would never come back. Mrs Knott, the manageress, told Edie she wouldn't be required any longer, paid her a day's wages, and showed her out with the tag line, 'You'll never get anywhere with an attitude like that.'

'Stupid old cow,' growled Edie.

Lindsey was shaking her head at the account. 'Have you never heard the saying, "The customer is always right"?'

'That's stupid.'

'You're fond of the word, "stupid",' Lindsey countered. 'Does it ever occur to you that the rest of the world is doing all right whereas it's *you* that's making a mess of things?'

'I'm not making a mess of things! Got away from stupid old Hobston, didn't I? Walked straight into a job yesterday.'

'And walked straight out of it today.'

'Well, I'll get another one! No problem! Six weeks to Christmas – shops are crying out for staff. I'll find something tomorrow.'

There was enough truth in this to give Lindsey pause. She might have asked, 'Do you intend to have a series of one-day jobs?' but thought better of it. Edie was in enough misery as it was. It couldn't be any fun to start out in the morning full of bright optimism and come home the same evening with everything in ruins.

The saying, 'She's her own worst enemy', seemed to apply

here. But how could her outlook on life be altered? Since she was taken away from her rightful parents she'd lived with a surrogate mother who'd raised her on principles that no child-care expert could ever have recommended: sometimes given affection, sometimes ignored, learning all the time to strike first in case your enemy landed a lethal blow . . .

And, with no one else to turn to, no kindly aunt, no friendly neighbour, and all the time moving from place to place so that she couldn't make friends among her schoolmates . . .

But why am I having to cope with her? Lindsey felt the question rising within her. And the answer was, because no one else would take it on.

It's not for long, she told herself. In a week or two, she'll get the hang of at least pretending to like her customers, and she'll hold down a job and get a place of her own, and then it'll all be over.

So she told her unwanted guest she was going to do some catch-up work from the office. Then about eight she would make omelettes for supper, and if Edie felt like contributing to the effort she could put a salad together.

'Huh,' grunted Edie.

When at length they were about to sit down to the meal, Lindsey found the salad was nothing but lettuce and tomatoes. Concealing her irritation, she got out other ingredients and washed them under the tap, dried them on kitchen paper, and added them to the bowl.

Edie had already sat down to the table. When she served salad on to her plate, she paused. 'You've put other stuff in,' she observed.

'Yes.'

'I'm wrong again, am I?'

'Oh, for Pete's sake! If you just want to eat lettuce and tomatoes, go ahead. But for me, a salad should have something interesting in it.'

'What's this stuff?'

'Coriander.'

'It's not bad.' Edie munched a little and swallowed. She tried the omelette, which was flavoured with Caerphilly cheese. 'Not bad,' she repeated.

Lindsey nodded in acceptance. She was wondering whether Edie would ever offer to do any of the cooking, and if she did, whether that would be a good thing.

'How come you eat such different stuff?' Edie asked.

'Different? What's different about it?'

'Well, everybody else eats take-aways.'

'No they don't.'

'Yeah they do! At the supermarket, I was always entering up frozen stuff in packets, and right next door there was a hamburger place and it was always full, know what I mean? I mean, I was at the checkout, I saw what folk were buying. Coriander? Nobody ever asked for coriander.'

'If you were to get supper one evening,' Lindsey said, 'what would you put on the table?'

'We-ell – not salad in winter, that's for sure. And if I was gonna do eggs, I'd do egg and chips.'

'Peeling the potatoes? Frying the chips?'

'You're joking! From the chippie, of course.'

Lindsey chose her words carefully. 'Edie, if you don't like the same kind of food, you could eat in a cafe before you leave the city.'

'Oh.' A long pause. Then Edie said in a surprisingly small voice, 'I kind of like this kind of stuff.'

Lindsey could have replied, 'Then stop carping.' But she didn't. It seemed to her she had won a point, begun a change, however slight.

Next day's news was that Edie was working at the till in a One-Pound-Bargain shop. She worked all day Saturday and from eleven till five on Sunday. On Monday she was fired for refusing to help a customer put her purchases in carrier bags. 'I wasn't hired to help a stupid old dodderer stow her things away! She was holding everybody up!'

'Edie, if you ever stayed long enough at one place to establish employee's rights, you could perhaps sue for wrongful dismissal. But until you hold down a job for at least a month, you'll be thrown out the minute you make yourself disagreeable.'

'Disagreeable! I'm not disagreeable!' cried Edie, with every appearance of believing it.

'You think it's full of charm to call an old lady "a stupid old dodderer"?'

'Well, I didn't call her that to her face, did I?'

'But you hassled her.'

'She was holding everybody up!'

'But that's how you behave if you're old and uncertain.'

'Oh, come off it, you don't know what it's like in a shop! Folk wandering about, picking things up, putting 'em down, never knowing their own minds for two minutes together. Then they argue with you about the change, then they want you to help them get out the door. You just don't know what it's like, coping with difficult people.'

Lindsey let a moment pass. Then she suggested, 'Ursula Guyler? Graham Walker? You?'

'Me?'

'You don't think you're difficult?'

'Me?' It was a totally new thought. 'I'm not difficult. I just speak my mind, that's all,' Edie declared. This bossy girl with her easy life – what did she know?

Her next job was in the stock department of a down-market chain store. In a basement area she had to unpack the T-shirts and sweatshirts, slip them on hangers, and put them on designated rails for transport upwards in the goods lift. She lasted three days at that. She was asked to leave after telling the supervisor that the T-shirts were a load of rubbish, that the whole building smelt of mice, and that the window display on the ground floor was a mess. It was the last remark that sealed her fate – the window-dresser was the supervisor's husband.

She landed something else at once, though – a job in a temporary shop selling Christmas decorations.

Because she had been unwilling to leave her on her own in the evenings, Lindsey's activities had been somewhat curtailed over the past two weeks. It was now past mid-November, and the pre-Christmas party season was beginning to gather momentum.

'I got the tickets for the Grove Charity Ball,' said Andrew

as they lunched on a damp, cold Wednesday. The ball was the Monday of the following week.

'Oh, did you? I wish you'd asked me first, Andrew.'

'Why? We went to it last year and you liked it.'

'I . . . well . . . this year it's not so convenient.'

'Why not? You knew it was coming up, surely?'

'I never thought of it.' At his enquiring glance she added, 'I've had a lot on my mind lately.'

'Yes, I've noticed.' He studied her. Now that he came to think of it, she didn't seem as attractively cool as usual. Moreover, on this miserable winter's day, her nose was pink and her dark brown hair had been damped down by the drizzle. 'You've been quite absent-minded from time to time, Lin. What's up?'

'Oh, nothing, really.'

'Come on, sweetie, there's something. Tell Uncle Andy.'

'Well, as a matter of fact . . . I've had a bit of a problem at home.'

'What, you mean up north with your parents?'

'No . . . it's that . . . I have someone staying with me in the flat.'

He was totally taken aback. 'Really? Since when?'

'A couple of weeks.'

'Relative? One of your brothers?'

'No, as a matter of fact . . . it's a girl.'

'A girl? Anyone I know?'

'No . . . yes . . .' The longing to have a confidant overcame her, the need to have advice, assurance, someone to sympathise. 'As a matter of fact . . . it's Edie Maybury.'

'Who?' Two weeks had gone by since the name Maybury had been mentioned and for the moment he didn't catch on. Then he said, in horror, '*Edie Maybury?*'

'Shhh . . .' She glanced about guiltily at the other lunchtime customers. 'Yes.'

'Are you out of your mind?'

'Listen, Andrew, I know it seems odd, but she had nowhere to go and she turned up here—'

'Here? Where?'

'On the steps outside the office. So I had to find her

161

somewhere to stay and the best I could think of in the situation was to take her home.'

'You must be mad!' This, in his clear tenor voice, caused quite a stir of interest among the others in the restaurant.

Lindsey reached a hand across and touched his with a gesture that was half warning, half pleading. 'Andrew, I had to handle it then and there. It was the middle of the night. What could I do – leave her there to be harassed by some man looking for a prossie? Let her be picked up by the police? Think of the publicity – Millionaire's Kid in Clink.'

'Well . . . if you put it that way . . .' Certainly no one would have wanted that. The quiet offices of Higgett, Ollerenshaw and Cline had suffered the equivalent of an earthquake during that series of encounters with the press. 'But when was this?'

'Couple of weeks ago.'

'Get rid of her.'

'I can't do that, Andrew. She's got nowhere to go and she hasn't any money.'

'You mean she's living off you?' he asked, in a very cold tone.

'Not exactly. She gets temporary jobs and she pays a bit when she can.'

'It's unheard of! When Old Ollie hears he'll hit the roof.'

'But he won't hear—'

'You think not? It's conference this afternoon.'

'You're not going to tell, Andrew?'

'I've got to, Lin. This is madness.'

'No, it isn't, because after all we're not in contention over her any more—'

'But if Mrs Guyler found out!'

'She won't. Why should she? No, listen,' Lindsey begged, 'Andrew, it's only temporary, until she finds a permanent job, and then she'll be off on her own.'

'But why should you be . . . ? There are places – organisations – you could get in touch with Shelter.'

'Good God, Andrew, don't you think she's been through enough without sending her to a charity set up?'

'"Been through enough" – what do you mean, "been through

162

enough"? She's a scheming little cat, and she got what she deserved.'

'But she's Ursula Guyler's daughter.'

'No she isn't.'

'She *is*, I tell you.'

'As long as Mrs Guyler refuses to acknowledge her, she isn't. And you shouldn't be meddling.'

'But she *came* to me, Andrew. I couldn't just walk away.'

'I don't see why not. You must have realised it was a ridiculous thing to do, to take her home. And now that you've told me, you've made me a co-conspirator. My advice to you is to show her the door at once. Tonight, when you get home. Hand her her baggage and tell her to get lost.'

'But Andrew—'

'Why is it your responsibility? You're risking everything! Old Ollie would have your scalp if he knew.'

'But you won't tell him, Andrew. You won't, will you?'

He hesitated. She'd been special to him for a couple of years now, they made a good pair, she went along with his ideas and shared his tastes, and one day when it came to settling down she'd make an ideal wife.

'You promise to get rid of her?' he demanded.

'Well . . .'

'Promise! Otherwise I hand on the news to Ollie this afternoon.' They had to keep their voices low, which made it seem as if they were engaged in some sinister plot. Lindsey was somehow trapped in an argument she'd never expected; she'd thought Andrew would . . . well . . . if not approve, at least support her.

She could see he meant what he said. Unless she fell in with his advice, he would tell Ollerenshaw.

'Well . . . All right.'

He blew out a breath of relief. The girl would be sent packing and he'd forget he'd ever been told about it. It was knowledge he preferred not to have. He glanced at his watch.

'And the Grove Charity?'

'Yes, okay,' she agreed.

'Wear that slinky green thing,' he suggested, glad to turn their minds to other things. 'You always look great in that.'

That slinky green thing had been to every grand affair of last winter and Lindsey had been planning to buy a new evening dress. Tomorrow, late shopping night, she had intended to go to a boutique where she liked the clothes. But first there was today's weekly conference to get through.

Her heart was in her mouth once or twice, but Andrew offered nothing but minor technicalities in the discussion period, and it ended as always with requests for more efficiency about billing and accounting. She went home very relieved, but with no real intention of telling Edie to leave.

Oh yes, she'd promised Andrew she'd 'get rid of her' – and she fully intended to do so. But she hadn't said when. As a solicitor Andrew should have listened for the small print, she told herself.

She found she was disappointed in him – almost angry. He'd seemed so heartless, so hide-bound. Did he really think you could deal with a human being as if she were an empty packet or a piece of junk mail?

In this mood she was pleased with Edie's efforts to provide their evening meal. The girl had bought goodies in a high-class delicatessen and set them out with a salad consisting of more than just lettuce and tomatoes. She'd even bought a packet of Bahlsen biscuits for dessert.

While they ate, Lindsey mentioned that tomorrow night she'd be late home because she was going to buy a dress.

'Oh? Where?'

'Have you noticed Petronella, in the arcade?'

'Oh, yes – nice things. That's the kind of shop I'd like to work in.' Edie sighed. It was a pretty place, with gilt-framed cheval mirrors to view yourself in, and – a sure sign of poshness – only one outfit ever in the window display, with no price tag.

Lindsey was about to speak but checked herself.

'What?' asked Edie.

'Never mind.'

'No, what were you going to say? Something about working in Petronella?'

'It's just that your style and theirs don't seem to match.'

164

'How d'you mean?'

Lindsey hesitated. Could Edie really not see that a firm like that would never hire a salesgirl who wore black denim clothes and chalk-white make-up? Petronella was all expensive elegance, touched with romance that reminded you of classic films like *Now Voyager* or *Les Enfants du Paradis*.

Luckily the kettle boiled at that moment so she was able to escape to make the coffee. When she sat down again Edie said, 'Are you going to a lot of things where you wear a dress like that?'

'Quite a few.'

'Christmas parties? I bet there are some posh parties in the city.'

'Oh, I'm never in the city for Christmas. I always go home.'

There was a dull silence.

Christmas. Lindsey always went home for Christmas. But what was Edie going to do, left alone in a flat in a suburb outside town, with practically no money, and no friends or relatives to turn to?

There were hotels where they held Christmas parties for those who would otherwise be on their own. But the mere idea of suggesting Edie go to one was absurd. A fish out of water, that's what she'd be.

No use telling her she could have friends in. She didn't have any friends.

The coffee was ready. She poured it. Edie opened the packet of biscuits with fumbling fingers. She offered it to Lindsey, who selected one and put it in her saucer. Edie herself took a biscuit and sat waiting to hear her fate, to learn what was to happen during the two weeks when the rest of the world went home to their families.

Should she say, 'It's all right, I'll sort something out for myself?' But Lindsey would know it was bravado.

She hated this, this being at a disadvantage. Her upbringing had been so strange that she didn't know how to cope with what everybody else took for granted. 'What're you doing for Christmas?' 'Oh, usual thing, turkey and crackers with the family.'

Christmas with Ma Maybury had taken various forms – the two of them together but getting on each other's nerves, or a week in Munich for the Christmas Fair while her mother romanced with a new boyfriend, or a Christmas on her own at eighteen when Ma Maybury was working in a funfair at Blackpool.

She had never been able to say, as Lindsey just had, 'I always go home.'

At length she said, 'I could prob'ly get taken on as a temp in a hotel over the Christmas period – waitressing or something.'

'You mean, work all the time?'

'Why not? Good money.'

Lindsey tried to envisage it. She herself would be in Northumberland with her parents and her childhood friends, eating her mother's good food, going to the Christmas carol service, unwrapping presents. Edie would be slaving away in a strange hotel surrounded by strangers.

Impossible.

'Edie,' she said.

'Yeah?'

'Edie, I could ask . . . I could ask my parents if I could take you with me.'

'Take me?'

'To Ellenham. You know, outside Newcastle.'

'To stay over Christmas?'

'Most of it. It wouldn't be a big thing, like Christmas in the city, though. It's a small place, it's mostly family gatherings, church events, that sort of thing.'

'Yeah? It's like that in Hobston,' Edie remarked, remembering how she'd seen the Christmas trees alight in other people's window and wished for one in their house.

'Not much fun, then?'

'Well, in Hobston . . . I didn't really know anybody.'

'Except Graham.'

'Oh, him.'

'Would you want to come?'

She tried to think of a way to say, 'Oh, yes, thanks a million.' What came out was, 'Better than being on me tod here in Bromsgrove.'

166

'Well, if you'd like to come, I could ring and ask.'

'Yeah, why don't you?'

'But first . . . Edie . . . There's something I have to say.'

'Go on then.'

'You won't be offended?'

'I dunno, do I? What're you gonna say?'

'It's about . . . about . . . Well, Ellenham is a little place. Quiet, conventional. People are easily shocked.'

'So what?'

'Your appearance . . . the way you dress . . . your make-up . . .'

'What?'

'I don't think they'd take to it.'

Edie was dumbfounded. She knew her appearance was unique to her, and was proud of it. If other people didn't like it, let them look elsewhere.

But . . . it occurred to her . . . where else was there to look in a small place like Ellenham? If they looked elsewhere, would they exclude her from Christmas? And if they did, that made the whole thing pointless. This sudden chain of reasoning made her go cold.

She found that she longed to go to this little town in the north and be included in their family celebrations. For once, just for once, to sample what it was that they all seemed to value so much.

Lindsey took up the conversation again. 'I'm sorry,' she said. 'I shouldn't have said any of that.'

'No, if that's the way it is, it's okay.'

'I thought earlier . . . You know, when we were talking about Petronella . . . you didn't understand when I said your styles wouldn't match.'

Edie pursed her lips. 'Wrong style for them?'

'Totally.'

'But this is me.'

'So you say.'

'Well, of course I do. It's me, the way I am.' Lindsey was shaking her head so she insisted, 'It is.'

'I think it's a defence.'

'You what?'

167

'It's a way of saying, "Take care, I'm the Black Avenger and if you cross me, I'll make you pay!"'

'Don't be daft!'

Lindsey sipped some coffee, bit into her biscuit, then said, very tentatively, 'I've only seen you once without your armour.'

'My *armour*?'

'The black gear. The white face. The raven locks. You hide behind them.'

'I do not!'

'Think not? You don't trust people, so you test them – they've got to reach behind the facade to find the real you. And very few have bothered, so you go on not trusting them.'

'Thank you Miss Trick-Cyclist. So what's your prescription? A few hours on the couch, tell me about your sad childhood and hey presto! I start wearing pink or lilac – and everybody takes a shine to me.'

'There's nothing wrong with wearing black. But the hair and the make-up – Freud would say you were pretending to be dead—'

'*What?*'

'Because you don't like your life.'

Edie could feel the blood rushing up behind the white cream on her face. She felt strange – angry but weepy, confused, flustered, almost as if she were about to burst into sobs. But if she did that she would lose the argument. And she didn't like to lose.

'I'm not pretending,' she said angrily. 'I don't bother to pretend!' Then suddenly, as if it were forced out of her, 'And if you want to know, I do hate my life.'

Lindsey was frightened at what she was doing. She'd embarked on this because she felt her parents would disapprove of the get up. She didn't want to spoil things for them, nor did she want Edie to feel unwelcome. Somehow she had to convey to her a need for change. Now she was sorry she'd made the attempt. But once embarked, she told herself she might as well go the whole journey.

'If you hate your life, why don't you try to change it?'

'I did, didn't I?' Edie said challengingly. 'I contacted Shula –

I thought I was gonna find a family, *my* family, and everything would be super. But that didn't work, did it? And then I thought Graham would help me change things but he was a mega-mistake. Now I'm here, ain't I – trying for a decent job in a new place, but it's no picnic, know what I mean? I keep driving into the buffers.'

'And have you asked yourself why?'

'Oh, you're gonna tell me to improve myself, buy a book about how to make friends and influence people.'

'A book might help,' Lindsey said with a fragile smile. 'But if you want my opinion, the first thing you should do is make it easier for folk to get close to you.'

'I don't want anybody close to me! They only let you down!'

'Yes, that happens. But that happens to everybody, Edie. You're not the only one. We all make misjudgements, it's the human dilemma.'

'Oh, the human dilemma – why don't you talk so us ordinary types can understand you?'

'I'm sorry. If you think I'm talking rubbish, I'll stop.' And she would have been glad to stop. Although family problems were her chief business at the office, this was too personal, too close to the bone. She longed to say to Edie, 'Oh, grow up!' but that would be less than helpful.

Edie shoved the biscuit packet around on the table top, angry with herself that she'd bothered to buy it. A sulky silence ensued. She wanted to do or say something horrendous – but how could you fight with someone who apologised to you?

She said at length, 'Do you trust other people? I mean, all the time?'

'Of course not. I'm a solicitor. It's my business to look hard at everything.'

'But?'

'But on the other hand I don't see the sense in scaring people away. That way you never get to be close to anyone. When *you* go behind your defences you cut yourself off from the rest of the world – even though it doesn't really help you. In fact it's a hindrance.'

'You're telling me I should wear Rosy Dawn make-up and everybody will love me?'

'Well, at least they might want to get to know you.'

Edie picked out a biscuit, stared at it, threw it down, and stalked out of the kitchen, leaving her coffee untouched on the table.

Very sorry for having ever begun the conversation, Lindsey felt even worse now it had ended. But perhaps it was a conversation that had to be gone through at some stage. After she'd cleared away the remains of the meal and drunk the last of the coffee, she telephoned home.

Her mother was surprised to hear she wanted to bring a friend. At first she thought it might be Andrew, of whom she'd heard quite a lot. But no, it was a girl.

'All right, pet, if you want to – plenty of room, of course, Gil won't be coming from Italy so she can have his.'

'I ought to warn you, Mum . . . She's not the easiest of people.'

'Oh, get on with you – there's too much going on at Christmas for anybody to be difficult!'

So that was settled – if Edie decided to accept the invitation.

Just before ten, when Lindsey was thinking of going to bed, Edie came into the living room. She closed the door and stood with her back against it.

'Okay, then, you're on,' she said.

'What?' said Lindsey, looking away from the wildlife programme on TV.

'This Christmas thing.'

'You've decided to come to Ellenham?'

In the dim light it was difficult to distinguish the other girl. She was clad in the T-shirt and bikini briefs she wore for sleeping, but there was something else.

Perhaps it was just because she was getting ready for bed. But she had washed off the ghostly make-up.

Fourteen

K eith Holland rang one evening towards the end of November. 'Just thought I'd keep in contact,' he said. 'How's tricks?'

'Fair to middling.'

'Oh dear, that doesn't sound enjoyable. More trouble with the Guyler thing?'

'You know I can't talk about that, Keith.'

'Okay, so let's talk about your private life. Having lots of pre-Christmas office parties?'

'There are a few. I was at a charity ball last Monday.'

'Ooh! Sounds impressive. Was there a photographer there? Because if so, I want to see the pix of you in your ballgown.'

'Nothing doing. How about you? Busy?'

'Oh, indeed, yes, Cartfield is a hotbed of activity as Christmas draws on. Bazaars, fairs, carol services, and the village pantomime.'

'You don't need to tell me, it's like that in Ellenham, only we've never attempted a pantomime as far as I recall.'

'Ellenham, that's just at the other end of the wall.' He paused. 'Your family's there?'

'Oh yes.'

'You wouldn't by any chance be going home for Christmas?'

'As a matter of fact, I am.'

'Well!' There was vast satisfaction in the exclamation. 'That's only about fifty miles off! How long are you going to be there?'

'Most of the so-called festive season. Why?' But she knew why.

'I was just thinking . . . It would be nice if we could join up at some point.'

171

'That's possible.' She waited to see what would come next.

'Well, invite me, dammit!'

'Mmm.'

'What d'you mean, "mmm" – is that a yes or a no?'

'It's an "mmm". After all, it's my parent's house, there'll probably be about thirty people going in and out over the two weeks. I can't just invite people without checking.'

'Go on, be a devil. Say I can come. I promise to bring my own mince pies. And you can always send me an e-mail saying "Stay away" if your mother doesn't like the sound of me.'

'You are absurd,' she said, laughing.

'No I'm not,' he said in a very serious voice. 'It's a long time since that day in Lichfield.'

'I suppose it is.' Such a lot had happened, she'd hardly had time to think back on it, but it came up fresh in her memory now. Andrew had summoned her back – Andrew, at his most managerial. At the charity ball he'd spent a lot of time mingling – she really hadn't enjoyed it much. The idea of a long comfortable talk with Keith was very pleasant.

'Let's say I'll ask my mother if it would be okay to have you there, perhaps for lunch one day.'

'Great,' he said. 'I'll send you a list of the dates I can be free. Don't forget, as editor of the world's most important news-sheet, I still have to meet deadlines.'

Laughing, she said goodbye.

'Who was that you were talking to?' Edie enquired, looking up from her magazine.

'Oh, just a man.' It struck her then that she must put some conditions on Keith's visit – nothing to do with numbers of guests or the availability of mince pies. He must promise not to meddle in the Guyler affair if – or more likely when – he met Edie.

December came. The leaves of the calendar seemed to fall away like leaves in a high wind and it was the day before Christmas Eve. Higgett, Ollerenshaw and Cline had their Christmas party, Edie left her shop full of decorations and was once more out of a job, and the two women boarded a train for Newcastle.

Edie was wearing her usual black leather skirt and denim jacket, but under the jacket was a pale blue sweatshirt with a polo neck. Instead of bare legs, she wore opaque black tights. Her hair had somehow been freed of its matt black dye over the last month or so and was now a shining light brown – still short and badly cut, but pleasing to see.

Yet it was in her face that the greatest change had come about. Gone was the clown-white cosmetic, gone the ring of black around the eyes, and gone the maroon lipstick. Bare of make-up, her skin was pale, fair but with a hint of creaminess, translucent, healthy.

Day by day, the changes had occurred, sometimes with a little interval between. First Lindsey had noticed that Edie's hair seemed to be losing its flat, dead look. It dawned on her that daily shampooing was washing out some product that had produced the zombie effect. The steel hooped earrings disappeared. Then the eye-pencilling was left off. Then the chalky cream. The last thing to alter was the ruby lipstick.

She had too much sense to make any remark about the changes. She sensed that if she said a word Edie would flare up and there would be a row. But it was almost as if her boarder had a time schedule in which to produce an effect. It was easy to guess that the target date was Christmas.

One worry to Lindsey was about clothes. Edie couldn't afford a whole new wardrobe and once or twice Lindsey had been on the verge of offering the loan of one or two items. But their styles were so different – Edie in one of Lindsey's business suits was a laughable idea, and as to off-duty clothes, she wore mostly jeans and shirts and sweaters, rather yuppie if the truth be told – but then being a solicitor was a yuppie business.

When Edie brought home the blue sweatshirt, it was in a crumpled carrier bag along with some other things. Edie stood in the living room, scowling but nervous. 'I bought these in a charity shop,' she said. 'Tell me if they're all right for your soppy pals in Ellenham.'

With that she emptied the carrier bag's contents on the sofa, to reveal the sweatshirt, a narrow cotton-knit top in solid white, a man's shirt in black and dark green checks, and a very creased wine-red blouse that was clearly pure silk but lacking buttons.

'Five quid I paid for this lot,' she reported. 'I made a bargain with the old girl in the shop – if you think they're no good. she'll take 'em back and let me have another five quid's worth.'

'But they're fine, Edie. Once that blouse is washed and ironed and we sew on some buttons, it'll look lovely.'

Edie stared. 'Really?'

'Yes, and listen – can I lend you a tie to wear with the black and green shirt? I've got just the thing, Black Watch tartan, you might like it.'

She waited with bated breath for the response. She was expecting to be told she was being bossy again. But after a moment Edie said, 'Would that be chic? Or would it be butch?'

'Let's try it and see.'

They spent the rest of the evening trying on clothes, crossing back and forth between Lindsey's room and Edie's. Edie was pleased, though a little surprised, when Lindsey didn't tell her to throw out the T-shirts that had been her main wear all her life.

'Try the grey one under the blouse. No, don't fasten the safety pins, let it hang loose – there – now that's chic.'

They tried it with one of Lindsey's tops, a muted pink. That looked good too. The silk blouse was voted the Best Buy of the Week. A few of Lindsey's belongings managed to creep in among the bundle of things that Edie eventually hung up in the wardrobe in the spare room.

So now it was a different version of Edie Maybury that was on her way to Ellenham. She immersed herself in a magazine so as not to have to make conversation. The fact was, she was dead scared.

In the first place, she was going to meet new people. She'd done that a lot in her life and never found much of a welcome. Then there was the point that her expectations were very high. She knew she was going to be disappointed in her dream of being included in an old-fashioned family Christmas. That sort of thing didn't really happen, she kept telling herself. It was only in TV advertisements that the mother and father and children sat down round a big table and pulled crackers and wore paper hats.

Through these worries there was the thread of her new look. Because she'd spent about seven years hiding behind the Dragons and Dungeons appearance, she was frightened by the nakedness she felt now it was gone. Was this what she was really like, this rather skinny, pale, insecure creature tagging along with a solicitor-type who'd probably have been happier without her?

Lindsey had her worries too. Although Edie certainly looked different – and in her opinion better – she still sounded the same when she talked. Assertive, tactless, not 'cultured' . . . She wondered how her somewhat conventional father would respond to some of Edie's opinions.

When they left the train at Newcastle she greeted John Abercrombie with veiled apprehension. 'And this is Edie,' she said, ushering her forward.

'How d'you do? Had a decent journey? Let me have your luggage – oh, is that all you've brought?' He was loading things into the boot, anxious to get away from the short-stay area used by those picking up and setting down. As they drove out into Westgate Road he brought his daughter up to date on matters domestic. 'Your mum will be glad to see you, she wants you to make that plum sauce for the goose.'

'I came home for a rest, not to be a kitchen slave,' Lindsey protested, from the back seat.

'You jest, surely. Nobody, but nobody, rests while the Abercrombie Christmas Caravan is in motion.' He glanced at Edie. 'You like goose, Edie?'

'Er . . . goose? . . . Never had it.'

'No? Best thing in the world, but a devil of a problem in the roasting – my poor wife's got a special roasting tin for the Christmas goose but of course it's banished from the kitchen the rest of the year so every December I have to go up into the attic and root about for it . . .' And so with his cheery chatter about their home life the drive to Ellenham passed without Edie having to say more than yes or no.

Mrs Abercrombie greeted her daughter with a hearty kiss and a long hug. To Edie she awarded a handshake using both hands. 'Come in, come in, I bet you're dying for a cup of tea. Or something stronger? John will bring in your luggage and take it up, don't bother. Lindsey, Bob's here, just pop your head into the conservatory, he wants to cut a chunk off that parlour palm and I'm *sure* that's not the right thing to do.'

Lindsey did as she was bid, then spent longer than she intended with her brother, arguing whether or not the ancient palm needed pruning or whether it should be moved so that it could grow taller if it wanted to. When she got back to the living room she found Edie on a step-stool pinning up branches of holly at her mother's direction, and being addressed as Edie.

When dinner time approached, she led her guest up to the room she was to occupy. It was at the back of the house, looking over the garden towards a stand of trees. Had it been daylight, Lindsey remarked, they could have seen the landscape around the Roman wall.

But Edie wasn't interested in the Roman wall. It was the room that interested her – entranced her, might have been a better word. It was small, with walls painted ivory white and curtains of dark yellow linen. The bed had an oaken headboard engraved with a cherub to watch over the sleeper, the bedspread was of matching tailored linen. The floorboards were polished oak over which lay a honey-coloured rug, very old but with something about it that told her it was precious, Oriental perhaps. Books were stacked on the shelves, not tatty magazines and comics such as Graham had hoarded but a mixture of textbooks, novels, encyclopaedias, and children's classics.

'Who generally sleeps here?' she asked.

'My brother Gil, but he's been in Italy for a couple of years now.' She opened the door of the old wardrobe to display a few garments in plastic moth-proof protectors. 'If anything of his is in your way, just push it aside. Dinner will be about half an hour.'

She turned to go. Edie seized her by the elbow. 'Lindsey—'

'Yes?'

176

'Do I have to . . . you know . . . dress for dinner?'

In the question Lindsey heard the echo of old black and white films on TV. She didn't laugh. 'No, no. But I thought you'd like to unpack, freshen up a little.' Just before she went out she added, 'We will all be dressing up a bit for Christmas dinner, though. That's when the silk blouse comes into play.'

'Right.'

When Edie unpacked, she hung the blouse on one of the hangers alongside Gil's rugby sweaters. She and Lindsey had found little matching buttons for it and Edie had sewn them on with painstaking neatness. The day after tomorrow she would wear it to a family Christmas party. She took hold of one sleeve and held it against her cheek for a moment. Its texture was soft, gentle, friendly – like the atmosphere of the house.

She knew she must take care to do nothing to disturb that atmosphere. So over the days that followed she was reticent, unexpectedly quiet.

'Can't think why you said your friend Edie was difficult,' said Lindsey's mother. 'I think she's shy, of course, but she's probably not used to a family like ours. An only child, is she?'

'Yes.' That was certainly true.

'Poor little lassie. What does she do?'

'She's . . . er . . . in retail.'

'Really? I only ask because she seems fascinated by my books.'

Alicia Abercrombie had a large collection of books on arts and crafts. Before her marriage she'd intended to go into fashion design, but living in a village in the north of England and with three small children had put those plans on hold. She'd found an outlet for her talent in the making of costumes for the many plays, pageants, charity parades and fancy dress parties that took place. Though Ellenham was a small place, a lively community lived in and around it.

Over the years new fabrics, new techniques, and new equipment had made demands on her. To meet these she'd gone to adult education classes when she could, but her chief resource had been books. She had books on making papier mâché

177

masks, on how to sew man-made fabrics, how to design a Chinese dragon for six dancers, and the concocting of special glues for special needs.

Edie had first picked up one of the books from the shelf in the living room simply to hide behind it. But it was about dressing small children for a nativity play, and the pictures and diagrams began to captivate her. She felt as if her fingers wanted to get to work, especially on the wings for the angels. She imagined herself folding the stiffened gauze, fixing it to the soft wire, and she knew that if she'd ever been asked at school to take part in the drama club, she'd have volunteered to help on the production side. Dressing the stage of the nativity play – she could imagine herself putting up screens, cutting out stars, spraying glitter here and there to make a mood of magic . . .

By the day after Boxing Day, Edie had read every book on the shelf in the living room and had been invited by Alicia into her workroom, a shed at the far end of the garden into which even Lindsey had seldom been invited.

Edie loved the old house, with its conservatory tacked along one side where Lindsey's brother was always busy, giving the plants their yearly re-potting. She loved the bookcases that appeared in every room and along the upstairs corridor. She loved the scent of the bowls of pot-pourri, the smell of baking bread from the Aga, the row of coats hanging in the hall which anyone might borrow if the weather turned sour. She loved the chats with Mrs Abercrombie about the skilful use of a staple gun when it came to making scenery, about turning everyday country clothing into outfits for *Oklahoma* cowboys.

'I think she's got a genuine feel for the applied arts,' Mrs Abercrombie told Lindsey. 'Did you say she was in retail? What does she do, window-dressing?'

'No, she's on the sales side.'

'Mmm . . . Perhaps in fact she hasn't done anything in that line. It all seems new to her. She's sort of astonished at how much you can do . . . If she takes it up as a hobby, she might like it a lot. I let her help me with those terrible cowboy costumes I'm making for *Oklahoma!* She worked out how to make the "chaps" fit over the trousers, she made a special belt, it works beautifully. Fiddly – I couldn't see how to do it.'

'I seem to recall,' Lindsay said, thinking back, 'that her father was a packaging designer.' For that had been Billy Guyler's original career.

'There you are then. It's inherited.'

On the following day, Keith Holland was coming to lunch. Lindsey had warned him that Edie Maybury would be there, at which he'd been justifiably astonished.

'You invited her home for Christmas?'

'Well, she had nowhere else to go.'

'But how could you even know that?' He added at once, 'You've been keeping in touch with her!'

'Yes, I have.'

'Why? Has Mrs Guyler had second thoughts?'

'No, she hasn't, and I want it clear that if you come to Ellenham, you're not to attempt any journalistic ploys.'

'Is that a condition?'

'It is.'

'All right then, no ploys.'

It turned out that he would have little opportunity because Edie was spending most of her time in the workroom solving the problem of frilly petticoats for the farm girls of *Oklahoma!* But they met, of course, over lunch.

Because her mother was busy in her workroom, Lindsey had done the cooking: a rich thick soup from the bones of the goose served with home-baked soda bread, pilau rice with a huge salad, and baked apples for dessert.

'My compliments to the chef,' Keith said when the coffee was served.

'Yes, very nice, dear,' agreed her mother. 'It's nice to get away from left-over plum pudding and mince pies.'

'Oh, Lindsey's good at this kind of thing,' Edie remarked. 'Salads – she's always putting different things in salads.'

The remark passed apparently unnoticed. But when the costume-makers had gone back to the workroom, Lindsey and Keith set out for a walk towards the top of Beacon Hill. He said, 'That was odd, what Edie said about your cooking? Do you invite her to your place a lot?'

'Well . . . as a matter of fact . . . she's staying with me.'

'What?' He was totally taken aback.

She smiled and walked on a pace or two, wondering how much to tell. In the end she said, 'It's complicated, but the long and short of it is, she's been at my flat since the middle of November.'

'Correct me if I'm wrong,' he countered, 'but aren't you hired by Mrs Ursula Guyler, who strenuously denied that that girl is anything to do with her?'

'You're quite right.'

'Lindsey, what are you *doing*?'

'To tell the truth, I don't quite know. I just feel that . . . she's had a raw deal. I couldn't just let her sink without trace after things went sour.'

He made no response, and when she turned to look he was frowning a little. 'You think she really is Ursula Guyler's daughter, don't you?'

'I think it's more than possible.'

'So you have some special interest in her, then?'

'Well, yes.'

'Enough to want to know how she came to be in the predicament she's in?'

'Of course.'

'Because, as a matter of fact, I've been giving that a lot of thought.' He gave a little apologetic laugh. 'Don't forget, I'm by nature and training an investigative reporter. When all that stuff hit the headlines about her claim to be Mrs Guyler's daughter, I found myself wondering why she was snatched in the first place.'

There was a stone dyke running along either side of the lane in which they were walking. They went to lean on the mossy stones, staring out at the hillside where sheep moved like white fur hats against a rich green backcloth.

'It was a strange business,' Keith remarked. 'No ransom was ever demanded, so it wasn't a kidnap for money. It could have been for revenge, a business rival, but that seems unlikely – Mrs Guyler's company wasn't as big then as it is now so it would hardly have caused any financial envy. And look who the poor kid ended up with – this oddball of a foster-mother, who according to the newspaper story never seems to have been able to earn a regular income or make a proper home. So she wasn't taken because of who she was or for her mother's money . . . or that's what I think.'

'I've always thought that the woman Edie calls Ma Maybury took the toddler for a whim, in a moment of emotional madness.'

'Almost like shoplifting, you mean.'

'But from some deep need, something that does seem to happen sometimes.' She'd read of women who, after losing a child of their own, felt impelled to find a substitute on whom to shower their love – but Ma Maybury seemed to have had very little love to shower.

'I've been wondering if Mrs Maybury had some connection with Cartfield,' Keith suggested.

'Of course she had – she got the names for the birth certificates from a mother and child in Cartfield.'

'Yes but –' and he held up a finger – 'how did she know about them?'

'I beg your pardon?'

'You're a woman who's taken a kid away from her parents and kept her. Now it's time to register her for school – if she doesn't the neighbours will tell the school attendance officer and she wouldn't want that because she can't account for the child. So she applies for birth certificates and so on. But how does she know what names to apply under?'

'Well,' said Lindsey, thinking, 'I always thought she did it the way it was done in that thriller.'

'You say that. It's a sort of shorthand way of describing it. But how was it done in the thriller? If I remember rightly the chap goes round looking at gravestones until he finds a dead man who'd be about his own age if he was still alive. But it might take a long time to find a gravestone for *a mother and child.*'

'Oh . . .'

'Yes.' He nodded once or twice in affirmation of the problem. 'I think Mrs Maybury remembered a death that occurred in Cartfield, a mother and a little girl of about three. I think she came to the cemetery and looked at the gravestone, to make sure. But how did she know it was there?' A pause. 'I think she was living in or around Cartfield when the accident occurred, and it had stayed in her memory.'

'But . . . was it so outstanding as a news item? Why should she remember it so well?'

'Because it was a hit and run driver, and the police tracked him down eventually by matching paint scrapes from his truck. It was quite a triumph for the local cops, I assure you – there was a lot about it in the regional paper. I looked it up in their archives.'

'She lived in the district?' Lindsey said wonderingly.

'I think it's better than a fifty-fifty chance.'

They straightened from their leaning positions, looked at each other, and their gaze became prolonged, changed and deepened so that they seemed to be reading each other's innermost thoughts.

He took her in his arms. They were eye to eye. He said, half laughing, 'I must tell you that I've been plotting this from the outset.'

'Not much of a plot – a close encounter on a wintry hillside!'

'This is just stage one.' He dropped a kiss on her nose. 'Stage two requires a warmer environment, so let's go back to the house.'

'The house has my brother Bob in it, fussing about in the conservatory. And my father will be back from his office soon, he only went there to check on the post.'

'Ah. In that case, come to Cartfield tomorrow.'

'Can't do that, we're all going to Coldstream tomorrow to visit cousins.'

'Say you've got something else to do.'

'Can't do that either. Edie would be left on her own amongst my cousins, whom she doesn't know. She's finding it hard enough to cope with the gang here in Ellenham.'

He sighed, then kissed her lightly on the lips. 'In that case I'll come to Birmingham. When are you going back?'

'New Year's Eve.'

'And I've got all the local new year sports results to get into the paper next day. Well then, let's say I'll be in your neighbourhood Wednesday of next week?'

'You will?'

'At the Normanton again.'

'Is this an assignation?'

'It's a delight – something to brighten up those terrible January days.'

'Keith . . .'

'What?'

'Is this going to get serious?'

'Who knows?' he asked, and kissed her with passion.

She found herself responding. Wrapped in each other, they knew nothing of the bitter wind, the gathering dusk.

Yes, she thought, this might be going to get serious.

When they let each other go, they turned back to go home. They'd been going to look at the view from the hilltop but darkness and gathering mist made it pointless.

As they walked, Lindsey's thoughts went back to their previous conversation. 'Do you really think you could find out anything about Edie's Ma Maybury?'

'It's my business. I could at least try.'

'But Keith – not for publication.'

He nodded agreement. 'I'd have to talk to Edie, get some clues.'

'I'll speak to her. Before you leave, after dinner?'

'I think I'd better make a start for home by about eight, in case this mist is going to get worse.'

'I'll set it up.'

Dinner was at seven – a casserole that had been simmering all afternoon in the Aga, with Mrs Abercrombie's good Christmas cake for dessert. When coffee was brought in, Lindsey's mother took herself off to her workroom again, Mr Abercrombie and Bob volunteered to do the washing up, so Lindsey, Edie and Keith had the living room to themselves.

'What was it you wanted to ask me?' Edie enquired in puzzlement, looking at Keith.

'I wondered if you'd like to know why you were taken away from that beach in Wales when you were a kiddie,' he replied.

'What?' She was startled.

183

'Haven't you wondered?'

'My God, of course I have! And I know the reason – that woman was a nutcase, know what I mean?'

'You think she did it in a moment of insanity, is that it?'

'What else? She didn't really *want* me, you know. I was a nuisance to her most of the time. I bet she found me a pain in the neck almost as soon as she got me home.'

'Then why didn't she hand you back? A reward was offered.'

'Oh yeah – and get herself arrested? No fear. Ma Maybury wasn't *that* daft.'

Lindsey said nothing, merely observing the dialogue. Edie turned to her. 'Why're you letting him interfere?'

'He thought you'd like to know how it all happened. I thought you ought to have the chance to discuss things. Keith can do some investigating, if you'd like him to.'

'Well, I wouldn't! The less I think about my life with that weirdo, the better! That's all behind me now. I don't seem to match up to anybody else's family, but I don't want to be reminded of the one that's gone!'

'All right,' Keith said with a shrug.

'Did you put him up to this?' Edie demanded of Lindsey. 'You'd no right! But that's just like you, trying to live my life for me! Leave me alone!'

She got up from the armchair and stormed out.

John Abercrombie's head appeared round the living room door a moment later. 'Something wrong?'

'Oh, just an argument,' Lindsey said.

'Really? She's such a shy type, I couldn't believe it when I heard her raise her voice. Nothing serious, I hope.' He disappeared back to the kitchen.

'A shy type?' Keith repeated.

'She's touchy.'

'Abrasive is the word I'd use.'

'We don't know what she's had to put up with in the past, Keith. Distrust is second nature to her.'

He took her hand. 'You're so kind-hearted . . . In fact, in every way I find you irresistible.' Then he picked up his coffee, drank it up, and rose. 'I'd better get going. Come and give me a farewell kiss.'

'Not on your life. My papa will want to shake hands with you as you leave – if you think I'm going to kiss you under his eye, you're mistaken.'

'Then kiss me now.' He gathered her up, and she did as he had bidden her. It was a long kiss. Neither of them wanted to draw apart.

But he had to get going, as he'd said, for the mist was getting thicker and though the roads in this part of the world were light on traffic, it would be a drive at slow speeds, and with fog lamps switched on.

Mr Abercrombie and Bob came to the door to see him off, as Lindsey had prophesied. Mrs Abercrombie was still at the far end of the garden in her workroom. Edie had joined her so she didn't appear either. With wishes for a happy New Year they parted.

Next day they all went to Coldstream as arranged. Edie was quiet, even quieter than she'd been since they first set out for Ellenham. She chose a moment after they'd got home at mid-evening to drop in on Lindsey in her bedroom.

'Why did you let that nosey-parker friend of yours start on about Ma Maybury?'

Lindsey bristled at the description of Keith but kept her cool. 'He suggested it. I thought you ought to have the chance to consider it.'

'Well, you were wrong!'

'I see that now. I apologise.'

'Well.' It was said in a sulky tone, as if she didn't accept the apology. Then she said, all at once, 'Why do you *do* that?'

'What?'

'Take the wind out of my sails! I think I'm going to have a real old row with you, and you say you're sorry and it all goes quiet.'

Lindsey's irritation subsided. She laughed. 'It's because I don't enjoy unnecessary rows.'

'But it's the way I was brought up! Know what I mean? You have to stand up for yourself!'

'Oh, I agree with that. But on the other hand, why waste

185

energy on being angry when I don't need to? *You're* cross with me about Keith, but I've got nothing to be cross about.'

'Aren't you cross because I called him a nosey-parker?'

'No, you're entitled to your opinion.'

'But he's your boyfriend! You just let me say things like that about him?'

'He's not my boyfriend.'

'Oh yes he is,' Edie said with certainty, and went to get ready for dinner.

If there had been a row brewing between them, Lindsey had defused it.

When they returned to Birmingham, Edie was laden with books presented to her from Mrs Abercrombie's collection.

She was reading one of them in the evening after they got home. All at once she looked up, fixing Lindsey with a serious gaze from troubled blue eyes.

'Lindsey,' she said with hesitation, 'how would a dimwit like me go about studying this art thing?'

Fifteen

Lindsey was immersed in sorting the mail she'd brought up from the lobby. She thought she'd misheard the question. 'Art thing?' she repeated vaguely.

'Making costumes and things. Like your mother.'

'What about it?'

'How do you get to do it?'

'Well, Mum does it because the local people ask her.'

'But they knew *she* knew how to do it.'

'Yes.'

'Well, how did they know that?'

'Because she's been doing it for years.' Lindsey said, baffled.

'But how did she come to it in the first place?' cried Edie, throwing up her hands in annoyance.

'Oh! You mean, how did she become qualified? Well, she went to art school.'

'Art school. That's a special school.'

'Yes, where they teach painting and drawing and sculpture, stuff like that.'

'Whereabouts?'

'Good heavens, there are lots of them! Mum went to the Slade School, and there's one called St Martins, and there's the London School of Fashion, I think, and of course every university has an art department.'

'University . . . ?' She pursed her lips. 'That's the sort of thing, then – like university?'

'Oh yes, on that level. Why?'

'I was wondering . . . I was thinking . . . it'd be good if I could get in on it, Lindsey. I think I might have a bit of a turn for it, know what I mean?'

187

Lindsey set aside the mail. This was the very first time Edie had ever shown any ambition other than to land a job in a shop.

'You feel you'd like to study art?'

'Yeah. Not that heavy stuff you were saying, stuff like sculpture – statues and all that. But how to do things for a show, or to put in a shop window, 'cos some of the Christmas windows I saw in the shopping malls were awful, and I've often thought the ones at the old supermarket could have done with a good tidy-up. Never understood before why they bothered me so much but after doing that stuff with your mum, it seems to have sort of come clear.'

'Well, that's . . . that's interesting, Edie.'

'Could I go to art school?'

Lindsey tried to sort out her thoughts. First of all, it was great that Edie seemed to be trying to do something with her life. And that having come into contact with 'art' for perhaps the first time, she didn't all at once decide to become a second Van Gogh.

Yet her new-found ambition presented problems.

'Did you get leaving certificates when you left school, Edie?'

'Certificates?'

'GCSEs. A levels.'

'Ho, A levels! You're joking of course.'

'Well then, GCSEs – did you take any of those?'

'Got two – English and economics.' Lindsey received this in silence, which Edie mistook for criticism. 'I could mebbe have got more!' she flashed. 'But I never got any encouragement, did I? Always moving from one town to another, a new school every year or so, the one I finished up in, old Ma Maybury never even went to the parents' evenings when they were trying to sort out what s'tifficates I should try for.'

Lindsey met the angry glance with a calming wave of the hand. 'I was just thinking . . . you'd probably have to have more to get into art college. I don't know how they select students – when I applied to university you had to have enough points to be on their list and then there was an interview.'

'You had loads of As, I s'pose!'

'Well, I was going to study law, Edie. And to tell the truth, I only have vague memories of what the other girls at school had to provide – a couple of them did go on to art school, I think, but I don't really remember what they . . .' She paused. 'I think they had to have a portfolio.'

'A portfolio? That's a folder sort of thing, with papers in it?'

'It's just a term, Edie – you have to show a collection of work so the selection committee can decide whether you have any talent.'

'Oh, Lord,' groaned Edie. 'I've never even thought of doing stuff like that. All I've done is that bit with your mum in her workroom.'

'She thought the things you did were very good.'

'Did she say that to you?' Her delight was evident. 'I thought mebbe she was just being nice to me when she said I had talent.'

'No, she meant it. So perhaps we should think about it seriously.'

'But only the two GCSEs . . .'

'You could get more.'

'What, go back to school? How'm I gonna do that at twenty?'

'Evening classes—'

'Oh, don't talk to me about evening classes. They had some at the town hall in Hobston, and I thought I'd do myself a bit of good by going, and it was this old geezer chuntering on about parish history.'

'But you could take special classes to get GCSEs.'

'But it'd take for ever!'

'Well, it might take a couple of years.'

'A couple of *years*!'

Lindsey got up, came across the living room, and sat down across the table on which Edie had set down her book. 'Think about it, Edie. To get into a college you have to have qualifications and, I think, a body of work that you can show. At the moment you've got nothing. You can't just go out tomorrow and expect to walk into a decent art school. If you really want to do it, it might take you two years. So what? If it's really important, you'd still only be twenty-two when you applied for a place.'

Edie stared at her in sullen disappointment. What did she know, this bossy woman who'd had such an easy life, a lovely family all around her, a lovely home where her mum cooked great meals instead of getting everything out of packets.

'We could get some information about entry requirements,' Lindsey went on. 'Then we'd know what you ought to do to work towards them. It would be hard.'

'I'm not afraid of hard work!'

'No, but it'd mean sticking at it – not giving up – and it'd be tiring – evening classes after a day's work.'

'I'm not going to those evening classes that the local council sets up! A load of rubbish, and everything at a snail's pace!'

Lindsey had no way of knowing whether that was true or not. But an alternative had suggested itself. 'There are day classes,' she said. 'Commercial set ups – the slang term is "crammer", they give you intensive training to pass exams.'

'Ah! Now you're talking!'

'But Edie, they cost money. You'd have to get a part-time job to help pay for it, and once you'd got the job you'd have to behave yourself . . .' She hesitated before going on. 'No getting crusty with customers, no answering back to the management! You'd need to stay in work to pay your way.'

'Um,' said Edie. 'An evening job, night work? Office cleaning, usherette, barmaid – barmaid might not be bad, tips could mount up, waitressing too, but that's fierce on your feet, then of course there's always all-night supermarkets, I know all about supermarkets.' A flood of enthusiasm coursed through her. She could do it, find a job, get the qualifications, make some things or draw up the designs for them, what's it called, a portfolio . . .

'Could we go to a cyber-cafe and look it up on the web?' she demanded, getting up and making for the door.

'Edie! It's seven o'clock on New Year's Eve, I don't think any of the cafes would be open, and anyhow we're going to a party.'

'A party?'

'Yes, every year the residents here go down to the lobby

190

with a plate of something and a bottle of something else, and we dance a bit and sing 'Auld Lang Syne' and go to bed about three.'

'Oh.'

'And then tomorrow we don't get up until something like midday and in the evening we might go out and see a show. That's the plan.'

Edie felt mutinous. It was as if her urge to start studying for a career were being written off as unimportant.

Then Lindsey said, 'On the second of January, though, you go into Birmingham and sort out a job – doesn't matter what for the moment, we just want some money coming in. But after you've landed something you can go to the library or the city council and find out about art college entrance, and get a list of schools that specialise in intensive study.'

Edie produced a wavering smile. 'Well, that doesn't sound too bad,' she said. 'Know what I mean?'

The New Year festivities were of a kind unknown to Edie. Hitherto, a pub had always been involved: either Mrs Maybury went to the Golden Lion or the Plough, or whatever local they happened to be near that year, leaving Edie in the care of home-staying neighbours. Or later, when Edie advanced towards her teens, she was taken along to the local, having been warned, 'Stay there in the corner with your soft drink and don't bother me.'

Later yet, with Graham, of course the pub had been the centre of celebration. Of the fifteen New Years that Edie could remember, not one had been spent with a group of rather quiet people who danced somewhat sedately to salsa and drank a couple of glasses of champagne on the stroke of midnight before heading for bed.

The first working day after the holiday, she landed a job at the twenty-four hour hypermarket, late evening shift, 9 p.m. to 3 a.m. Lindsey was horrified.

'How are you going to get home?' she demanded. 'There's no train at that hour and a taxi would cost—'

'Take it easy, take it easy, there's an all-night bus service.

One an hour and there's a stop right outside the store, of course.'

'An all-night bus!' Lindsey had used them once or twice during her student days, and had never thought them alluring.

'It's okay, I asked and there seem to be about four others on the staff that take the bus. Safety in numbers, know what I mean?'

In other respects the job was desirable. Edie had filled out an application in the personnel office. When the man behind the desk spotted the word 'Yes' on the line asking for computer experience, he'd almost grabbed Edie and hugged her. At the mini-supermarket in Hobston she'd divided her time between the checkout and the computer stock register; the personnel manager was delighted.

By the time he'd worked out overtime rates for night employment, possible extras for Sunday day work, and the bonus involved in handling the stock computer, her pay came to almost twice as much as she'd earned in Hobston.

To Edie it seemed a fortune. To Lindsey, it was a sum unlikely to fund private tuition as well as living expenses. But she said nothing of that. It was important not to rain on Edie's parade.

There was something endearing about Edie's enthusiasm. It reminded Lindsey of her own schooldays when September was close and there was the excitement of the new pencil-case, the drawing up of timetables for homework, the trying on of the one-size-larger school blouses.

This was what Edie was feeling now, and perhaps for the very first time. Instead of being hauled off to a new town and dragged unwillingly to a new school where everybody else would know each other and the teachers, she was going of her own volition to a school of her choice.

The choosing of the school and the subjects to study engaged them for the whole of the next weekend. Lindsey, because she often handled cases concerning family problems, had contacts in education – she'd more than once had to find a college that would take young Charlie for yet another attempt to get him through exams.

'Chepperton College gets good results,' she told Edie. 'But what I've heard is that they work their students very hard.'

'I'm not afraid of hard work,' Edie said yet again It was something of a refrain with her, the one thing she knew about herself of which she could be proud. Lindsey nodded in agreement. Certainly the few days since she started at the Brunswick Hypermarket bore it out – off on the bus to start at nine each evening, home by 3.30 in the morning, getting up again by the time Lindsey was leaving for the office at 9.30. And already starting on a self-programmed study of some of the literature on Lindsey's bookshelves.

The GCSE subjects Edie had chosen were English literature (''cos after all that's just reading books and going to plays, isn't it?'), computer studies ('I know quite a lot already. Know what I mean?'), and, of course, art ('there's these modules, I don't really understand 'em but two are compulsory and I'm choosing calligraphy for the third 'cos that's just handwriting').

Lindsey listened and made sympathetic sounds. But her mind was elsewhere. On Wednesday Keith would be in Birmingham, and she was wrestling with the problem of whether or not to see him.

Once back in her usual surroundings, the episode with Keith in Ellenham seemed illusory. Could she really have responded with so much eagerness to his kisses? No, of course not, because she was bound by a relationship of almost two years to Andrew.

Yet there had been a slackening in that bond over the last few weeks. Ever since he had summoned her back from Lichfield to deal with the trouble over Graham Walker and the Guylers, they hadn't been comfortable with each other. She thought he had been interfering and, more importantly, wrong – he had given bad advice to the Guylers.

But worse yet had been his manner when she told him about Edie. First of all he had seemed quite heartless about the girl's possible future. And almost as bad, he'd given Lindsey orders. 'Get rid of her!' he'd said.

Well, who was Andrew Gilmore to issue instructions?

As she thought about these things, she noticed that there was no loving tone to them. But there . . . Every affair had its ups

193

and downs, therefore she shouldn't think she and Andrew were on the way to a parting.

She saw him, of course, at the office and they were always polite and friendly to each other.

Less than a week into the new year, Mr Ollerenshaw called Lindsey into his office unexpectedly.

'Now, Lindsey, this is a serious matter that I'm going to broach with you. I . . . er . . . couldn't quite believe it when I first heard it, but tell me now . . . It is true that you are harbouring the young woman who caused so much trouble to Mrs Guyler?'

Lindsey, who had brought in some papers that she thought might be in question, looked up to stare at her boss.

'Harbouring?' she echoed. 'What do you mean by that? She's not a criminal!'

'That's by no means certain,' said Ollerenshaw in a tone of rebuke. 'Whether that is a fact or not, she is certainly persona non grata with one of our most important clients. I must therefore ask you to break off any association with her immediately.'

'I'll do nothing of the kind!'

He was amazed to hear her refuse. He almost gaped. 'Miss Abercrombie!' he said in a tone of ice. 'You will do as I tell you.'

'Not where my private life is concerned, Mr Ollerenshaw.'

That gave him pause. He knew that if he pursued this matter to the bitter end, it might come to dispensing with the services of a very valuable member of the firm. And that might open the way to a claim of wrongful dismissal. And if that happened, there would be unwelcome publicity, which might include the mention of the name of Edie Maybury – and *that* would put the cat among the pigeons.

A moment of rapid thought caused him to alter his manner. He acknowledged to himself that he had no right to interfere in her private affairs. Some of the staff members led lives that he disapproved of but he turned the proverbial blind eye. Should he do the same here? But there was the problem of Mrs Guyler. If Mrs Guyler ever learned that one of his junior colleagues was giving a home to her bête noire he trembled to think what she might do.

He started again. 'Now, Lindsey, this is a very serious matter.' He saw an expression flit across her face which told him he'd already said that. 'Mrs Guyler would not approve. I'm sure you agree on that point.'

'Mr Ollerenshaw,' Lindsey said, 'if you want to know what I really think, it's my opinion that Mrs Guyler will one day regret her attitude to Edie Maybury. In a way, I feel it's my duty not to let Edie come to grief – and she was very near that when I offered her a temporary home.'

'Temporary!' said Ollerenshaw with relief. 'You do agree that it must come to an end without delay?'

'It will come to an end in its own time,' she said. She was thinking that the financial strain might prove too much.

'But you intend to let her remain on your premises?'

'On my premises,' she said, stifling a laugh. 'Yes, I think I must insist in being allowed to give a room to whoever I want to.'

'But . . . but . . . it would be advisable not to let Mrs Guyler know,' he ventured, much less dictatorial in his style.

'That seems to be the case.'

'I disapprove,' he said. 'I state this for the record. I disapprove. It alters my perception of your judgement, Lindsey. I want you to know that I disapprove.'

'I accept that, Mr Ollerenshaw.'

'Very well. We'll consider the matter closed until you can tell me the girl has gone.'

'I understand.'

She went out, still preserving the calm she'd shown during the interview. But she was furious. She stormed up the stairs two at a time and barged into Andrew's office, slamming the door hard behind her.

He looked up in astonishment at her entrance. 'Lindsey! What's wrong?' A flush coloured the usually pale skin, the calm hazel eyes were burning with indignation.

She came up to his desk, leaning forward to stare into his face. 'Did you tell Ollerenshaw that I'd got Edie staying with me?'

'Me?'

'I've just had a damn-fool interview with him about it, and the only person who could have told him is you.'

''I didn't . . . well . . . you know . . . . we were at a new year thing . . . I may have had a little too much to drink . . .'

'You *told* him?'

'I don't honestly remember . . . I think I may have said something because he came to me yesterday and said, did I really mean what I'd reported about the Maybury girl, and when I said, what did I report, he said, was she staying with you at your flat, and you see, Lin, I had to say yes, because she is, isn't she?'

She stood up straight. 'You're a rat,' she said.

'No, now, look here, Lin – it was bound to come out sooner or later.'

'No it wasn't! I told you because I thought I could trust you!' She shook her head at herself. 'How could I have been so silly? You and Old Ollie had a few drinks together and you thought to yourself, "Here's a way to get into his good books."'

'No, that wasn't it at all! He was saying that you'd done a good job with the Guylers and I think I said, that if they only knew what you were up to—'

'Oh, you did? You thought you were putting in a good word for me, is that it?'

'Well, I suppose I felt . . . you know, what you're doing is awfully risky! If they got to know—'

'If they get to hear of it I'll know who told them! But –' she paused, pointing an accusatory finger at him – 'don't do it, Andrew. If you imagine it would put you in good odour with them, think again – they'll take their legal work away from Higgett, Ollerenshaw and Cline like a shot and Old Ollie will have your head on a platter!'

'I wasn't thinking of telling them,' he muttered.

She gave a little shrug. 'I'd really like to know what you *were* thinking. You must have known Ollerenshaw would haul me over the coals. So of course I'd know you'd sneaked to him about it.'

'Sneaked?'

'What else do you call it?'

'I call it showing some sense!' he retorted, firing up. 'You've behaved like a sentimental idiot over this Guyler thing from the start, and it's time you sorted yourself out. There's no place for sentiment in the law!'

They were having a blazing row, in very loud voices. The phone on Andrew's desk rang. He turned to it in surprise, but picked it up. 'Hello?' He listened a moment then said, 'Okay, thank you.' He looked at Lindsey. 'That was Bob Griswold down the corridor. He says he can hear our lovers' tiff and would we please cool it.'

'Right.' She turned for the door. 'Let's cool it. Let's put the whole thing on ice, shall we? I'll avoid you and you avoid me – agreed?'

'Agreed,' he replied. 'I should have known better anyway – office romances are a mistake.'

'How right you are!'

She marched out. She was still so angry that she could hardly contain herself. She snatched up her coat from the downstairs rack before the eyes of the startled receptionist, and stalked out into the bleak mid-morning.

Walking briskly, she marched through the shopping centre. The January sales were on, with crowds eddying about, but she scarcely noticed them. She eventually found herself on the little island where the representation of Tony Hancock looks out on the world with puzzled eyes, and there she sat down.

It was cold. The traffic rushed round her in the busy square. A few pigeons pecked about.

She found her eyes filling with tears.

I really cared about him, she told herself. I thought he cared about me.

Was it true that he blurted out the news about Edie because he'd had one too many brandies? Or had it been a half conscious desire to take her down a peg or two?

Andrew was ambitious. He wanted to become a junior partner and she and Andrew were the most likely candidates for promotion when the financial year began again in April. Could he have been sabotaging her chances?

It doesn't matter why he did it, she argued. He betrayed a confidence.

197

This conclusion was inescapable. She delved for a Kleenex and mopped her eyes. After a moment or two she sat up straight and murmured to Tony Hancock, 'Now I've worked that out, where do we go from here?'

Well, it was all over between her and Andrew. After the things they'd said to each other this morning, there was no chance of a reconciliation. And besides, she didn't want one.

With this decision she got up and was on the move again. She walked for about half an hour, eventually reaching the front steps of the office again at about eleven thirty. She looked up at its imposing entry, at the windows behind which advice on major business matters was being debated. She thought, One day I'll leave all this. One day I'll go somewhere else and practise law like my father, knowing everybody and their family and taking a close personal interest in every detail.

It was only much later, when she was packing up to go home, that another thought occurred to her.

Now she didn't have to worry about being disloyal to Andrew if she went to meet Keith Holland at the Normanton. Now she was free – free to go forward, without ties, without guilt.

Keith rang on Tuesday. 'Just to remind you that I'll be in Birmingham tomorrow,' he said in a light-hearted tone.

'Yes. I'm looking forward to it,' she replied.

'You are?' His voice changed to something much more earnest. 'Does that mean what I hope it means?'

'We'll find out tomorrow, won't we?'

'Well, thank the Lord for that! I was afraid you might have decided it definitely wasn't going to be an assignation.'

She found herself smiling. It was such a lovely word, full of old-fashioned romance. 'You know there are attributes that go with it. Roses, candle light, champagne . . .'

'Look here,' Keith rebuked her, 'this has all got to go on my expense account. You'll get chrysanthemums in a pot and Australian Chardonnay, and I don't think they allow candles in the Normanton. And let me warn you, the fixed-price dinner is at eight, though I might spring for drinks in the bar at seven thirty.'

She was laughing as she broke the connection. She had a feeling that however the evening might end, she was going to enjoy it simply because he made her laugh.

She gave a lot of thought to her dress. Nothing too formal, of course, it was just a dinner for two in a medium-grade hotel. She chose a dark blue shift of fine wool, nothing special. But she gave a lot of thought to her underwear, which must mean something.

She found he really meant it when he said the table d'hôte menu came on at eight. And just to go along with his scenario, she actually ordered from it. But neither of them seemed to have much appetite. Their waiter became quite concerned. 'Is there something wrong with the food, sir?' he asked Keith.

Keith shook his head and sighed. 'If music be the food of love, bring us some of that,' he suggested.

'Beg your pardon?'

'Never mind.'

Around nine o'clock a pianist began to play in the bar. 'There you are!' said Keith. 'Music, just as I ordered.'

They went to the bar to listen. A young man – perhaps a music student from the university – was playing 'Claire de Lune'.

'Very classy,' said Keith. 'I was expecting something more along the lines of that song from what's its name – that show your mother's doing the clothes for.'

'*Oklahoma!*'

'That's the one.'

'And what was the song – "The Surrey with the Fringe on Top"?'

'I was thinking more of "People Will Say We're In Love".'

'You surprise me – I wouldn't have thought you had much interest in shows from the forties.' She wanted to tread carefully around the message in the song title.

'You forget – I'm a reporter, so I actually attended some of the rehearsals of the Ellenham and District Dramatic Society's production of that fine old musical. I even told my readers I thought it would be worth the fifty-mile drive to see it.'

'You've been to Ellenham?' she said in surprise.

'Sure thing. When you're serious about a girl, you want to get on good terms with her family.'

She let a moment go by. 'Are you telling me you're serious, Keith?' she asked.

'I know it's difficult to believe, but I have a serious side. I find it difficult to believe myself, because a career in the newspaper world tends to go along with deep disillusion. Yet here I am, wanting to convince you this is the most important thing that ever happened to me.'

She didn't know how to reply. To tell the truth, she was taken aback. She'd thought she might be about to enter into an affair – happy in the expectation, pleased with the thought of physical enjoyment, a cheerful entanglement that might somehow compensate for the miseries and anxieties of the past few weeks.

Love? Was he talking about love?

Perhaps she should draw back. It was more than she wanted to undertake.

But when he rose from his chair and held out a hand, she put hers in his and went with him. When she saw champagne in a silver bucket and two dozen red roses in a crystal vase in his room she began to laugh

'You said you couldn't afford all this!'

'To the devil with expense!' he cried melodramatically. 'Anything, anything to entrap you!'

'Am I entrapped?'

'Let's find out,' he said.

He proved to be a passionate lover, yet very caring, always thinking of her pleasure before his own. To Lindsey, it was a revelation. She found she could give herself up to each moment, never wondering if she was measuring up to his demands. It came about as if it were all destined.

Somewhere about eleven o'clock Keith opened the champagne. Sitting up in bed, they drank, and in her mind Lindsey knew it was an unspoken toast – to what, she was uncertain. It was a new beginning, perhaps of the greatest thing that had ever happened to her. But this strange fluttering in her heart might only be excitement, the thrill of the moment. It was too early to tell.

They parted after an early breakfast served in his room. He found himself wanting a promise that they would meet again soon, that he would be the only man in her life. Something in her manner as they shared a goodbye kiss told him he mustn't put that into words. She wasn't ready for a commitment.

So instead he said, 'Sorry I couldn't come up with any candles.'

She kissed him briefly on the nose. 'You are an idiot,' she said, but there was great fondness in her tone.

She had to race home to change and arrive in reasonable time for the office. Edie was fast asleep in her room. They scarcely saw each other, their timetables were totally opposed because of Edie's night-time job. But at the weekend they shared a sort of brunch, and had time to talk.

The new term began at Chepperton College in eight days. Lindsey had already verified that there were vacancies in the courses which Edie wanted to take. The director of the college requested a personal interview for this late-applying student, and it was at that point that Edie began to be nervous.

'He'll take against me! People in uppity positions always do! What's he gonna ask me, Lindsey?'

'It'll be about what certificates you've already got, and what your aims are – things like that.'

'So am I gonna tell him I went to about twelve different schools and only got two GCSEs – and not very good ones at that?'

'Why not? It wasn't your fault. And besides, your references from the Hobston shop are quite good – they say you were efficient at the computer stuff and made redundant during staff reorganisation – that's because they can't say they got fed up with you over the Guyler business.'

'You think it's okay?'

'Edie, they'll have students there whose parents have had them at twenty schools and are in despair over them. You're not as handicapped as you think. And besides,' she added, 'I got my mother to e-mail them with a letter of recommendation.'

'You never!'

'I did. She said you had a lot of talent that had never received any encouragement. So I think you'll be all right. Just bear one thing in mind.'

'What?'

'Mr Justin doesn't want trouble in his school. So try not to look like trouble.'

Edie made a great effort. She wore jeans newly purchased from a charity shop, her dark red silk blouse, a sweater borrowed from Lindsey, and absolutely no make-up.

'I just sat there saying "Yes Mr Justin, no Mr Justin" and then I handed over the cheque and more or less curtseyed and got out of there!'

'Good for you.'

'It's gonna be classes on four days a week. He says I've gotta go to a studio near the Bull Ring for the calligraphy thing, and that'll be extra but I've got to discuss that with the studio manager.' She hesitated. 'It's a big thing, Lindsey, isn't it.'

'But we knew that.'

'Yeah, but I didn't realise *how* big.'

Lindsey made no reply. It was a big thing, no mistake. And the possible financial implications were beginning to worry her.

But the only thing to do was to try out the plan and see if it worked. She thought six weeks would be a good sample of the possibilities. End of February, she told herself. By mid-February I'll know whether we can cover the costs, whether Edie's enthusiasm is going to last out, and whether her health is suffering from the strain. By the end of February it might be time to look at Plan B.

Except that she didn't have a Plan B.

Nevertheless, as the weeks went by, it became clear something would have to be done. Textbooks proved very expensive, equipment for the art work cost more than Lindsey had expected. Edie had to stay in the city from mid-morning classes until the end of her night shift at the supermarket, so she had to eat in cafes and pubs which meant extra expense. And then there was the problem of clothes. Edie was content to buy outerwear from charity shops, but underwear and tights had to come from chain stores. There was also the problem of a good coat for the continuing cold weather.

Lindsey gave it a lot of thought, setting out the problem on paper as she usually did with her legal work. Edie's salary was being used up in her day to day living. Lindsey had paid her tuition fees, and had no expectation of getting the money back. She had used money from her savings account and, though she financed the books and art materials from her salary, it meant that she wasn't replacing the money she'd taken out.

She had plans of her own for which the money in the bank was intended. One day she wanted to set up her own law practice; that was what the savings were for. But if she had to finance Edie much longer, her own ambitions would have to be postponed.

In the end it came down to this. Sooner or later Edie would have to get financial help. There were grants she could apply for, but whether she would have success in that, no one could tell. Besides, a grant might not be made available until the beginning of the next academic year, which wasn't until September.

There were student loans, but that meant going to official-dom, with the danger of having to explain about her birth certificate.

The logical place to go was to Edie's parents the Guylers – Lindsey was sure in her own mind that Edie was the long-lost daughter Julie, though the Guylers resisted this suggestion. But Lindsey thought a case could be made out that they owed Edie something – that they had raised expectations which had not only been unfulfilled, but quite cruelly dismissed. She felt she could argue a case for a payment of some kind, enough to see Edie through for at least six months, perhaps longer. During that time Lindsey would sort out the possibility of a grant from an educational charity.

All that was needed was the equivalent of a bridging loan. But how to get it from the Guylers? They ought to be approached in a formal manner. Perhaps she could get Mr Ollerenshaw to write to Ursula. No. Old Ollie would have a fit at the mere idea.

Perhaps she herself should write. She could say that Edie had approached her and asked her to make contact. No. Edie was dead against having anything to do with the Guylers. They'd thrown her out with the rubbish. However, Lindsey could write without telling Edie anything about it. We-ell . . . Letters were easy to ignore. She could telephone. But then Ursula would simply put the phone down.

Lindsey set up and discarded these proposals during the last days of February. In March she saw in the *Birmingham Post* that Billy Guyler's golf club were running a Spring Charity Match, with all the proceeds to go to a children's hospice. Billy Guyler was named in the list of players.

Billy Guyler? Ursula was unapproachable. But Billy was a different matter, particularly if she were to encounter him in the midst of his friends, where he'd be unwilling to make a scene.

She looked up the Old Park Golf Course on a map of the city. It was on the northern outskirts, beyond Great Barr. The match would be held over the Saturday and Sunday of the next weekend. Spectator tickets could be bought at the lodge gate, ten pounds each for charity, light refreshments available.

It was too difficult a trip for public transport, so Lindsey hired a Peugeot Meridien from her local garage on Saturday. She felt she'd better go on Saturday in case Billy got knocked out in the first round. She could only pray that Ursula wouldn't be there.

There proved to be a good turn out of spectators trooping round after the players and being supportive of husbands, brothers and sons who were taking part in the tournament. No women players, Lindsey noted, although there were plenty among the supporters – but fortunately not Ursula Guyler. Lindsey recalled that Ursula's favourite pastime was shopping, and Saturday was such a good shopping day.

As she'd rather expected, Billy was one of the first to be knocked out and was driving back to the clubhouse in a golfmobile by mid-morning. At first that was a dilemma. Lindsey couldn't get into the clubhouse.

But she waited, and by and by Billy reappeared, smartly

clad in a covert coat against the March wind. He was going to spectate.

Lindsey walked up to him, and was facing him before he realised who it was.

'Mr Guyler.'

'What—? Good Lord, Miss Abercrombie!' He was amazed. 'What are you doing here?'

'I need to speak to you.'

'What about?' he asked, even more amazed.

'I want you to speak to your wife about Edie Maybury.'

Emotions washed across his gentle, indeterminate features – consternation, repugnance, dismay.

'N-not on your life!' he stammered.

Sixteen

H e was poised for flight. She caught him by a sleeve. 'Don't run away.'

'I can't speak to you.'

'But you must,' she insisted.

'There's nothing to say about that girl.'

'Oh yes there is. It's important, and I'm not going to give up, so let's just get on with it.'

He seemed to wilt at her insistence. 'Not here,' he said, glancing around in alarm. 'Shula's dropping in for lunch.'

'My car,' she suggested. 'It's in the spectators' area, she's got no reason to go there.'

He hesitated but, short of wrenching himself out of her grasp, saw no way out. 'All right then.'

They settled themselves in the back of the little car in opposite corners so that they could look at each other.

Billy broke into speech at once. 'Shula and I have agreed we would never talk of that episode ever again. She's admitted to me that she's been wrong all along to go on hoping to find Julie. We've agreed to put all that behind us.'

He said it as if he felt it a wonderful thing, that his wife should admit she'd made a mistake – wonderful, admirable, and not to be gainsaid.

It sounded different to Lindsey. 'That's a bit hard on Edie though, isn't it?' she suggested.

He stared at her in bewilderment. What could she mean? 'That dreadful girl!'

She could hear Shula's tones echoing in the phrase. 'She's not so dreadful. You don't know her,' she replied. 'You never really tried to know her.'

'Oh, we got a good idea of what she was up to! And now

she's at it again – she's somehow enlisted you in some scheme to screw money out of us.'

'That's a rotten thing to say!'

She was so clearly angry that he found he regretted his aspersion. A faint flush crept up under his skin. There was a painful silence. 'We-ell . . .'

'It's true I'm going to ask you for money. But Edie knows nothing about it.'

'I don't understand.'

'She's studying for GCSEs at the Chepperton College in Birmingham. She wants to get enough qualifications to go on to university. But it's costing more than we expected—'

'Studying for GCSEs?' he broke in. 'You're joking!' It was so clearly a lie that he couldn't understand why she said it.

'Ring up the college and ask,' she said calmly. 'She started in January.'

'But how do you know this?'

'I'm . . . I'm in touch with her.'

'But why? I can't see why you'd do it!'

'I'll tell you why,' she said, understanding that something like shock treatment was needed to get him past his bewilderment. 'I found her crying her heart out in the middle of the night on a pavement in Birmingham.'

'What?'

'With hardly any money and a few clothes in a rucksack.'

'Good God!'

'And do you know why she was there? Because she'd had a row with her boyfriend—'

'That dreadful young man!'

'Had a row with her boyfriend,' she persisted, 'because he'd gone behind her back in sending that demand for money.'

'That awful letter, asking us if we "liked being hated"!' His face screwed up in horror at the recollection.

'As far as I can tell, she knew nothing about it. They seem to have had a quarrel over it that went on for a couple of days and then he threw her out.'

'Oh dear.' He heard himself say it, and realised how paltry it sounded. But it came from a real sense of shock, of a wish not to have to hear this.

'So that's why I took a hand. I felt she needed a friend.'

'But she's not the kind of girl you can be friends with!' he protested, recalling Edie in all her hard antagonism. 'And how do you know she's not just out for what she can get?'

'Because she's working nights in the big hypermarket so she can take classes in the daytime. And her nose is in a book when she isn't struggling with pictorial composition.'

'Pictorial composition?'

'I told you you never got to know her.'

'But pictorial composition is part of an art course,' he said, recalling his own student days.

'Right. She wants to go to art college.'

He shook his head. 'It's some sort of scam. That girl is just using you to get at Shula and me.'

'I tell you, she doesn't even know I'm talking to you. And I wouldn't be, except that the whole thing is costing more than I expected and it's difficult to make ends meet.'

'You mean she's managed to get you to pay for this—'

She cut him short, not wanting to let him make some unkind accusation. She wanted to keep everything as calm as possible. 'I paid her tuition fees, yes. And I hope, starting with next term, that I'll have got some sort of grant from somewhere. But in the meantime she needs a decent coat because it's cold coming home on the bus at three in the morning.'

'Oh, come on, you're making all this up!' He almost made violin-playing movements with his hands, to show contempt for this sob story.

She frowned at him. 'Mr Guyler, am I the sort of person who makes things up? Is that the impression I gave you while I was trying to sort out the mess Shula got you into?'

'The mess Shula . . . ? How dare you say that! It was that dreadful girl—'

'Stop calling her that! She's what she was turned into by sixteen years of living with that ersatz mother!' Lindsey almost let irritation drive her into a confrontation. She told herself to keep cool. 'Then along comes Shula,' she said, 'holding out the key to the kingdom of real family life – but she never even lets Edie unlock the door, she leaves her standing outside in the cold.'

'But Shula knew that girl couldn't be Julie.'

'Shula refused ever to think about it,' Lindsey asserted. 'To me, she seemed like a customer buying a car – "If I can't have it in peacock blue I won't have it at all." But Mr Guyler, this wasn't a car, it was a human being she was dealing with.'

'Look here, I won't have you blaming my wife! You've no idea what she's been through over this.'

'I *know* she suffered,' Lindsey agreed gently. 'I saw it. But I also saw that she was defending something all the time – her view of Julie, a dream child who no longer existed.'

'But our little Julie could never have grown up so hard, so aggressive.'

'How can you know that? I see a lot of family situations in my work, and I can tell you, I often hear that cry – "He was such a darling little boy, how could he treat us so badly?" Lovely children can change into heartless money-grabbers, sweet little girls can go straight to the bad.'

'You can plead for her as much as you like,' he said, trying now to explain the uselessness of it. 'But Shula and I have agreed that it was all a mistake and we're just going to put it behind us and forget it.'

'The ostrich position.'

'What?'

'Head in the sand.'

He was hurt. 'I don't think you should sneer at us.'

'I don't know whether to laugh or cry,' she said. 'This has been such an enormous thing in your life. Honestly, Mr Guyler, are you so rock-like that you're never going to wonder how Edie gets on? Are you never going to say, "Perhaps we were wrong"?'

'No, never.' He said it with total firmness.

'And Shula? Is she as determined that she's in the right?'

'Yes, she is. She knew from the minute she spoke to that dreadful girl that she couldn't possibly be Julie.'

'She never wonders?'

'No, never.'

'You talk about it, and she's always certain you did the right thing?'

'I *told* you, we agreed never to talk about it.' But he

knew he'd said the wrong thing the moment the words were out.

'So if you never talk about it, how do you know she still feels the same?'

'What?'

'If you're both so busy hiding from the idea, how do you know what she thinks?'

'That's ridiculous.'

'At least speak to her about it, Mr Guyler. Edie needs help—'

'She's not going to get it from us.'

'You're going to go through the rest of your life, never forgiving her for being kidnapped and turning out a difficult girl?'

'Never forgiving her?' Billy echoed. He knew he sounded bewildered, and that was, in fact, how he felt. Yet there was something else, a terrible emotion that surged up and died back. Was it remorse?

'That's what it is, isn't it? Shula had impossible expectations and she can't forgive Edie for not living up to them.'

'That's just some silly psycho-babble!' He had rallied. He wasn't going to let her upset the delicate balance he and Shula had achieved by putting it all behind them. 'You think you can persuade me by accusing my wife of . . . I don't know what . . . stupidity, prejudice . . . Shula's not like that. She wanted to love Edie. She tried, we both did, and all we got was abuse, threats and undeserved criticism in the newspapers.'

'But perhaps it's time to try again. Edie has changed, has had time to get over the hurt she felt.'

'The hurt *she* felt!'

'And now it might be easier for you all to get together.'

'No!'

'Speak to Shula,' she begged. 'Give her the chance to think again.'

He was shaking his head violently. 'I can't,' he said. 'I can't speak to Shula about that girl. It's out of the question.'

'I'm not asking you to say she must accept her as a daughter. But I think you both owe her something – something in the way of reparation, a gesture at least.'

'No.' He opened the door on his side and began to get out. He felt the blessed cold fresh air on his face, grateful to feel it, to get away from this determined young woman. Over his shoulder he said, 'I don't want to hear another word about this, because if I do I'll have to complain to Mr Ollerenshaw.'

Lindsey sat for a while after he'd gone. 'Well done!' she said to herself in irony. 'You handled that beautifully.'

She was glad she hadn't discussed it with Edie beforehand. To have to report that Billy Guyler and his wife had so completely shut her out of their lives, out of their very thoughts, would have been yet another rejection at a point when it might be very harmful. Edie was at the outset of something new. The last thing she needed was a blow to her self-confidence.

Sunday was spent with Keith. Among other more sensual pleasures, they went to look at the daffodils on the banks of the Avon. Edie was at home struggling with the techniques of collage. When Lindsey got back there were scraps of cloth and paper all over the living room.

Soon, she reflected, the flat wouldn't really be big enough. The spare room was average in size, but there wasn't really room for an easel or a worktable and the spread of many sheets of A1 paper. Moreover, it faced south so that the light wasn't the best for an artist. Yet there must be many other students in the same sort of plight; Edie would just have to manage.

Monday was a busy day at the law firm, with a succession of clients. As she was eating a sandwich lunch at her desk, a call came through. 'Mr Guyler on the line for you,' said Meg.

Ah, thought Lindsey. But she immediately quelled the little surge of optimism. He might be ringing to warn her he was about to report her to Ollie.

But no. There was appeasement in his voice. 'Miss Abercrombie . . . Lindsey . . . I've been thinking over some of the things you said on Saturday.'

'Yes?'

'I'd like to be . . . I don't know . . . better informed . . . You took me so much by surprise that I didn't take in a lot of what you said.' And that was the simple truth, because when he tried to bring it to mind, it whirled around him like a dust-devil.

'I understand.'

'Could we meet?'

'Of course. Let me look at my engagements. There's a space tomorrow morning.'

'Not at the office! I was thinking more of . . . you know . . . a drink and a chat.'

'I see. Where did you have in mind?'

'Somewhere quiet . . . A bit off the main drag, if you know what I mean.'

Somewhere that Shula won't think of going, Lindsey amended inwardly. 'How about the Grange Wharf?' It was the former coaching inn to which she'd taken Edie, out along by the canals.

'Where's that? Oh, never mind, I'll look it up. Could you make it this evening?'

'Well, that's a bit—'

'I've got a committee thing in the city this afternoon, it would make it easier for me if it could be this evening. I could come straight on from that.'

'All right. What time?'

'Let's see, committee'll be over around four thirty, five. Say five thirty?'

'In the bar of the Grange Wharf at five thirty – okay.'

'Thank you, Lindsey.'

As she put down the phone Lindsey reflected that his manner had betrayed him. He was meeting her without telling his wife. Well, that was all right. She'd have preferred it if Billy Guyler had had the courage to speak to Shula, but any advance was better than none.

She was a little late at the rendezvous. Billy was sitting on a bar stool fidgeting with a glass that might contain a gin and it. He was in informal clothes, a loose windcheater hiding the slight bulge at stomach level. She noticed that he had the beginnings of a double chin too. But his thinning hair was expensively barbered and smelled of some expensive dressing. He liked to look well turned out, although he didn't try to compete with the glamour of his wife.

212

He stood to greet Lindsey without offering his hand. 'Let's take that corner over there,' he said. 'What'll you have?'

She asked for Dubonnet then followed him to the table. The place was almost empty, too early for the shopping visitors to be back from the malls. All the same, Billy spoke in very low tones.

'I'd like to know a bit more about what you said,' he began, leaning towards her over the table. 'This business about taking exams – did you really mean it?'

'Yes, of course. Edie is aiming at taking a university course called "3D Art" – I'm not sure what it is, and to tell the truth Edie only got to know about it once she'd started at Chepperton.'

This was something he knew a little about. 'It's a contemporary idea, suitable for . . . well, staging things in three dimensions. Would be useful in theatre design, puppetry, other things – I don't keep up with it as much as I ought to, I've gone right away from the design side of the firm.' He sipped. 'What makes her want to do that?'

'She saw some stuff my mother was doing—'

'Your *mother*?' His voice rose in astonishment. He set down his glass with a thump. 'She's met your *mother*?'

'Yes, why not?' she said, although there had been all sorts of reasons why not, before she and Edie actually set off for Ellenham. But this wasn't the time or place to go into that.

'But . . . but . . .'

'She came home with me for Christmas. I felt I had to ask her otherwise she'd have been all on her own.' She eyed him as she told him this, wondering if she was pitching it with too much pathos. 'My mother does the costumes for the local amateur dramatics. Edie gave her a hand. She proved to have quite a talent for it.'

'And that's why she . . . ?'

'I imagine so. And my mother wrote a letter of recommendation to the college which helped get her accepted at short notice.'

'A letter of recommendation . . .' Billy was utterly staggered. Lindsey's mother – a total stranger – had taken the

213

trouble to come to the aid of Edie Maybury, whom they'd been so glad to get rid of.

'Yes. My mother thinks highly of her.'

'Of that dreadful girl?'

'Mr Guyler, stop saying that. She's changed a lot – the all-black mind set is gone, so is the "hit first" outlook. She's not an ordinary girl, I'll give you that, but she's not any more dreadful than a lot of the kids I hear about from clients.'

'But she's . . . she's always up in arms about something.'

'These days she's too busy to be in an argument with everybody and besides, she can't afford to risk losing her job.'

'Yes, her job. Is it really true she's working nights at a supermarket?' The very idea made him shudder. Billy had never much cared for hard work and though he figured on the pay roll of Gylah Cosmetics as an executive, most of his tasks were social. The mere thought of working all night was anathema.

'That great big one, the Brunswick, open twenty-four hours, you know it?'

He shook his head. 'Never been there.' He paused, seeking the words for his question. 'That must be very hard?' he ventured.

'Oh, very. There's not a *lot* of business at two in the morning, she tells me, but all the same she has to be awake, and she has things to enter into the overnight stock computer. It seems when the management change prices, put in bargain offers, that sort of thing – some of that gets done in the middle of the night.'

'It sounds awful.'

'It's nothing I would like to do,' Lindsey agreed. 'But she has to be free for classes in the daytime.'

'And she's been doing this how long?'

'Since January.'

'And you said . . . did you say . . . that you're paying for her tuition?' This was the worst part. Someone had taken over what perhaps should have been done by the Guylers. After all, it was only money: they could have done it without in any way committing themselves to a close relationship.

'I paid for the current term. It was all done in a bit of a rush,

214

and I didn't want anything to . . . to delay things, to put her off. But I can't finance the whole two years. I'm going to look into the possibility of an educational grant from a charity—'

'No, no!' He startled himself by how much that offended him.

'Why not? If you're afraid something might come out about your trouble with her, don't worry – grants like that are confidential.'

He was silent a while then looked at her rather miserably. 'You don't think much of me, do you?' he said.

'What makes you say that?'

'You thought I was just against the charity thing because something might come out about us – the Guylers.'

'Was I wrong?' she countered.

'I was thinking . . . feeling . . . that she ought not to have to go to a charity.'

Lindsey drew in a slow, silent breath. He was becoming involved, wanting to have some influence over what happened in Edie's life. It was what she had hoped for the minute she heard his voice on the telephone.

'There doesn't seem to be much alternative,' she pointed out. 'If we applied for a government loan, I think some difficult questions might arise over birth certificates and so forth.'

Billy Guyler hesitated. 'What sort of money are we talking about?' he asked.

Aha. 'To cover tuition fees for the summer term and leave a decent margin for books and clothes – about two thousand pounds.'

'But what about food, lodgings? Do her wages at the hypermarket cover that?'

This was the time for the knock-out blow. 'To put you completely in the picture, Mr Guyler,' she said matter-of-factly, 'she's living with me.'

He sat back in the upholstered banquette in utter consternation. Slowly he coloured up until he felt hot with what might have been shame.

'Oh,' he gasped. 'Oh. You took her in? You looked after her when we . . . when we . . .'

She decided to let that lie. He might have been going to say,

215

'When we had rejected her.' That was in fact the truth, but why upset him further?

She went back to the financial point, to give him time to recover. 'Her wages are a source of pride to her. She's doing a lot better than she did in Hobston. But she's still buying her clothes in charity shops, and—'

'No, no,' he interrupted, 'this is wrong, I can't have this!' He felt strangely perturbed, he felt tears in his eyes.

She waited. She longed to ask, 'So what are you going to do about it?' But it had to come from him. He must never be able to say that she had forced his hand.

'I could make some money available,' he said at last.

'You could?'

'You know you said . . . on Saturday . . . that we could have done something, made some financial gesture.'

'I remember saying something to that effect, yes.'

'Well, I could supply – it couldn't be two thousand in a lump sum because . . . because . . .'

'Why not?'

'Because when we come to do our tax returns Shula would see it on the bank statement.'

Lindsey suppressed a sigh, but understood what he meant. 'Your wife isn't to know,' she said.

'It would be better not.'

'You didn't tell her about our talk on Saturday?'

'No – really – Lindsey, you've got to understand, she can't bear to have the girl mentioned. I *couldn't* do it.' It was the simple truth. He couldn't do that to Shula.

Since he first met Shula, she had always been the one in command. Seeing how the advent of Edie Maybury had brought her low had been a shock to him. It left him without a leader, without someone to revere and admire. However, in the last couple of months something like the former Shula Guyler had emerged. She seemed strong and capable again. All the same, he didn't want to put her to the test.

He became aware that Lindsey was waiting for him to go on. 'I couldn't get it out of my mind, what you said,' he resumed, 'so I thought I'd . . . I mean, it seems so wrong. We've got money, and she needs money, poor kid, but Shula . . . Well,

216

it's easier if I provide it sort of bit by bit, Lindsey. Would that be all right?'

'Anything you can do, we'd appreciate.'

'I thought I could wangle a weekly allowance – I could hide it in among the business expenses – you know I do a bit of public relations, liaise with some of the people at the top—' He broke off. 'I sound like a wimp, don't I?'

She put out a hand across the table. He hesitated then took it. 'Mr Guyler, I admit I think it would be better if your wife knew all about it. But you live in that marriage, I don't. So all I'm thinking is that you're being kind, and I appreciate it.'

'Don't tell Edie about the money!' he said in a sudden panic. 'Don't tell her it's from me!'

'But why not? It would mean a lot to her.'

'No, no, please, you must promise! It might raise false hopes, she might try to get in touch. Then we'd have all that old agony again. No, don't tell her the money comes from me.'

'All right.'

'It's going to have to be in cash. I'll post it to you at your office. Let's say I get it at the cash machine at the golf club – I practically always play either on Saturday or Sunday, I'll drop it in the post box there, it should reach you by Monday, Tuesday at the latest.'

'Thank you.'

He got up. 'I don't think I deserve any thanks,' he said with a weary shake of the head. 'But it's the best I can do, Lindsey. And I want you to know that . . . that I appreciate . . . I feel you've behaved with amazing generosity . . . a sense of responsibility that we should . . . well . . . never mind, that's all past now.' He produced a faint smile and a nod of farewell, and then he was gone.

217

Seventeen

It was just after midnight. The public address system was sending out a cheery medley of show tunes over the aisles where few shoppers now moved. Edie had just come back from her meal break. At checkout four business was slow, so she took out her book surreptitiously to read. It was *Silas Marner*, borrowed from Lindsey's shelves, and she was finding it hard going.

She became aware that she was being observed. She looked up and turned her head towards the stacks. A figure disappeared round a corner. She shrugged and returned to her book. Then she felt the gaze on the back of her neck. She turned. Just the suggestion of a male-sized foot, whisking away behind the special offer of Windward Islands bananas.

Some pervert, she thought to herself. Not uncommon. She glanced up now and again but he was nowhere in sight. Unless that was him, peeking out from behind the tinned goods. Now he seemed to be spying on Nell at checkout ten, the mid-point of the unattended row.

She turned back to page one-one-nine. This George Eliot was a woman, so Lindsey said. Some funny notions she had, for a fact. Here was this old guy, takes on a kiddie who turns up out of nowhere. Oh yes, a likely tale. Still, you had to admit, you wanted to know what happened.

Billy Guyler went through the checkout with a box of chocolate mints to account for his presence. He looked at the girl – smallish, dark, wearing a name badge which said Nell on her brown and orange checked jacket. He glanced at the other girl but her head was bent over something. Taller-looking than Nell, wispy toffee-coloured hair held back not very tidily in a scrunch, name badge indecipherable at this distance.

Taking his change, he made for the doors. There he paused to look back. He was wondering whether he could return to look at the other girl's badge when a middle-aged man in a security firm's peaked cap strolled towards him. Billy fished out his car keys, to show he was on his way to the parking lot. The security man waited until he'd gone out of the swing doors, clearly on guard against dodgy customers. And quite right too.

Billy had come into the store on impulse. He was on his way home from an evening with some pals at the bridge club when almost without his being aware of it the car had turned right onto the exit for the hypermarket. Now as he drove away he was asking himself, 'Was that Edie, that girl on checkout four?'

If so, Lindsey Abercrombie hadn't underestimated the change in her. But it might have been someone quite different. There must be more than two girls on duty, and hadn't he been told that Edie did something with the stock computer? That must be behind the scenes, in the offices. The girl in the checkout could have been anyone.

Well, he hadn't wasted much except one pound fifty on a box of mints, which he had thrown in the wastebin in the car park. Shula would think he'd lost his senses if he came home with the offering of a box of supermarket mints.

Had he lost his senses? What on earth was he doing, playing hide and seek among the rows of groceries at midnight in a hypermarket? All just to get a glimpse of Edie Maybury, the girl he'd been so tremendously glad to see the back of.

'I only want to see justice done,' he said to himself. 'Perhaps we treated her badly, blaming her for the things done by that dreadful young man.'

He drove home, musing about past events, wondering if he and Shula should have acted differently with Edie. He might have been more independent in his judgement, perhaps. But Shula . . . After all, it was Shula who had felt it most profoundly. Nights without sleep, appetite gone, her usual self-assurance turned into a defence that was almost manic, so that one hardly dared say, 'It's a nice day' until she'd already passed judgement on it. She *couldn't* be wrong, even on the slightest things.

Those had been dark, dark days. Christmas had been ruined. They'd gone to Morocco, to a splendid hotel with a fitness club, and there Shula had taken the complete make-over course. Wrapped in seaweed, or using the exercise bike, or 'relaxing' with pads on her eyes – eight days of non-communication. He'd taken refuge on the golf course. He realised now that he should have tried to talk to her.

Well, he had talked to her – in the end. When they were home again. Over dinner one night she'd suddenly jumped up and run out. He'd found her in the morning room, sobbing. And that's when she'd told him she was going to close the whole business off for ever, never think of it again, give up all idea of ever finding Julie.

'I should have stopped years ago, Billy. I think it was an obsession. I just wouldn't accept the fact that I couldn't find her – I wouldn't believe what the police said years ago, that she was probably dead.'

'Ssh, darling. Ssh.' Arms around her, trying to comfort this Shula, so different from the one who ruled his world.

'So I've made up my mind. She's dead, and I must stop torturing myself with the hope of ever finding her.'

'Yes, love. You've been through enough.'

'And we'll never speak of it again, Billy. You'll forgive me for being so stubborn and silly, and I'll forgive myself for putting you through all that. That's how it'll be from now on.'

'All right, dear. Of course, whatever you say.'

'I'm making you a solemn promise, dear. From now on it's all over. We're going back to what we used to be, aren't we?'

'Yes, back to the good old days.'

'That's it, the good old days when we'd never heard of that dreadful girl.'

'Right.'

But the truth was, they *had* heard of that dreadful girl, and she'd turned their lives upside down. Shula had been put through hell on earth, so of course he must do everything he possibly could to protect her.

Yet here he was, coming away from what might have been a

too-close encounter with the girl – and actually regretting that he hadn't been able to make sure he'd seen Edie.

And wanting to try again.

'What's the matter with me?' He addressed this query to the reflection in the rear mirror, but got no response. All he knew was that he'd like to see the girl – he'd very much like to see her, just to ensure that what Lindsey Abercrombie said about her was true.

Changed. No longer black as the Maltese Falcon in her clothing and her outlook. That could have been her, that girl in the checkout. But it had been impossible to see the name badge, and he couldn't get back to the store during the night shift for quite some time. What excuse could he give to Shula for sallying forth at midnight? Their ways were rather set, they were inclined to be off to bed early on most nights.

The school, of course. In the daytime Edie attended classes at Chepperton College. It would be a lot easier to be in the neighbourhood of Chepperton College about lunchtime, to see the students coming out in search of hamburgers or pizza.

What was he thinking of? Why on earth should he be so mad keen to see this kid? No, no, he must put the whole idea out of his mind.

Having decided this, it was all the more extraordinary that a week later Billy Guyler was standing in the fitful March sunshine on the pavement opposite the large old house used for the college. If anyone should ask, he had a perfectly good reason to be loitering there: opposite the college was a photographic shop, in whose window he was studying the digital cameras while at the same time watching for the reflection of any students to appear from the building. They came out singly and in groups. It all happened faster than he'd expected. The girl he'd been trying to inspect in the supermarket didn't seem to be among them.

Wrong day? Or didn't she have a class that morning?

He strolled away to the cafe at the end of the road. He walked past, glancing in. A crowd of students just inside the door was forming a queue past the food display. He walked on, turned the corner, crossed the road, turned back, crossed again to the same pavement and walked past the cafe again.

And saw her.

She was sitting with two other girls about the same age, listening with a faint smile to something that was being said. They seemed to be sharing a meal, a large bowl of salad. It was clear they were good companions, perhaps even friends.

She seemed to belong there among them. They shared something more than their food – a sort of generic look, casual, comfortable, jeans and sweatshirts and jerseys.

The girl he thought of as Edie had fairish hair pulled back with a piece of black ribbon. Her hair had the look of being recently grown longer, and was not quite long enough for a ponytail. She was fresh-skinned, blue-eyed and wearing only a little lipstick. She was frowning now, shaking her head in disagreement, and he saw in the drawn brows something of the strong will he associated with his former enemy.

All at once he found he couldn't bear any more. He hurried off, retrieved his car from the car park and drove to the business appointment that had brought him into Birmingham today. In the parking area of the advertising firm, he drew up and switched off. Then he sat for a long time, staring through the windshield at nothing.

Well, now he could be reasonably sure that the tuition money he dispatched to Lindsey Abercrombie was being put to good use.

The money arrived regularly, usually on Tuesday morning in an envelope bearing the crest of the golf club and marked in large capitals, PERSONAL. The amount varied, but was seldom less than a hundred pounds. Once there was three hundred pounds with a note saying, 'Backed the winner in the US Masters'.

Lindsey had smiled over it, but had then been caught by a moment of anxiety. Was it difficult for Billy Guyler to find actual cash? Was he having to descend to more subterfuge? But then she made herself accept Billy's methods. As she'd said to him, he had to live inside his marriage with Ursula Guyler, and that couldn't be easy. Perhaps it was lucky for him he was a follower, happy enough to have his life arranged for him. Except for this, he had probably never in his life gone against his wife's wishes in any important matter.

Easter was approaching. Chepperton College would close for only the bank holiday Monday, but Lindsey wanted to go north for the weekend on Thursday evening. She had no qualms about leaving Edie alone at the flat. She had friends of her own now, or at least fellow students and a couple of women from the hypermarket with whom she shared meal breaks.

'I'll be fine,' Edie had assured Lindsey. 'And if you're worried I'll burn another saucepan, I promise to eat cold meals.'

In fact, Edie was rather looking forward to having the place to herself. She had a project for the art class which necessitated spreading eight sheets of the large A1 paper on the floor, and only the living room was big enough for that. Even in the living room she'd have to move the furniture about.

She was going to make a 3D representation of Hobston on market day. She'd done some sketches, giving them a childlike simplicity, very bright colours, an effect of wonderful things just beyond one's grasp. Too flighty, she warned herself. But what the hell – you had to try things, and after all it might work.

She was sitting at the checkout thinking about it and automatically passing bar codes across the reader when the customer spoke.

'Edie?'

'That's my name,' she responded with practised cheeriness, looking up.

Billy Guyler was gazing at her.

She gasped and half turned, almost as if to call for help. Then good sense returned. She said in a calm tone, 'Mr Guyler. What can I do for you?'

He was the last of a group of customers who had gone through the checkout in one of the little rushes that occurred in the store when the hospital or factory staff changed shifts. He had tacked himself on to the end of the queue with a bunch of flowers on which there was a special Easter offer. 'At least,' he told himself as he selected them, 'I can give them to Erika the housekeeper as an Easter gift.'

'Could we have a talk?' he asked.

'What about?'

'About . . . an apology for the way we behaved.'

She was too amazed to reply. In her mind she'd long ago written off the Guylers as people she ought never to have bothered. She'd even got to the point where she blamed herself a little. She should have seen that it was no go from the outset and simply backed away. But no, idiot that she was, she'd hung on because . . . well . . . never mind about that.

So here he was, Billy Guyler. Offering an apology?

She shook her head. 'Never mind,' she muttered. 'That's all finished.'

He stood dithering at the spot where the carrier bags hung. He'd always been a bit of a ditherer, she recalled.

'I'd feel better if you'd let me . . . explain a bit . . . that's if I can.'

'No, no, never mind,' she said.

The security guard came up. 'Problem?' he enquired.

'Not a bit, Terry. Everything's okay.'

'I was just having a word,' Billy said. 'About the flowers.'

'Yes, I was telling him there's a packet of preservative powder inside the wrapping. You put it in the vase, you know.'

'Oh, I see,' Billy said in a grateful tone. 'But will it harm the flowers?'

'Not a bit, sir. Helps to make them last longer.'

Terry wandered away, not in the least interested in the life-span of cut flowers. As soon as he was out of earshot Billy burst out, 'Please let me talk to you. It's been on my mind for weeks, and I'm finding it hard to live with.'

'Why should I care?' she almost said, but she caught it back, as she'd learned to do these past few months. She didn't rush into cruel speech these days, or at least not often. So after a minute's pause she said, 'I get a half hour meal break at eleven forty-five. There's a MacDonald's the other side of the furniture area – how about going there for a cup of coffee?'

'See you there,' he said, and hurried away before the security man got anxious again.

He put the flowers in his car, then paced the car park among the halogen lamps until his watch showed him it was time. He hurried inside again, found the restaurant, and hovered by its entrance on the main floor. Edie arrived only a few minutes later, this time without the store's staff jacket. He thought she looked nice in her blue denims and fawn jersey.

He was unaccustomed to such places. She urged him to a table, said, 'Milk? Sugar?' and was off before he could respond.

There was almost no one in the restaurant. The shift-changers had gone home to sleep, the next group hadn't arrived yet. He watched Edie chat to the staff at the counter, collect the tray, and walk towards him with a long-legged, graceful stride.

She handed him the plastic beaker and let a handful of cream cartons and sugar packets spill on the table as she sat down. 'Bit of a change from the Old North Star Hotel,' she remarked.

He didn't want to be reminded of it. That had been their first meeting and they'd made a hash of it.

'Shouldn't you be eating?' he enquired.

She shook her head. 'Can't get used to eating at this hour of the night. I leave something sort of simple ready to eat when I get home, and that helps get me off to sleep.'

'I don't know how you do it,' he said. 'Night work. Turning the world upside down.'

'You get used to it.' She unlidded her coffee and sipped. 'How did you know where to find me?'

'Lindsey told me.'

'Lindsey?'

He nodded, and to delay explanations he too tried his coffee. It was better than he expected. After a sip or two he ventured: 'Lindsey approached me over the financial aspect.'

'The financial aspect of what?'

'Your studies.'

Her brows came together in a frown. She gave a little shake of the head. 'How d'you mean?'

'Well, it's going to cost a bit, studying for GCSEs and going to university.'

225

'But Lindsey's going to get a grant from an educational charity.'

'But not until the beginning of the next school year.'

She thought about it. 'Lindsey's in money trouble?'

'Oh, not exactly. But she's feeling the strain a bit.'

'She never said.' There was protest, muted anger, in her words. He could hear an echo of the old Edie.

'No, instead she contacted me. I was very put out about it at first, but now I'm glad. I think we owe you something by way of amends for the way we treated you.' He had so much wanted to say that, to gain a little credit for daring to go against his wife.

'We? Who's we? You and Shula?'

He hesitated too long. She understood that 'we' didn't come into it, that it was only a manner of speech. 'Not Shula,' she said. She shrugged. After a moment she added, 'This is weird.'

'I'm sorry. I didn't mean to let you know any of this.' But of course he had. Why else was he here? 'It's been a while since Lindsey came to me, and at first I just wanted to see if what she told me was the truth. She said you'd changed—'

She shrugged. 'About time.'

'I've been to the shop before, you know, but I couldn't see your name tag. And then I went to the college, and there you were, the girl from the hypermarket, so I knew it had to be you – I mean, I knew you were Edie.' He shook his head. 'That should have been the end of it, really, I suppose. But I found I wanted to tell you . . . to explain if I could.'

'Explain why you disliked me?'

He sought for the words. 'We saw you as a bad lot, yet here you are, holding down a job, going to college, looking sort of . . . well . . . you're not what we thought you were. So I wanted to make some sort of amends for being so wrong.'

'Okay,' she said.

He stared. 'Okay?'

'What else do you want me to say?'

'I thought . . . I don't know.'

'Shula isn't offering this apology, is she? It's just you?'

He went scarlet. She studied him, feeling the first impulse

of pity. Poor guy, it must have taken all the courage he had, to go against that awesome woman. To go to all the trouble of finding her and now this face to face apology – not an easy thing. She wasn't sure she herself would have been up to it.

'Okay, you've done this on your own. That's all right, Shula's not the type to admit she's in the wrong. Know what I mean—' She broke off, smiling and shaking her head.

'What is it?' Billy asked, puzzled.

'My pals at college tell me not to say that. They say it's very un-cool. Probably they're right, I think I caught it off Ma Maybury.' She shrugged. 'But as I was saying, thank you for trying to sort it, and I don't hold any grudge against you.'

'Thank you.'

They sat in silence for a moment. The public address system was giving them 'Alexander's Ragtime Band'. Always light-hearted brisk music for the night shift. It was so totally out of keeping with their thoughts that it was almost painful.

'How are you getting on with your exam subjects?'

'Not too bad. Reading a lot of books I'd have thought were weird a few months ago, but you get the hang of them if you stick with them. The art thing is different. Lindsey's no help there. She can scarcely draw a straight line, and as for explaining what some of the terms mean . . .'

'She . . . er . . . she told me you were living with her.'

'Yeah. A really nice place. I pay her out of my wages, you know, and I get stuff here at staff discount so I take that home to help the budget.' She paused. 'I sort of didn't quite realise . . .'

'What?'

'That she was hard pressed.' She nodded to herself. 'True, enough, she handed me a cheque to pay the college fees . . . And the text books – you've no idea how that mounts up.' She blushed faintly. 'I should have seen it. Heavens above, I know what it's like to be hard up, I grew up with it.'

Billy reached out to pat her hand which was lying by her coffee beaker.

'But you see,' she went on, trying to find an excuse for herself, 'the way she lives . . . It's so different to what I've been used to . . . It just didn't occur to me she was hurting for money.'

Billy summoned his courage. 'If ever you're in need of cash – you know, for books, or something to wear . . .'

She was drawing back in negation. 'It would put you in trouble with Shula.'

'Well . . .' Something almost like boyish glee flashed across his features. 'What she doesn't know she won't grieve over.'

Edie refused to join his mood. 'You're doing enough already, this business with Lindsey. I think even that could land you in trouble, but—'

'No, no, I've worked out a scheme, it's no problem, and honestly, Edie, if you ever need anything . . .' He fished in his pocket for a pen. 'I'll give you my cellphone number. Any time you're in a fix, just give me a buzz.'

'And you'll do what? Rush up with your cheque book?'

Her tone had sharpened, and his enthusiasm vanished at once. He looked crestfallen. And Edie was ashamed. Poor chap. A wife he loved, but couldn't match in strength of will. A desire to do something he felt to be good and generous, but she was thwarting him.

She took the hand he had stretched out to pat hers. 'I'm sorry,' she said.

'No, I'm the one that's sorry.'

'It's just that I don't like being your guilty secret.'

'No, I understand.'

'Tell you what. I won't take the phone number but mebbe you'd like to ring me some time. You've got Lindsey's home number? You'd probably have to leave a message 'cos the pair of us are seldom in the place, know what I— But that's okay.'

He hesitated. 'What would I be . . . ringing for?'

'Might meet now and again, eh? Stand me a lunch somewhere, cup of coffee if you're going to be here shopping some night?'

She'd had no idea it would mean so much to him. He seemed suffused with pleasure. 'That would be really nice,' he said breathlessly. 'That would be lovely.'

'Okay. Now I gotta go, I only get half an hour. Bye now!'

With a brief pressure on his hand she was gone. He turned

in his chair to watch her. He was prey to a surge of conflicting emotions.

If only . . .

If only she had looked like that when they'd first seen her, they would have accepted her. If only they hadn't been so prejudiced against her by her manners, her clothes, her outlook, if only they had given her the chance to change.

If only she had never been taken from them, she would have been a daughter to be proud of. If only he dared to speak to Shula about her, she could be their daughter now.

He realised he was thinking about her as if she were Julie. But Shula had said Julie was dead, part of an obsession of which she was now ashamed.

Sighing, he rose to his feet to go home. To go home and say nothing.

Edie had plenty of time to go over that unexpected tête-à-tête in her mind. Trade in the store was slack and *Silas Marner* failed to hold her attention.

Making amends, he'd called it. And he'd gone to a lot of trouble, first of all making an agreement with Lindsey about money and then coming in person to find her.

She had the feeling he sort of approved of her now. She looked in her handbag for her compact and surveyed herself in the little mirror. 'There's been a change in you,' she sang to herself. Nothing very much to look at now, to tell the truth. The old Edie had a lot more character in her all-black get up and her gruesome war paint, but this one was a lot more comfortable to live with. She looked back now and realised she'd never have been accepted at Chepperton College if she'd turned up in that gear for the interview.

Nor would daddums have come anywhere near her.

She brought herself up short with that sarcastic thought. She was assuming that Billy Guyler was her father.

Well, she'd always thought so. She'd always been sure in her own mind that Billy was her father and Shula her mother. No matter how they angered her and up-staged her and rejected her, she'd always been sure of the truth – they were her parents.

But she'd put them out of her mind. She'd put old Ma Maybury out of her mind, too, determined to make a better life than anything ever offered by that volatile woman. It had been harder to erect barriers against the Guylers because they were a sort of dream family to her – rich, elegant, successful, the opposite of the pseudo Mrs Maybury in every way.

Well, okay. She was never going to make it with both of the Guylers. But Billy was nice. Billy might never be able to take over the role of . . . what was that phrase Lindsey had used the other day? Paterfamilias, something of the sort. It seemed to mean some grand male figure. Billy was never going to be *that*. But he was kind, he was caring, it would be nice to see him now and then. And if, in her own private thoughts, she sometimes called him . . . what? Dad? Daddy? Papa?

Impossible. He would always be Billy to her. She grinned to herself and put away her mirror to deal with the approaching knot of customers. As she began to pass their purchases over the reader, she was thinking to herself, 'I'd better tell Lindsey about this.'

Lindsey didn't know whether to be pleased or worried at the news. 'But you can't have anything against me seeing him now and again, Lindsey,' Edie protested.

'Not at all. It's just keeping it a secret that bothers me.'

'Well, me too, to tell the truth. Poor guy, he gets so embarrassed when he talks about Shula . . .'

'Let's just see how it goes, shall we?' Lindsey had good reason for this injunction. Keith had been on the phone only the previous evening, with some news.

'You remember I told you I'd like to do some investigating into the woman who took on the identity of Mary Lois Maybury?' he asked.

'I remember. And I think I asked you to leave well enough alone.'

He gave a chuckle. 'That was then, this is now. You've got the kid staying with you and turning from a sow's ear into a silk purse.'

'A winsome phrase.'

'I have a turn for a good phrase. Don't forget, I'm a newsman. Do you want to hear what I've found out?'

'I don't believe there's any way I could stop you from telling me. You want to boast, I can hear it in your voice.'

'I think I've got enough evidence to build up a good case.'

'A good case of what?'

'You're not taking me seriously. For that, I'm not going to tell you.'

'Oh, go on, Keith. I was only teasing.'

'It'll wait till I see you,' he said.

And he proved adamant. But it was only one more day to wait, for she would be in Cartfield and in his arms tomorrow evening.

Eighteen

First things first. Lovemaking before lectures. It wasn't until the morning of Friday that Lindsey remembered there was a narrative of some kind about Edie. Over breakfast, looking out over the river from the window of Keith's narrow cottage, she at last enquired, 'Now what's all this about "a good case" in the Guyler thing?'

'Ah.' Keith spread honey on his toast, giving it his full attention, so that she tapped her coffee cup with her spoon to make him look at her. 'So you really want to know?' he said with feigned indifference.

'I admit it, the suspense is killing me.'

'It'll take a while to set it all out. Let me put the kettle on for fresh supplies of coffee because we may need it.' He turned in his chair, reached out a long arm, and flicked the kettle's switch. The kitchen was so small he could practically do the washing up without moving from the table.

'Best Beloved, as Kipling used to say to his listener, this epic tale begins with a woman called Betty Trenton. At the time of the accident that killed Mary Lois Maybury and her baby, she lived in Cartfield – or at least, in a mobile home on the outskirts.'

'A traveller?' asked Lindsey.

'Well, those who knew her say she was a bit of a hippie. Her livelihood was in making handicraft things – wreaths of dried flowers, pot-pourri in little willow baskets, that sort of thing. That's how I tracked her down, I asked around for someone who did that sort of thing and it turned out that from time to time she'd hire a stall in the open-air market, or take a pitch at a car boot sale. I got onto her through the market office in Cartfield.'

232

'I don't remember telling you that was how she made her living?'

'Simpleton,' he chided, with the sudden grin that she found so engaging. 'That was in the newspapers when Edie and her boyfriend sold her story to the *Globe*. I looked up the files and made lots of notes before I even started to look for her.'

'And you started in Cartfield,' Lindsey ventured, 'because you thought she must have been there, to know about the accident that killed Mrs Maybury and the baby.'

'Right. Well, once I got a name for this wreath-maker, I tracked her back a bit. She was in and around Lancashire, Yorkshire and parts north for quite a few years before and after she came to Cartfield. She often moved with a group of others but she wasn't a Romany or a traveller, she joined them and left them as she felt inclined. Her main stopping places were market towns.'

'But this must have been twenty years ago. You mean to say you still found her tracks?'

'There are quite a few people who remember her, and not many speak well of her, I'm sorry to say.' He shook his head as he considered some of the opinions he'd heard.

'That's sad,' Lindsey murmured. 'And this is the woman who stole little Julie?'

'I think it is.'

'But just finding out where she'd been, what she did—'

'Best Beloved, listen patiently. I told you it would take some time to tell. This Betty Trenton had a boyfriend, a soldier called Louie or Lew – something like that. I'd take a bet that she met him while he was stationed at Catterick. Some of the old ladies I spoke to made haughty remarks about her and said she'd had quite a few boyfriends, but it appears Louie was the love of her life. They seemed to meet mostly in pubs, but he stayed with her when he got a weekend pass.'

'Stayed where?'

'At that time she had a place near Barnard's Castle. Anyhow, Louie seemed quite happy to have a home to go to off-barracks and she was boasting to her friends – well, her acquaintances, because she doesn't seem to have had any real friends . . .' He paused, looking back at the picture of this rootless, unhappy woman from so long ago.

'She was boasting?' Lindsey prompted.

'That they were going to be married.' He got up, went out of the kitchen, and came back in a few moments with a thick notebook. After glancing through it he stopped at a page and read, 'Mrs Hainey says Betty went on and on about getting married and settling down. Says she never believed a word of it. Miss Biggs, post office, states Louie had "a whole harem of other women".' He looked up at Lindsey. 'From this you'll gather he was a handsome chap, and I think he was several years younger than Betty. And alas, most people say that Betty wasn't particularly good-looking and certainly lacked charm.'

'What you're going to say is that he ditched her.' Lindsey was trying to get the feel of these events of the past. In her work, she'd often come across situations like this – an older woman determined to entrap a younger man.

'Not exactly. He got posted overseas to one of those places in the Middle East – Dubai or somewhere like that. Everybody I spoke to says that at first he never had the slightest intention of coming back to the flat he was sharing with Betty. But Betty refused to accept that. She told everybody that he'd come back because he'd promised to marry her.'

'Promised?'

'Nobody believed that either, but then she produced chapter and verse – she'd found out she was three months pregnant just as he was being flown abroad, he'd promised to do the decent thing, and she was moving to a place a few miles off where she'd been promised a council flat because she was expecting a baby. When his three-year stint overseas ended, they'd settle down together.'

'But the hospital report – after her death—'

'Wait, you'll find out. She showed her friends one or two letters Louie had sent, talking about getting out of the army and finding a job – I think he may have been trained in engineering, people said he talked about opening a repair shop of some kind.'

'How do you get these folk to tell you these things?' she marvelled.

'Have you forgotten? I'm an award-winning journalist! Anyhow, she moved to this place in Yorkshire but didn't get a council flat. She had a share of a little house in a town called Kingslowry. She stayed put there, and once again it was, "Louie will marry me when he gets home", and then in fact, Louie *is* coming home.'

He stopped, looking at Lindsey with an expectant gaze. 'What?' she asked.

'Louie is coming home and expecting to see his little daughter, now aged two and a half.' He waited, watching her.

Lindsey's mind seemed to be up against a blank wall. She sought about for the response he seemed to expect. 'I don't understand,' she said at last.

'Betty Trenton didn't have a baby two and a half years old. She never applied for a council flat in Kingslowry on grounds of her pregnancy. She never attended any pre-natal clinics and I can't find any notification of her ever being delivered of a child.' He paused, and added sadly, 'I think the whole thing was a fantasy, a ploy to keep Louie tied to her.'

'But she – she must have *known* it wouldn't – I mean, when he came home, what was she going to say?'

'Who knows?' Keith sighed. 'Perhaps she meant to kill off the imaginary kid before he got back. Edie, she'd named her – and I suppose she got snaps of other folk's kids to send him, it wouldn't be difficult, would it? At a pub perhaps – kids left out in the garden or the playground – mothers and fathers taking pix, she perhaps offers to take a snap with both parents and their baby, then says, "Take one of me". There she is, with somebody else's baby. She sends it to Louie, "This is our little Edie on the baby swings in the park."'

'It's . . . terribly depressing, Keith.' She found a lump rising in her throat.

'It gets sadder. Louie's being flown home a bit early after getting some virus or something, the gossips I spoke to said unkind things about the ailment which may or not have been true – in other words they thought he'd caught something from a lady of pleasure.'

'Good grief they really didn't like him much, did they?'

'Seems not. Well, he's expecting to see his daughter, Betty's left it too late to write to him about how poor little Edie got pneumonia and died. So what does she do?'

Lindsey drew in a slow breath. 'She goes to a holiday beach and steals Julie Guyler.'

'More or less the right age, approximately like the descriptions she's been sending him and if she doesn't quite match any photographs, well . . . kids change so much when they're so small, don't they?'

'But how did she account for the non-existence of the child before Louie came home? She must have had neighbours and friends – acquaintances—'

'One elderly lady who's a regular in the Golden Crown at Kinslowry told me about it. She remembered it well, it all seemed so romantic at first. Apparently, Betty went to her cousin's and brought the babby home. Edie had been living with the cousin because the cousin – she even remembered the cousin's name, Josie – "Josie was married and had two kiddies of her own so it was better for the little girl to be with her." You remember, Betty Trenton travelled about to markets and car boot sales. Not fair on a little girl, to be dragged about the country like that, now was it? Much better to have a stable family life with cousin Josie.'

'You make it all so real, Keith!'

'It *was* real, it happened. The poor crazy woman needed a baby to show to Louie so she went out and stole one. On precisely the date when Julie Guyler disappeared, Betty Trenton turned up in Kingslowry with a baby girl nobody had ever seen before. But you see, no one ever suspected the kid wasn't Betty's because there was all this fairy tale she'd been spinning to herself and everybody else for two or three years – about how Louie was coming home and opening a shop and they were going to be married and all that. Besides, the kiddie looked as if it belonged to Betty – dressed in hand-me-down type clothes she probably bought at a car boot sale – she got rid of the frilly little sunsuit Julie was wearing.'

Lindsey was trying to keep track of the probabilities. 'Keith, there's no word of anybody called Louie in the story Edie tells of her life.'

'No, it all fell apart.' He shook his head. 'Perhaps when

236

you're stuck miles from home in the Middle East, the idea of going back to a loving wife and a little girl might seem great. But I imagine Louie had no real longing for domesticity, and the kid probably cried a lot – wouldn't you, if you were in a strange place with people you didn't know and no lovely bedroom of your own and no gentle nanny to comfort you in the night? Poor little Julie, she must have been breaking her heart. And driving a wedge between Betty and Louie. So Louie took off.'

'Dear God,' breathed Lindsey.

'People I talked to say Betty Trenton nearly lost her mind.' He turned over a few pages of his scribbled notes. 'The doctor put her on sedatives. The woman who shared the house with her, in the downstairs flat, she more or less looked after baby Edie for five or six weeks. Then Betty seemed to pull herself together a bit, joined a group of travellers who were going to Appleby for the horse trading, and that was the last they saw of her in Kingslowry.'

She sat in silence. After a long moment she said, 'We're lucky something didn't happen to Edie.'

'There was a danger, perhaps,' he conceded. 'But Betty went away with a group of people. It's not so easy to do anything bad, or walk away from your kid, when you've got twenty or thirty others around. Safety in numbers – it may have been Edie's salvation.'

Lindsey was hugging her arms around herself as if she were chilled to the bone. 'It's ghastly,' she whispered. 'It's appalling. And of course now we understand why Betty never could be a loving mother to her. Edie was a continual reminder of how she'd lost Louie, wasn't she?'

'And probably a big part of the reason why Louie walked out. I imagine there were many times when Betty thought about abandoning her somewhere on her travels. But then a couple of years later, when Edie gets to school age, they end up in digs somewhere where there's just enough interest from the neighbours to make it important to send her to school. So she remembers the fatal accident to Mary Lois Maybury and the baby Edie, and that's when she arranges for the birth certificates. They adopt those identities. After that, I suppose

237

it seemed not such a bad idea to Betty to keep those names and stick together – with the phoney birth certificates and so forth, she can apply for child benefit, that sort of thing.'

Lindsey had no argument against his assessment of Betty Trenton's mind. She was silent, and he left her to her thoughts. Then she said, 'Wait a bit. There's a flaw in this. It could never have worked the way you're suggesting, because Julie was the wrong age. Louie would have noticed.'

'You mean she was a year older than the baby Betty was supposed to have had.'

'Exactly. According to your timescale, she told Louie she was three months pregnant, so the baby should have been born six months or so into his stint in Dubai. He did a three-year tour?'

'Most of it. He got sent home a bit early to recuperate. Hence the sudden need for a baby daughter.'

'So Edie should have been two and a half years old. But when Julie Guyler was snatched, she was nearly three and half.'

'Lindsey darling,' Keith said, shaking his head at her. 'This is a young man of about twenty-six, who's lived most of his life in military barracks. Show him a toddler in a frilly party dress – is he going to say, "That child is more than two and a half"?'

'We-ell . . .'

'No, of course he isn't. And bear in mind this is a child suffering from severe shock – frightened, bewildered, probably in tears most of the time. I think she was nothing like the little angel he'd been picturing so he'd soon lose any desire to get close to her.'

'That's true.' She gave it more consideration. 'But Betty could never have hoped to get away with it if Louie *had* married her. She had no birth certificate for the baby at first – even when she was on her own with Edie, the time came when she had to produce one and that would have happened just the same if Louie was on the scene.'

'I don't think she ever looked that far ahead, Lindsey. That was one of the things people said about her – she was impulsive, she made spur of the moment decisions, often quite

238

rash. I think she was like Scarlett O'Hara – what was it she said? "I'll leave that till tomorrow."'

'"I'll think about that tomorrow."'

'There you are.'

Lindsey got up and began to clear away the breakfast things. Keith sat watching her with sympathetic amusement as she tried to find the cupboard for the bread crock, the right shelf for the honey jar. But by and by he saw how troubled she was. He went and put his arms around her from behind. She turned to him, hiding her face against his shirt front.

'It's just so awful . . .'

'I know.'

'I can't seem to get my head round it.'

'I understand.'

'I knew of course that Edie wasn't Mrs Maybury's child – the hospital report and so forth – I knew that Edie was probably the little girl stolen from the Guylers – but that was – I don't know – academic knowledge . . .'

'Perhaps I shouldn't have told you.'

'No, it's right that I should know. Edie sort of dragged me into her life, after she split up with Graham Walker. I think I've got to know things like this if I'm to help her. But after what you've told me it just seems so – so . . .'

To her own dismay she began to cry. Keith held her closer, murmuring words of comfort. She tried to stop but somehow the tears insisted on trickling down her cheeks.

When at last she recovered, she summoned a shaky laugh. 'I'm sorry, I've made your shirt front all wet.'

'Plenty of dry shirts upstairs, love.'

'Let's go out. I feel the need for some fresh air to blow the misery out of my head.'

'You've taken it too much to heart, Lindsey.'

She remembered that Andrew Gilmore had accused her of getting emotionally involved. It appeared to be true. She said, 'The thing is, you made me see it from Edie's point of view. I'd never been able to think of her as a *victim* before – she's so pugnacious, so ready for a fight. But that's *now*. When she was a three-year-old . . .' And she began to cry again.

Eventually they went out for the remedial fresh air. They

walked along the river bank, admiring the small clumps of daffodils that had come out to greet this cold Easter.

As if she were continuing a conversation already under way, Lindsey said: 'Often when I read about cases like that – child abduction – I feel some sympathy with the abductor. She's often someone who's recently lost a child of her own, isn't she, and you say to yourself, "Poor thing, she's not really responsible for what she's done." But not this.'

'No, Betty Trenton did it to help with a trick she was trying to play on the man she wanted to marry.'

'It's just so callous!'

'Totally self-engrossed. Never a thought of what it would mean to the child, to the parents.'

'I wonder she didn't go for the reward. After Louie left them, I mean.'

'That puzzled me for a while. But if you think it over . . . she was in an acute depression when Louie disappeared out of her life. She probably couldn't think about anything practical, like money. And then when she came to herself a little, she wanted to get away from Kingslowry, with its memories of Louie and the misguided hopes of a wedding. So she sets off with her group of travellers or whoever they were. If she thinks about the reward, it's probably a bit scary.'

'You mean because the police would be involved? I'd imagine the Guylers would have promised not to call them in.'

'But Lindsey,' he countered, 'the Guylers had been in the public eye. If they got their little girl back, *somebody* was sure to notice and sell the story to the press. So the police would be sure to know sooner or later.'

'I hadn't thought of that,' Lindsey acknowledged. It hadn't occurred to her that people sold items of personal news to the press. 'Yes, I expect Betty Trenton didn't want to take a chance. And then you know, Keith, as time went by, perhaps she found she'd got used to having the poor little soul around. Perhaps little Julie would be calling her mummy. Edie did say that sometimes Ma Maybury was nice to her.'

Keith gave her a little hug round the shoulders. 'Softie,' he whispered into her hair.

The subject kept recurring throughout her stay in Cartfield.

240

When she was packing for the return to Birmingham on Monday afternoon, Keith watched for a while in silence. Then he enquired, 'What do you want to do with the information I collected? I've got it on tape, and I've typed up a brief summary if you want it.'

'I've been thinking about that. You know, darling, almost none of it would stand up in a court of law. It's hearsay, mostly.'

'Right. But it was never intended for a court of law. I just wanted to track back and find out who Mary Lois Maybury really was. I think I've done that, although not up to the standards of a courtroom.'

'In my heart I'm convinced that Betty Trenton is the woman who called herself Mary Maybury and was Edie's so-called mother.'

'Yes.'

'And I'm convinced that the so-called Mrs Maybury took Julie Guyler from her parents and called her Edie.'

'I agree.'

'I always have been convinced that Edie is the Guylers' child. If you look at Edie now, there are things that remind you of Ursula Guyler. Her eyes and her skin colouring, and the way she walks.'

'I only got a glimpse of her at your mother's, and of course only know Ursula Guyler from newspaper photographs. I'm prepared to respect your views on any family resemblance. But on other grounds, I'd say that Edie is almost certainly Julie Guyler. The way the dates coincide – the kidnapping and the appearance of the little girl at Betty Trenton's house in Kingslowry . . .'

'Yes.'

'So what are you going to do?'

Lindsey sat down on the bed beside her overnight bag. 'One of my problems is that the Guylers are my clients. They never hired me to prove that Edie is their daughter. On the contrary, Shula would prefer me to prove the opposite.'

'You're not going to tell them?'

'I don't know. Shula may be dead set against it, but Billy . . . I think Billy would want to know.' She explained how she had contacted Billy in hopes of getting him to talk to his wife about financial help. 'He was too scared even to think of it! But he felt he ought to do something for Edie, and since then he's provided an income.'

'Well, that's encouraging.'

'And he actually made contact with her a couple of days ago.'

'You didn't tell me that.'

'Keith, I had no idea you were going to find this whole life story about Betty Trenton. And since you told me I've been trying to come to terms with it and work out what it means for Edie. And,' she ended with a sigh, 'I think it's going to mean very little.'

'But I thought you just said that Billy—'

'Billy's suffering from pangs of conscience. I think he may be feeling that perhaps he *is* Edie's father. But facing up to Shula with that sort of thing is quite another matter. And as for going myself to Shula with this information – I think she'd have me thrown out the minute I mentioned Edie's name.'

'So that's Mr and Mrs Guyler ruled out. What about Edie? Are you going to tell her?'

She nodded. 'I think I must. This is her life we've been talking about – how it was shaped, why it was changed. She deserves to know. But she won't do anything with the information.'

'Why not?' he enquired, surprised.

'Because she's perfectly well aware that Shula won't want to hear any of it.'

'But she could tell Billy.'

'She could, but I don't think she will. You see, she's been there while Billy simply hovered in the background during their big disagreements – and now he's got in touch with her but he's done it behind his wife's back. I think she feels sorry for him, Keith. She wouldn't want to inflict a burden like this on him.'

'How do you mean, a burden?'

'This information of yours makes it almost certain that Edie is their daughter. He couldn't tell Shula, she's put an embargo on ever mentioning the subject again. He'd have to keep it a secret.' Lindsey sighed at the recollection of his alarm when she contacted him at the golf club.

'But according to you, he's already keeping a secret. He's giving money for Edie's upkeep.'

'Ye-es.' She got up and resumed her packing. 'But to tell the truth, I'm in constant expectation of Billy blurting that out to his wife. He's just not the type to have a guilty secret of any kind. And I think Edie feels the same.'

'What a loving, trusting family,' Keith said with a grim smile.

'Oh, I see it all the time, Keith. People at loggerheads with their nearest and dearest . . . And Edie is neither near or dear where Shula Guyler is concerned. So I don't expect Edie will pass on your information.'

He hesitated. She eyed him and said, 'What?'

'If she *does* confront Mrs Guyler with it and there's a big bust-up, you will let me have an exclusive on the story?'

'Keith!'

'I'm sorry, I know it sounds terrible, but it would be a great exclusive, Lin darling. The *Globe* would pay thousands—'

'How can you be so mercenary!'

'But it's not just the money, Lin, it's being in there *first*!'

'You're incorrigible.'

'But lovable with it.'

'Yes, I have to admit. Very lovable.'

They kissed, and somehow the kiss became lengthened into something more, so the packing was delayed for quite a time.

On the following day, Lindsey called the office to say she wouldn't arrive for work until the afternoon. She pottered around the flat, and by and by there were sounds from Edie's room. Lindsey put on the kettle for coffee.

Edie appeared yawning and stretching, then screwing her eyes up at sight of Lindsey. 'I heard you clanging about. Not gone to the office?'

'I'm going in later. Coffee in about ten minutes.'

'Real coffee?' At Lindsey's nod, Edie sped off in the direction of the bathroom, reappearing minutes later with the sleep washed out of her eyes and her hair more or less brushed.

'Did you get back late last night? Is that why you're having an easy morning?'

'No, I stayed at home on purpose to speak to you.'

Edie took the coffee mug that Lindsey held out. She frowned a little but sat at the kitchen table. Always at the back of her mind she had this apprehension that Lindsey would ask her to leave. There was no real reason for her to put up with a long-stay visitor. So she thought the talk that was coming would turn out to be an invitation to find somewhere else to live.

'Are you awake enough to pay attention to what I'm going to say?'

'Wide awake.' But she felt a little less anxious. The tone, though somewhat formal, wasn't loaded with 'I hate what I'm going to say but I must say it.'

'Keith gave me some information over the weekend that I want to pass on to you. It's about your mother – that's to say, about the woman who brought you up.'

'Ma Maybury?'

'Her real name was Betty Trenton. Keith found out a lot about her.' Lindsey paused, then picked up an envelope from the worktop. 'He typed up the main facts, so I'll leave you in peace to read this through. Then if you want, you can ask me questions and if I know the answers, I'll tell you.'

Edie took the envelope. Lindsey went to the window to gaze out at the tree tops, giving her lodger space in which to read and assimilate the news. She didn't turn back until she heard the rustle of the sheets of paper being folded and put back in the envelope.

'Well,' Edie said. 'Now we know why she did it. I've always wondered, you know. She certainly never did it because she longed for a little girl to love and care for.'

'No, that's pretty clear.'

'She couldn't have thought she was going to get away with it,' Edie said. 'I mean, if this guy Louie had actually married her.'

'Keith and I talked about that. He says people who remembered her said she was apt to rush into things.'

'Too true. Like the time we went to Munich for the Christmas markets, and we ran out of money practically the first day.' Edie shook her head. 'Act first, think afterwards if she thought at all. Know what I—' She broke off. 'Well, anyhow, that's that.'

'You're going to leave it at that, then?'

'Can't see what else to do.' She paused, studying Lindsey. 'Oh, you're thinking that it makes it pretty well watertight that she stole a kid to show to Louie, showed up with her the very day that Julie went missing so as I was that kid, I'm Julie. Yeah, that seems quite likely.'

'You don't want to do anything about it?'

Edie summoned a smile. 'I tried that, remember? Presented myself to Shula, and got the boot.'

'But things are different now, Edie. Billy Guyler is trying to get to know you – that's what he's doing, isn't it?'

'Seems so.'

'Couldn't you pass on Keith's information to him? Get him to show it to Shula?'

'What, and have her slaughter him?' Edie gave a curt laugh. 'Do me a favour! I know and you know, that Shula can't stand the thought of me.'

'But that was when you were playing the part of the Big Black Angry Bruiser. Things are different now.'

'Yeah, and *I'm* different now. Last year when I first went, all of a tremble, to meet the great Mrs Guyler, I would have given anything for her to wrap me in a big hug and say, "My darling chee-ild!" Now I see that she and I would never get on. I don't like her any more than she likes me. What do I need her for? Answer me that!'

Lindsey was silent for a long moment. Then she said, 'I believe I've said this before. Parents and children don't always get on. Freud said it a long time ago, "The family is the battleground." All the same, the information Keith has put together is important. Perhaps the Guylers deserve to know it.'

'They're not going to hear it from *me*.'

'You really mean it – you're not even going to tell Billy?'

Edie didn't want to ask herself that question. She said quickly, 'He's got enough of a burden as it is, doing this money thing without telling the boss lady.'

245

'It's the fact that he offered his help that makes me think he deserves to know the Betty Trenton story.'

Edie understood what Lindsey was implying. 'All right,' she agreed, 'he feels pretty sure I'm his daughter. And I am, of course. And the information about how Betty Trenton came to need a baby girl seems to bear all that out. But then he's got a problem – does he want to gain a daughter and lose a wife?'

'It needn't come to that—'

'I'm not going to risk it. The poor guy has as much as he can handle already.'

'Okay,' Lindsey said. 'It's your life and you've a right to handle it how you want to. But I felt you should know the story of how things went the way they did.'

'Yeah. Thanks. That's one more thing I owe you for.'

'You owe Keith, not me. If you ever want any more of the background, give him a ring, his number's on the telephone memory, button four.'

Edie nodded, but without the slightest intention of ever following it up. She could understand why the boyfriend had wanted to carry out his investigation – after all, he was a newspaperman. But for herself, she'd decided months ago that she must forget the Guylers. That had been a mistake, one of the many stupid things she'd done after Ma Maybury died. Now she was in a new life, and the Guylers were never going to play any part in it.

Except, of course, that Billy Guyler had different ideas.

246

Nineteen

Billy had invited Edie to lunch one Sunday. Shula was safely off at the health club, and he himself was supposed to be watching a golf match at the club. He took her to a quiet pub out on the Warwick road, previously scouted to ensure no one with a lot of money might patronise it. People with a lot of money might have been people who knew him.

On a previous meeting he'd asked her to bring samples of her work. Having himself once had talent, he was eager to know if Edie had any. She brought a big plastic carry-folder, from which at the coffee stage she produced some samples.

'Nothing much,' she said in embarrassment. 'I'm still trying to get the hang of the art thing.'

He took the items from her one by one. There was a collage showing a street market in very vigorous colour, a sketch for what looked like a room interior or perhaps a stage set. With that went three or four tiny figurines made from papier mâché and clothed with scraps of cloth, very neatly stitched to make dresses for the girl figures and a suit for the man.

'I couldn't do more than one pair of trousers,' she confessed with a faint flush. 'They're awfully hard to make at that size. Next time I'll try it all on a larger scale.'

'It's supposed to be theatre?' he asked.

'No, it's a shop window – I was gonna do furniture, mebbe even a vase of flowers, but I'll have to scale it up a bit. It's called Design for Living.'

He was impressed. Not by the idea of the window, nor by the unoriginal title, but by the determination and skill shown in the making of the little figures.

247

He said as much, but she shrugged. 'Early stages,' she said. 'I'll have another go at it soon.' She delved into the carrier, to produce samples of calligraphy.

Billy knew a lot about lettering. When he was a packaging designer, one of the things that lifted his designs above the average was the elegance and impact of his word placement. It was he, years ago, who had designed the logo still used for Gylah Cosmetics – a soft cursive style with the first letter enlarged and widened to include most of the others.

Edie had taken two or three brand names and re-styled them. They were perhaps too inclined towards flashiness but he remarked to himself that after all, he too had done some flashy things in his early stages. But it was the setting of a well-known quotation from St Paul's Epistle to the Phillippians that stopped him cold. She had lettered it in one of the standard black italics, not very large, but with the significant words outlined again in blue. 'Whatsoever things are *True*, whatsoever things are *Honest* . . .'

There was something there. A simplicity, an eye for space and emphasis, an instinctive understanding of the importance of the message.

'This is good,' he said, his voice thickening a little with the shock of knowing she had real ability.

'My tutor at the print studio says it's fussy.'

'Well, he wanted you to do it in black and white, I expect.'

'D'you think the colour's wrong?'

'No, I like it.'

She smiled in satisfaction. 'I think it's cool, myself.'

He went back over the samples she'd brought. They pleased him. He felt a surge of certainty. She was his daughter, she'd inherited the talent he no longer used.

He called for a refill of their coffee cups, offered the last of the wine he'd ordered. She shook her head and he fussed about pouring it into his glass. Then he said, 'You know, Edie, I'm going to do something about things.'

'What things?'

'Well, about how you stand in the world, about how you come to be where you are now.'

'I don't get you.'

'I'm going to hire a detective, see if he can find out how that woman came to bring you up.'

'Hire . . . ?'

'Yes, I want to have . . . you know . . . chapter and verse if I can get it. Who she was, what she thought she was doing. Might take a while but once I know that, I think it would be useful.'

She smiled. 'Save your money. Somebody's already done all that.'

'What?'

'Editor or something of the paper in that town where the real Mayburys lived – Cartfield.'

'He's done some tracking?'

'Oh, I think you could call it chapter and verse. Ma Maybury in all her glory from the time she fell in love to the time she found she needed to produce a baby for the boyfriend to see.'

'What!' Billy was astounded. 'He's got her life story?'

'Certainly has.'

'And you know all that?'

'Yeah, Lindsey gave it to me at Easter. Her boyfriend – Keith, the newspaperman – had typed it all out on his computer for her.'

'But Easter was weeks ago, Edie!'

'Yeah, so what?'

'But you didn't tell me!'

Oh dear, she thought, now I've done it. She put out a hand towards him. 'It doesn't matter, Billy.'

'Not matter? Not matter? How can you say that! Edie – Edie – it might make all the difference!'

'Who to?' She put her fingers gently around his. 'Come on now, pal, calm down. It's just words on paper. It may be true, it may not be – who can say?'

'But what do you think? Do you think it's true?'

'Oh, yeah, Ma Maybury and her weirdo world in every line of it. But I still say it makes no difference, Billy.'

'It makes a difference to *me*,' he said. His heart was thudding in his chest. Armed with that, he could fortify his courage and speak to Shula. Chapter and verse, how their Julie came to be taken and turned into Edie Maybury – evidence, well, not exactly evidence, but convincing surely, because Lindsey had handed the report on to Edie and she wouldn't have done that if she didn't think that it stood up.

His thoughts raced on. A clarification, an explanation, a *reason* for their loss, something that would speak to Shula, thaw the wall of ice behind which she'd retreated.

'Have you got it? Can I see it?' he demanded.

'I don't carry it around with me,' she said, with a little laugh. 'But I've got it at home.'

'Send it to me. I've got to see it.'

'Billy, what good is it going to do—'

'I've got to see it! To know *why*, to sort it out at last . . .'

Edie was studying him. Last year, when she got in touch with Ursula Guyler through the television programme, she'd been trying to find a mother. It seemed odd when she looked back that she'd never given much thought to a father. Yet here he was, in turmoil, hardly able to cope with the idea that there was some meaningful background to the story of her life.

It was dawning on her that the loss of his daughter had been as much a tragedy to Billy Guyler as to his wife. Yet he'd stepped back, or at least to one side, to be a support to Shula, to hide his own grief because she needed him to be what he'd always been, second fiddle to her strong personality.

'I'll bring it with me to the store tomorrow night,' she said, giving in. 'Can you drop by?'

'Of course – we'll have coffee again – Edie – this is tremendous – I can't tell you!'

'Ssh,' she said, 'people are looking. Don't make so much of it, Billy. It's just stuff from the past, but if it means so much to you I suppose you've got to read it.'

He wanted to go on talking about it but he was flustered and stirred up. In any case, time was passing and she had homework for tomorrow waiting for her at the flat. He drove her to a bus stop in Birmingham from which she could make her way home, then himself drove away aimlessly. He felt quite unable to go home and talk to Shula – he would blurt it all out, and that would be a mistake, because when he broached the subject he wanted to be armed with facts, yes, facts, unassailable facts.

He built up the investigative report in his own mind to

a resumé of hard evidence. It was going to make all the difference.

When he did read it, it did indeed make a difference. To him. He saw in it the tragedy that had befallen Julie – little Julie, sunny, trusting, open-hearted. He recognised it as truth, perhaps not capable of positive proof but accounting for that day, that dreadful, unforgettable day, when Julie had been taken.

The report was economically written, filling only a few pages. Edie watched him read it and saw the tears filling his eyes. Poor guy, she thought to herself. Perhaps I shouldn't have told him. Too late now, and in a way, she was glad he knew, because they'd been growing closer and now she felt that the closeness had a special quality. Father and daughter, was that it?

'I'm going to show this to Shula,' he said.

'No, don't!'

'But I must, Edie. She's got to know – to see how it was—'

'Don't do it, Billy.'

'But you're our *daughter*!'

'Billy, that's not the point. She doesn't like me.'

'But she will, she must.'

'No, you're wrong. Lindsey said it – something about the family being a battleground. Mums and dads don't necessarily like their kids. So I think you've got to keep this to yourself. It's good and bad, you see – it's good that you feel convinced in your own mind, and I am too, but it's bad because it leaves Shula out of the loop. And I don't think she'd want to come into it – and you see how bad *that* would be.' He was shaking his head. She said again, 'Keep it to yourself, Billy.'

But it was time for her to go back to the checkout, so she rose, dropped a kiss on the top of his head, and hurried off.

When he got home Shula was preparing for bed. Sitting in front of the dressing-table mirror in a pretty azure-blue negligee, creaming her face, she looked tired but relaxed. 'Did you lose a lot, dear?' she asked with faint humour. The informal bridge club played for ten-pence pieces.

All at once he made up his mind. 'I didn't go to the club,' he said. 'I went to meet Edie.'

251

'Edie?' For a moment the name meant nothing to her. Since the beginning she'd thought of the girl as Ediemaybury, all in one word; Edie by itself was too friendly, too accepting. More recently she'd become 'that dreadful girl'.

Then the meaning came home to her. She turned on the tapestry stool to face him. 'Edie M-Maybury?' she stammered.

'Yes. Our daughter.'

'Billy!'

'I've been seeing her since Easter.'

'But you never—'

'I didn't tell you because I knew you'd get in a state. But the time's come to have this out, Shula. That girl is our daughter.'

'She's not!'

'Yes, she is.' He took Keith's report from the inside pocket of his jacket. 'Read this.'

She made a sweeping gesture with her hand. 'I don't want to read it. It'll only be lies.'

'It's the truth, Shula. Please read it. It's the career of the woman who took her, and *why* she took her.'

'Oh, you've fallen for another of their tricks,' she raged. 'Billy, will you never learn? She and that awful boyfriend.'

'They broke up. She didn't agree with what he did, those threats.'

'She *says* so, and you believe her.'

'Yes, I believe her, because she's working nights in a supermarket to pay for lessons.'

'Oh yes? What else did she tell you? She's got an invalid sister who needs an operation? That's the usual yarn.'

'Shula, will you take your head out of that cardboard box and *listen*? She's changed, she's turned her back on all that weird black stuff, she's let her hair grow normally, and you know what? Her hair's fair, just like Julie's would have been.'

'Don't you talk to me about Julie!' She jumped up, her voice had grown shrill. She pulled her gown close to her throat, as if to protect herself from some polluting element. 'You never suffered the way I did when she disappeared! You don't know what it's like to lie awake night after night imagining what might have happened to her. You read such dreadful things . . .

I thought he'd probably killed her, but I couldn't give up, I wanted to *will* her to stay alive, but now I realise – We talked about it, we agreed, she's dead, she's been dead for years, we agreed we had to accept that.'

'She's not dead, Shula! She's a nice, ordinary, twenty-year-old girl trying to sort out her life, working all hours of the day and night.'

'You believe all that? It's just another trick.'

'It's true, I've seen her, sitting at the checkout in the middle of the night.'

Suddenly Shula laughed, breaking into his tale with a terrible harshness. She glared at him, blue eyes full of contempt. 'You've fallen for her!' she cried. 'You old fool, she's taken you in! The male menopause, is that it?'

Billy's breath left his body. He drew back from her as if she'd struck him. After a long minute he found enough voice to reply. 'You should be ashamed of yourself,' he said softly.

With that he picked up the envelope from where it had fallen and left the bedroom. Shula was left standing in front of the dressing table, its three mirrors reflecting the image of a woman turned to stone, one hand out-stretched as if to call back the man who had gone.

At length she sank down on the stool. She bent forward, arms about herself as if to hold in the emotions tearing at her.

How could he? It was a betrayal. He'd gone over to the enemy.

Billy, usually so lacking in initiative, had taken steps without her knowledge, had been meeting this – this brat, this slut. How could he do it! What on earth had caused him to seek her out? And for how long?

Since Easter. It was May now. Weeks and weeks. Secret meetings, and he said she was pretty . . . Pretty and young, that was the cause.

She straightened, turned, looked at herself in the gold-framed mirrors. Mid-forties, in good condition, skin almost unlined, hair encouraged to be blonde and well-styled, chin still firm . . . She touched her chin with one hand. No sagging . . . yet. Firm and well-defined. But not young. Not any more.

It had happened to so many wives of her acquaintance. The

253

successful marriage in a world where success was of the utmost importance, where one or both partners had to have ability far above the norm. But at the height of his career, the husband longs for something more, something that might bring back those earlier years devoted to climbing the ladder. So he seeks out a younger woman, and there everything comes apart.

But those men at least had chosen a new partner who was only a successful rival. Billy had chosen Edie Maybury. Because he was too shy, too inactive to seek out some young beauty. He cloaked his need by telling himself he was befriending his daughter. Their daughter.

Now she wished she'd read whatever was in the envelope he'd held out to her. But he'd taken it with him when he walked out. Well, it would be only a pack of lies, anyway. But that was Billy, of course – easily taken in, which was why she'd had to be the controlling influence in the business – he would fall for almost any story he was told if it sounded halfway reasonable.

Easy enough to get someone to concoct something attractive, to play up to his desire to be 'a friend'. Perhaps there really was nothing sexual in it, perhaps he really fancied himself in the role of father, the benefactor bringing goodies into her life, her poor deprived life, working in a supermarket, toiling, moiling . . .

She stared at herself in the mirror to find she was crying. Tears were rolling down her cheeks, sliding easily over the moisturising cream, trickling over her chin, that firm chin . . .

What was she going to do? Her solicitor . . . That young woman, Lindsey Abercrombie. She'd done well that last time, when that awful young man tried stupid threats.

But that would mean . . . telling her about it.

She couldn't do that. The idea of putting it into words to another person was unbearable. 'My husband's making a fool of himself over a girl young enough to be his daughter . . .' Who in fact claimed to *be* his daughter . . .

It was the kind of joke that men tell each other in bars. 'There was this middle-aged bloke, falls for a pretty young thing, kids himself it's all fatherly affection . . .'

No, she couldn't talk about it to anyone. She would have to

deal with it herself. The usual advice was to wait it out, to be patient until the strain of keeping up with someone so much younger finally told the man he was making a mistake.

Ursula had patience. She would wait. She'd control herself, utter not another word of recrimination. When he came to his senses she'd never say, 'I told you so.'

But in the meantime? How to live the day to day life?

She tried it from every angle. Cool civility, the let's-be-grown-up approach. She used that in business a lot – but then she didn't have to meet business acquaintances in the bedroom, or across the breakfast table.

The everything-is-normal approach. 'We have a business to run so let's just go on as usual.' Would that work? Billy was never too involved in the business, he might not be bothered about how they ran it. And moreover it was she who ran the firm.

For hours she sat thinking. There seemed to be a dozen ways to go, but down each avenue she foresaw problems. If he had really gone out and found a mistress, it would have been easier. This screen he was hiding behind was too delicate for most of the manoeuvres she considered – a touch too rough and the screen might topple, to expose – what? Billy as self-deluded, corrupt? The idea was too shocking to bear.

It was early in the morning when she went to bed. Billy hadn't come back. She'd heard him moving about in one of the spare rooms and knew he'd decided to sleep there. In her bed, with a strangely empty space alongside, she lay awake. She forgot to set her alarm, for the first time in twenty years. It was almost dawn when she slept.

When she awoke it was bright daylight. She'd overslept. She sprang out of bed, startled, disoriented. Why was she so late? Why hadn't Billy roused her?

Then she remembered.

She rang for Erika, the housekeeper, who came almost as if she'd been waiting outside the door. 'Is something wrong, madam? You don't usually—'

'Bring me some coffee, Erika. And tell Mr Guyler—'

'Mr Guyler has gone out, madam.'

'What?' She glanced at her clock. Nine thirty-five. Well,

of course Billy would have gone to the office – or had he appointments on the social side today? His organiser would be at the office, of course. He might have gone out to a breakfast meeting – that had become fashionable in recent years and meant you could sit around for an hour or more drinking orange juice and eating American muffins. She herself hated it, which was why Billy usually took it on.

Erika departed for the coffee. She came back with a silver pot on a silver tray, with a porcelain mug, a rosebud in a silver vase, and a white envelope.

'Mr Guyler asked me to give you this, madam,' she said, touching the envelope.

The room seemed to move in a swinging circle around Ursula. The housekeeper made an anxious move towards her, but she steadied herself.

'Thank you, Erika, that will be all for now.'

'Shall I serve breakfast, madam?'

'In about forty minutes.'

'Thank you, madam.'

Erika went out, very worried indeed. Loud voices last night, *der Herr* sleeps in another room, rises early, eats nothing, packs things from his dressing room, writes a note, and drives away. What could it mean but big trouble?

Ursula tore open the envelope the moment the door closed.

Dear Shula
I feel that we need some time apart. After what you said last night I don't think I could speak to you without distaste. I'll be at the Lamont if you need me but I think we should keep our distance for the time being.
Yrs
Billy

A douche of cold water.

She sat down on the side of the bed, the letter dropping from her hand. She was gasping for breath. Billy wrote that? Billy Guyler, known for his unwillingness to take action of any kind?

It was the decisiveness that shocked her most. Without

hesitation, he had gone. They had almost never been apart – occasional days when she had business in London or Paris, the week in hospital when she was having the baby, but even those separations had been discussed, prepared for. That he could simply walk out . . . Such a thought had never occurred to her.

For many minutes she sat immobile, letting feelings and ideas course through her. First there was the unexpected sense of loss. Then guilt, because she'd clearly said something very bad to him, but what, she couldn't now remember. An urge to apologise came next but almost at once she repelled that, letting anger take over.

How dare he? Sneaking behind her back, seeing that dreadful girl, letting himself be hoodwinked by some new scheme, expecting anyone with any intelligence to read the fake report that would somehow validate her claims . . . Did he think she was as big a fool as he was?

Well, let him take up residence at the Lamont. The Lamont was an excellent hotel but he'd soon miss the familiar comforts of home. Billy wasn't adventurous. He'd soon be back. Probably, at this very moment, he was sitting down to a hotel breakfast and wishing he could have Erika's Austrian version of scrambled eggs.

She was wrong. Billy had had a continental breakfast sent up and was now telephoning Lindsey Abercrombie's flat. He knew Lindsey would have left for work and that Edie would soon be starting her day. He left a message on the machine: 'Please ring me without fail before you leave for college at this number – just press re-dial. It's very important that I speak to you.'

Edie, coming sleepily into the living room just before ten, saw the light blinking, switched on, and heard the message. 'Just wait a minute,' she said to the machine. 'I need a cup of coffee.'

She put breakfast blend into the coffee-maker in the way she'd learned since coming to live with Lindsey. Before that, morning coffee had been instant and hot water. She dabbed cold water on her face to wake herself up then took her mug to the telephone.

Billy picked up at the first ring. 'Edie? Thank you for answering so quickly. Edie, can you take the day off from college?'

'Eh?' she said. 'What for?'

'We need to talk, seriously. I'm at the Lamont Hotel – do you know it?'

'Sure thing. What are you doing there so early?'

'I'll explain when you get here.'

'But Billy, isn't the Lamont the sort of place where your up-market pals might see us?'

'That doesn't matter now, Edie. I want it all out in the open. Can you come?'

With a sense of impending doom, she agreed to meet him in about an hour. She knew, just from the tone of his voice, that something terrible had happened.

Twenty

Lindsey couldn't but be aware of Billy's message because Edie hadn't erased it from the machine. When she heard it, it made her anxious. She was relieved as well as surprised when Edie walked in at about six o'clock.

'I've been with Billy Guyler most of the day,' Edie said, throwing her handbag and jacket onto a chair.

'Yes, I heard his message on the tape.'

'Yeah. Well, the long and the short of it is, he's staying at the Lamont because he's had a big barney with Shula.'

'*Staying* there?'

'It'd be called a trial separation if they were pop stars. But mebbe that's going a bit far – he's staying away from her for the time being and it's like as if he's a champagne bottle with the cork popped,' she said fondly. 'Can't stop, full of plans, I only hope he doesn't have a terrific let down in a day or two.'

Lindsey had been in the midst of salad-making. She went back into the kitchen to put the iceberg in the spinner. Over her shoulder she said, 'I'm just guessing, but does this have anything to do with Keith's information?'

'Good guess.'

'You told him?' she said, rather troubled.

'Last night. At least I gave him the notes so he could read for himself.' Edie, having followed her to the kitchen, began abstractedly to set the table for a meal. 'I felt I had to, Lin. He was going to hire private detectives to hunt up stuff, and I imagine he was going to keep it all a secret from Shula, so I thought it'd be better just to give him what we've got and be over with it.'

'I see.'

'You think I was wrong?'

'No, I think people should know things – "let there be light", that's my motto. I was surprised, that's all. I had the feeling you'd probably not pass on the information.'

'Because I couldn't see what good it would do – yeah, that was my view. She's never going to like me, you know, so what's the point?'

'Oh, she could change, Edie. People do.'

'Well, she hasn't had an overnight transformation, know what I—'

'Perhaps that was a bit too much to expect.'

'In fact, she had quite the opposite. Billy didn't tell me much about it because he didn't want to hurt my feelings, I think. But I got the impression she said some nasty things.'

Because she's afraid of you, thought Lindsey. Aloud she said, 'In a word, she took it badly.'

'Mega badly. So Billy said ta-ta early this morning and his address for the time being is gonna be the Lamont. We got together in the lounge and had coffee. That's a really, really lush place. With the coffee they had these mini-Danish – absolutely smashing. He was sitting there trying to tell me tactfully that Shula had flipped when he told her he'd been seeing me, and I was going, "Oh dear" and "What a shame" between scoffing the Danish.'

'You don't seem very bothered about it?' Lindsey remarked, stifling a laugh.

'Well, I've seen Shula doing that kind of stuff, haven't I? Let her get on with it, I say. But of course –' her voice changed, something like pity entering its tone – 'there's Billy. He says he wants it all out in the open, he's going to acknowledge me as his daughter, and so on and so on. I tell you, he was talking a blue streak, and I was trying to calm him down but I don't think I made much headway. And when at last I was saying goodbye he told me not to tell you.'

Lindsey was surprised. 'Why not?'

'Well, he pointed out that you're really Shula's solicitor and you might pass something on to her.'

'Of course not – not unless she asked me a direct question. But she won't.'

'You don't think so?'

260

Lindsey shook her head. 'She won't be saying anything to anybody about the break up, not if she can help it. It's such a come-down for her, isn't it? By the way, does she know you're staying here?'

'No, he never got a chance to explain how he came to get in touch with me or anything of that. Seems she just went up in smoke the minute he said he'd been in contact. After that it was open warfare. So, except for the fact that he's now at the Lamont, she doesn't know anything. And he wants it kept that way.'

Lindsey suppressed a sigh. Of course, Billy wanted to avoid conflict if he could, but nothing was to be gained in her opinion by keeping things secret. The sooner Shula could be told the story of Betty Trenton and her reasons for stealing the baby, the more likely she was to begin moving towards acceptance of her daughter.

But she reflected that in a way, even the innocent Billy Guyler might be enjoying the sense of power he now had. He knew things Shula didn't. He had learned the background to the abduction. He had what amounted to proof that Edie Maybury was Julie Guyler. And he was the one who had reached out to their daughter, he was the one who wanted to come to her aid.

Edie went to the living room for her handbag. Lindsey was taking down the omelette pan from its hook when she came back. 'Before you get started on whatever you're gonna do,' she said, 'will you take a look at this?'

Edie produced an envelope with the crest of a High Street bank. Lindsey took it and looked at the contents. They were the papers asking for the signature of the new account holder.

'He'd been to the bank before I got to the hotel – it's practically next door. He'd opened an account in my name. When we'd talked all morning he said we'd just pop next door before we went to lunch and get the account going.' Edie looked at Lindsey with a frown of anxiety. 'I said I didn't think I ought to do it, and we had a bit of an argument, and then I said I'd have to ask you first before I signed anything.'

'You want my opinion?'

Edie disregarded the query. 'You can see he's put in a lot

261

of money for openers. I mean, he's taken that out of his own account and plonked it in this new one. Everybody at the bank will think I'm some bimbo he's got involved with!' She coloured up at the thought.

'Well, that's a possibility,' Lindsey agreed, unable to suppress a smile, 'but if he's serious about having it all out in the open everybody will soon know he's accepting you as his daughter.'

'Oh, Lord, why did I ever show him that report?' cried Edie, crushing the papers and throwing them on the draining board. 'There's going to be all kinds of ructions – and I'm not allowed to tell you, but he's got all sorts of other ideas – honestly, Lindsey, I dunno if I want to get into all that again.'

Lindsey sat down at the kitchen table and gestured to Edie to do the same. It was time for some serious consideration. 'Let's look at this calmly,' she said. 'Billy now knows the story behind the abduction seventeen years ago. Everything points to the fact that you are the grown-up version of the little girl who was abducted, therefore you are the daughter of Ursula and William Guyler. You think so, I think so, he thinks so and for what it may be worth, Keith Holland thinks so. You agree so far?'

Edie nodded.

'Billy feels impelled to do something about it. He wants to bring you into the family, but his wife is against it. So instead, he wants to go it alone and treat you as if you were his daughter. He wants to do things for you, to look after you, to make up for all you've missed.' She paused. 'Seems natural enough to me . . .'

'Well, I suppose so.' But she looked dubious.

Lindsey forged ahead. 'He wants you to have some money. You don't want to take it – partly because you're embarrassed but also, I think, because if Shula gets to know of it, she's going to be reinforced in her view that you're a gold-digger.'

'Yeah.' Edie gave a little grimace. 'You're not slow on the uptake, are you!'

'But on the other hand, the money would be awfully useful, Edie. And you *are* his daughter.'

'Mmm . . .'

262

'You don't have to make up your mind this minute. Think it over.' She waited a moment but got no response. 'And now,' she went on, 'I'm going to make a cheese omelette, and the question is, are you going to eat with me because if so it'll have to be a big one.'

Life resumed its normal tenor that evening. Edie went to her job, Lindsey looked through some documents she'd brought home, and when Keith rang about ten she gave him a resumé of what had happened. 'Billy Guyler might be in touch with you, Keith. I gather he's avid to know as much as he can.'

'He only has to ask. I can fax him some of my notes, the verbatim quotes from people who knew the late Betty Trenton.'

'Poor man, he's in a terrible quandary! He wants to acknowledge Edie yet he knows it will antagonise his wife. And he loves Shula, you know. It was a tremendous shock to him when he realised she'd been in the wrong all the while.'

'It'll be a heck of a story when it breaks,' Keith said in the eager tones of an investigative journalist.

'Keith!'

'All right, all right, I promise to be good.'

Days went by, however, in complete peace. Lindsey rather dreaded that Ursula would get in touch, but no – there was silence from that direction. Edie went to classes, went to work, chatted about daily life when they encountered each other, but rather pointedly said nothing about Billy.

It was well into June when Billy Guyler himself telephoned Lindsey. 'Miss Abercrombie, I'd like to make an early appointment to come to your office for a discussion on a legal matter.'

Lindsey hesitated. 'Are you asking me to act as your solicitor?'

'Not at present. I would like a mini-conference, with you in the chair. I'll be inviting my wife to—'

'Your wife!'

'Yes, I want both my wife and my daughter to be present for a serious discussion but it needs to be run in a formal style – to avoid hubbub and emotional outbursts.'

Lindsey very much doubted if she or anyone else could control Ursula Guyler if she wanted to make an emotional outburst. She was very unwilling to be involved in this affair, and her lack of enthusiasm must have communicated itself along the telephone line because Billy said, 'Please Miss Abercrombie – Lindsey – you tried to help us in the past, won't you do it again?'

'But I was totally unsuccessful.'

'This time I think it'll be different. This time even Shula will have to take it seriously.'

'Mr Guyler, I really don't think—'

'Do it for Edie,' he begged. 'She's had such a hard life so far, help me to make it better for her.'

She wasn't able to resist that plea. 'All right,' she said. 'What do you want me to do?'

'Give me an appointment and I'll let Shula know.'

'You're in touch with her?'

'I'll send her a note,' he said, with a sigh that let her know he'd had the phone slammed down on him more than once.

She looked at her organiser. There was a space in two days time, Friday morning. She entered Billy's name adding 'and others'. She preferred not to think of who was implied by 'and others'.

'I'll have to tell my boss about this,' she warned him. 'Shula's business is very important to this firm, Billy.'

'Yes, I understand. But they can't actually forbid you to see me, can they?'

'No-o, I imagine not.' She really wasn't sure, but she planned to be diplomatic over this. 'See you at eleven o'clock on Friday.'

Clearly Billy's note to his wife was hand-delivered, because that afternoon Lindsey's phone rang. 'What on earth is *this*?' demanded Ursula without preamble. 'An appointment in your office on Friday? What's it about? How dare you agree to a thing like this?'

'Mrs Guyler, I've no idea what it's about. I'm doing it in the role of *amicus familiae*—'

264

'Don't use legal jargon on me! If you're helping Billy to play some trick on me.'

'He asked me to set it up so that there could be a calm discussion.'

'But he's bringing that awful girl!'

'Yes, and he must have a good reason.'

'If he thinks I'm going to agree to making any money settlement or anything of that kind—'

'I've no idea what's in Mr Guyler's mind, Mrs Guyler. Really. All I know is, it must be important because he wouldn't be doing this otherwise.' Wouldn't be daring to do it, she almost said.

'What's got into him?' wailed Ursula. 'He's never behaved like this before!'

He's never had to fight somebody for something important, thought Lindsey, but she only said, 'I hope you'll come to the meeting?'

There was a long silence. Lindsey almost thought the line between them had broken down. Then Ursula said in a tight voice, 'All right, I'll come. But if that chit tries any of her tricks with me, I'm walking out.'

'We're going to try to prevent anything unpleasant, Mrs Guyler,' Lindsey said in her most reassuring tone.

Now that it was agreed, she had to inform Mr Ollerenshaw. Thankfully, the day of the weekly staff conference was past so she sent him a personal memo. To her surprise there was no response. Towards the end of the day she checked with his secretary. It turned out that Mr Ollerenshaw had had to leave for Bristol on urgent client business, and would stay there until the weekend. So, in fact, Old Ollie was unaware of the forthcoming meeting of the Guyler family.

On thinking it over, Lindsey decided not to telephone him at his Bristol hotel. She didn't want him quacking warnings at her over something that was now inevitable. Besides, she was determined to go on with it, either here at the office or at some other venue. Billy was about to make some decisive step and for Edie's sake she wanted to hear it explained.

She didn't see Edie at the flat, but there was nothing unusual in that. They seldom converged during the working week. On Friday morning she half expected Edie to emerge from her room before she herself left for the office but when she tapped at her door, simply to say, 'See you later,' Edie was still asleep.

Eleven o'clock approached. Billy was the first to appear, looking tense and nervous. Next came Edie, clearly as nervous as Billy, but better at concealing it. Lindsey had booked the conference room where there was a hot-plate for coffee. She served it, so that they sat there toying with cups and saucers, and still Ursula Guyler didn't appear.

At eleven fifteen the receptionist rang to say Mrs Guyler had arrived and was asking to speak to Miss Abercrombie in private. 'Oh, no,' groaned Billy fearing the worst. Lindsey tried to look encouraging before going out to greet her.

'Are they here?' Ursula burst out the moment Lindsey came into the hall.

'Yes, having coffee.'

'I don't think – it's not as if – I didn't sleep a wink last night!' she cried. Her voice was full of uncertainty. 'I must look a mess.'

'Not at all,' Lindsey soothed, although in fact she looked worn and tired behind her expert make-up.

'I don't want to see her!'

'What harm can it do? She's just a girl, Shula, and you after all are an experienced woman of the world.'

This deferential, almost fawning flattery had the desired effect. Ursula straightened her shoulders, patted her hair, and allowed herself to be ushered to the conference room.

With her came extreme unease. Billy leapt up, came to greet her as if to give her a kiss, but she leaned away from him. She kept her eyes averted from Edie who was sitting quietly at the table.

Edie had made a special effort today. She was wearing carefully pressed jeans, the famous dark silk blouse from the charity shop, and a matching ribbon to tie back her hair. Her only make-up was a little eye-liner to accentuate the keen blue eyes.

'Would you like coffee?' Billy quavered.

266

'No I wouldn't like coffee, I'd like to know what the devil I'm here for!'

'Sit down, please, Mrs Guyler,' Lindsey said formally. 'Everybody, please settle down. We're here to talk quietly. This is an informal meeting and it should be free from hostility.'

'Oh yes? I'd like to know how you expect to achieve *that*!'

'I'm going to achieve it by having you sit down and behave like a businesswoman,' Lindsey said, hardening her tone.

'Oh, like a businesswoman? Is that it? Business? I'm going to be asked for money, am I?' But she took a place at the conference table, two seats away from anyone else.

Lindsey sat down at the head of the table. To tell the truth, she was at a loss. Generally, when she was having a client conference, she had at least some private notes to guide her. But on this occasion she hadn't the last idea what was coming.

She looked at Billy. 'Mr Guyler, perhaps you . . . ?'

'Right.' He cleared his throat. 'What I want to say is that over the past weeks I've had a lot to think about. Lindsey approached me just after Easter with some news about Edie that had an effect—'

'Oh yes, that was clear,' muttered Ursula.

He ignored her. 'I found out that the things Lindsey told me were true. Edie –' he glanced towards her but his wife's eyes stared stonily at the table – 'was employed at the Brunswick hypermarket to pay for classes at Chepperton College. I checked it out, it was all exactly as she said. So without prejudice I provided some funds – I felt we owed her at least that much—'

'We? Who's we?' Ursula enquired.

'We – you and I – the people she'd approached in the hope that she'd found her family.'

'In the hope of screwing money out of them!'

'Mrs Guyler – Shula – please! I think it would be better if you let your husband finish his explanation.' To tell the truth, she herself was quite eager to hear what he had to say.

Billy gave a nervous smile, gulped in a big breath, then went on, 'Lindsey's friend, Keith Holland, undertook a search into Edie's background. He wanted to get on the track of the woman who brought her up, the woman we know of as Mrs Maybury. It turned out her name was Betty Trenton, who needed a toddler for reasons it would take too long to explain for the moment. She went out looking for one and she took Julie. You can read about it there.'

He opened a thin leather document case and took out the notes that Keith had faxed him. He pushed them across the table towards his wife. She ignored them.

He waited a moment for her reaction. When none came, he cleared his throat and struggled on. 'When you . . . decided . . . not to look at the papers a couple of weeks ago, I concluded it was time for me to take action on my own. I've done that – at least, I've done some of the things, the important things . . . But now I want you to agree, Shula. I want you to accept the rest of my plan – I want it to be *our* plan.'

'This is getting us nowhere,' Ursula said, smacking the palm of her hand down on the table top. 'Is this all it's going to be? More waffle to make a case that we owe this girl something?'

Billy flushed. 'I'm sorry if I've waffled, I'm not all that good at business procedure, as we both know, Shula.' He kept his glance away from her, but everything in his voice was pleading for her help. When none came, he paused to gather his thoughts. 'I suppose I knew nothing would convince you except hard evidence, so I've *brought* you some.' He slid his hand into the document case and came out with a typed and signed document stapled to a second sheet. 'Hard evidence, Shula.'

He had to stretch his arm to offer it to his wife. She was frowning, blue eyes stormy but troubled. Almost as if against her will, her hand reached out. She took the document, glanced at the first sheet, drew in a sharp breath. She turned hastily to the second sheet, read it swiftly, then looked up. Not at anyone at the room, but beyond them, at the window.

There was a moment's tense expectation.

She tore the sheets of paper in two, rose from her chair in one angry movement, and stalked out of the room.

No one said anything.

At length Lindsey rose, collected the torn papers and, after asking Billy's permission with a glance, scrutinised them. The top sheet bore the heading of a well-known private hospital; the second sheet was a scientific report, lines of formulae that Lindsey passed over without being able to make much of them. A few salient words caught her attention, but it was the last two sentences that mattered.

The DNA test from blood samples provided by the two subjects display codons of compatibility which establish definite profiles of consanguinity. There is no doubt that the subjects are very closely related.

Twenty-One

Edie had not said a word throughout the episode. Not a word had been addressed to her. Now she said, 'That went well.'

Her father made a sound that was half a laugh, half a sob.

For her part, Lindsey was at a loss. She looked from one to the other. Billy was in a state of shock. He'd been so certain that his wife *must* be convinced by the evidence that he'd expected a happy family scene. He met Lindsey's eyes now, and simply shook his head.

She went to her office and came back with the brandy bottle and some glasses, and poured. Billy was about to refuse but she said, 'We need it, Mr Guyler.' He picked up his glass and swallowed a mouthful. A little colour came back under the outdoor tan on his cheeks.

Edie let her glass stand on the table in front of her. She was studying Billy, concern in her gaze. A swift sidelong glance at Lindsey conveyed the message that she'd half expected this discourse to end badly.

What should happen now? Lindsey waited for some hint, but Billy seemed incapable of speech for the moment. She gave him a smile of encouragement, he sipped a little more brandy, and summoned some words. But it was to his daughter that he spoke.

'I'm sorry, dear.'

She shrugged.

To Lindsey he said, 'Edie was always a bit doubtful . . .'

'It's my gypsy background,' she quipped. 'From Ma Maybury and her fortune-telling pals.'

They were both clearly hurt at what had happened. Edie was hiding the fact, but Billy was incapable of pretence at

270

this moment. Lindsey had a sudden desire to rush out, find Ursula Guyler, and shake her until her teeth rattled.

She tried for reassurance. 'Perhaps when she thinks things over . . .'

'Don't hold your breath,' said Edie.

'It's got to have some effect,' Lindsey insisted. 'Scientific evidence—'

'But she doesn't like me,' Edie cut in. '*That's* the point. She may be saying to herself now, "Okay, she's our daughter – but that doesn't do away with the fact that she's a bad lot."'

'Oh, now, Edie dear—'

'Don't try to pretend it's not like that, love.' Edie sighed. ''Cos it is.'

Lindsey sought for something constructive to say. 'What did you plan on doing,' she ventured, 'if everything had . . . you know, gone well?'

'I'd booked table for lunch at the Richelieu. For three . . .'

'Well, here we are, three of us . . . and the conference room will be wanted by one of my colleagues in about ten minutes.'

'Right!' Edie sprang up. 'Come on, Billy, I think Lindsey's inviting herself out for some nosh.'

It was only as they were headed to the outer suburbs of the city that Lindsey thought about the Richelieu. Set in part of what had once been an engineering tycoon's mansion, it was a splendid restaurant often praised in the glossies. She knew Edie had never been to so exclusive a place. She wondered if she should give a word of warning, but Edie was sitting in the front of the BMW with her father while she was in solitary splendour in the back.

Well, she'll have to get used to it, she thought. Billy seems to want to take her around and show her off.

Edie raised her eyebrows a little as they rolled into the parking area, and perhaps a little more when the head waiter looked up from the reservations book to greet them with an enormous smile. But her only remark was a whispered, 'Coo-ol!'

The reason for the welcoming smile was soon obvious. Billy had told the management that this was a celebration so there

271

was Krug on ice when they sat down at a table with a view over the parterre. Their waiter poured the wine at once, handed menus, then withdrew so they could decide what to eat.

'Well,' Billy said, raising his glass, 'here's a toast . . .' He hesitated. Exactly what were they celebrating? The fact that he'd just had yet another row with his wife of over twenty years?

'Absent friends,' prompted Edie.

He gave her a glance of gratitude and affection. He was thinking, She's a nice girl. That was a forgiving thing to say. And then he thought, Shula, if you only knew what you're missing . . .

The champagne had its inevitable effect. They grew less tense, more mellow. Edie gave up trying to make sense of the menu and left it to the others, and though truth to tell she didn't much take to the bisque, which proved to be a soup she thought fishy in both senses of the word, she was prepared to have a go at anything.

Lindsey knew they had to make some decisions. She waited until the Bavaroise to broach the subject. 'Shula's mind is still unchanged,' she remarked. 'What happens now, Mr Guyler?'

He shook his head. 'I can't believe she's being so *stubborn!*'

'She doesn't like me, Billy,' Edie repeated. 'It's my fault, of course. We got off on the wrong foot and it seems we're not going to change step now . . .'

'She doesn't know you. Not the *real* you. If she'd only . . .'

'It may happen,' Lindsey said, trying for a note of hope. 'But perhaps not in the immediate future.'

'The future. Yes, that's what we want to talk about. I was saying to Edie that, of course, once we'd made things straight with Shula, she'd be coming home. I meant, home to our house, you know. But I see that's not going to happen.'

'No.'

'But Edie was always a bit reluctant about that – weren't you, pet?'

Edie nodded. 'There's this noticeboard at the store,' she began. 'In the staff room. All sorts of stuff, "Take This Management Course" or "Learn Judo" but there's advertisements

272

for places to live. And one of them's for what they call a Businesswomen's Residential Club. I thought that might be sort of decent-ish.'

'You want to move out?' Lindsey asked, and tried not to sound too pleased at the thought of having her flat to herself again.

'We-ell . . . I hope you don't—'

'Your place is too far out of Birmingham,' Billy broke in. 'No offence, but it's all right for you, Lindsey, you have easy office hours and the train service suits you fine. But Edie's classes involve her in a funny timetable and anyhow . . .'

Anyhow you want to do this for her, thought Lindsey, and was totally in agreement. 'It's fine,' she said soothingly, 'I think it's a great idea.'

'And I want her to give up that job at the hypermarket,' he went on. 'It's too much for her. And besides . . .'

'And besides, he thinks it's beneath my dignity,' Edie said, laughing. 'Billy Guyler's daughter, working nights at a checkout? In two words, Im Possible.'

'Well, it's not the best arrangement,' Lindsey said. 'You hardly get time to think of anything except work, classes and sleep. When was the last time you went for a stroll in the park? Or round the clothes shops?'

'I'm doing all right,' Edie said with a stubborn tilt of the chin.

She looked so like Shula at that moment that Lindsey and Billy exchanged a glance.

'No you're not,' Lindsey said. 'You're focusing so hard on getting your GCSEs, you're going cross-eyed.'

'Cross-eyed? Cross-eyed?' A combination of emotion, champagne and weariness gave Edie a fit of the giggles. 'I am *not* cross-eyed. Mebbe a little bit pie-eyed, as Ma Maybury used to say when she'd had a couple of gins. Here's to old Ma Maybury – may she rest in peace!'

'What we need now is lots of coffee,' Billy said, signalling the waiter. 'So it's agreed, then, you'll give in your notice?'

'And become a lady of leisure?'

'Become a student.'

'I already am a student, Billy.'

273

'Yes, but I want you to be a student who gets some fun out of life. You see, Lindsey,' he said, turning to her, 'there's this bank account. I can't get her to accept it.'

'She'll think I only went to that clinic and did the DNA thing to screw money out of you,' Edie said, her voice cracking a little.

'You mean Shula.'

'Yes, Shula, who else? Lemme tell you, Billy, you should think hard about what you're doing. 'Cos she may never forgive you for all this.' She took in the restaurant, the champagne, the three of them at their ease, with a wave of her hand. 'You see, Billy, I think it's gonna come down to this . . . You can have me as a daughter, or you can have Shula as a wife. But I think she feels you can't have both . . .'

'Hush,' he said. 'It'll be all right.'

'You think so?' She turned to Lindsey. 'Do *you* think so?'

Lindsey had no idea, but she gave an encouraging nod. Billy took it up at once, without allowing time for any more doubts.

'I wondered if you would act as trustee?'

'Trustee?'

'For the bank account. Edie keeps on saying she doesn't like to take the money, but if you think about it, it's not much compared to what she should have had all these years.' He paused. All these years. More than seventeen years of doing without, all because a self-centred woman needed a baby girl to show off.

Lindsey understood what he was thinking. And in fact she agreed with his view. Edie's efforts to catch up with her education would be greatly helped if she could have an easier life outside the college. To work almost every night and to study almost every day, without let up, would take its toll. Her father's money could be an enormous help.

'I couldn't undertake a trusteeship in the legal sense,' she said. 'Not without talking it over with my boss – and I think he'd be—' she broke off, she'd been about to say horrified.

'Against it,' Billy supplied, 'because of Shula being a big client.'

'Yes.'

'But could you . . . sort of . . . be a guardian, have Edie as a protégée . . . unofficially?'

'Hang on,' said Edie. 'This is me you're talking about, isn't it? Don't I get any say in this? Who says I want a guardian, eh?'

The coffee came, the waiter poured, they sat in silence until he'd gone. Edie resumed, 'No offence, Lin. Nothing against you personally, y'know.'

'No, you just feel you have to fight your corner and have your say.'

'*Right*. And anyway you've done enough already, now hasn't she, Billy?'

'Well . . . yes . . .' He picked up his coffee cup and looked at his daughter over it. 'But who else is there?'

'I dunno. I don't want the money in the first place.'

'Edie, it would be a good idea to take it,' Lindsey said.

'What?'

'You really need it. Billy's right about the night work, you ought to give it up. And you should have a place of your own. Now, since you're never going to get any kind of a job that would pay for that and your tuition – and you know, Billy's already paying for your classes . . .'

'Well, yes, but you did that without ever asking me first.'

'Yes, and I don't apologise for that. You're not going to say you wish I hadn't?'

'Ha . . . I'm too tiddly to be having this argument,' Edie said. 'And you're such a clever-clogs you'd tie me up in knots even if I was sober.'

'So you agree you need the money?'

'Did I say that?'

'Yes, of course you did,' Lindsey said, laughing.

'I didn't. You're trying to get me mixed up. Of course I'm already mixed up, what with Shula walking out on me and too much shampers, but what I always say is, what's life without a bit of a mix-up.'

'So that's settled, then,' Billy said, taking his cue from Lindsey. 'You'll sign the papers for the bank account on the understanding that Lindsey will keep an eye on it?'

'I s'pose I will. Not now, 'cos I don't think I could spell my name at the moment – Gosh, that Krug stuff is strong, isn't it? And I don't think the coffee's doing much good. Billy,' she turned to him, 'Billy, thank you for a lovely lunch and everything, but I think I ought to go home now. It's been a tiring day so far.'

As he drove them to their flat, Lindsey called the office to say she'd be late back. Edie was led indoors and into her room, where she fell on the bed and went straight to sleep, fully clothed. Lindsey took off her shoes, dropped a throw over her, and went out quietly.

'Is she all right?' Billy asked as she came into the living room.

'She's fine. Just a bit overcome.'

'She's a decent girl.'

'Yes she is.'

'Shula should just get to know her . . . .'

Lindsey gave a little shrug, then went to put on the kettle for the coffee they'd missed out on at the Richelieu. He followed her to the kitchen.

'I'm asking far too much of you,' he said with heavy regret. 'But who else can I ask, Lindsey?'

'It's all right.'

'If I went to some other solicitor, would that be better?'

'Perhaps. But I think it would be difficult to keep it all quiet. I think the press might get word.'

'Yes, and we don't want all that again.'

'No. Never mind, Billy. It'll sort itself out, eventually.'

'You think so?'

How could she tell? All she wanted to do was give him some reassurance.

They sat down with their coffee at her kitchen table, where he laid out the documents from the bank. They agreed she would get Edie's signature that evening, that she'd go with her to look at the Businesswomen's Club next day, that if there was a vacancy she'd see Edie enrolled or booked in or whatever the term might be, and that she'd help move Edie and her belongings and art work there when required.

'I'm not going to be around so much,' Billy said. 'In the first place, I don't want her to think I want anything in exchange

276

for the money.' He coloured at the idea. 'And in the second place, she needs some time to get used to taking control of her life. First there was that dreadful woman, then there was that dreadful boyfriend.'

'And then me, though you're too polite to say so.'

'We-ell . . . After all, she's not a teenager, Lindsey. It's time she tried out some of the more enjoyable things in life.'

'I know what you mean.'

'But if ever there's a problem – about funds, or planning for the future.'

'Yes, you'll be the first to hear.'

He drove her back to the city and dropped her at her office.

The news that there had been a fracas in the conference room was all over the place.

Andrew Gilmore came to Lindsey's room to ask about it. 'Is that right, you had Billy Guyler in this morning, and his wife came too?'

'Yes, quite right.' No use trying to deny it.

'What was it? Divorce? If so, Berrinton will be very glad to hear it.' Berrinton was the firm's divorce expert.

'We didn't get that far,' Lindsey said. She was wondering if that would be the result in the end. If so, it was entirely to be regretted. They loved each other. The crisis they were going through now had nothing to do with the loss of love – but if Ursula Guyler remained adamant it might result in a definite separation. Asked to choose between them, Billy might choose Edie – because he felt he owed her so much.

'I heard he brought the other woman with him,' Andrew went on. 'A snip of a girl, Meg says.'

'I wouldn't put too much trust in that if I were you, Andrew.'

'How did the missus find out about it? I bet she's in a rage at Billy falling for someone young – that's the bit that always hurts, I imagine.'

'We didn't cover that sort of thing,' she said. It seemed to have eluded everyone that the conference room had been booked not for their client, Mrs Guyler, but for Billy.

'I don't know what Old Ollie is going to say when he hears,'

Andrew went on. 'He'll do anything Mrs G. wants, of course, but an angry divorce case isn't really his favourite thing.'

'Me neither.'

'Oh, come on,' Andrew begged, 'give us some of the inside info.'

'You know I can't discuss confidential matters, Andrew.'

He gave her one of his friendliest smiles. 'You've grown a bit distant recently, Lindsey.'

She too smiled, rather coldly. 'If I remember rightly, you were the one who put distance between us after Ollie had me on the carpet.'

'Oh, well . . . You know . . . That was only tactical manoeuvres. I didn't mean for it to go on so long.'

'You didn't?' She left unspoken the fact that it had been months since they had so much as shared a pizza. Andrew felt the weight of the wordless rebuke and flushed a little.

'Office politics are the devil,' he muttered. 'Let's kiss and make up, Lin.'

'Not just at this moment,' she said. 'I'm busy.'

He frowned, shrugged, and turned for the door. 'Suit yourself,' he said in a huffy tone, and went out.

The afternoon flew by. Lindsey stayed a little past the rest of the staff to catch up on e-mails and phone calls. When she got home it was almost seven, and Edie was sitting sorrily in the kitchen with a cup of black coffee.

'I've got a headache,' she said.

'Have you taken some aspirin?'

'Yeah, so far no good. That Krug . . . !' She gulped some coffee. 'Did I make a fool of myself?'

'Not at all. You simply got a bit . . . cheerful.'

'Oh, did I? I rang the store to say I didn't feel well and wouldn't come in. I think they were a bit browned off. I've taken a lot of time off recently.'

'Well, that doesn't matter, does it? You'll be giving up the job.'

'Will I?' She looked genuinely puzzled. 'I know we had a long talk, but I can't seem to remember what we said.'

'We said you should give up night work because it was too

tiring and you needed your strength for your classes. We said you'd be moving to a businesswomen's club—'

'I remember *that*.'

'And we said you'd accept the bank account to cover the cost of living expenses.'

'Um,' said Edie. She rubbed her aching forehead. 'I know it was a long conversation but did I really agree to all that?'

Lindsey smiled. 'You were dithering,' she said. 'But, Edie – take what Billy's offering.'

'But it's such a lot!'

'He has a lot of guilt to get rid of. This is his way of making amends. Let him do it, Edie. He needs to do it.'

Edie said nothing. Lindsey began on the process of preparing an evening meal. She moved about, making as little sound as possible in consideration of the headache, but in the end she needed to chop parsley and the knife on the board would make a racket.

'How's the head?'

'Throbbing.'

'Go into the living room. I need to do some crashing about.'

'You're not making anything for me, are you? I couldn't swallow a mouthful.'

'Okay.'

'Lindsey . . .'

'Yes?'

'You really think I should take the money and everything?'

'I really do.'

'All right then, you're on.'

Twenty-Two

The Businesswomen's Club was out on Summer Lane, in what appeared to be a converted warehouse. Loft-living was very popular, it seemed. It was divided into studio flats, some bigger than others. The one on offer was at a corner of the second floor, up a concrete staircase that dated from the original use yet had been made attractive by the astute hand of an interior decorator.

'Do you like it?' Lindsey asked as they looked around the room.

'Okay by me.'

'No, really, Edie – do you think you could live here?'

'It's fine,' she said. 'By the time I get my stuff here . . .'

Her stuff didn't actually amount to much. Two duffel bags of clothes, a large assortment of artwork, and a cardboard carton full of books. Lindsey was taken aback by how little Edie actually owned.

They'd been to the bank to open the bank account. Edie, rather scared, had signed a cheque for a month's rent in advance plus a membership fee. 'So you can move in,' remarked the manager, 'on the seventh of July.' And so she did, in a taxi with Lindsey as helper.

When it came time to say goodbye, there was a strange atmosphere. Lindsey felt rather like a mother handing over her five-year-old on her first day at school.

'Well, I'll leave you to sort yourself out, put your books on the shelves and so on.'

'Yeah.'

'How about if we meet tomorrow for a pub lunch?'

'I'd like that.' It was said with eagerness. Behind a facade of calmness, Edie was having something like a panic attack. She'd never actually been on her own before. There had always been someone – Ma Maybury, Graham Walker, Lindsey . . .

'All right then, ring me tomorrow when you're ready and we'll go somewhere.'

'Okeydokey.'

'Bye for now, then.'

Lindsey glanced back as she went out. Edie was walking through the vestibule and about to climb the concrete staircase. She looked . . . fearful, lonely.

Well, it had to be. Billy had put it into words. It was time for his daughter to sample some of the normal things in life, such as leaving home, going out on your own.

That evening Keith telephoned Lindsey. He was dying to know what was going on, but she evaded his questions. 'However,' she said, 'I can tell you this much. Next time you come to Birmingham, you can stay with me.'

A pause. 'You mean Edie has moved out?'

'That's what I mean.'

'Well, splendid!'

'I thought you'd think so.'

'Could I perhaps come tomorrow?'

'Not tomorrow, Keith – I've a date for lunch tomorrow.'

'Monday then?'

She laughed. 'Don't you have a newspaper to run?'

'Never mind the paper! This is important.'

'All right, then, Monday.'

It was strange being able to expect him at her flat. For months now, she'd had to think about someone else within her living space. Now that someone else would be the man she loved.

The thought brought her up short. Did she love Keith?

There was something between them – there was no doubt of that. She liked him tremendously. He made her laugh, he sympathised when she told him her problems, he was a considerate and ardent lover. Now that Edie was gone, it seemed Keith would be often at her flat. He would play a larger part in her life. Did she want that?

She thought about Andrew Gilmore, who'd once seemed so

important. Perhaps it was best not to become too dependent on anyone . . . Yet it was such a tremendous pleasure to look forward to Keith's visit. Surely it was all right to share at least part of her life with him?

Yes, why not?

And she began going round the flat, tidying up, checking the food supplies, the wine, looking forward with delight to having him there among these familiar surroundings.

When he arrived on Monday Keith engulfed her in an embrace that lasted for a long time. Then he let her go to inspect her home. It seemed incredible that this was the first time he'd seen it.

'I hope you realise how long-suffering I was while you had your lodger,' he teased her. 'Many's the time I wished her in Timbuktu.'

'Well, that sort of . . . just happened. I never meant to get stuck with her for such a long time.'

'So now she's gone. Where, exactly?'

'To a residential club.'

'Which one?'

'Why d'you want to know?'

'So that I can rush out and interview her, of course.'

'So of course I'm not going to tell you.'

'Huh! If I really wanted to know I could find out in half an hour. There's only so many places she could be in Birmingham.'

'I never said she was in Birmingham.'

'So she's gone elsewhere?'

'Never you mind!'

'Do I take it that since she's not gone home to be with Mama and Papa, there's been no loving family reunion?'

'You can take it how you like, my dear investigative journalist. Is that why you rushed here so fast – to cross-question me about Edie Maybury?'

He grinned. 'No, I had something completely different in mind.'

'Such as what?'

He moved towards a door along the little hall. 'Is this by

any chance the bedroom?' he enquired, and held out his hand to her.

Later, when they were sitting over the meal she'd prepared, he confessed he very much wanted to know what had happened in the Guyler affair. 'But not for publication,' he added quickly. 'I just feel a sort of link with it – after finding out about the Betty Trenton side of it.'

She shook her head. 'I really can't talk about it, Keith.'

'Well, can you at least tell me this – is Edie all right?'

'I think so.'

'On a score of one to ten, how all right?'

'About five or six.'

'That's not scoring very high.'

'Well, you can't score very high in a game where one of the players keeps walking away.'

'Ah. Which one – Papa or Mama?'

'Keith, I really can't talk about it.'

So with a shrug he let it drop. And because they had other and better things to occupy them, they didn't give any more thought to the Guylers.

But the next day when Keith had gone and the workaday world had taken over, her mind turned back to the problem. Should she be doing something to help resolve it? But it wasn't strictly her business as a solicitor – her client, Ursula Guyler, hadn't asked her to take any action.

So the days went by. Mid-July was approaching. One morning her office phone rang and the receptionist said, 'A Mrs Bergenstal to speak to you, Lindsey.'

'Who?'

'Bergenstal, I think she said.'

'Never heard of her.'

'She says she's calling from the Guyler residence.'

'The Guylers? Put her through!'

She thought it might be some doctor – a psychiatrist, she said to herself, from Vienna with a name like that.

'This is Lindsey Abercrombie.'

'Ah, Miss Abercrombie – here is Erika.'

'Who?'

283

'Erika, housekeeper at the Guyler house.'

'Oh, Erika! How do you do? Is something wrong?'

'Very much wrong, I think. I didn't know what else to do so I am calling you. Is this all right for me to do?'

'Of course – please – what's the matter?'

'The matter is that Mrs Guyler is making herself very sick. She eats nothing, she sleeps bad, she takes the sleeping pill and it makes her worse. *Der Herr* does not come back, she picks up the phone to call him then she slams it down. A strong woman, but I think she is breaking under this.'

'Has she seen a doctor?'

'From where do you think she gets the sleeping pills? Of course a doctor. "Doctor, I am nervy, I don't sleep good," so he prescribes, but she doesn't tell him what is really wrong and so it goes on, worse and worse.'

Lindsey hesitated. 'What do you want me to do?' she asked, perplexed.

'Madame, I want you to come and talk with her. I could think of no one else. She is not the woman to tell anyone her troubles, you know? But already you are . . . what is it . . . *unterrichtete* . . . aware of the problem, no?'

Only too aware, thought Lindsey. Aloud she said, 'She didn't ask you to call me?'

'*Aber nein!*' Erika's voice rose at the mere idea. 'She tells me, "Nothing is wrong, I am fine", but every morning I throw the breakfast in the bin and every evening I throw the dinner in the bin and how can it be nothing is wrong when every day she loses weight and looks more sick? I am very worried, Madame. I owe to Mrs Guyler, she has been good to me. I think it would be wrong to let her go on in this way. So I tried to think of someone who could talk with her and you – you are the one I think of.'

Lindsey could hear the desperation. 'What is it actually you want me to do?'

'Come here. Come to the house. Make her see good sense. I only know a little part of what it is that troubles, but it is to do with the daughter, *nicht*?'

'I'm afraid so.'

'The daughter . . . Madame, I lost a son. I came here with him, a charity provides the money so that he could have

284

medical treatment. But the doctors . . . Well, it was the will
of God, but I say to myself, "Madame could have a daughter,
why does she turn away from her?" To lose a child . . . I know
what that is. And to find again the child, that is a great, great
blessing. No matter that she is not what you expect, she is your
child, and you must try to love her, try to be her mother again.
I believe it is this that is making her so sick, that she fails so
badly . . . But it isn't my place to speak to her of it. So I beg
you to come, Madame, and try to help her.'

'Very well.' Impossible to withstand the passionate appeal.
'When should I come?'

'Oh, soon – the sooner the better or she will waste away to
a shadow. Come this evening, Madame!'

'Will Mrs Guyler be at home?'

'Why not? She goes nowhere. Sits at home, late into the
night, watching the terrible programmes on television, no
parties any more, no dressing up to go out to premieres. Ach,
she will be at home, so please, come, come!'

'All right, I'll be there.'

As soon as she'd disconnected she regretted her agreement.
Try to help her? She'd tried already, by letting Billy hold a
family gathering in her office. What good had it done? Ursula
had simply walked out.

In her own home, might things be different? There, she
might feel less threatened – and she certainly had felt threatened when Billy handed her the DNA documents. She'd
retreated, hurried away from a situation she simply couldn't
handle. But at home, in familiar surroundings and with only
one young woman as antagonist . . . ?

No, Lindsey checked herself, I'm not an antagonist. However much Ursula's stubborn denials might irritate her, she
was in essence an unbiased adviser, must be dispassionate but
helpful.

Helpful? What could she say that she hadn't already said?

She shook her head at herself. She should never have
given in to Erika. And yet – someone had to do something. And she'd seen Ursula in so many moments of crisis
that perhaps she'd gained some experience of how to handle
her. Besides, her work with family law had given her some

285

insight. A psychiatrist she was not, but she'd become perceptive of the routes by which others struggled out of turmoil. Perhaps she could act as at least some sort of guide to Ursula.

So she'd go, and she'd try to offer help, and there was some slight hope that Ursula might listen if the whole thing could be kept calm, quiet and well-intentioned.

All the same, Lindsey felt qualms all through the rest of the day and they were still in full force when she presented herself at the door of the Guylers' house.

Erika opened the door to her, at once seizing one of her hands in both of hers. 'Thank you, thank you,' she breathed. 'You are so good! I shall never stop being grateful to you for this. Please come in, she's in the drawing room, she scarcely touched her food and it was all of things she likes . . .'

She led the way along the hall, tapped at a door, went in and announced, 'Miss Abercrombie has come, Madame.'

'What?' cried Ursula, jumping up from her chair, completely startled. 'How dare you show her in! I don't want her in my house!'

Erika stood her ground like some sturdy Austrian herd dog facing a snow storm. 'I was given no instructions of that, Madame,' she said, and ushered Lindsey in.

Lindsey advanced, with much less courage than Erika had shown. She was trying to think what on earth to say.

'Did Billy send you?' Ursula demanded in a harsh tone. 'If you're here to plead his cause, don't bother.'

'I haven't spoken to Billy in days, Ursula. How are you? You don't look too—'

'Never mind how I am! As if you care, anyway! Out! I want you out!'

Lindsey had been going to say that Ursula didn't look well. And indeed, she did not. There were dark circles under her eyes, the bones of her face were more prominent, and the usually perfect hair showed signs of needing a visit to the hairdresser. Her clothes might be said to be perfect – a heavy silk caftan of dark blue with little matching slippers. Yet the long gown seemed somehow too big for her.

'Don't you want to know why I'm here?' Lindsey asked.

'Oh, that doesn't take much working out! If Billy didn't send you, *she* did.'

'She? Edie?'

'Who else? Didn't get what she wanted last month so now she's trying a new tack.'

'What do you think she wanted last month?'

'Money, of course – that's what it's been about all along.'

'Shula, if she wanted money she could make it by selling her story to a tabloid – MY HARD-HEARTED MUM by Julie Guyler.'

'Don't call her that! She's not my Julie!' The name struck at Ursula like a knife. Deep within her, grief awoke as if it was only yesterday she'd lost her. My baby, my baby, mourned the inner voice that was never completely stilled.

'No,' agreed Lindsey, 'she isn't.'

Ursula stared at the words. Then she slowly sank down on the nearest chair. 'So – so you agree she's not my daughter?'

'I didn't say that.'

'Yes, you did. You just said—'

'Can I sit down?' Lindsey asked. 'If we're going to have a conversation, I'd rather not stand as if I was giving a lecture.'

Ursula gestured at a chair. Her fury at Lindsey's arrival had vanished. This young woman was going to tell her something that would release her from the bonds she'd been struggling with for so long – she was going to tell her that Edie Maybury was an impostor and with that news, Ursula would be able to demolish the foolish fantasies her husband was harbouring.

Lindsey sat. A major point gained, to be able to sit and converse like a human being. 'I agreed she wasn't your Julie. She isn't. She's the girl Julie grew up to be, Edie Maybury. She's your daughter, all the same.'

'No. That's a lie. I don't want to hear any more.'

'You must, Shula. Don't back out now.'

'No!'

'Yes, *yes*, Shula. The scientific evidence is compelling.'

'Scientists can be wrong!'

'You mean you think the courts are wrong when they accept DNA testimony?'

'I don't know anything about the courts. I only know that

I feel in my heart that she's not my baby, never could be my baby!'

'Of course not. And that's the trouble, isn't it? You've been longing for a pretty three-year-old toddler.'

'Don't be absurd! Of course I knew that she'd be eighteen years older.'

'Yes, the grown up version of little Julie – sweet, biddable, loving. Instead you got a rough and tough young woman who didn't think much of you.'

'What do you mean, "didn't think much of me"?' Ursula blurted, astounded.

Lindsey shook her head at her. 'Did you think you were at your most lovable at the Old North Star Hotel? Looking down your noses at her, refusing to accept her young man.'

'That dreadful boy!'

'It wasn't endearing behaviour, was it?'

'But they were both so awful.'

'They weren't exactly your cup of tea, but if you could have detached yourself from the dream you'd had – of finding a lovely, princess-like girl who would live up to all your expectations.'

'I only wanted my own daughter back,' Ursula said, and began to cry.

To some extent it was a relief. It put an end to the pointless raking over of old coals. But Lindsey didn't know what to do. She'd had people break down in her office before now, and there she could always supply a tissue, a glass of water, a comforting murmur. Here in Ursula's home she was at a loss.

She'd reckoned without Erika, who must have been listening outside the door. In a moment the housekeeper was with them, providing a clean handkerchief, going to the drinks table for a glass of something restorative, nodding at Lindsey over the head of the sobbing woman.

'*Ruhig, ruhig, sei nicht so elend,*' she murmured. 'Everything will come right. Here is Miss Abercrombie, who will make it good again. *Komm, Liebling*, drink the sherry, it will do you good.'

Ursula obeyed, like a child. She sipped, sipped again, wiped her eyes with the handkerchief, made a little gesture of dismissal at her housekeeper, and gave Lindsey a watery smile. Erika went out, with a little nod of approval at Lindsey on the way.

There was a little silence. Lindsey waited for Ursula to break it. At length, with a wan smile, Ursula said, 'Well, I feel a fool.'

'It's all right to have a little weep, Shula.'

'It's supposed to make you feel better but all I feel is stupid.'

'Let's start all over again. First I must apologise for barging in uninvited.'

'Oh, I bet you were invited. Erika's been hanging over me like an anxious hen for days.'

'Well . . . she's very worried. You're making yourself quite ill, the way you're going on.'

'I can't help it. My head feels as if it's in a vice. I suddenly don't know where I am for minutes at a time. I lose track of conversations at the office . . .'

'Perhaps it would help you to talk it out.'

'Isn't that what we've just been doing?'

Lindsey suppressed a smile. 'I've been talking and you've been protesting.'

'We-ell . . . You've been *accusing*!'

'Perhaps I have. You think I was wrong in what I said about your attitude to Edie?'

There was a long hesitation. 'You said I had to accept the DNA results.'

'Well, wouldn't it make more sense than acting like an ostrich about them.'

'You mean I have to believe that girl is my daughter.' There was utter reluctance in her voice.

'She is, Shula.'

'You really believe she is?

'Of course. And I believed it long before Billy went to the clinic to get the tests done.'

'No.' Ursula was shaking her head. 'She can't be Julie.'

'There!' Lindsey cried, almost in triumph. 'You've said it! She can't be Julie – she can only be herself, and that's the girl she's *become*.'

'But Lindsey, she's turned into someone I could never like!' And there it was, admitted at last. The girl was her daughter. She'd grown more and more convinced of it as time went by. Yet it couldn't be so, because she simply didn't, couldn't like her.

Lindsey sighed. 'I said this to you before, I think it was almost at the outset. You don't have to like her. Lots of family members don't like each other.' Ursula hunched her shoulders and muttered at that. 'But you should stop being afraid of her.'

'I'm not afraid of her!' No one was going to say she was a coward and get away with it.

'Then why are you cowering at home and not trying to sort things out, at least between you and Billy?'

'*He's* the one who walked out!'

'But you could make him walk back in again by just picking up the phone.'

'No, no.'

'Why not?'

'Because it would mean . . .' What would it mean? So many things she couldn't accept, so many changes and innovations. 'I'd have to agree . . . He's taken on Edie as if she . . . she means a lot to him.'

'I think that's a given now, Shula. Billy likes having a daughter.'

'I'm not competing with a twenty-year-old!'

Lindsey said nothing. After a moment Ursula blushed, shaking her head at herself. 'Why did I say that?' she mourned.

'It's out in the open now, isn't it? Part of the problem has been that you're seeing Edie as a threat. Billy tells you she's changed, and when you eventually come across her in my office you try not to look at her, but you can't help but know she's not the horror-film character you first met. She's a rather nice-looking, ordinary girl.'

Lindsey waited. Ursula at last said, 'I suppose she is.'

'But she's his daughter, Shula. He's not falling for her. It's nothing like that.'

'But men are so soppy about daughters,' Ursula replied. And with a deep sigh, 'Especially about new-found daughters.'

'And you're not up to dealing with that?'

'Well, I . . . I . . .'

'You're not used to it. You've been the only woman in his life for so long that you can't take it.'

'You make me sound a self-centred idiot!' Ursula cried.

'Sorry, sorry. I'm not a marriage counsellor, I'm just doing the best I can. What's your take on it? Why are you so scared of Edie?'

'Who said I was scared of her?'

'Well, if you're not scared, what's the reason you find the DNA evidence so hard to take?'

'It's nothing to do with being scared,' she protested. 'I just . . . I was so hurt that he went behind my back and had that test done!' And her eyes filled with tears again.

Lindsey said nothing. It was a thought that hadn't occurred to her. After a moment of mopping her eyes, Ursula resumed, 'I just felt completely . . . at a loss. I've been all at sea ever since this thing started. I never expected it to make me feel so fuddled and upset and when Billy produced that report . . . It was . . . as if he'd slapped me . . . Oh, I can't explain, I know I sound crazy.'

'Would you like my opinion?'

'Ha! Isn't that what I've been getting?'

'I mean, on what to do next.'

Ursula frowned. 'No, thank you. You've done quite enough, thanks.' Some ghost of her usual common sense stirred and took command. 'I know I've been a fool but it's my business, I'll sort myself out on my own.'

'Right you are.'

'Don't sound so unconvinced!'

'It's just that you've made yourself quite ill . . . It wouldn't be good if you went back into that sort of state.'

Ursula was taken aback. 'You're really quite concerned, aren't you? I mean, it's not just that you're a solicitor trying to sort out a problem, you're quite bothered about me.'

'Of course.'

'Does that get put on the bill?'

'Now, Shula,' Lindsey reproved. 'Stop it. I think you're past that stage.'

'What stage?' But she managed a faint smile. She'd proved she was still capable of carrying the attack into the enemy's camp. Although Lindsey Abercrombie wasn't an enemy, after all.

'The stage I meant was where you're hitting out at everybody,' Lindsey said.

'Is that what I've been doing?'

Lindsey got up. 'I think this is a good time for me to say goodnight. If you're asking yourself sensible questions, you should be able to get sensible answers.'

'Oh . . . wait . . .' Her sense of what was fitting suddenly asserted itself. 'I never offered you a drink, or anything.'

'That's okay. I just need to ring for a taxi.'

Ursula actually laughed. 'I bet Erika's doing that this very minute! Hovering at my elbow all the time, trying to foresee every need. You know, I think I owe her a lot. You too, perhaps.' She offered Lindsey her hand, and they shook. 'Well, so long then. I'll give it all a lot of consideration.'

'That would be good.'

'Better, at least, than doing the ostrich bit.'

'Right.'

Lindsey went out, to find Erika hovering in the hall. They exchanged glances but not a word was spoken until the housekeeper was watching her step into the taxi.

'Madame,' she said in a fervent voice, 'thank you.'

Twenty-Three

A cloudy day, but warm and sultry, the air almost too heavy to breathe. Edie came out of the college doors at about four in the afternoon, glad to think that in a few days the term would end.

Chepperton would then close for a couple of weeks for necessary repairs and refurbishment after a year's almost continuous use, daytime and evening, six days a week. Then it would re-open for the summer school, crash courses for those who needed to catch up on basic learning.

Edie had intended to enrol for those weeks, but Billy had persuaded her to go instead to an adult education centre in Wales. There, she'd take part in an amateur production of *The Little Prince* by Oscar Wilde.

Edie had read the story and her verdict, murmured to Lindsey, was that it was 'kind of soppy'. Still, she hoped to take part in designing costumes and sets – the sets not much use to her because they'd be largely done with curtains and lighting, but the costumes . . . ?

She was heading along the pavement thinking about the little plastic figures she'd made. This evening perhaps, she'd try out the scraps of cloth on them to see if the colours were right. Next would come the fiddly job of making the tiny garments – her sewing was adequate but she still wished her sketching was good enough to convey what she meant; making figures and clothing them could *really* be a pain.

A Mercedes was drawn up alongside the kerb. Its driver's door opened and someone stepped out in front of her. Help, thought Edie in amusement, I'm being kidnapped.

'Hello, Edie,' said the kidnapper in a nervous voice.

It was Ursula Guyler.

They stood confronting one another, blocking the pavement with their presence and the open car door. A pedestrian walked around them tut-tutting.

'Would you like to . . . hop in the car, Edie?' Ursula suggested.

'What?'

'We're blocking the path.'

'Oh . . . yeah . . . well . . . all right.' She went round to the other side and got in the passenger seat. Ursula got in, released the brake, and drove off.

'So am I being taken for a ride?' Edie asked in a gangster voice.

'We're going to the shops.'

'We are? What for?'

'We're going to buy you a dress.'

'A dress?'

'A party dress.'

'I'm going to a party?'

'Your birthday party.'

'I've had my birthday,' said Edie. 'It was in June.'

'No, that was your Edie Maybury birthday. Your Julie Guyler birthday is on the twelfth of August, which means you're a Leo, and everybody knows that Leos have to show off a bit and as it's your twenty-first, it's got to be a really nice dress.'

She'd been talking rather fast and breathlessly, to fill what might have been an awkward hiatus. She glanced with some trepidation at her daughter, who was gazing through the windscreen at the traffic lights and shop signs.

After a moment Edie said, 'I've never had a dress.'

'Never?' Ursula countered, amazed.

'Not that I can recall. There used to be a snapshot we toted around in a box of stuff from one town to another and that showed a kiddie in a frilly frock, but it got lost somewhere. I think that was me in the photo, but I don't remember the dress.'

'So what did you wear to school and whatever? School uniform?'

'The schools I went to?' Edie said in scorn. 'Nah! T-shirts

294

and a denim skirt in summer, sweatshirts and jeans in winter.' She gave a sidelong glance at Ursula and to rub it in added, 'They usually came from jumble sales and that sort of thing.'

It had even more effect than she'd intended. Her mother's mouth quivered, and she blinked once or twice as if to get rid of a tear.

'What brought this on?' Edie enquired, but in a gentler tone than before. 'This urge to scoop me up and make me a birthday girl?'

Ursula hesitated. 'It's been sort of . . . building up. The last few days I've driven past the college a couple of times, wondering if I'd see you.'

'And?'

'And today I did see you, and knew it was you despite—' She broke off, making a little gesture that took in Edie's clothes and hair. 'And it seemed silly not to . . . meet.'

'But we'd met already.'

'This time it's different.'

'Certainly is. I'm not quite sure what to make of it.' That was an understatement. Edie was thunder-struck.

They were in a main road where there was a pub with a parking area. Ursula turned in, parked neatly, and switched off. The engine ticked into silence.

'What now?' enquired Edie.

'I can't talk about important things and attend to traffic at the same time.'

'Are we going to talk about important things?'

'Yes, we are. It's time to sort things out.' Ursula gave an unsteady laugh. 'I admit I've been a stumbling block and I'm apologising.'

'I see.'

'What I'd like,' she went on, 'is for us to get to know each other. We got off on the wrong foot and I confess I was to blame. I've given it a lot of thought – in fact I've thought of practically nothing else for weeks – and it seems to me that if we could . . . you know . . . meet and chat and go shopping and do what other mothers and daughters do . . .' She paused. She was hoping for a sign of agreement but Edie made no move. 'What do you think?' she asked.

Edie went to quite another aspect. 'Did you talk this over with Billy?'

'Ah . . . No . . . I wanted to do this on my own. Then you see I thought I could go to him and say you'd agreed to try a new start and he'd forgive me . . .' Her voice trembled into silence.

They sat saying nothing. Ursula was afraid to speak again. She'd never been good at expressing emotion, and at this moment she was too overwhelmed to find any more words.

'Billy would be pleased,' Edie ventured in a musing tone. 'He's been really down.'

'Has he? I haven't . . . been in touch.'

'I know that. He's been eating his heart out.'

'Oh, dear,' said Ursula, and put her hands over her face.

Edie couldn't tell whether she was crying or not. She looked at Ursula, trying to make out if any tears were creeping between the fingers. After a moment she put out a hand and touched Ursula's shoulder. 'It's all right,' she said.

Ursula shook her head without taking her hands away from her face. 'No it's not,' she mumbled. 'I've made everybody unhappy. I've been an utter *fool*!'

'Mmm.' Edie felt she couldn't in honesty disagree with that. But she said, 'Well, I didn't help, did I? Gruesome Gertie, I was.'

Ursula took away one hand to give a little glance at her. 'That terrible white make-up!'

'Theatre stuff, you know. I think they use it for the ghost in *Hamlet*.'

There was a giggle from behind the covering fingers. 'Dracula, more like.'

'Well, you know . . . it seemed a good idea at the time.'

'I can't think why,' Ursula said, sitting up with some return of composure and patting at her hair. 'You've got a nice skin, I can't think why you wanted to hide it.'

'You all right now?'

'As right as I can be for the moment. This is a difficult time for me, Edie.' She glanced at her and away. 'I'm not used to eating humble pie.'

'Caviar and champagne, more your style?'

'That's it. And that's been part of the problem – I like things to be nice, you know? And I couldn't come to terms with the idea that you were . . . well . . .'

'Not nice.'

'Oh, I'm sorry, I didn't mean that.'

''S all right,' said Edie almost airily. 'I read a thing in my literature class – "the hour of thoughtless youth" – that was me then, if you see what I mean. Wherever me and Ma Maybury settled, nobody seemed to like us much, so as soon as I had a bit of money from a job I began to build up a sort of defence – I s'pose all that black gear was my armour, eh? Bad luck I chose that sort of stuff, I could've gone for the outdoor look, or mebbe even been a DIY type because I'm good with my hands . . .'

'A sort of disguise?'

'Yeah. Well, I'll meet you halfway on it – I wasn't especially attractive and I put you right off, didn't I?'

Ursula sighed. 'Let's say neither of us was at our best.'

'You're on.'

'So is this a fresh start?'

'Buying a dress? For me it certainly is,' Edie said, laughing.

So Ursula re-started the car and they drove to the shopping centre, each wondering how this was going to turn out.

Later in the day Edie rang Lindsey.

'Oh, hi! Getting ready for end of term?'

'Yeah, I've taken a lot of stuff home from the graphics studio already. Listen, Lin, big news. Today I went shopping and then had tea with Shula.'

Lindsey was surprised, and then not surprised but very pleased. 'Well, well . . .'

'She wanted to buy me a party dress.'

'What for?'

'To wear at my twenty-first birthday party.'

'You're having a party?'

'Shula's setting it up. You're invited. Twelfth of August.'

'Can't do it. I'll be in Italy.'

'Oh, so you will. Well, that narrows down the guest list. It'll be me and Shula and Billy, I s'pose.'

'And you're going to wear the dress? What's it like?'

'Baby blue silk organza. Knee length. With a frill.'

'A frill.'

'Round the hem. It's narrow, though.'

'Well, let's be thankful for that.'

'She was so keen on it, I hadn't the heart to say no.'

'Mothers do that,' Lindsey explained. 'Perhaps you'll have to get used to it.'

'Does your ma buy you things you don't like?'

'Not any longer. I've educated her. But it takes time, you know.'

'The next thing is she wants me to go to a beauty salon. Have my nails done.'

'No harm in that.'

'But then she'll want me to have streaks in my hair, same as her.'

Lindsey laughed. 'Remember, you used to have yours dyed flat black.'

'So I did. Well, there you are, funny, isn't it? Flat black was bad, gold streaks are good. We'll see.'

Lindsey cleared her throat as a signal to talk seriously. 'Do I take it that she and Billy have got together again?'

'Right on. She rang him on her mobile when we were having tea in this posh restaurant. I decided to go and powder my nose when she got to a certain point – it was all "darling" and "dearest" and that sort of stuff. Do your ma and pa go on like that?'

'Hardly,' said Lindsey, thinking of her austere and rather taciturn father. 'But they do throw in the occasional "dear". Of course, this telephone call was a different thing, Edie. Making up. You're entitled to go a bit over the top at a time like that.'

'If you say so. I haven't had any experience with parents.' She sighed. 'It's all so *weird*, Lindsey. Like hearing a foreign language.'

'But nice.'

'Well, yes,' she agreed, though her tone held some doubt. 'Anyhow, Shula went flying off to the hotel to see Billy and I get the impression he'll have moved back home by tomorrow.'

'That's good.'

'So I expect they're probably going to ask me to move in with them.'

'You think so?'

'It's what Billy's wanted from the first. Live in their house, be their darling daughter.'

'It doesn't appeal to you?'

'I dunno. I'm just getting used to coping on my own. Dunno if I want Shula at my elbow saying "Use more moisturiser" or "I'll enrol you in the health club".'

Lindsey was nodding in understanding. 'But don't forget, Edie, she's got about eighteen years to catch up on – eighteen years of not doing things for you.'

'She says there's a room I could use for my work.'

'You mean you're tempted?'

'But I get space for my work at the graphics studio.'

'You don't have to decide right now, Edie. Wait a bit, see how it goes. You're off to this summer school anyhow, aren't you?'

'Yeah, that's when my birthday pops up. She's coming to the school, collecting me, we're going to some famous restaurant like that one we went to – the Richelieu? – seems there's these classy places dotted around for folk that like classy food. Billy was already going to be in the neighbourhood, he's playing golf at Llanelli or somewhere. So she's going to fix it all up, and we'll have shampers again and I'll get woozy and agree to almost anything, won't I?'

Lindsey laughed. 'Decisions, decisions! That's what family life is like, love. You'll have to sort it out as you come to it, bit by bit. I'll admit Shula could be overpowering if you let her, but . . . well . . . you'll learn how to handle her.'

'Think so?'

'I haven't a doubt.'

'To tell the truth . . .'

'Yes?'

'I'm a bit scared. In case I muck it all up somehow.'

'No, no. You'll be fine.' Lindsey was sure of it, and put all her assurance into her voice. After a moment she added, 'Would you like to come to the flat? Have a sandwich and a chat?'

299

'Not tonight,' Edie said. 'I'm worn out. It's been a bit of a whirligig, today.'

'I can imagine. Come tomorrow, then.'

'Can't. Shula said she'd like me to come to the house tomorrow evening, for dinner and to see if I'd like one of the spare rooms.'

'Ah.' It was clear that Edie wouldn't be as dependent on Lindsey as in days gone by. She had her own family now. Lindsey felt a strange sense of relief, as if a burden had been removed from her back. She was a little ashamed, and said quickly, 'Okay, then, ring me whenever you feel like it.'

'Yeah. Thanks. Lindsey . . . ?'

'Yes?'

'You're a peach.'

On this complimentary note, they disconnected.

Lindsey was looking forward to her holiday in Italy. She hadn't mentioned to Edie that Keith Holland was flying out to spend a few days with her there. Her brother Gil worked in Bologna but had a mountain *casina di caccia* which he was lending them. The cool mountain air of the Apennines, the leisurely pace of life – how she longed for them after this difficult and crowded year.

Life at the office hadn't been good. Reverberations over the Guylers' row had gone on for days. Mr Ollerenshaw, arriving back from his business trip to Bristol, had believed the general gossip about an impending divorce so that when Lindsey contradicted it, he was at a loss.

'Then what was going on in the conference room while I was away? My information is that Mrs Guyler stalked out looking very angry, after some audible turbulence in the room.'

'There were some emotional remarks. They had nothing to do with a divorce.'

'Then who was the young woman who attended the gathering? I have it on good authority that she was the third party in the divorce.'

Lindsey stiffened. She was tired of being told information

that was nonsense. '*I* am the only authority on this, Mr Ollerenshaw. The girl was *not* the other woman in a divorce triangle.'

'Then who was she?'

There was no point in trying to keep the information from him. Billy Guyler had been proclaiming defiant intentions to make everything public. So she said, 'The girl is Mr Guyler's daughter.'

'I beg your pardon?'

'His daughter, and Mrs Guyler's daughter. The missing Julie, known for most of her life as Edie Maybury.'

'*Edie Maybury*? She was here?'

'Yes.'

'The girl who held Mrs Guyler up to public scorn in the spring?'

'Yes.'

Ollerenshaw's eyes went cold and hard, his voice turned icy. 'Miss Abercrombie! Do I take it that you have *kept contact* with this person?'

'Yes, I have.'

'When I specifically ordered you not to?'

Lindsey decided on direct confrontation. 'My opinion was that you didn't quite understand the situation, Mr Ollerenshaw. In family matters, all parties can be at fault and in this case, Mrs Guyler's attitude—'

'Mrs Guyler is our client! Her attitude is our attitude. It was clearly against her wishes that you should take any part in helping that young woman.'

'But Mr Guyler doesn't share that view.'

'Mr Guyler is not our client.'

'Excuse me,' she said, letting some temper show, 'our client is actually the company, Gylah Cosmetics, and Mr Guyler is a partner.'

'Don't bandy words with me, young lady! There's no question that Mrs Guyler *is* Gylah Cosmetics. You had no business doing anything specifically for the husband.'

'You must allow me to differ from you there, Mr Ollerenshaw. Ursula Guyler came to me on a family matter, and a family matter can't be handled in isolation. I felt it was my duty to

301

keep contact with all three if and when I could. The girl, who was a key member—'

'A key member! An impostor!'

'No, Mr Ollerenshaw.' Enough, she thought. 'DNA tests have established that she's Billy Guyler's daughter.' She paused to let that sink in then went on, 'I should be wary of calling her names. Mr Guyler is extremely protective of her, and if he heard what you just said, he'd call it slander and perhaps bring an action.'

Old Oliver coloured up, opened his mouth to say something, then closed it. Wrathful at what he saw as insubordination, he sat in silence for a long moment. Then he said with a frown, 'She is his daughter?'

'And he so acknowledges her.'

'Good God.'

She could see he was dumbfounded and seized her opportunity. 'Mr Ollerenshaw, this young woman hasn't received the best treatment from Mrs Guyler. We excuse that to some extent because Mrs Guyler is experiencing great emotional distress. However, we oughtn't to make matters worse by accepting unsubstantiated gossip.' She gave her boss a meaningful look, to make sure he got the point. 'Mrs Guyler is *not* suing for divorce. There *is* no other woman. Their affairs are in a state of confusion and it's true that Mrs Guyler is angry, very angry.'

'With you,' interjected Old Ollie, rallying. 'For befriending the girl, contrary to instructions.'

'With herself,' said Lindsey. 'Perhaps you haven't had as much contact with people in trouble as I have. Contract law tends to be argued out between solicitors, whereas I see open distress very often. Where the Guylers are concerned, my view is that we should exercise caution and remain ready to help, because it's quite clear to me that Billy Guyler is *not* going to give up his daughter. The Guylers may separate, they may not. I hope they won't.'

Old Ollie took this in with unwillingness. He said, 'You should have kept me informed.'

She didn't reply, as she might have, that he had given her direct instructions to turn her back on Edie Maybury. Had she obeyed him, Billy Guyler would never have been reunited with

302

his lost child. Neater, of course, from Mr Ollerenshaw's point of view, but even he surely wasn't prepared to say it was a preferable outcome.

He was extremely uncomfortable at what he was hearing. He asked a few questions about Billy Guyler's association with the girl, nodded now and again, and let Lindsey go. She got the strong impression that although he couldn't actually find fault with what she'd done, he was very displeased.

That was in the aftermath of the family gathering in the conference room. A few weeks later, it became known that Ursula Guyler had been seen around the up-market shops with a young woman who had a noticeable resemblance to her. A sort of uncertainty developed in the office. What did it mean? What might it mean to the firm? Was Ursula Guyler pleased with them, or not? And what was Old Ollie going to do?

No actual, official acknowledgement had been made of Edie's status. Edie herself had asked for that to be put on ice. 'It'll only make the reporters flock round us,' she confided to Lindsey. 'Do we need that?'

Lindsey couldn't but agree. In the midst of a relationship so new and delicate, too much public attention might do harm. All the same, an announcement in the personal columns of the broadsheets might have been helpful to her. At work there were sidelong glances; conversations stopped abruptly when she came into a room. The staff were discussing her situation – would Old Ollie ever be able to forgive her for not keeping him totally informed about the Guyler affair? For putting him in the wrong?

Her feeling of being somehow in disgrace was borne out later when, just before the summer holiday season, the annual bonuses agreed by the auditors were announced. At the Wednesday staff conference she learned that she herself had achieved a decent bonus but the wished-for invitation to a partnership hadn't been extended. However, Andrew Gilmore had been made a junior partner.

It was a rebuff. She had offended Mr Ollerenshaw and he intended to punish her. She was angry, because it seemed childish and prejudiced – but then he had never really been keen on having a woman in the office except in a secretarial or housekeeping capacity.

So as August shuffled in with all its stuffy heat and discomfort, she looked forward to a break during which she could think things through. She longed for the Italian highlands, the spare simplicity of the little hunting lodge, and the whimsical good nature of Keith Holland.

She drove in her rented Italian car to meet his plane at Bologna airport. As she watched his rangy figure come through arrivals she felt a surge of delight. They hadn't seen each other in almost a month. The farming community in his part of the world were going through a particularly hard time. He'd been busy reporting their troubles and interviewing agricultural experts, sharing the uncertainties about the future.

But he'd left all that behind him for the moment. Only pleasure showed in his face as he surveyed her. She was bare-legged, in sandals and a summer dress. 'Lindsey, you're a sight for sore eyes. Or, as they say in this part of the world, *"Com' e bella la signorina!"* Impressed?'

'Impressed but not surprised.' They hugged and kissed. 'I might have known you'd speak Italian better than I do.'

'Comes from weeks of trying to get an interview years ago – I was on the trail of an Italian film director holed up in the Veneto with somebody else's wife. Well, how are you, my lovely legal lady?'

'All the better for seeing you. I see you're clad in holiday gear.' He was in Docker slacks, heavy shoes, and a worn linen shirt. 'How was your flight?'

'Never mind my flight. Where is this mountain castle of yours, Rapunzel?'

'Castle! Two rooms and a vine arbour – and the grapes from the vine are uneatable.'

He threw his travel bag in the back and got into the car. As they drove out towards the mountains, he looked about eagerly. One of the things she liked about him was that he was interested in everything, and was never bored or indifferent.

He loved the hunting cabin as soon as he saw it. 'How could you be so unjust to it!' he cried. 'It's like a little eagle's nest.'

Perched as it was on a tiny grassy shelf, it had a superb view: winding narrow roads in the higher mountains to the east, leading up to stony peaks where villages clung like clumps of lichen to the crags. Below, hidden by the contours of the mountainside, was a lake, from which hydro-electric power fed energy to the area. The cabin, despite her disparagement, had light and even heating for the cool of the night, and her brother Gil had installed modern amenities but no telephone.

It was an ideal hideaway for two people weary of the pressure of everyday life. They spent the daylight hours walking in the quiet valleys and the nights in each other's arms. But the idyll could only be brief. Keith had to be in Cartfield for press day, so she drove him back to the airport for a late-night flight on Monday.

They arrived in time to have a drink together in the bar. She found herself saying, without preamble, 'I've decided to leave Higgett, Ollerenshaw and Cline.'

He set down his glass untouched. 'What brought that on?'

'I've got at cross-purposes with the boss.'

'Old Ollie?'

'Yes, him. We've never really seen eye to eye – I think that at heart he doesn't like the idea of women solicitors. Anyway, I've decided to pack up and go elsewhere.'

Keith didn't say, 'Isn't that rather rash?' or show any doubt about her decision. 'Got anything fixed up – another job?'

'No. I've been sort of . . . letting it all simmer. What I'd really like is to go more or less on my own and do family law.'

'Plenty of it about,' he acknowledged, picking up his wine and sipping while he studied her over the rim of the glass. 'Hard, though – to go on your own?'

'Yes, probably. But . . . in a firm like HO and C, it's so big and there's so much back-biting – office politics, you know. I'm not good at that kind of thing. I know it's silly, but I find it a bit distasteful.'

'I imagine you'd find plenty of families in Birmingham needing legal advice.'

'I thought of leaving Birmingham.'

'Leaving?'

'I was getting tired of city life and being here in the Appenino has confirmed it – I want to live in the country again.'

> 'It's oh, once again in the north I would be,
> For the oak and the ash and the bonnie ivy tree,
> They flourish at home in the north countree.'

So he understood. He knew she was a north-country girl and felt the longing to go back to it. 'Somewhere quiet,' she mused. 'I thought perhaps County Durham, some country town, not too big . . . . When I get back I'll start looking.'

'Cartfield is very nice,' he suggested hopefully. 'Not in County Durham, of course, but it has its good points.'

'No, no – too much distraction in Cartfield.'

'Lindsey!' he begged. 'Don't call me a distraction!'

She shook her head at him. 'I'm still thinking about it,' she said. 'Don't try to make me do things I'm not ready for.'

His narrow face assumed an expression of exaggerated hope. 'If and when you settle in County Durham, may I come and see you when you've been practising law for ten years or so?'

'I'll let you know.'

He sighed. 'You must be an absolute whiz at drawing up legal documents – you're so hard to pin down!' Then he brightened. 'All the same, "the north countree" is closer than Birmingham. It gets my vote.'

She promised to keep him informed of any and all decisions as they parted. Now that she'd put it into words, her thoughts about leaving Higgett, Ollerenshaw and Cline hardened into a resolve. When she went to finish her holiday with a stay at her brother's flat in Bologna, she rang her mother to discuss it.

'Well, that would be nice, Linnie,' murmured Alicia Abercrombie. 'To have you closer to us . . . But that's not the main issue, is it? You feel you're ready for this big change?'

'I've always wanted to specialise in family law. And I've given it a lot of thought. The way things are going in agriculture,' Lindsey said, 'farming families might have a lot of problems in the near future. It would be good to be there, Mum, ready to help.'

'That's true, dear. Let me put your father on. He'll probably have ideas about it.'

Her father heard her out, approving on the whole, offering sound advice on the financial side. 'You'll need a friendly bank. Come for a weekend when you get back,' he suggested. 'We'll talk it over, maybe have a drive around, looking at possibilities.'

The 'possibilities' would have to be rather inexpensive. To tell the truth, having Edie as a house guest had cost her some of her savings. She kept hoping that one of the Guylers might recognise that fact and offer reimbursement, yet she certainly wasn't going to broach it herself. But on the whole, she was confident of a bank loan to set her up on her own or to buy into some small country law practice.

When she got back, September was approaching. At the weekend she went home as suggested, and on Saturday she and her parents made a tour of the towns she'd singled out. She'd looked at advertisements in the broadsheets and specialist magazines, noted the addresses of firms offering either office space or some kind of partnership. She wasn't looking for 'big time' law. She wanted somewhere with enough population to give her a clientele but with countryside around it and space to breathe.

She found the right niche with an elderly partnership in a small market town. John and Walter Prackley told her they were planning to retire. Bachelor brothers only a year apart in age and so alike they might have been twins, they explained their intentions. 'We want someone sensible and competent, willing to take on more than just the legal problems of our neighbours,' John Prackley said. 'We want to feel that our friends will be in good hands when we go five years from now.' Keen amateur archaeologists, they'd already bought a croft on one of the Shetland Islands and were going to write a book about Viking settlements

Lindsey had taken to them at once. She felt sure she could work with them during the run-in period, and the price they were asking was within her financial scope. What remained to be seen was whether the practice would generate enough income to pay back the bank loan and give her an income.

'You're really going?' Edie Maybury asked, looking around ruefully at the signs of packing in Lindsey's flat.

'Yes, I'm signing the papers tomorrow. It's a two-man firm in Daverton, on a river that flows into the Derwent eventually. The Derwent?' she said as Edie looked lost. 'It's a big river in County Durham. There's a good rural community around the town, some former mining villages, and some farms struggling to keep going in these hard times.'

'Hard times? Is that good for a law firm?'

'My dad asked the same thing, Edie. "Will they be able to pay their legal bills?" But I prefer to ignore that.'

Edie had brought some of her handiwork to show off to Lindsey. The residential summer school had been a great success, giving her some items she could include in her portfolio for her exams next year at the college. She was busy, sharing much of her time with her father and mother but still holding out against 'living at home'.

'I'm not ready for that yet,' she'd protest. 'Perhaps I never will be.' But she'd brought herself to understand they needed her – she was part of the restoration work that had to go on between Ursula and Billy Guyler.

She didn't want to lose Lindsey. In a way, Lindsey was closer to her than her newly acquired parents. But she, who was always talking about her independence, had to acknowledge that Lindsey had every right to go away and do her own thing.

'You can come and visit me any time you like,' Lindsey suggested. 'The place I'm renting has spare rooms, and it's not far, you know.'

'It jolly well is – over a hundred miles!'

'But now you've got your driving licence, you can whiz up north on the motorway.'

Edie nodded, but sighed. She knew she wouldn't make the trip very often. She had so much on her plate these days. What a difference from her childhood, when time seemed to stretch boringly ahead of her, with nothing to do and no one to do it with.

Well, she was lucky. She knew that and reminded herself of the fact every day. And though Lindsey was going away, they'd still be friends.

That was something she was learning – people weren't all that difficult to get to know, friendships could arise almost without effort, and all the more easily if you shared some interests. Her fellow students were friends, and there was that fellow who'd joined in September, nice-looking guy, she wouldn't mind getting to know him better . . .

Lindsey's resignation had caused consternation at Higgett, Ollerenshaw and Cline. Even when he heard through the grapevine that she was signing papers with some tatty little country practice, Mr Ollerenshaw was still hoping to persuade her to change her mind. He invited her to have sherry in his office.

'Miss Abercrombie . . . Lindsey . . . is it wise to go? You have made a place for yourself in this firm.'

'But not a very rewarding one,' she intervened. 'I have to tell you I've felt ill at ease here.'

'Oh, surely not! For what reason?'

'There was criticism that seemed to me rather unnecessary, and a lack of understanding.'

'Lindsey, I hear you,' said Ollerenshaw. 'I confess I was wrong over the Guyler situation but you must understand I belong to the old school. I like matters that can be dealt with according to the rules.'

'Exactly. So I feel I must go elsewhere and try out my school of thought, which takes more notice of the human aspect.'

'Ah . . . That would be difficult for me to do, speaking for myself, but if you would consider staying on? The department of family law, which developed under your aegis, might be allowed to expand.' He looked hopefully at her as he said this, wondering if it was the best ploy.

'I appreciate the implication, but it might be hard to get permission for some of the methods I prefer. I've found it difficult here. I wanted to work in the best interest of the client which sometimes meant stretching the strict legal framework.'

'But a legal firm is not a psychiatric clinic, my dear girl.'

'Certainly not. But it ought to have been clear to all of us here that, for instance, Mrs Guyler was in an extremely tense emotional state. Her case couldn't be handled by simply accepting her instructions.'

'Mrs Guyler, I may say, cannot speak too highly of you these days,' Ollerenshaw broke in, unwilling to accept the implied reproach. 'A very satisfactory outcome. If it would persuade you to stay, I may say the senior partners would be willing to give you a free hand in any matters that concern Mrs Guyler's . . . er . . . family.'

'Thank you, but I've always wanted to go out on my own one day, and now seems a good time.'

Ollerenshaw sighed. He was having to admit to himself that he'd made bad choices. To have given a partnership to Andrew Gilmore was a mistake, it should have gone to Lindsey Abercrombie. Too late to remedy that now, the firm couldn't afford another junior partner.

'Let me just say,' he began again, 'that we are not advertising your post. If you should decide in the near future that you would like to return to us, your desk would still be there waiting for you.'

'Mr Gilmore would still be on the firm?'

'Oh, certainly.' Aha, he remembered someone saying there was an attraction between those two.

'In that case, Mr Ollerenshaw, I shall certainly not be coming back.'

'You don't wish to work with Mr Gilmore?'

'Decidedly not.'

He was vexed. Had he misunderstood the hints he'd been given? 'I had the impression that you and he got on rather well?'

'That may once have been the case but as the French say, everything changes. No, thank you, Mr Ollerenshaw, but I think it's time for a new beginning.'

Andrew had tried to dissuade her from leaving. 'You're making a big mistake,' he told her when he heard the rumours. 'You've turned yourself into a big noise around here now that Mrs Guyler's singing your praises. Get her to recommend you to her business pals and you could pile up the money.'

310

'No, Andrew, I've made up my mind to go.'

'Well then . . . if you really mean that . . . How about if you recommend me to Mrs Guyler? It'd be quite a feather in my cap if she chose me out of the partnership.'

Lindsey suppressed a sigh. 'Mrs Guyler is quite capable of making her own choices,' she said. And wondered how she'd ever thought him lovable.

Daverton was rather an austere little town. The Prackley brothers had found her semi-permanent accommodation in a holiday cottage, vacant now that winter was approaching and perhaps, if next summer proved as disastrous as the one recently ended, available to buy. She arrived on Sunday, driving north from Birmingham in a rented van with her belongings – clothes, some food supplies, but mostly books.

Her own car was still in the garage in Ellenham where she'd left it on accepting the job with Higgett, Ollerenshaw and Cline. Even on her first interview there, she'd realised that the sleek silver Corolla would be little use in a city like Birmingham. But here in Daverton she'd need it – and driving might become a pleasure again. Life would be quite different in Daverton.

She found that though she'd taken a cursory look at the place on an earlier visit, she'd missed the fact that the sparsely furnished holiday home had no book shelves. She sat down in one of the elderly armchairs, and felt her eyes fill with unexpected tears.

What was she *doing* here? In this cold, half-empty cottage in a town where she knew nobody? Why had she given up the familiar – and lucrative – routine of the big city? Had it all been a fit of pique, because Andrew Gilmore had been given a partnership and she had not?

For some moments she sat there, listening to the faint creakings of the little old house as it resisted a cold November easterly wind. Through the window she could see clouds scudding across a slate blue sky, and in the garden of the cottage a few bare-leaved bushes swaying in the breeze.

But among them was a Bourbon rose, bearing a late-autumn

flush of blooms. Its full-petalled flowers tossed and turned, resisting to the end the loss of finery. She watched it for a while, then sat up straight in the sagging chair. 'Right,' she said to the rose, 'I get the message – stop snivelling and get on with it.'

She went round the cottage, turning on all the heating she could find, opening the windows a crack to get rid of the musty smell. She brought in her belongings, and sought out the carton containing the wine she'd brought from the Appenino. She opened a bottle, poured some into a mug adorned with the message 'A Present from Scarborough', and held it up in a toast to the Bourbon rose.

'Here's to the firm of Prackley Brothers and Abercrombie,' she said to the empty house. 'God bless all who litigate in it.' Then she unpacked, piled her books in the room she meant to use as her study, cooked up some microwave food, made up the bed in the master bedroom and fell into it.

Her first day at work was extraordinary. The office was in a substantial house in Daverton's main street, with an old wrought-iron lantern hanging over the doorway. When she arrived, the elderly receptionist, beaming, handed her a pile of mail which by the feel of it consisted of greeting cards. When she entered the room assigned to her, she found it full of flowers, from the Guylers, from Edie, from her parents, her brother and, most importantly, from Keith.

John and Walter Prackley were totally at a loss, hovering in the midst of this celebration. 'You have some good friends, Miss Abercrombie,' they remarked.

One set of friends was about to prove their worth. There was a parchment envelope among the thin greeting cards. Inside was a letter on the notepaper of Gylah Cosmetics signed by its joint owners Ursula and William Guyler. Amidst a great deal of legal verbiage it conveyed the news that from that day forward all Gylah Cosmetics' legal business would be conducted by Ms Lindsey Abercrombie at Prackley Brothers and Abercrombie, Solicitors of Daverton. There was a contract, dense with clauses specifying the usual requirements as to duties, rights and retainers but with a note attached in Shula's writing – 'I know you want to specialise in family law but we're your family now, so sign this, dear.'

Lindsey sat with the papers spread out on the Victorian desk provided by the Prackleys. She was alight with pleasure, gratitude and relief. The contract ensured her livelihood for the foreseeable future. She looked around the little office and its array of flowers, seeing it brightened even more by this vote of confidence. She felt tears gather and said to herself sternly, 'None of that, we went through all of that yesterday.'

Walter Prackley cleared his throat. 'Er . . . should we show you some of the matters under consideration at present? Joseph Spence is coming in this afternoon with his son, they're in a disagreement over the compensation they should be getting from the government . . .' He gestured towards the door so she rose to follow him to the main office shared by the two brothers.

As they came out, someone came in at the main door of the building. The receptionist began a polite enquiry but Lindsey cried, 'Keith!'

He advanced towards her, smiling and holding aloft a bottle. 'Thought I'd bring something to break over the bows of the good ship Legal Lady.' He glanced at the two elderly solicitors, 'How do you do, I'm Keith Holland, friend of the accused.'

'Er . . . how do you do . . .'

'Glasses?' he suggested.

The receptionist, Lorna, leapt up. 'I'll fetch them!' Nothing so interesting had happened in the ten years she'd been with the Prackleys.

'How did you get here?' Lindsey said, half laughing, half crying.

'Drove, of course. Up at dawn, champagne in a carton of ice specially frozen the night before, helter skelter over the Pennines and here we are. I hope you're admiring my organisational skills.'

The Prackley brothers exchanged a glance. Mad, they were telling each other. Is this the kind of friend our new partner goes in for?

But Lorna had found a collection of odd glasses in the kitchenette and was placing them on the hall table among the helpful leaflets offered to clients. Keith opened the champagne, poured its festive bubbles into glasses, and offered them round. Everyone stood looking at Lindsey.

'A toast,' suggested Lorna, who'd ensured there was a glass for herself.

Lindsey didn't know what to say. This was serious, not to be shrugged off with the ironic words she'd used yesterday.

Unexpectedly, John Sprackley spoke. 'To the future, to all our futures and the good things waiting there.'

'To the future,' echoed his brother and the receptionist.

Lindsey said nothing, neither did Keith. He held out his hand to her, she took it.

The bachelor Sprackleys looked at each other. Oh, it's like that, is it? was their unspoken comment.